A BETTER LIFE

Also by Lionel Shriver

Mania

Abominations: Selected Essays from a Career of Courting Self-Destruction

Should We Stay or Should We Go

The Motion of the Body Through Space

Property

The Mandibles: A Family, 2029–2047

Big Brother

The New Republic

So Much for That

The Post-Birthday World

We Need to Talk About Kevin

Double Fault

A Perfectly Good Family

Game Control

Ordinary Decent Criminals

Checker and the Derailleurs

The Female of the Species

LIONEL SHRIVER

A BETTER LIFE

THE BOROUGH PRESS

The Borough Press
An imprint of HarperCollins*Publishers* Ltd
1 London Bridge Street
London SE1 9GF

www.harpercollins.co.uk

HarperCollins*Publishers*
Macken House, 39/40 Mayor Street Upper
Dublin 1, D01 C9W8, Ireland

First published by HarperCollins*Publishers* 2026

1

Copyright © Lionel Shriver 2026

Lionel Shriver asserts the moral right to be identified as the author of this work

A catalogue record for this book is available from the British Library

HB ISBN: 978-0-00-880010-9
TPB ISBN: 978-0-00-880011-6

This novel is entirely a work of fiction. The names, characters and incidents portrayed in it are the work of the author's imagination. Any resemblance to actual persons, living or dead, events or localities is entirely coincidental.

Printed and bound in the UK using 100% Renewable Electricity at CPI Group (UK) Ltd

All rights reserved. No part of this publication may be reproduced, stored in a retrieval system, or transmitted, in any form or by any means, electronic, mechanical, photocopying, recording or otherwise, without the prior written permission of the publishers.

Without limiting the exclusive rights of any author, contributor or the publisher of this publication, any unauthorised use of this publication to train generative artificial intelligence (AI) technologies is expressly prohibited. HarperCollins also exercise their rights under Article 4(3) of the Digital Single Market Directive 2019/790 and expressly reserve this publication from the text and data mining exception.

For the two Katies in my life—gleeful outliers both. We will win in the end, if only because we've had so much more fun, reliably at the opposition's expense.

Mankind is divisible into two great classes: hosts and guests.
— *Max Beerbohm*

AUTHOR'S NOTE

In 2023, the mayor of New York City proposed a program much along the lines of what I have christened Big Apple, Big Heart. The mayor's program never materialized. It has been made manifest in this novel. That program, my characters, and the Bonaventuras' only-slightly-made-up house in Ditmas Park are fictional inventions. All other news stories, figures, and details, to the best of my ability, hew to reality.
Lionel Shriver

1

"That's the most ridiculous idea I've ever heard": possibly more than Nico had said to his mother in six months.

"You're too young for a curmudgeon," his sister Vanessa jollied from across the round kitchen table. "At least give her proposal a chance."

"Yeah, think about it for a second," his older sister, Palermo, said. "Hear her out."

Worse than unthinking, Nico's explosion of derision ran counter to his recent efforts to harness the unsuspected power of *neutrality*. He'd spent a goodly portion of his college education studying methods for the conservation of energy, and having no opinions whatsoever was efficient. Lately he sought the serenity of not merely keeping his feelings to himself but also of having no feelings. The rare moments he'd managed absolute agnosticism had been more relaxing than Xanax. To maintain a perfect absence of positions on anything whatsoever, from the legitimacy of the state of Israel to the viability of plastic recycling, was to wear a cloak of invisibility. Surprisingly, the elixir of pure neutrality induced sensations of formidability, unspent potency, and omniscience. It made him feel sorry for all the little people and their *views*. Yet any donning of mental beige contravened his twenty-six years in this family, with opinions spewing out the ass.

"Accepting our share of responsibility—" their mother began.

"Why are they our responsibility?" Nico asked. *Neutrality* would take work. It was alien to his genetic makeup. He should probably practice not giving a shit on something smaller first.

"Because they're here," Palermo said.

"We didn't ask them to come here." Why was *he* on the defensive? Ever since the divorce, it was the three women against one.

"Have some compassion," his mother said. "These people have been through things you can't imagine."

"Totally," Vanessa said. "And they're desperate."

"See, I was talking to Helen Levitt across the street," his mother said. "A ghastly woman, I'd no idea how ghastly until this last year. She railed about how progressives 'should put their houses where their mouths are.' Invite newcomers into their own homes instead of burdening the city. Fine, she was nasty and xenophobic. But I also thought: maybe she's right."

"So, what," Nico said phlegmatically. He'd already lost this argument because there wouldn't be an argument. "Like, a whole family or something?"

"We have five bedrooms," his mother said. "Plus your lair in the basement, for just you and me."

"If it's too much space," Nico said, "why'd you fight Dad so hard to keep the house?"

"Principle," his mother said curtly.

Palermo told her brother, "You're the one who's capitalized on Mom getting the house."

"Give the kid a break," Vanessa said. "It's normal to be at sea in your twenties. You had a hard time at his age, too."

"For good reason," Palermo said.

A point Nico conceded. As usual, his elder sister was dressed head to toe in black, and not even a deep, striking black; her jeans and limp cotton shirt were washed-out. For the era, the monochromatic garb was intentionally stock, because she didn't want to call attention to herself. Beneath the drab exterior she still had a nice figure, but she did everything she could to disguise the fact. She cut her hair carelessly close and jagged; she probably hacked it off in the mirror with a razor blade. Even her slender profile was joyless; she had no interest in food. As for her habitual harshness, she'd earned it. Palermo always held herself tightly, as if policing her own expectations. Having reset her aspirations to nearly zero as a senior in college, she demanded that everyone else just suck up their disappointment, too.

Although the two got on well, his sisters were chalk and cheese. Vanessa was a bright-sider who wasn't disappointed in anything or anybody, including herself. For example, Vanessa was overweight for barely five feet tall. But she didn't give two hoots about her weight, and she advertised this indifference with every step she took.

"Maybe we should start small," his mother said. "Take in one boarder to begin with."

Who was this "we" starting small? Palermo lived in Queens, Vanessa in Bay Ridge. The only party who could make the subject of that sentence plural was Nico himself. He'd not volunteered, either; he was being drafted. "I've seen those lines, curving around the block near Grand Central," he said. "It's mostly guys."

"*Of military age*, as Fox News would say," Palermo said sourly.

"I'd be a bit nervous, Mom," Vanessa said, "if you took in a grown man."

"This 'Big Apple, Big Heart' program must be carefully vetting the folks housed with locals," his mother said. "If anything goes wrong, the *New York Post* will have a field day."

"*Dad* will have a field day," Palermo said.

"Mind you," their mother said, "your father won't like this idea one bit." She announced the advisory with relish. Nico couldn't imagine any move his mother might make that would annoy her ex-husband more.

"Let him fume," Palermo said. "Vanessa and I haven't spoken to Dad for, what—eight years? Almost nine."

While his sisters were competitors in this breath-holding contest, Nico did, on occasion, meet with his father in Manhattan. He didn't lie about these assignations; he wasn't forthcoming about them, either. Their sporadic dinners were on the down-low. The spicing huggermuggery of being a double agent was almost worth submitting to Dad's ritual chastisement—but not quite. Nico had already stashed away his mother's crackpot proposition to use for conversational spackling. Next time, his father could be so disgusted by his ex's ostentatious altruism that for a few blessed minutes he'd forget to rag on his only son for being such a letdown.

"It would be safer to request a single female," his mother supposed. (Just what this household needed: more women.)

"In that case, I think it's a wonderful idea," Vanessa gushed. "I'm proud of you, Mom. Real charity, not a load of talk."

"Remember," his mother said, "I haven't been all talk for months."

Oh, certainly not. Gloria Bonaventura had single-handedly mobilized the Ditmas clothing drive for "our newest New Yorkers." She'd convinced multiple nearby supermarkets to put out donation bins for canned goods and "culturally appropriate" foodstuffs like tortillas and rice. She and the other seraphic members of her book club regularly drove into Manhattan to distribute pizzas to the lines around the Roosevelt Hotel in midtown, once a pretty flash joint, apparently, with chandeliers, the works, and now the city's central intake center as well as home to hundreds of foreign families—although his mother and her fellow Saints of the Sixteen-Inch Pie had sometimes to weather objections that the pizzas were all plain cheese. What, no pepperoni? His mother found such complaints disarming: "People are the same everywhere! They have incredibly strong feelings about food!" These worthies always bought too many pies for only one slice apiece but too few to give everyone on line at the Roosevelt two, so his mother always brought leftovers home, the crusts soggy under the sauce and hard on the edges. He ate the slices anyway, because the unacceptable alternative was to buy his own pizza.

"It's a little embarrassing," his mother was saying, "but there's a financial upside. Every day, the city spends hundreds of dollars per person to lodge these poor migrants in hotels and shelters. So they'll pay us a hundred and ten dollars *per night*—while still saving the city a bundle, so it's win-win."

Nico asked, "Is the income taxable?"

"And everyone claims he's not a grown-up," Vanessa said.

"Doubtless, Nico, what isn't?" his mother said. "So what say you on my proposal, Palermo? You haven't weighed in."

Palermo shrugged. "Sure. Sounds great. Seems, you know, super civic. I'd consider doing the same thing, except Byron and I don't have an inch of extra room in Corona."

What a disappointment, Nico thought. Palermo must have been crushed that she couldn't install a total fucking stranger in her apartment—who spoke no English and had no money, no friends or family, no work, and no clue how to navigate New York City. That meant, damn, now she couldn't sit at dinner with Byron every night awkwardly pointing and smiling and miming "Would you like some more?" while wondering what on earth had compelled her to wreck her home life just to impress her mother.

"Same here," Vanessa said (aw, shucks!). "I've only got the one bedroom, and even Kumquat gets stir-crazy. But if you need anyone to shop, or get the room ready, or fill out paperwork—it's the city, you *know* there's going to be paperwork—I'd be glad to help. Anything to make this thing fly."

"And you, Nico?" his mother asked. "Might you come down from 'ridiculous'?"

This whole convocation was fake. Supposedly, his mother had gathered "the family" (minus one) to come to a joint decision. But being foregone, it wasn't a decision. Vanessa was a soft touch by temperament—she thought the best of everybody, which was broadly appealing but also explained why she and Nico were not that close— while Palermo, temperamentally a tough cookie, was a soft touch on principle. That is, an official heart of gold in respect to "the vulnerable" gave her license to rip political opponents' throats out. Either way, both sisters' votes were predetermined. Their mother could have skipped this theater of consultation and announced her intentions on Facebook. It didn't matter what he thought. It so didn't matter that he found the pretense of soliciting his opinion no little insulting.

"You're gonna do what you're gonna do," he said flatly, neglecting to add: *but on your head be it*.

After wispy kisses from Palermo and rocking bear hugs from Vanessa, his sisters took their leave. Nico loitered sullenly at the table while his mother cleared the dinner dishes. The kitchen and adjoining breakfast room had been remodeled to look like a sprawling Midwestern farmhouse in the 1940s—you know, where a kindly matriarch in a gingham apron would sterilize Ball jars by the dozen to preserve big batches of homemade pickles and jams to last through a long, brutal winter. He'd no idea why anyone would pay extra money to make brand-new cabinetry look dated. Even at sixty-two, his mother was boringly scrupulous about her figure, and she sure as hell never made jam.

Yet a rigid bearing and angular countenance did Gloria Bonaventura's character a disservice. A touch of roundedness might have gentled the censorious, withholding impression she sometimes made, much as the curve at the corner of their wraparound porch eased the architectural sternness of right angles. In truth, his mother was naturally generous. Unfortunately, she mostly exercised her magnanimity on people she'd never met.

"I don't think our sponsoring a migrant will have much impact on you," his mother said.

Our sponsoring—again with the first-person plural. Nico had a gut feeling the arrival of some arbitrary foreigner would have a greater effect on his life than his mother was pretending, which was why she felt moved to claim otherwise.

"But I hope you'll make her feel welcome," his mother added. "Show her around the neighborhood. It's not as if you're terribly busy."

"I have stuff to do. And I don't speak Spanish, or Chinese, or African."

The ignorant kicker was deliberate, and he enjoyed her predictable reaction: "No one speaks *African*."

"Listen, why is it *migrant*?" he asked. "Only a couple of years ago, it was *immigrant*. Then suddenly it's *migrant*, from the *Times* to CNN. You didn't used to say 'migrant' either."

"I don't know. It's shorter."

For the "far-right" podcasters whose fulminating videos Nico followed behind his mother's back, the little matter of two to three million annual entrants pouring over the southern border—formerly dubbed "undocumented" (implying American bureaucratic dereliction) and now "irregular" (like mis-manufactured towels)—had tripled subscription rates and lit the comment sections on fire. Blind to its own irrelevance, an imperious legacy media wouldn't have tweaked the language in which this radioactive issue was framed solely to spare the proles an extra syllable. Traditionally, "migrants" were poor, undereducated schmoes who trooped into your country or region to do hard, thankless seasonal work and then went home. So maybe, Nico speculated, the dropping of that inbound suffix was meant to cloak these new arrivals Stateside in the appealing linguistic fiction that they were ever going to leave.

"I realize this is a big gamble," his mother said. "We're reaching into a grab bag with our eyes closed. We don't know who'll show up, and maybe we won't get on. This could turn out to be a total catastrophe! But if you never take a chance, you don't do anything."

"What's wrong with not doing anything?"

She sighed. "Also. There's one other issue." Loading the dishwasher, she could avoid looking him in the eye. "When we renovated the basement for your grandfather, we put in the full bathroom, kitchenette, and TV so he'd feel more independent. He was already so apologetic about imposing on us. When Daddy passed before he could move in, it obviously made sense for you to stay there after graduation to get your bearings—"

Nico was way ahead of her. "You want to put the *migrant* in my basement. What do you expect me to say? *Great?*"

"I expect you to understand that someone who hasn't enjoyed any privacy for months would be grateful for effectively her own apartment. You can shift your belongings to your old bedroom upstairs. It's less space, but you'll have the run of the house."

"Won't she?"

"Of course. We wouldn't want to seem unfriendly."

"Why should I schlep all my crap upstairs, when I live here and she's a guest?"

"A paying guest—"

"She won't be paying. New York taxpayers will."

"Which doesn't include you. Though thank you for your concern. I have to say, one benefit of this Big Apple, Big Heart business is that we've finally found a topic that engages you. I can't remember when you were last so talkative."

Nico wasn't *engaged*. He was cross. He lifted his place mat begrudgingly so she could wipe the table. "Any idea how long this *mi casa, su casa* arrangement will last?"

"I don't know how long the program is budgeted for. Who knows, our first experiment could be short-lived. Most migrants are anxious to find work and establish their own home."

"In the most expensive city in the country."

"Yes, even here. As a rule, migrants are resourceful. Resilient. They're natural problem solvers. Our creaming off the most aspirational people in other countries is a kind of stealing. A porous border would be a policy of fiendish demographic genius, if only it were intentional."

Just as Nico knew better than to interrupt his mother's set-piece opining, he knew better than to differ. Yet while she'd been Florence Nightingaling for their country's gate-crashers the whole last year, Nico was prowling the internet for evidence that her munificent parkas, pinto beans, and pizza pies were treacherous, if not treasonous. Thanks largely to YouTube (here's looking at you, Victor Davis Hanson), he'd steadily assembled a cache of counterargument, much as Ukrainians were stockpiling an arsenal for their upcoming summer offensive. Yet he never took his mother on. At the most, he made sideswiping sorties and immediately withdrew, employing the hit-and-run tactics of a guerrilla force picking off stray soldiers in an advancing army. Closer to cowardice, merely shutting the fuck up hardly qualified as *neutrality*, a lofty yet nearly unattainable aspiration he may have fully achieved for only a few seconds at a time. Still, constantly repressing criticism of his mother's unconditional hospitality—on behalf of a native-born population she'd no right to speak for—at least required a certain fist-in-mouth discipline.

Like, if every "aspirational" foreigner cost the city hundreds of dollars per day, who was doing the stealing, really? And if the multitudes cascading into the country were "natural problem solvers," they all seemed to have arrived at the same inspired solution: dump their problems on someone else. For reasons Nico didn't understand, the fact that his own circumstances gave him no moral leg to stand on only made his unfocused resentment more intense.

"Hey, why do you assume that sponsorship program will ever wrap up?" Nico posed innocently. "The numbers are only rising. Now they're staying in our basement—"

"One person, Nico, and I haven't even filled out the application yet."

"It's just . . . you're providing a pretty powerful pull factor for the tons of foreigners who haven't packed their bags yet: an en suite, a kitchenette, and a sixty-five-inch Sony. So why won't they just keep coming? Over the border, and also to New York?"

His mother sat back down, and now she did look him in the eye. "The world is pretty unstable right now, kiddo. Ukraine. Sudan. Dysfunctional, corrupt governments in Central America. Haiti has *no* government. Venezuela's economy has collapsed—"

"Yeah, I *know*—"

"—Not to mention Afghanistan. We should be flattered so many refugees would rather live here, and we should be relieved there's somewhere for them to go."

"The world's always been unstable, Mom," he said, patronizing her right back. "Haiti finally gets a government, somewhere else will fall apart—"

"You need to get your head in gear, sweetie," she said, patting his arm. "Or your heart. Marshal a little kindness. Toward *one person*, that's all. I sometimes worry you're crawling up your own posterior down there. It'd do you a world of good to think about someone else."

Once she'd gone to bed, Nico did think about someone else: his mother. Why did he put so much effort into assembling the case against her latest pet cause? Why not just let her have her little "white savior narrative," as Palermo would say? Was the bug up his butt really a matter of *Mommy isn't paying attention to me!*—when surely what he wanted most was to be left alone?

Though he'd not been irremediably scarred by the divorce, he could have skipped it; his mother's commitment to a sequence of crusades like this one, subject to his father's escalating ridicule, closely correlated with his parents' split. Clearly something about this rampant goodness of hers got his goat, and now her plan to physically drag in any old itinerant off the street had upped the ante. Vanessa aside (the exception who proved the rule), he didn't believe in goodness, not pure goodness anyway. There was always some creepy secret reason anyone did something superficially high-minded. The nicest gloss he could put on his mother's turning this place into a third-world flophouse was she was trying to set an example: see, Nico? This is the kind of principled action your *more admirable* parent undertakes when adhering to *deeply held beliefs*. But her displacing family for a foreigner was maternally perverse. Mothers were the guardians of home and hearth. They owed their primary allegiance to blood ties. Besides, this more-the-merrier horseshit didn't seem staged for his sisters but seemed aimed with the utmost pointedness at her youngest, her only son. She knew he treasured sameness, and she'd have known he'd despise finding some fish-out-of-water stranger at the breakfast table day after day without pretending to ask. *She's messing with your world on purpose,* he intuited, *because she doesn't know what else to do.*

After a couple of late-night beers in a finished basement already slipping from his possession, Nico grew morose. The family court judge had let him choose to live with either parent for his senior year of high school.

He'd picked his mother, though he'd never announced why: because he felt sorry for her. His father could have taken the rejection; spurned, his mother would have been crushed. He'd never gotten around to determining which parent he truly preferred. It didn't matter whether he "loved" his mother more; it only mattered that she thought he loved her more. If that sounded a trace condescending, from the age of seventeen he'd questioned who was whose protector.

Whenever anyone got a load of the Bonaventuras' family home in Ditmas Park, they made errant assumptions. In a borough where renting a closet cost six grand a month, the house was huge, with two sprawling floors and a full attic you could stand in. No cheek-by-jowl Brooklyn brownstone but a freestanding Queen Anne built in 1905, the stately structure was set generously back from the street on a corner lot, its grounds bushy with hydrangeas and rhododendrons. It was replete with goofy fairy-tale turrets, dormer windows, and a columned wraparound porch that cried out for craft beers and Scrabble boards. (The porch was in large part lost on them. By the time it was warm enough to laze on the swing or bounce in the springy chairs with green-and-white-striped all-weather cushions, the mosquitoes were unbearable.) The house sponsored all those fiddly "period details" women creamed over—complex wooden cutouts lacing the roof of the porch, antique etched glass in the ground-floor doors. The exterior was clad in blue-gray wooden shingles with trim in Lipstick Red; the latter pick was brave, if selecting a paint color could ever qualify as requiring courage, and his mother seemed to have gotten away with the boldness of the choice. The bedraggled lawn sign for BLACK LIVES MATTER (and who had ever said that they didn't matter?) marred the retro aesthetic somewhat, but at least it demonstrated that the homeowner was thriving sufficiently to feel badly about it.

The interiors lived up to the grandiose facade. Oak flooring was inset with darker accents of mahogany. Window sashes were deep enough to balance a dinner plate. The baseboards and cornices were all "original." The massive curly-maple table in the dining room no one ate in would also have been impressive, if it weren't always covered with insurance documents and old *New Yorker*s still wrapped in cellophane. The rooms were dotingly kitted out in love seats, divans, and worn, overstuffed leather armchairs. Dark-wood bookcases were crammed with hardbacks. Anyone faintly acquainted with New York real estate would have leapt to the conclusion that the Bonaventuras were crazy rich.

The tenderness was out of character, but Nico was sympathetic with his mother's frustrations on this point. Sure, when the houses in this small neighborhood were first constructed early in the twentieth century, they must have been swank. But according to his parents, by the 1970s the whole city was a dump, most Brooklynites were still darkly complected, and this area's crime rate was through the roof. No one wanted to live in monsters that were ruinous to heat, especially if shivering several blocks to the tacky, depressing avenues of Flatbush or Coney Island for a pint of milk meant getting held up by a junkie at knifepoint. Old houses, his father said, "yearn to fall apart," and without owners who could afford the upkeep many of these impractical anachronisms fell into disrepair. Apparently buying this place in 1992, shortly after Vanessa was born, was like homesteading in the Wild West. Even these traditional liberal Democrats (at the time; of Dad and Democrats later) bought a gun. The house was a wreck, and their Realtor thought even the fire-sale asking price of $160,000 was too high. The roof leaked. Half the windows were smashed. The lawn was all dandelions and crabgrass. The appliances were rusted out; the floors were stained and water-damaged; pigeons were roosting in the attic.

The behemoth fucking ate money. To keep the renovation bills down, his father did much of the work himself—sanding and refinishing the floors, cutting wooden curlicues with his skill saw to match the few old ones on the porch facade still intact—a big reason he was so pissed that Mom got the house in the divorce. The division of spoils was relatively fifty-fifty—Dad walked off with the stock portfolio and kept his 401(K)—but the settlement took no consideration of all the time, labor, and love he'd poured into the property for decades. By Nico's first memories in the early aughts, the house was habitable, and the crime rate was starting to drop. But Dad was still making improvements right up until the day he left for good.

The point being: when a risk pays off, everyone forgets that you still took a risk, which by definition might not have paid off. The neighborhood could instead have continued to decline, leaving his parents and their two young children in a battened-down fortress plastered in ADT signs, from which they dared scurry only to collect the Colt 45 empties and spent hypodermics that the locals cast contemptuously in their yard—and good luck recouping even the $160K purchase price in an urban snake pit. While according to Nico's idle Googling this place would now sell for a cool $2.5 mil, his mother could only cash in by moving out. Meanwhile, she hectored him to turn off lights and take shorter showers. Winters, she set the thermostat at sixty—cold enough to ensure discomfort, warm enough to preclude a compensatory self-pity. Every summer, she refused to install central air. She got alimony, which before the divorce she'd claimed she didn't believe in, and she came into a modest inheritance when his grandfather died, as he and his sisters had also. But Toys & Trinkets, the crafty online retail business she'd run from home for years, didn't bring in beans. Her noble proposal to take a migrant off the mayor's hands may have been more motivated by that $110 per diem than she let on.

His mother's frustrations weren't limited to every passerby's assumption that the owner of her house was a billionaire. Nico was a frustration. Now four years out from college graduation, her son was still living at home and pursuing neither gainful employment nor volunteer work. The rarity with which she pestered him to start designing a game plan for his future was clearly strategic, lest he dig in his heels and clam up. Still, when she couldn't control herself, she lamented the fact that his current stall was at such odds with "the boy she thought she knew."

He'd been an exemplary high school student. He got the grades, he got the test scores, he joined the clubs. Constitutionally, he was a short-termer—good at achieving a realizable goal an inch from his nose, but lousy at taking the long view. In any event, he looked back on his hackneyed desire to get into a "good school" with contempt. He couldn't remember asking himself if he cared, truly *himself* cared, about going to college in the first place. The ambition hadn't originated on the inside. The boy his mother "thought she knew" was driven to please.

Furthermore, confirming he was way dumber than his parents and teachers had alleged, he'd bought wholesale into his country's glib formula for winning the college admissions game: earnest study + fanatical test prep + an overkill of extracurriculars both broad and a little quirky + savvy reading up on tips for making your essay stand out from the pack (when the rest of that pack was acting on the same tips). But imagining that anyone named Nico Bonaventura had a crack at the Ivies in the 2010s was hilariously naive.

He wasn't a legacy candidate; his father went to Bennington, his mother to Smith. Whatever its in-august status in 1992, Ditmas Park no longer qualified as deprived. All the top schools had an excess of applications from New York. His parents were too wealthy for him to qualify for scholarships but not wealthy enough to seem like potential big donors down the line. He didn't have a sob story (truly determined to gain admission to the rarefied ranks of higher education, he'd have run out in front of a bus). His test scores were near the top, but not, like those of his high school's Asian math whizzes, perfect. The coup de grâce: he was white.

His parents might have spared him that blizzard of form-filling: "Honey? You haven't a prayer. You fit the profile of exactly the candidates every selective admissions office in this country is bending over backwards to reject. Remember that Borough of Manhattan Community College accepts anybody." Because not only were all his first choices nonstarters, but so were the second-tier "safety schools"—Carnegie Mellon, University of Michigan, Vanderbilt, Rensselaer. He was left with third-tier, or no-tier. Meanwhile, word spread at his high school that *certain students*, who everyone knew full well were academic mediocrities at best but who also displayed the, ah, *qualities* that these fastidious admissions officers were looking for, got into Brown (irony alert), to Yale, and to Cornell. The whole college scramble was a con, and having jumped all those hoops like a performing seal—joining the chess club, studying the oboe, taking that AP course in International Relations—left him feeling humiliated. Yet if he were looking for consternation on his account, he wasn't getting any from his mother. When he identified the prickly matter of *hue* as the reason his applications were unavailing, she shut him down: "Maybe it's good for your historical education to find out what it feels like."

So he enrolled at Fordham—yeah, yeah, also a "good school," sort of—with an inevitable shortfall of enthusiasm. But he might have run out of something, and run out too early, at Columbia or Princeton, too. This impression of driving on a depleted tank helped explain why he opted for Fordham's four-year engineering physics degree, with a concentration in electrical, rather than the five-year program, which was more demanding. He wasn't sure he could last five years. He wasn't sure he could last four.

His mother and sisters blamed Covid. They assumed his life being put on hold for two years had interrupted his momentum and stopped a promising young man in his tracks. Clearly, imposed stasis was soporific, paralysis habit-forming. But he'd graduated a good ten months before the first order to "shelter in place." Whatever happened had happened before Covid, a period that he anyway recalled as glorious, like a long glide downhill on a bike; considering that the disease had furnished an off-the-shelf excuse for his mystifying "stall," he wouldn't want to appear ungrateful. So it would have been late summer in 2019—back when he explained anything to his mother, back when he was nicer—that he haltingly spelled out to her why he hadn't already applied for internships, entry-level engineering positions, or master's programs.

In his college application essays, he'd expressed an eagerness to pursue a career in sustainable energy, which of course his mother applauded. But, uh . . . But, uh . . . Now that he knew more about it, he told his mother nervously (and not nearly this cogently), the whole renewables paradigm didn't add up. So long as you still needed fossil fuel backup to kick in during what the Germans called *dunkelflaute,* intermittent wind and solar would only moderately reduce carbon emissions, and a whole parallel energy infrastructure was too expensive. Batteries still weren't scalable, and even if they became scalable, they'd require more rare earths than the planet provided—most of which had been co-opted by China. Open-pit mining for not only lithium and cobalt but also critical and less discussed elements like neodymium and dysprosium was filthy, polluting, and often dependent on child labor. No one considered the energy it took to produce all those panels and turbines, and no one knew how to recycle the hardware once it was shot. So there were already vast graveyards of wind farm blades, rotting in the sun like the carcasses of elephants in safari parks. This stuff didn't last nearly as long as it was supposed to, and it was mostly made in China with energy from coal—

Somewhere in here she stopped him. "Well, if so many challenges remain, your talents are sorely needed, right?"

She had a point, and he'd been relieved when she cut him off. Because he was lying. The problem, if it was a problem, which he continued to doubt, was far deeper. His own energy was not renewable.

The light bulb moment might sensibly have occurred at graduation, the tassel from his stupid hat tickling his cheek as he studied the bleary haze of his personal horizon. Instead, he hit the inflection point a few weeks earlier. There was no reason this single instant—when sitting on the lawn of Edwards Parade, gnawing a barbecued-chicken wrap, and staring absently at Keating Hall—should have occasioned a revelation of any sort. But presumably you had to take your epiphanies where you found them. The message was irrefutably clear and enchantingly simple. This insistence did arise from inside, plausibly for the first time in his life:

I don't want to be an engineer.

That was it. Signally, this discovery did not arrive in tandem with a replacement aspiration, such as *I'd love to organize microloans so that female entrepreneurs can buy sewing machines in India* or even *I yearn to become a trapeze artist.* No. He had no interest in being an engineer, and he had no interest in being anything else, either.

Nico had taken one elective in creative writing freshman year, a mushy course he soon transferred out of. But before he cut and ran, the instructor delivered the ironclad rule for storytelling: "Always make your character *want something*."

He made a rotten character.

2

Enlightenment prior to graduation had made Nico's remaining classes and exams an agony. Only an aesthetic commitment to the completed set and a veritably textural aversion to the ragged edge kept him from dropping out. That and low enthusiasm for facing his parents' flabbergasted ire. He could stand up to them, sure, but the parental showdown was a sport for which you needed to be in tip-top shape.

The real purpose of Nico's single-minded pursuit of admission to the college of his choice was to avoid thinking about *being* in college. The real purpose of his blinkered determination to earn an engineering degree at Fordham was to avoid thinking about *being* an engineer. Neither aspiration had originated at mission control. Focusing on achievable-goal-an-inch-from-your-nose the better to evade critical examination of said goal was a coping strategy that loads of people adopted in perpetuity. Finally, decrepitude arrived, and the one-inch-away goal was simply to stay alive, the supplements and surgeries and senior citizen yoga classes likewise an avoidance of asking why you would even want to stay alive. Yet this long-haul survival technique of feverish, beaverish distraction—of focus on process over product, journey over destination—only worked if you stayed very busy, which explained why everyone in his surround stayed very busy. His mother had been right on one point: now he wasn't busy.

Stereotypically, unemployed stay-at-home adults barricaded in disorderly bedrooms and rarely took showers. They were grumpy, incommunicative, and hypersensitive. They spent most of their time online but were secretive about the content, often falling down radicalizing "rabbit holes" (a now-ubiquitous expression whose origin was as perplexing as its abrupt disappearance was bound to become in a year or two). They kept unsociable hours, often not arising until midafternoon. They neglected to get dressed. They developed mental health problems—rather, as the inane contemporary construct had it, they "had mental health"—usually vague, unfalsifiable ailments like depression or anxiety and preferably both. They either starved themselves or gained weight. Their key point of uniformity: they were all disconsolate. No one else in the household knew how to jolly them out of their emotional pit. Many a parent at wit's end pushed their inert, moody, either literally or figuratively self-harming progeny to "see someone," if only so that they or their offspring might be seen to be "doing something." But even if this disappointment of a grown kid capitulated, therapy, with its usefully indeterminate duration and usefully indeterminate objective, would function only as more delay.

Nico pleaded guilty to being incommunicative, and obviously he was no stranger to YouTube. In fact, he celebrated having come of age in an era that allowed you to effortlessly spool through hour after hour, only to look up in surprise that not only was it already dark but it had apparently been dark for some time. In his view, the likes of YouTube allowed for the satisfaction of the very open-ended curiosity, both practical and intellectual, that formal education was meant to encourage and instead actively squelched.

Yet Nico was anything but disconsolate. One reason he limited discourse with his mother was to conceal from her the alarming extremity of his contentment. He took showers. He made his bed, just as Jordan Peterson told him to. He slept serenely, because his mind was untroubled. He woke naturally circa 10 a.m., not at three in the afternoon. He had a good appetite but stopped eating when he was sated, and his weight never varied by more than a pound or two. It would never occur to him to spend all day in a bathrobe. He wasn't into the exercise whathaveyou, but he did take long walks, sometimes to Manhattan and back, and these many hours of silent noticing were far more edifying than any college course; thanks to these day-long peregrinations, he was more up to speed on the nitty-gritty of New York's "migrant crisis" than his mother had any idea. He wasn't into reading books, either, but he read plenty of Substacks and online magazines, including, furtively, on occasion, his father's. Averse to the tyranny of shaving all those reeds, he'd abandoned the oboe, but he enjoyed singing. Neither his mother nor his sisters had ever pushed him to "see someone." You didn't usually badger people to seek psychiatric treatment because they seemed too happy.

Sure, he watched his share of porn, cycling through a selection of old reliables, in preference to falling down the *rabbit hole* of acceleratingly sicko vids of bestiality and poo. He'd experimented with a few mano a mano clips and kept the best ones in the rotation, though he'd never flown into a tizzy over his "identity" or "orientation" or "gender." Gay fucking was just one more kink, and a pretty lame one. It was only pictures, and he'd never put a hand on another guy's cock.

As for women, at Fordham he did have that on-again, off-again thing with Kayla—who was never exactly his "girlfriend," a formal designation grown archaic anyway. Besides, by his junior year, no more resistant to international manias that any other hopelessly unmoored institution, naturally Fordham was in the grip of #MeToo, a crusade whose copycat handle reduced to "Wait, I want in on it as well!" Now that pity conferred a higher status than achievement, white girls had latched on to "sexual harassment" as their sole (and rather slender) grounds for getting people to feel sorry for them. But the pathos came at a price, not that the girls themselves paid it. Nico's friend Cole from organic chemistry got caught up in a fake rape case with some dish who decided five days after the fact that she wasn't cool with their fumbling rendezvous. Following the summary judgment of a university kangaroo court that never let the guy say a word in his own defense, much less cross-examine his accuser, Cole was kicked out of school, which meant no other remotely selective college would accept him, either. The lesson-once-removed wasn't wasted on Nico: flesh-and-blood females were too much trouble.

Besides, by senior year, Kayla had announced she was "nonbinary." He'd said what the fuck does that mean and she'd said neither fish nor foul and he'd said, no, I mean what does it mean you want to do in *bed*. She couldn't even answer. She had no idea. But he was relieved, in the end. Sex with humans was too complicated and too awkward, and he disliked the persistent impression that he didn't know what he was doing. If he was honest with himself, he preferred getting off on his own. It actually felt better—you could squeeze exactly *here*, for *this* long, and then rub *here*, for *that* long, and speed up *just this much* exactly *now*, all without having to direct some other party who never quite understood your *nonverbal cues*. You could say whatever filth came into your head aloud and the only lingering embarrassment was with yourself; on the whole masturbation lark, Self got a free pass. He had a regular Appointment Wank around midnight, which amounted to the only commitment on his calendar that bound him to a schedule of any kind.

Nico had inherited $75,000 from his maternal grandfather, and after four years he still had most of it left. When your only expenditures were the odd takeout and six-pack, a rainy-day fund of that size would last quite a while. Although his reserves would run out eventually, that prospect was distant, and he was sure to think of something. Besides (not to be morbid), *in the fullness of time*, as they say, there was always, you know, the house—whose proceeds would be considerable, even divided three ways. Meanwhile, he didn't experience this period of his life as delay. Delay of what? He didn't experience this period of his life as a period, period. It was simply his life. He wasn't putting anything off. The stillness, the sumptuous monotony of his days, the luscious absence of demands, the paucity of engagements, the wide-open space both inside his head and without together conjured the hypnotic illusion that time had stopped. There was no future to plan for because the future and the present had fused. He was suspended, without a care, in an eternity.

Yet one threat to this hovercraft serenity loomed large: the Big Apple's big, stupid heart.

Vanessa's instincts were sound. There were scads of paperwork, although the authorities seemed more concerned with vetting the sponsors than the unknown quantities who'd presumably acquire keys to local homes. The application wanted to know about pets in case of allergies, fire safety, childproofing, and mold. Was your property on a flood plain, did it have any compromised extension cords. You had to upload a recent gas safety check. The spare room at issue needed one window of minimum dimensions; sent downstairs with a tape measure, Nico was disappointed to learn that the window on his basement light well qualified.

While Vanessa entered answers in the city's intrusive forms, their mother ranted about the governor of Texas. The guy was busing shedloads of his state's visitors-for-life to Democratically controlled cities like New

York and Chicago, aiming to mock their sanctimonious status as "sanctuary cities," which refused to enforce federal immigration law. (In fairness, the governor's main beef was with the primary party not enforcing federal immigration law: the federal government.) Northern municipalities were getting a mere taste of what Texans had put up with on a far vaster scale for decades. The tiny border town of Eagle Pass (pop. 29,000) was now receiving New York's total migrant intake of the last year within two weeks.

Nico dared to note mutedly to his mother and sister that the governor was only delivering what the city had claimed to want. At the start of this inundation, their mayor had been all smiles, announcing how joyously New York "welcomed newcomers with open arms." Besides, their mother was always talking up these "resilient" pilgrims, who could help fill a labor shortage. Shouldn't we be thanking Texas for gifting us so many migrants, then—or even begging for more?

"In the long term, all these new residents will grow the economy," his mother said. "In the short term, thanks to Texas, it's too many too fast."

Yet according to Nico's scrolling, the abundance of these arrivals were beelining to Gotham with no help from Texas, because word was out: unlike most cities in the known universe, New York had codified a "right to shelter." Anyone who showed up was entitled to a place to stay. And three meals per day. And another phone, should God forbid anything happen to yours. Even better, the "right to shelter" wasn't time limited. They had to put you up *forever*. Maybe "the world" still didn't owe you a living, but New York City owed you a living for sure. The mayor moaned about this sudden influx of broke people "destroying New York City," but he was helpless in the face of his moronic predecessors. Imagine passing all these holier-than-thou bills while being totally unprepared for the fact that, when you advertise free digs, free grub, and free Wi-Fi, a fair crowd will take you up on the offer.

Had the whole fiasco remained a spectator sport, Nico might have gladly leaned back to enjoy the show. But as of an email in his mother's inbox toward the end of May, current events were about to arrive in his living quarters, and on the wrong side of the sixty-five-inch TV screen.

"Her name is Martine Salgado," his mother announced while Nico fixed a sandwich from last night's roast chicken; he liked having a kitchenette for cold beer, but he preferred the main kitchen because it had food in it. "She arrives on June sixth. Doesn't say what time."

He'd been hoping the wheels of bureaucracy would churn slowly, but it seemed the city could move double-quick when getting shed of even one freeloader.

"Where's she from?" he asked. "How old? Any English?"

"They only provided her name."

"That's rich. They made you give them everything but a DNA sample."

"After all the protests I've joined, I'm astonished I passed the criminal records check," she said lightly. "Anyway, you'd better start packing up downstairs."

Just then, Nico resolved to form a covert resistance of one. True, he didn't have a snowball's chance of stanching the avalanche over his country's southern border by so much as one unaccompanied toddler. On his lonesome, he was helpless to defend against the outsiders imposing themselves on the deranged hospitality of his native city. But he drew the line at the threshold of his own family's house. Given the fifth column problem, he'd be no more successful at protecting the integrity of the Bonaventuras' private borders than the hapless authorities protecting the national ones. But he was not going down without a fight.

Vanessa and Palermo descended that weekend to help their mother prepare for the arrival of their new charge. Rather than assume a sullen aspect, for which he'd have been taken to task, Nico took refuge in *neutrality*. This entailed wearing a blank expression while stacking his boxers in a laundry hamper, marching upstairs with a roboticism he tried not to overdo, and speaking little.

Still covered in Arctic Monkey posters, the walls of his old bedroom seemed to close in. The fact that he now spurned the keening indie band as a bit of a buzzkill gave this room a whiff of the mold that Vanessa had just assured the city didn't fester here. The nostalgia that conventionally attends adult return to a boyhood bedroom might have kicked in more powerfully had he spent the last four years farther than two floors away. Oh, presumably he had a "happy childhood." But having only had the one, he had no means of comparison, and being a kid was way harder than grown-ups ever seemed to remember. That sensation he had in bed with Kayla of not knowing what he was doing: it permeated his boyhood every day, and without the upside of blowing his load. To the degree that he was ever actively happy rather than barely managing amid a miasma of lesser, subtler emotions that he didn't even have names for then, that was over by age nine, after Palermo devastatingly deserted her little brother for the University of Denver.

The real problem: this oppressively familiar venue underscored that he was *living at home*. It threatened to suck him back into the hackneyed adolescent orneriness and resentment (of *what?*) that he'd been trying to rise above. The implicit regression contrasted with the man-cave feel of the basement, kitted out with a sectional sofa, a massage chair whose gyrations raised his midnight Appointment Wank up a notch, an exercise bike–cum–clothes hanger, a broad antique desk that beat the daylights out of the tiny third-grade-style one here, and a separate outside entrance that kept his movements from being monitored—all of which he'd now bequeathed to a stranger with itchy feet. If his previous hang's impression of self-sufficiency was an illusion, he'd had no problem with living a lie.

When Nico rejoined his sisters in the basement, they were stripping his bed. The sheets stacked on the exercise bike were the sea-green ones with a satin sheen, a bazillion-thread-count set that for Nico was off-limits. The prodigal had to use the worn-out white ones, with fitted bottoms whose elastic was shot. His simple blue bedspread was rumpled on the floor, while lovingly draped over the bike's handlebars awaited a handmade quilt, a prized heirloom from their maternal grandmother. In two oversize bags from Target he found four new pillows, one pair memory foam and the other goose down—since who knows what their princess-and-the-pea arrival might get her best night's rest laying her head upon.

Picking up the pattern, he was no longer surprised to find plush, guest-only towels in the bathroom. The shower stall was stocked with unopened bottles of volumizing Scots-pine shampoo, hydrating tea-rose conditioner, and Cornish-hedgerow bath gel. Arrayed beside the sink: a pot of moisturizer called "skin caviar," antibacterial lemongrass hand soap, Optic White Renewal toothpaste, two new Oral-B toothbrushes—soft and medium—as well as two dispensers of dental floss—waxed and unwaxed. And the can was spotless. Gone were the smears of shaving cream around the sink and the soapy buildup on the shower door. Those maniacs had even gone at the tile grouting, mildewed for years. You could've served punch from the toilet bowl, while the fixtures were polished like sports trophies.

When he emerged, his sisters were on either side of the bed, cornering and smoothing the top sheet. Somehow their athletic pounding of the pillows was the limit.

"This woman may be fresh from a homeless shelter," he said. "She won't get her nose out of joint because her pillows aren't fluffed."

"The idea's not only to take up slack for the city," Vanessa said, "but also to be nice."

Lined up on the kitchenette counter: salted almonds, rosemary potato chips, whole-grain crackers, and corn nuts. Chilling in the fridge: bottled water (sparkling and still), clementines, a selection of Mexican cheeses, and *Nico's* six-pack of IPA. "What, no champagne?"

"We thought about it," Palermo said defiantly.

"But you're furnishing the amenities of a five-star hotel's minibar."

"It's a small outlay in our terms," Palermo said. "No woman should plunge into a tailspin because she can't afford shampoo. The pocket money for asylum seekers is a joke."

"How do you know she's an asylum seeker?"

"I think they're pretty much all asylum seekers," Vanessa said.

"Well, doesn't that tell you something?"

"Tell me what?" Vanessa asked. From childhood, his younger sister had been perfectly lacking in guile. The innocence was charming. But it also meant she projected guilelessness onto everyone else, making her a danger to herself.

"You can only seek asylum if you're fleeing persecution," he said. "Not because you're plain old poor, or want a job, or your country sucks and you'd rather live in the United States."

"There's no such thing as 'plain old poor,'" Palermo said. "Destitution is soul destroying." It was a mystery why *she* knew what poverty was really like and he didn't.

"Most of these people enter the country under false pretenses," Nico insisted, tired of Palermo treating him like a kid. She'd never credit it, but he was way better informed about this stuff than she was. "I don't care how poor you are. Doesn't qualify you for *asylum*."

"If we issued more work visas," Palermo said dismissively, "they wouldn't need to bend the rules. Now, clear off and let us finish. You can't have dusted down here in months."

On the evening of June fifth, the sisters returned to prepare a huge pan of chicken enchiladas with red sauce. The elaborate operation entailed individually shredding two family packs' worth of poached chicken thighs with the jousting of two opposing forks, and the red sauce got all over the stove. Once the women got down to rolling the enchiladas, Palermo had to sit down, because, you know, her back.

It was always hard to remember that she was in constant "discomfort," as doctors dubbed agony, because she never mentioned it. Subject to the same torture, Nico would have never shut up about it. But Palermo didn't try to extract special concessions. True, she was being a real pain in the ass about this migrant business, which brought out the proclivity for self-righteous hectoring that progressives never seemed to register was not their best feature. Still, he should be more mindful that she was always suffering, which must have put an edge on her. In her place, had anyone given him the slightest guff, he'd have ripped their face off.

For the big day, they still had no ETA for "this Martine person," a locution that Nico favored, if only because the implied distaste was too elusive to call him out on. The sixth was a weekday, when Palermo would usually be putting in a good ten hours at Corona Construction, the home repair and renovation outfit her husband ran; obviously with the back thing she wasn't putting up Sheetrock, but she answered the phone, ordered materials, and kept the books. Byron claimed she was indispensable, but her taking one day off, she said, wouldn't send the company to the wall. Vanessa had located someone to sub at the after-school program in Sunset Park she'd helped found called Peanuts, which provided sports, games, and tutoring for disadvantaged primary school kids with working parents. The operation was more trying than most people appreciated. Vanessa played the pandemonium down, but he'd been there: many of the children were poorly behaved, loud, sometimes abusive or even violent, and they weren't all toilet trained. He'd no idea how she could stand it.

Both sisters would help form the greeting committee that would welcome Martine Salgado into the family. Vanessa had an unlimited appetite for new people, whereas Palermo, the savvier of the pair, probably wanted to ensure the lodger was sound. Throughout this crapshoot, what no one acknowledged was that most people, wherever they were from, were either annoying or extremely dull.

The atmosphere, the literal atmosphere, in the five boroughs on June sixth objectified Nico's private sense of foreboding. An uncontrolled wildfire in Canada had produced a murk of smoke, thick and massive enough to occlude all of Quebec in satellite imagery. Winds had pushed the smoke south, and it now enveloped the city. Technically, according to NY1, the skies were cloudless. Yet by noon the tint overhead was as red as a sunset. The haze was so dense that you could look up at this "clear" sky and stare at the sun, shrunken to a sullen disc of vermilion. Public advisories to stay indoors and avoid exertion had been ceaseless and hysterical.

The feeling, then, was of exceptionalism, like a school snow day, as if normal rules did not apply. Brooklyn's motorists seemed to have gotten that message, for as the family loitered on the front porch awaiting "this Martine person," the speeding, honking, and sideswiping along commonly tranquil Ditmas Avenue were extraordinary, as if the drivers had been bitten by zombies. Dark, rubescent skies midday felt apocalyptic. Surely the sooty, glowering firmament was an ill omen.

At last, around 5 p.m., when the women were as discouraged as Nico was growing hopeful—that in the eleventh hour the city's absurd attempt to dump its unworkable "right to shelter" on ordinary, hard-pressed New Yorkers had been rescinded—a white van pulled up out front. As Nico trailed behind, his mother and sisters hustled eagerly down the porch steps. Should his hanging back betray hurtfully that he wasn't into this arrangement, tough.

Nico couldn't help but notice that the woman who bounded from the passenger seat wasn't as stocky as many of the Hispanics waiting outside the Roosevelt Hotel; she had a waist, and she wasn't ridiculously short. Twenty-eight? Hard to say. As she jabbered fulsomely to the driver in Spanish and blew him kisses, she retracted the side door and hoisted two enormous pink roller bags to the sidewalk. Turning to the Bonaventuras with a smile wide enough to have made her jaw ache, Martine Salgado, presumably, flashed such blazing ivories that maybe she wouldn't need that Colgate Optic White Renewal after all. She threw her arms open and exclaimed, "¡*Buenas tardes, mis nuevas amigas! ¡Gracias, muchas gracias por mi nuevo hogar!*"

Any New Yorker picked up bits of Spanish like it or not, and the grateful greeting scanned. Martine's booming voice must have carried down the whole block. So far this specimen jarred with Nico's preconception of a mousy, apologetic mumbler keen to be no trouble. Martine immediately identified his mother as head of household and wrapped her savior in a long embrace. "¡*Señora Bonaventura!*" Stepping back but keeping her hands on his mother's shoulders, she tilted her head. "I sorry. English, small. No so good. I try. Be better."

"*Bienvenida Señorita Salgado . . . esperamos que . . . muy feliz aquí.*" His mother, who'd also only learned subway-advertising Spanish, had been rehearsing her welcome for days.

"*Por favor,* you say me 'Martine.'"

"*Por favor,*" his mother echoed, "you say me 'Gloria.'"

Oh, *God.* It was nauseating. Now a Smith-educated design major was regressing to pidgin. When she introduced Palermo and Vanessa, she kept stooping and bobbing her head, as if she were in Japan. Nico's otherwise articulate, self-respecting mother always got this way whenever interacting with *people of color*: oversolicitous and underdignified, all with an undercurrent of terror. Both sisters received the overkill embrace, which Vanessa returned with enthusiasm. By contrast, Palermo arched in a visible recoil. She wasn't demonstrative by nature, and Martine must have been murdering her back.

Having remained on the bottom step of the porch, Nico took a moment to size up the newest member of the household. She wasn't bad-looking, with wild, curlicued black hair, wide, high cheekbones, and strong eyebrows. She had hips on her, but they were proportionate. Her tight jeans, blingy rhinestone belt, and strappy gold sandals with spike heels didn't look conducive to hiking the infamous Darién Gap or leaping onto cross-Mexican freight trains like The Beast. Yet her red muscle T exposed arms and shoulders that wouldn't have looked out of place on a professional mover. With male contemporaries, Nico disdained the conspicuously cut for having squandered their leisure time on mindless physical repetition. But it was doubtful Martine was a paid-up member of CrossFit, and on a woman those guns were intimidating.

When his mother urged him down the step to introduce himself, he shuffled forward and stuck his hand out, keen to escape a suffocating grapple. "Nico. *Hola.*"

"*Hola. Un hombre* . . . so handsome! *Gusto en conocerte.*"

Her grip didn't disappoint. If anything, she laid on the pressure a bit thick, keeping his hand firmly in hers an extra beat and looking him in the eye, as if to establish something. Her manner was gushy, even ditzy, but that gaze was steady and clued-up with a hint of warning.

"Nico," his mother said, "could you help Martine with her luggage?"

Their lodger had stepped back to take in her new circumstances. "Oooh, *su casa*! Is so BIG! ¿*Y muy bonita*, no? I no believe *posible*, must be dream! So *bonita*, maybe I cry, *sí*?"

"No need for tears!" His mother looked torn between pride and embarrassment.

Nico juddered a roller bag along the paving stones, while Martine followed with the second. At the outside entrance to the basement, he scuttled down the stairs to unlock the door and so facilitate his own displacement. But when he retrieved Martine's bag, he almost lost control of the case. The pink monster weighed a ton. "What's in this thing," he muttered, "assault weapons?"

"In my country"—Martine took the handle from him with her free hand—"that no so funny."

Your country? Nico thought, as Martine hefted both enormous suitcases down the steps to his vacated lair by herself. *If you still have a country, why don't I get to keep mine?* But he was sufficiently his mother's son to never advance such an impolite question out loud.

The Women encouraged their visitor to get settled, maybe have a shower (with Cornish-hedgerow bath gel), and come up for dinner at her leisure. Around seven thirty, Nico ran into her wandering the living room. She'd changed into a sleek aquamarine dress surprisingly stylish for a homeless shelter. Though she was clearly scoping the place out, Martine said, "Oh, Nico, *bueno*, I lost! ¿*Dónde está la cocina?*"

"This way." He led her toward the kitchen. She seemed to understand more English than she spoke. "On the way to El Norte," he asked idly, miming her luggage, "did you travel with both those huge bags?"

"No, no, *servicio. Con bagaje. Para inmigrantes. A Estados Unidos y de regreso. Es un gran negocio.*"

"Sorry, what?"

Pausing in the dining room, she loaded the translation app on her phone that would simplify the rest of the evening. Her excitable Spanish input was milled into a mechanical rise and fall: "Trucks piled high with immigrant luggage run up from Panama to all over the United States. They will deliver to any city you want them to. It's a big business, very lucrative, but for us not nearly as expensive as UPS or DHL. You can even track your bags online."

"How convenient," Nico said, but Martine foisted the phone on him. He hit the English button. "*Que conveniente*," the app produced, the sourness of his delivery lost.

Martine insisted on preparing the salad, though she washed way too much lettuce for five people, and she used up all the heirloom tomatoes from the Grand Army Plaza Greenmarket. She also insisted on setting the table, though because she didn't know where the plates, napkins, silverware, and hot pads were kept, helping her feel helpful was more trouble than setting the table themselves. Nevertheless, his mother looked to Nico with triumphantly raised eyebrows, as if to say, *See?* See what? The while, Martine chatted ebulliently in Spanish, the content of her monologue less the message than her tone: *I am injecting energy and renewal into this pale, phlegmatic household, and you will soon wonder how you ever got through the day without me.*

The enchiladas were a hit, if Martine's incessant ¡*Muy bien!* ¡*Muy auténtico!* was to be believed, though the dish could have done with a lot more cheese; his mother was afraid of cheese. Absent conversation, there was nothing to do but eat, which meant dinner proper took ten minutes. Nico could feel his mother and sisters beginning to panic. Cleanup would only take a few minutes more, and then what would they do with her?

Dabbing her mouth, Martine slipped out her phone, with which she produced a formal after-dinner speech in patient segments: "Thank you Gloria, Palermo, Vanessa, and Nico for taking me into your beautiful home. Thank you for a delicious meal. I come a long way, and my journey was very hard. But I am sure the whole time that my goal is worth the trouble. America is the land of freedom, the land of plenty. It is true what I hear: Americans are very nice. They give house, food, doctors, school, money. I am so happy I come to your country."

The other women glanced at each other, then went to their bags in the foyer. Their mother's "no phones at the table" rule was moot for the foreseeable.

His mother went first. "You're more than welcome, Martine, and maybe after all your hardship we can learn more from you than you can from us." *Blah-blah*, in Spanish. "Don't hesitate to let us know anything you need or anything you don't understand." Spanish. "But maybe you could start by telling us: Where are you from?" Spanish. This was going to be slow.

"I come from the neighborhood of Rivera Hernandez, in San Pedro Sula. Very, very poor. You can have no idea." Once Google had done the honors, Martine thought to add, "Honduras."

Oh, just great, Nico thought loudly enough that it almost got out underbreath. *Thank fuck we didn't get a boarder "of military age" who's a guy.*

Palermo helped Vanessa download the app, set the languages, and put the app in conversation mode; so much for any worries about how to occupy the evening. "What made you so desperate to leave your home?" Vanessa asked. "Was it mostly being poor?"

"In San Pedro Sula, I take in laundry from my neighbors," Martine's phone translated. "I make only fifteen lempiras per day. But if money is the only problem, maybe I stay."

Intending to boycott this halting, arduous interview, Nico let curiosity get the best of him. "You did the washing by hand?"

Google's irksome rendering of his question in a female voice emblemized the girlification of everything. God forbid that Silicon Valley would make the ghost in its machine a man.

"*Sí, sí. No lavadoras.*" Martine's phone elucidated, "In Honduras, washing machines are only for rich people."

Well, that explained those shoulders.

"But my husband," she continued; so much for getting any ideas. "He gets no work. He doesn't like that his wife brings in all the money. First he only drinks Salva Vida—beer. Not so bad. But then he switches to Flor de Caña—rum. He hits me." She pensively traced a scar on her forearm. "I try to make him happy, prepare nice food, but it's no good. He does not feel macho." The word duplicated in English. "I worry someday he hits me so hard he kills me."

"You look like a woman who can stand up for herself," Nico said. He sure wouldn't want to go up against those arms in a bar.

"I fight back, I make worse."

"Did you have any family you could turn to?" Palermo asked.

"Is more my family," Martine said, "turn to me."

"We're your family now," Vanessa said. "You can always turn to us if you need help."

"Thank you, Vanessa, you're very kind." Martine had returned to the app. "And since you asked, there is another reason I could no longer stay in San Pedro Sula. Groups of men. Often not men at all, but boys. Scary boys. Not children, more like wild animals. They are stronger than the police, and often the police are on their side. They fight with each other. Where we live, there is gunfire almost every day."

"We're familiar with Central American gangs." Palermo's English input displayed a trace of impatience. She may have found the inference that the likes of MS-13 and Barrio-18 were news to the naive Americans a measure insulting. "They're in the US, too."

"Not only in LA, either," Nico said. "They're on Long Island." *Isla Grande* sounded more magnificent than the reality in English.

Now Martine showed a twitch of impatience; they weren't going to impress a woman from Honduras with their street smarts. "One of these, yes, gangs"—*pandillas*—"they notice I have my own business. They say I must pay them 'rent.' But I already pay rent! With two rents, we have no money left. These boys, they are very dangerous. You cannot tell them no. I think, if I escape to the USA, I get away from two terrible problems at once."

"We call that 'killing two birds with one stone,'" Vanessa provided.

"Stanford has banned that idiom for 'encouraging violence against animals.'" Palermo's deadpan delivery obscured whether she found the new no-no funny.

"Will your husband be all right?" their mother asked.

"Do I care?" Martine said defiantly, then translated: "But they may leave my husband alone. He has no business they can take a piece of."

"Did you use a coyote?" Palermo asked.

"We no say *coyote*," Martine said in English. "We say *snakehead*." Back to the app. "It is a dangerous journey for a woman. You must hide any money in places I would rather not say."

"Did you walk the whole way?" Vanessa asked.

Martine suddenly switched gears, back to her sunny, animated mode. "This talk is too sad for a pretty summer night! In our beautiful house and after our wonderful food. Let us be happy I meet such charming new friends and join a new family." Martine folded her cotton napkin and stood. "Now, I clean *la cocina*."

Their mother quickly punched her phone. "You are our guest, not our servant!"

As Martine insisted on helping out, Vanessa had to instruct her on loading the dishwasher. The newcomer's awe at a machine that cleaned tableware seemed exaggerated. No way she hadn't heard of a dishwasher before. As the women put away the leftovers—tons of uneaten salad—something was bugging Nico that he couldn't put his finger on. It was always tricky to discern whether foreigners were full of shit.

"*Muy cansada!*" Martine said at last, laying her head on her hands.

Little wonder she was tired. While miraculous at first, Google Translate interminably dragged out every mundane interchange. Poorly articulated assertions came out as gibberish. At the slightest pause, the app cut you off, and you had to start again. Ideally, then, you formed your thoughts whole in advance, the way his mother said people typed before word processing, when revision meant mucking the paper with white goop. With computers, the process of writing, she said, had become less deliberate and more . . . What did she say? More "venturing into the dark," more "blind." That is, "more in the fingers, less in the head." With a typewriter, she said, you only launched into a sentence when you knew exactly what you wanted to say.

His sisters were off to their apartments, but not before loads more embracing and cheek kissing and exuberating with Martine about how great it was to have her here and what a wonderful time they were all going to have together and how they'd have to make plans to show her the city and maybe they should begin with the Botanical Gardens . . . All this jubilation, joyfulness, and jollity took Nico back to being eleven years old when, surrounded by empty booze bottles and half-eaten wedges of brie, two dozen of his parents' friends had hugged and kissed and danced and wept, because the first black guy—half-black guy, but they weren't picky—had just won the presidency.

Once Martine was safely ensconced downstairs, he wandered into the living room, where his mother had resumed knitting another one of the woolen animals she sold online.

"Doesn't it concern you," he ventured tentatively, "that Martine's story seemed a little, I don't know. Pat?"

"*Pat?* What do you mean *pat*?"

"It seemed, well, predictable. Constructed."

She stopped knitting. "Honestly, honey, I've no idea what you're talking about."

"Why wasn't her account more particular? Why wasn't anything she told us surprising?"

"I found Martine's history plenty 'particular.' And what's surprising? That an attractive woman with no defender made it here at all."

"Will you hear me out?" he implored. "During the Trump years, the standards for granting asylum were pretty tight. But now Biden has expanded the definition of 'persecution' to include being subject to domestic abuse or gang violence. Those two loopholes have opened asylum to hundreds of thousands of immigrants who wouldn't otherwise have qualified—"

"Why loopholes?" she said. "They're good reasons to offer someone refuge."

"It's just that most of the people crashing the border—"

"*Crossing*. You can't 'crash' through those murderous coils of razor wire in Texas."

"All these people have boned up. They're online. They know more about American immigration law than most attorneys."

"And why do *you* know so much about immigration law?"

"Given recent events in this house, it's in my interest to know about it. But here's the thing. Subject to domestic abuse and fearful for her life, *check*. Menaced by gang violence and extortion threats, *check*—"

"Martine might easily fall into both those categories simply because in Honduras gang warfare *and* domestic violence are horribly commonplace."

"But it's like she's lined up her story in advance, carefully crafted to match recent changes in asylum law. No surprise if tomorrow she tells us Honduras is murderously homophobic and she's come out as a lesbian."

"That's enough," his mother announced sharply. "Martine has given us no reason to think she's anything but what she appears: a good-hearted young woman grateful for our help and relieved to put a troubled past behind her. I'm ashamed to say that this presentation of yours was worse than cynical. It was bigoted."

Well, that was the times' traditional showstopper. He shouldn't have said anything. Sometimes he gave his mother too much credit.

3

By the time Nico arose the next day, Martine must have been up and at 'em for hours. She was already halfway through scrubbing the baby-blue kitchen cabinets, her shoulders bulging from another muscle T. The surfaces she'd scoured were a discernably baby-er blue.

"*¡Buenas días, Nico Niñito!*" she cried. She mimed sleep again. "*¿Dormiste bien?*"

"Fine." The grunted reply should have communicated in universal Esperanto that he was not a "morning person." Helping himself to the coffeepot, he took a sip and winced. This shit all but required a knife and fork. Though he preferred it black, a glug of milk only turned the mugful a sickly umber and tepid to boot. This wasn't his mother's coffee.

"*¿Quieres desayuna?*" their guest asked gaily, lifting the loaf from the artisanal bakery on Cortelyou Road. "*¿Huevos? ¿Mantener revueltos, fritos, o rancheros?*" She was remarkably generous with other people's food.

"No, *gracias*." Nico slumped with his undrinkable coffee and buried himself in his phone. So *niñito* meant "little boy." Charming.

Martine prattled, "*¡Debes mantener tus fuerzas! ¡El desayuno es la comida más importante del día!*"

Focused on ignoring her, Nico only clocked what all her beavering at the stove was about when she plunked a plate of fried eggs and toast before him. He didn't want it, but she'd been here less than a day, and he didn't want to seem rude. The yolks were too set and the toast was too dark, but the grilled tomatoes, fished from the leftover salad, were a nice touch.

Yet the presence of this peppy Latina was already destabilizing Nico's hovercraft repose. He felt irritable, when his demeanor on waking was commonly poised. Change of any kind rumpled something, which he tripped over like a rucked rug. With the jolt of a repaired moving walkway, time seemed to be moving forward again. It was horrible.

With great fanfare later that week, their "newest New Yorker" prepared a feast of Honduran dishes: *baleadas*, basically burritos; *catrachas*, the same ingredients but spread out; and *pupusas*, more tortilla things, but filled and oozing. At least she wasn't afraid of cheese.

After ooh-ing and ah-ing over the fancy appliances with all their settings and buttons, Martine promptly assumed responsibility for the household's laundry, and she ironed everything. Not just his shirts, but his T-shirts and boxers. She ironed his *jeans*. She ironed the sheets. She ironed the tea towels. She ironed the towel-towels, which made them stiff. All this obsessive flattening being a total waste of time didn't faintly constrain his mother's effusions of gratitude.

Martine soon accompanied his mother food shopping to ensure they were always stocked with the ingredients for her Honduran specialties: slightly different arrangements of beans, cheese, beef, and corn. The other pattern: everything was fried. Which would ordinarily have freaked his mother. Instead, she acted enchanted by this exotic new cuisine, when really it was just Mexican without the kick.

Having established the precedent, Nico now submitted to Martine's cooked breakfasts every morning. If he didn't leave the house, she'd be on him to come down for lunch. It wasn't the food he disliked; it was the debt.

"I thought she wasn't supposed to be our servant," Nico noted a few weeks into this pointless experiment, on a rare occasion he could speak to his mother in private. The sun was blazing, and the newly eco-conscious Martine was hanging laundry on the outdoor clothesline. He could seldom talk candidly about their lodger, because her comprehension of English was eternally uncertain and she was always *there*.

"I've told her repeatedly that she doesn't have to cook or clean or do our shopping," his mother said. "But she *wants* to pitch in. I appreciate the attitude. Migrants are constantly being tarred at takers, and Martine is desperate to give back."

"But she does more for me than I want her to. And the constant cleaning—is it really necessary? You've never been a germophobe who runs a white glove along the mantel. The scrubbing and polishing are exhausting to be around, and the whole house reeks of bleach."

"I think you don't like the fact she's showing you up."

"How?"

"You never carry a bowl to the sink, much less to the dishwasher. You take it for granted when *I* do your laundry. At best, you make your own sandwich and then leave the mayo on the counter."

"So I should compete with her over who can be more ingratiating."

"The word is helpful. Ingratiating is unkind. Oh, and by the way," she raised with unpersuasive casualness when he turned to go. "When you saw your father two nights ago—"

"Why do you think I saw Dad?"

"For whom else would you put on a collared shirt in the summer? And you didn't raid the fridge when you got home. Sorry, am I wrong?"

"Well, no." In the absence of a private entrance, his movements were too easy to track.

"Honey, I'm not put out. You know you can see him whenever you like." His mother's breezy tolerance was fraudulent. "I was just wondering whether you told him about Martine."

"Um—yeah, I guess. Was that okay?"

"Sure, more than okay. Our participation in the program is nothing to be ashamed of. I was just curious how he responded to the news." She'd averted her face, but not enough to hide that sly smile.

The "news" had landed in the middle of their restaurant table like a fifty-pound kettlebell dropped from the ceiling. Far better than a merely temporary diversion from the usual time-to-get-your-act-together-kid, the story of his mother's latest act of munificence had triggered his father's derision on a scale that consumed their dinner all the way through to three scoops of gelato.

"You could say he's not a fan," Nico allowed.

She'd given up on disguising the smile. "Well, isn't that just too bad."

At last, Martine did put one foot wrong. On an afternoon in latter July while his mother was out, the basement's new occupant took advantage of her proximity to the gardening tools stored on the side-entrance landing and voluntarily went at the landscaping all around the house. The job she did on the hydrangeas and rhododendrons with the cordless hedge trimmer put him in mind of the time his father took him to a proper Turkish barber on Flatbush when he was ten, because the cuts of the unisex hairdresser in Park Slope that his mother preferred were too soft and precious for a boy. Those electric clippers had been set at such a, so to speak, *barberous* level that classmates at school worried he had cancer, and he hadn't needed another haircut for a year and a half. In other words, Martine razed the shrubs to sticks.

His mother had watered, fertilized, and sculpted those plants since they were five inches high. Now, *maybe* folks raised in the tropics were accustomed to explosive flora that shot up into the stratosphere virtually overnight and had to be shown who's boss. But Nico was more inclined to perceive this literal hack job as revealing a side of their boarder hitherto unseen. He was tempted to call the butchery "passive-aggressive," except there was nothing passive about all those flowers mounded on the lawn like Ukrainian corpses in Bucha. So maybe it was just aggressive. Her aim had clearly not been to shape, coax, and nurture so much as to punish, dominate, and defeat. The carnage raised the question of what exactly Martine might be so pissed off about, not to mention how the rest of the time she could so successfully disguise a fury on that scale.

When Martine proudly displayed her handiwork, his mother's face would surely have appeared to "blanch" were it not for the strength of the summer sun. But watching his mother try to express a soupçon of displeasure was excruciating. Google Translate further moderated her temperate response, with all that enunciating and pausing between sentences. It was a lovely job, his mother assured their well-intentioned horticulturalist, and of course those bushes had been quite out of control. Martine's having taken it upon herself to impose some order on the grounds showed admirable initiative. But perhaps next time it might be optimal, that is, ever so slightly better, if Martine undertook a little consultation, that is, sought a bit of advice, a bit of *guidance*. But this was not to say that his mother wasn't delighted, everything looked great, and it was incredibly generous of Martine to do such hard, physically demanding work on their household's account. Even at the cost of further depleting his original $75,000 nest egg, Nico would have paid his mother serious money to simply fly off the handle, in her own yard, in English.

After all, what made this aristocratic reserve astonishing? Everyone imagined she was so sweet and kind and reasonable, but behind closed doors his mother had a terrifying temper. While eruptions of her personal Mount Vesuvius were relatively rare, the three kids never knew what would set them off. When sneaking a slug of gin from the liquor cabinet at twelve, Nico broke one of her Depression-era tumblers with ruby-red Art Deco crosshatching; her screaming fit was so extravagant that, showing him how beautiful and irreplaceable one of its sisters was, she knocked another one on the floor—for which he got the blame, too, just as it was his fault that she lost her voice. Why, for their mother the divorce itself was arguably one long act of sustained, self-destructive rage. Yet a mere acquaintance who ravaged thirty years' worth of gardening got a pat on the head.

His sisters dropped by frequently, taking Martine to see the sights. They went to the top of the Empire State Building; they ferried to the Statue of Liberty; they took the Circle Line—all the activities that real New Yorkers shunned. Marshaling suitably somber deportment, they escorted Martine to the 9/11 memorial.

The family's paperwork wunderkind, Vanessa helped Martine assemble documentation for a New York City ID, expressly brought in to give residents with "irregular" immigration status access to municipal services. Martine claimed that her passport had been stolen en route to the border, but she did still have her faded, flimsy paper Honduras national identity card; they downloaded documentation from Big Apple, Big Heart; and Vanessa put Martine Salgado on their mother's ConEd account to reach the four "points" required. Vanessa drove Martine to the Brooklyn Public Library at the northern end of Prospect Park in a state of some anxiety, because it was glaringly obvious that the Honduran ID was out-of-date (if not also fake, Nico did not say).

"The library was mobbed with migrants who didn't have appointments," Vanessa reported on return. "*We* had an appointment. So big deal the ID was expired. Did Martine herself expire? Did her birth date change, or had she suddenly not been born anymore? Stupid technicality, which they obviously overlooked on purpose. They *want* to give migrants identification. I overheard conversations from the other cubicles. Loads of people had shown up with no photo ID whatsoever, no proof of address, and they hadn't even filled out the application form. In comparison, Martine was a bureaucratic paragon." Happily, NYCID came with one-year memberships of three dozen cultural institutions, so when the usual trio went to MoMA and the Museum of Natural History, Martine's entry was free.

In short order, the whole family got nicknames, which Martine bestowed like garlands. Nico was stuck with "Nico Niñito," whose irresistible marriage of assonance and alliteration their guest invoked at every opportunity. Ditto "Vanessa Vivaz." At least the rhythm of "Gloria Ador*a*ble" worked in Spanish, whereas "Gloria Adorable" sounded retarded; actually, Gloria Ador*a*ble sounded like the refrain of a Christmas carol. But Vivacious Vanessa sure scored better than her sister; perhaps "Palermo Práctica" was coined when the wellspring of Martine's invention was running dry. Fuck being known as merely practical.

In fact, Nico detected a subtle but building competition between his sisters over Martine's favors—who could come up with the most offbeat museum, who got to introduce Martine to her first New York street pretzel, which of them had mastered fawning Spanish adjectives like *esplendida*, *maravillosa*, *magnifica*, and *deliciosa*.

Of the siblings, Nico was most often in Martine's vicinity, but he tried to keep his distance. She didn't make it easy. Had Nico been put up by strangers who didn't speak his language and whose motivation for sacrificing a whole floor of their house to a foreigner was anything but obvious, he'd have made himself scarce—withdrawing downstairs every evening, disappearing no-one-knew-where during the day. Instead, Martine did her nails in the living room. She cooked in the main *cocina* and took her meals at the family kitchen table. She even felt at ease waltzing into his bedroom to dust or to empty the trash can full of jizzy Kleenex.

For Nico, there was a huge atmospheric difference between ranging an empty home, or gliding past a parent house-trained to leave him alone, and sharing the space with an outsider who incessantly demanded interaction. Not to put too fine a point on it, Martine never shut up. During all that cooking and cleaning, she kept up a nonstop monologue in Spanish, whose intonations unerringly communicated eagerness, optimism, and goodwill. He had yet to detect any letup in this jubilation, whose constancy seemed unnatural, as well as at odds with the look in her eye when she first shook his hand out front. He begrudged the concession, but that look hadn't simply put him on notice in some way; her pupils had been flecked with an intelligence that should have made this prattling positivism impossible to maintain. He'd met his share of idiots in his day, but Martine's bubbly ebullience and tritely Latinate gesticulation seemed like a cunning imitation of an idiot. It seemed contrived, as well as deliberately designed to play to American stereotypes of the passionate, exuberant Hispanic; she could as well have broken out a pair of maracas. Her whole routine was ineffably off. The song and dance generated a mask, behind which she could be anyone. Not only did it feel like a schtick, but it also had the texture of a sleight of hand, a distraction. If so, distraction from what? Ironically, while his mother and sisters blithely took the woman's incontinent affections at face value, it was Nico's contrasting wariness that ascribed to their lodger the diabolical complexity of a real human being.

More uncomfortably still, the Honduran wore tight slacks, skimpy shorts, and revealing crop tops. She was forever butt-wagging from a ladder or bending over to pick up a carrot peeling from the floor with both cheeks practically in Nico's lap. He may have been flattering himself, but he was plagued by the suspicion that she dressed expressly for him. As if those two voluminous pink cases hadn't been sufficiently bursting, she'd already gone on a buying binge along Flatbush, returning with stacks of colorful flash fashion that she modeled not for Gloria Ador*ab*le but for Nico Niñito. The outfits she paraded across the living room with a hint of self-parody seemed consistently a half-size too small. Supposedly, she was married—though to a wife beater, so maybe the dickhead didn't count. Without intending to beforehand (if you will), during one of his recent Appointment Wanks at midnight, he got sidetracked into a hallucinogenic home video in which he was fucking Martine Salgado up the ass (and there were seamier details he preferred to forget). After he cleaned up, the standard embarrassment took longer than usual to burn off. Maybe he was being ridiculous, but it seemed as if the fantasy had been imposed on him. Its insertion in the part of his brain over which he exerted no control made him feel abused, like the inaugural victim of a male #MeToo.

After bringing Martine back from another I-heart-New-York adventure with Vanessa, who had to get home to her dog, his older sister didn't understand why they didn't just open some beers around the kitchen table. When Nico still insisted that he needed to get out of the house, she agreed to have a drink six blocks away at Manchego. He didn't know whom else to talk to, because he didn't usually feel the need to talk to anybody.

He and Palermo had grown somewhat apart, so she might not have appreciated how much he still looked up to her or quite why. When she was excelling as a gymnast in high school, he was only a little kid, and most of his adoration would have been wide-eyed and wordless. She was tall for the sport at its elite levels, but strong, graceful, and dedicated. She worked out on the balance beam or (her favorite) the uneven parallel bars every afternoon after school. She embodied the very desire and sense of direction that had abruptly evaporated on him at Fordham—assuming he'd ever enjoyed drive of his sister's variety, which was doubtful. By the time she was a senior, he'd troop from his elementary school down to James Madison High School's gymnasium to watch her practice, perching on the bleachers chin in hand, transfixed. Her long, angular face matched her long, angular figure, and what she could do was unearthly. On reflection, Nico rarely admired anyone these days, and he missed the sensation; the humility was strangely uplifting. Why, fiercely admiring someone else was credibly more satisfying than being admired yourself—though his many years of achieving nothing faintly admirable didn't allow for testing the theory.

Even then, the future Palermo Práctica was realistic and didn't necessarily expect to make the Olympic team. But getting into the University of Denver on an athletic scholarship was still a big deal; the school had one of the most competitive gymnastics programs in the country. From Colorado, Palermo sometimes sent the family videos of her routines at collegiate competitions, which he watched repeatedly, even if he was getting too old to have a crush on his own sister. She was hoping for at least a short professional career, maybe followed by a university coaching job.

Had she authored the story herself, she might have chosen to literally fall from grace on her beloved uneven parallel bars. But most of the major plot twists in your own stories you didn't get to write, and shortly before graduation Palermo's aspirations were prematurely truncated by a more quotidian car accident. His mother had been fixated on whether the driver had been drinking, but Palermo only cared about the fact of it. Her spine was a wreck. Once stabilized, she was transferred to New York to be closer to her family (then still a family); after being discharged, she returned to Ditmas Park. Subject to multiple operations, she was in and out of the Upper East Side's prestigious Hospital for Special Surgery for years.

Having also been in the car but comparatively unscathed, her boyfriend, Byron, moved to Brooklyn after he graduated, the better to help support what passed for her recovery. He stuck by her throughout the surgery redos, the ineffective pain meds, the grueling physical therapy. Once marginally functional, Palermo returned his loyalty by going all-in with his fledgling construction business in Queens. The end.

Not so fast. What made Palermo amazing wasn't a proficiency at gymnastics that more young women of every generation attained than the US Olympic teams required. No, his sister's emotional acrobatics if anything exceeded her feats on the uneven parallel bars, and it was her psychic triple backflip that earned her brother's eternal awe—though Nico had never known quite how to tell her this without risking her taking the compliment as an insult. For the immediacy with which she adapted to What Is at twenty-two was improbable, if not inhuman. Unless she condensed the turmoil into a bilious five minutes while he was out of the room, she seemed to skip altogether the toxic cocktail of bitterness, regret, grief, resentment, fury, and despair that ought logically to have followed such a lifetime disappointment. She never appeared to nurse, either, some absurd notion that she might someday return to her sport, not even as a ruse to kid herself through another set of pelvic curls. It was just, bang, that's over. Once she was minimally mobile, she tossed all her leotards, tights, hand chalk, and worn leather slippers in a box, which she had their mother deliver to a thrift shop that very day. She hunched to the curb to chuck her trophies unceremoniously in their outdoor trash bin. The only souvenir she kept of her decade-long passion was one tumbling mat, useful for physical therapy, and its continued if demoted presence in her surround seemed the source of neither affliction nor sentimentality. He never saw her cry, beyond a few leaked tears of pain that were involuntary.

With the crispness of changing a channel, she switched all the discipline she'd once applied to exhilarating exhibitions of power and finesse to dreary repetitions of primitive side bends and static wall sitting. Overnight, she replaced her holy grail of being able to execute a salto-forward-mount-to-hang-on-the-high-bar with being able to walk. She never talked about gymnastics.

For the last few years, when Americans were smitten with the formidable gymnast Simone Biles, Nico had instinctively sought to shelter his older sister, the construction company bookkeeper, from her compatriots' infatuation. Surely the astounding young gold medalist, who stuck at the end of her routines as if the mats were slathered with superglue, would make Palermo jealous. During the Tokyo Olympics, she walked into the den when the iconic athlete was on TV, and he lunged for the remote. His sister abjured blithely, "Leave it, dummy. What, I'm going to kick the screen in?" Then when Biles withdrew from the games due to "the twisties," Nico asked diffidently if his older sister was sympathetic. "Not especially," she said. "Why should I be?" As if the sport had nothing to do with her. Nico had also asked tentatively once whether she ever considered qualifying to coach. Palermo said, "No"—flatly, without rancor. When the monosyllabic reply didn't satisfy, she spelled out patiently, "Coaches have to be able to spot. That sometimes means catching a body in free fall. Gymnastics is dangerous. No responsible parent would entrust their daughter's well-being to a cripple." The word wasn't fashionable, but Palermo used it freely, and no one ever had the nerve to call her on it.

Were there such a thing as mature adulthood, it must have entailed perfect accommodation to reality. In some ways, Palermo was the model for Nico's eternally suspended present, during which he tried to confront its basics with the same frankness. He was a college graduate. He lived at home. He had no plans. He'd trained himself to refrain from justifying, apologizing for, or disguising from himself the plainness of his circumstance. He would not struggle against material fact.

He couldn't help but wonder, though, whether after falling for Palermo in her athletic prime Byron sometimes felt guiltily subject to a bait and switch. Her face had always been a bit odd, not quite symmetrical; she wasn't a classic beauty. But that lean, taut, sculpted body in college was peerless. Now she was merely skinny, with an incongruously soft belly that would have bothered her had Palermo allowed any insult to her vanity to bother her, which she probably didn't. She never applied makeup, and she kept her dark hair in that jagged, indifferent crop. She wore almost nothing but those black jeans, black T-shirts, and black sneakers.

Which was therefore what she was wearing when they ventured to Manchego. It wasn't far, but Nico had to slow his standard ground-eating pace to match his sister's trudge. The limp on the right side was routine, but every twenty steps or so she had to stop, because the hip had given way. "Is it bad?" he asked.

"Normal," she said. She'd been warned that she'd have to live with nerve pain for the rest of her life. He wasn't clear on what distinguished "nerve pain," aside from being particularly unpleasant—or as Palermo had put it, "unusually pure."

"So the home front seems to be ticking over," she said, once they were seated at a long marble table in their regular tapas bar on Cortelyou Road. "Mom's the queen bee of her book club. Now they all want to know where they can get their very own migrant, too—as if Mom has snagged a distinctive color of Ugg boots they can't locate on Amazon. Of course, what Mom's really snagged is *moral standing*. It's hard to find online."

He would need to be politic. "It's September. I don't see any sign that Martine is looking for a job or making any gesture toward establishing a home of her own."

Palermo guffawed. "I could say the same of you."

"I grew up there. She's a total stranger from Honduras."

"Not a stranger anymore."

"I wonder," Nico said obscurely.

"Three months or so isn't that long. Asylum seekers aren't allowed to work until at least six months after they apply, and Vanessa only helped her file at the end of July. Besides, she's a hoot. Learning more English. Mom appreciates the company, since you're as gregarious as a doorstop. Meanwhile, Mom's raking in thousands from the city. And I gather Martine's pretty helpful around the house."

"Too helpful," he said glumly as their beers and chorizo arrived.

"Lost me. Not sure there's such a thing as too helpful."

He would have to retreat and regroup. "Vanessa. You know how generous she is. She can't help it. Every time she shows up, her arms are full of flowers or some cake she's baked. I'm not like that. Neither of us is mean or stingy, but you're not like that, either. Vanessa is exploding with, I don't know . . ."

"*Love* is the word you're too embarrassed to reach for. *Love.* And you're right. You and I aren't exploding with love."

"She's always been like that. I watch people meet her, and at first all that gushy openness and goodwill are a turnoff, you know, a little *much*. And they also assume at the start—I can see it—that she must be stupid. But after only about ten minutes, they decide she's fantastic."

"Okay, I've seen that play out. And?"

"All I'm saying is I know what a good-hearted, naturally magnanimous person acts like, even if I'm not that kind of person and even if I find it a little weird. But with Martine? . . . It seems like a performance."

"Let me get this straight," Palermo said, licking chorizo oil from her fingers. "You're *objecting* that she does the laundry and the cooking."

Nico took a moment. "Yes." He continued in a torrent, "The feeling is that she's an honorary member of the family now and everyone's happy-clappy and nothing's stopping her from living there the rest of her life. Which as far as I can tell is what she intends."

Palermo laughed. "I think you're jealous. Martine's playing the part of the ideal live-in grown kid, and you're the useless-motherfucker reality."

"I've stayed out of Mom's hair."

"That's clearing a low bar. How about some *patatas bravas*? I'm still hungry."

"Listen," he resumed after the waitress left. "Martine. Does she give you presents?"

"Yeah, a few things. Like, she gave me this Saint Christopher necklace." Palermo fished out a quarter-size medallion beneath her T-shirt. "Bit trite, bit tacky, but she wore it up through Guatemala and Mexico for good luck—*para la buena suerte*, as I've learned to say. I didn't want to accept, because it meant so much to her, but she said she'd already found all the *buena suerte* she'd ever need by meeting our family. I was touched."

"She got Mom a cordless phone charger. Apple, the real thing. It's fifty bucks."

"I think Vanessa's been bowled over. We're all so used to her showing up with gifts galore that it never even occurs to us to get anything for *her*. Martine got her this big bright baskety bag decorated with straw flowers. Loud for my tastes, but Vanessa carts it everywhere."

"Well, last week she gave me a watch. It looks expensive, too."

"Don't be such a sucker. It's probably a knockoff from Canal Street."

"I don't think so," he said. "Where does the money come from? Refugee Cash Assistance pays around two hundred bucks a month. I looked it up. Lasts about ten minutes here. Wherever it's from, isn't it interesting she decides the best use she could put her resources to is plying the Bonaventuras with bribey little favors?"

"You are a piece of work, Nico. First, she's too helpful, and now she's too nice."

The *patatas bravas* arrived swimming in grease, but after Martine's cooking he was used to it. "I didn't want a watch," he said. "And presents are a burden."

"But you said from Vanessa—"

"Vanessa's presents aren't a burden because Vanessa doesn't mean them to be. From Martine, they're making a claim. You owe her. And that's the way she wants it."

"You could always give her something back."

"She'd just give me another fucking present! It's like she's making a down payment. And all this givey-givey camouflages the fact that she's getting free room and board in a two-point-five-million-dollar house in Ditmas Park as a reward for breaking American immigration law."

A mistake. Palermo visibly hardened. "There's nothing illegal about applying for asylum. As for the evil, manipulative motivation behind her presents, she's abashed by Mom's generosity and trying to express her gratitude. You could tear a page from that playbook yourself."

"You spent five years at home in your twenties," Nico mumbled.

"You didn't really say that. Tell me you didn't say that."

"Okay, okay! Not fair, and I didn't say that. But maybe in a way I'm in recovery, too."

"From *what*?"

He had just broken his hard-and-fast rule to never justify himself. He returned to facts. "I'm an almost imperceptible drain on Mom's resources: an increment more water and electricity. A few slices of bread from a loaf she'd otherwise let mold. The Wi-Fi would beam all over the house regardless. I pay for my own out-of-pocket expenses. My room would sit empty without me. On a material level, I fail to detect the urgency that I get a move on."

"Please. You know full well Vanessa and I don't ride your ass because you're inflating Mom's water bill. Honestly, we don't give you a hard time nearly enough. But since you're so keen that instead, Martine 'get a move on,' let's look at the balance sheet. She brings in three thou a month, so there's plenty left over after she takes a shower. Cooking and cleaning, more points. Makes domestic atmosphere livelier, bonus points—and you get demerits on that one. Keeps Mom company. Assures Mom she's Making the World a Better Place, while you just make her feel like as a mother she did something wrong."

"I was perfectly happy before Martine showed up," he said staunchly.

"Well!" Palermo cried, signaling for the bill. "Martine's showing up could be the best thing that's ever happened to you, then."

Glad for Vanessa's painstaking assistance with a baffling asylum application, Martine decided she should help other recent arrivals herself. Their mother put her in touch with a migrant liaison organization called the Inclusion Network. As a volunteer, Martine could explain to Spanish-speaking newcomers the multitude of benefits to which they were entitled.

With much leisure time at his disposal, Nico did a deep dive into all the programs to which Martine could connect IN's needy clients. Obviously, these pilgrims were owed housing on the very day they applied for it, at an average cost to the city of $394 per person per day. Martine could assure these sightseers that New York was also obliged to furnish them "a clean, well-constructed" mattress, a pillow, two clean sheets, a towel, soap, toilet tissue, a storage locker, and twice weekly laundry service.

She could detail how to sign up for Cash Assistance, which also entailed signing up for Medicaid—the financial enormity of which these wayfarers would only appreciate if they ever started paying American medical bills themselves. She could allay anxieties about not speaking a word of English, because the Human Resource Administration was legally required to provide paperwork and assistance in their own language. She could remind these budget travelers that they were always welcome to attend any public hospital's emergency room, regardless of their inability to pay. She could reassure finicky eaters that shelters must provide residents three "culturally relevant" meals per day, with snacks available 24/7. She could explain to families and single mothers how to take advantage of the Special Supplemental Nutrition Program for Women, Infants, and Children; in addition to items like diapers and infant formula, they were eligible to receive a list of foods running to nine pages in tiny print.

Martine could refer newcomers to a legion of legal charities that would file asylum applications on their behalf. She could instruct parents on how to enroll children in public school, including kindergarten and pre-K. She could provide the locations of food banks, soup kitchens, and pop-up cafeterias serving hot meals. She could apprise asylum seekers and refugees, aka everybody, that they were eligible for half-price Metro cards, free childcare, free school meals including breakfast, housing vouchers for reduced rent, utilities vouchers, $180/month Safety Net Assistance, free English classes, public library membership, mental health counseling, HIV services, discounted medications, and treatment for substance "misuse."

The list being arm-long, Martine might struggle to itemize all the

NGOs dedicated to assisting "our new neighbors." Nonprofits arranged weekly distributions of complimentary clothing, toys, books, and school supplies. They provided "TLC" goody bags to asylum seekers on arrival at the Port Authority bus terminal. Between "antihate" campaigns, the charities offered cooking classes, tutoring, and pro bono representation in immigration court. One outfit in Queens was giving all asylum seekers free bicycles.

Martine could guarantee that being "irregular" was no barrier to acquiring a valid New York State driver's license. She could apologize that these weary globe-trotters still couldn't vote in local elections, but only because the city council's bill to enfranchise noncitizens including "illegals" had been struck down by the state's Supreme Court. She could console them that their residence would still count as much as a citizen's in the apportionment of congressional seats by population, thereby bolstering the saintly Democratic Party's political power in their new state. And she could further incentivize the friends and relatives they left behind to lace up their hiking boots by recalling that two years earlier claims to have lost work during Covid qualified "undocumented" New Yorkers for one-time cash payments of $15,600 per person.

The one point of information she'd never need to underscore was that any babies they bore on the magic side of the Mexican border would instantly become American citizens, because they *definitely* knew that already.

Lastly, Martine could advise all these good people that receipt of these benefits was *not* dependent on their immigration status and did *not* involve getting a Social Security number; that the "public charge rule" barring immigrants from acquisition of visas or green cards because of their likelihood of becoming burdens on the state did *not* apply to asylum seekers, refugees, juveniles, or beneficiaries of the president's ever-expanding parole program; and that acceptance of any or all of these benefits in *no* way affected their immigration cases.

Thus, Nico concluded, the Bonaventuras' putting up one visitor would help ensure that there would soon be many more visitors, and that they would all get their rightful access to free stuff.

4

For Nico, one upside of these selfless endeavors on behalf of the "migrant community" was having the house more often to himself. Twice a week, his mother drove her fellow volunteer to provide logistical support for residents of the 140 hotels the city had now commandeered for Martine's brethren (though it was anybody's guess where that endangered species, the traditional Big Apple tourist hoping for dinner and a show, was now expected to lodge). For hours at a go, then, the frenetic Latinate voiceover switched to mute, and he could ease uninterrupted into the blissfully indefatigable offerings on YouTube. Small downside: he was the only one home to answer the doorbell.

Anticipating his lunch order of Koo Moo Yang BBQ pork, Gui Chai Chive Pancakes, and Panang Curry with Shrimp from DoorDash, Nico hustled to the front door. Roughly his age or a touch older, the dusky *hombre* on the porch was a good deal shorter than Nico (who may have been a weakling, but like most American men of his generation was well over six feet). Food delivery had been the exclusive purview of illegal immigrants from Central America for years.

Still, something was wrong with this picture. Empty hands by his sides, chin uptilted, the Latino was not carrying the signature brown paper sack in a plastic bag. Behind him, no moped awaited on the sidewalk.

"Something go wrong with the order?" Pointless. Delivery guys never spoke English.

The man didn't respond. His face was impassive, and he seemed to be sizing Nico up. Besides the missing chive pancakes, what else was wrong: demeanor. Which was not beseeching or apologetic, but closer to belligerent. Insolent, even. During an Indian summer in the eighties, he was wearing cargo shorts yet a turtle-necked tunic with long sleeves, below which the backs of his hands were scribbled in dark, inscrutable tattoos.

"Martine Salgado," he said at last. It wasn't a question. It was a demand.

Had Nico been thinking on his feet, he'd have denied that any such person resided here. After all, Martine claimed to be in flight from domestic violence. But Nico's constitutional wariness was all attitude. It didn't carry over into behavior. His life having been sheltered, his default assumptions about unknown quantities were almost as naive as Vanessa's. He was often leery of strangers because they might burden him with their problems, but it always took him too long to consider that they might be malign.

"Martine isn't here," Nico said. "*No aquí.*"

"Back when," the guy said.

"I have no idea."

"I wait."

Nico was standing before the wide-open front door, and the visitor simply launched past him into the house before he knew what was happening. The guy strolled unabashedly into the living room, casually checking out the heavy violet drapes with tasseled tiebacks, the mahogany bookcases, and the pink marble coffee table laid with pewter-and-crystal coasters, one of which he picked up, only to rattle it back to the marble as unworthy of his attentions. Even their neighbors rarely appreciated that his mother had assembled this stately decor with bargains from thrift shops and estate sales, so to this blow-in the interior would scan as "loaded." With sound architectural instincts, the uninvited guest navigated his way to the kitchen, as Nico trailed helplessly behind. The scavenger went straight to the refrigerator, located a Brooklyn Brewery IPA, and uncapped the bottle with a quick, practiced thwap of his hand on the counter's edge. He took a seat at the round kitchen table, landing unerringly in Nico's chair. He shut Nico's laptop, shoved it aside to clear space for his beer, and took out his phone.

Nico was at a loss. He hadn't asked this man in, and now he was stymied by how to get rid of the fucker. They hadn't taught courses at Fordham in Ejection of Not Overtly Threatening But Still Disturbingly Presumptuous Intruders. Not wanting to suggest conviviality, much less hospitality, he wasn't about to join the gate-crasher at the table. Awkwardly, then, he remained standing. This whole setup made him feel humiliated. More to the point, dominated. The fellow may have been on the short side, but he was compact and proportionate. He was clean-shaven and coarsely good-looking, with the faint residual pitting of adolescent acne. Even with the long-sleeved shirt, it was apparent that he sported a formidable musculature, the kind you got from long, boring, and intermittently conflictful stints in prison.

"Do you speak English?" Nico asked as the man thumb typed obliviously.

"Good enough," he grunted, not looking up. "I no have much to say."

"You know . . . Martine could be gone for hours. I'm not even sure she's coming back tonight. It might be better if, well, you could give me a message. Like, leave your phone number. So she could text you when she's available. I don't want you to have to waste your time."

"Me, nothing but time," he said, sounding a touch testy, as if Nico was making a pest of himself and it was Nico who was being impertinent.

The doorbell rang.

Nico was torn. He didn't like leaving this guy with his laptop. But taking it with him to answer the door would seem paranoid, maybe even racist. It might have been ludicrous to worry about being rude under the circumstances, but that's what years of soft, moron-ifying middle-class socialization will do to you. He left the laptop.

It was DoorDash. The deliveryman was standard issue: Hispanic, shy, no eye contact, eager to be gone. If only to keep watch over the intruder, Nico didn't know what else to do but return to the kitchen, where he unloaded the polystyrene containers and flipped open the lids. The interloper ambled over to survey the haul. Helping himself to the disposable chopsticks, he appropriated the barbecued pork—but not before taking two of the three chive pancakes and picking off the shrimp atop the curry to add them to his lunch.

Martine and his mother didn't get back until six. In the meantime, Nico retrieved his laptop and propped it on his knees after pulling a chair a distance from the table. But even with headphones, he was unable to concentrate on videos. He was constantly shooting furtive looks at this asshole who hadn't deigned to introduce himself, much less to explain his relationship to Martine, while blithely setting up shop in someone else's home. It rankled that Nico himself was agitated, yet asshole appeared at his ease. Two beers down, their home invader drifted to the adjoining bathroom—leaving the door open, thus treating his host to the loud rush of his manly stream. When Nico ducked into the can himself, piss was splattered all over the oak toilet seat, which the guy wasn't civilized enough to raise. Feeling responsible for the intruder's presence and uneager to hear from his mother about the mess, Nico set about wiping up the urine with wads of toilet roll. More humiliation. This prick had barged into the house, helped himself to Nico's pork dish, then whipped out his schlong and effectively pissed in his unwilling hotelier's palm. Still, after vigorously washing his hands, Nico didn't say anything. The reticence was instinctive, and for once not borne of oversocialized politeness. Keeping his mouth shut was probably smart.

"*¡Domingo!*" Martine cried as she let herself in the kitchen side door. "*¡Qué alivio! ¡Estás seguro! ¡Estaba muy preocupada! ¡Estoy tan feliz de verte!*"

She threw her arms around the guest and kissed him on both cheeks. "Domingo" was less demonstrative, eyeing the woman of the house behind Martine.

"Gloria Ado*rable, este es mi hermano,* Domingo," Martine introduced. "My brother, *sí*? Is so long! Our mother, she be so happy he okay!"

"Nice to meet you," Nico's mother said, shaking Domingo's hand limply; neither of their hearts seemed to be in it. "I mean, *Gusto de conocerte.*"

She'd been making an effort, but at sixty-two nothing stuck, and she'd probably just exhausted her new vocabulary. Amid the effusion of this household's last few months, the tepidness of his mother's welcome was conspicuous.

"*Hola,*" Domingo said lifelessly.

Nico and his mother shared a glance. He was unable to quite pack his own look with I'm-sorry-he-just-forced-his-way-in-I-had-no-idea-who-this-guy-was-and-he-gives-me-the-creeps. But he read her own uneasiness, and she probably got the gist.

Domingo's helping himself to another beer in the fridge spoke volumes. His mother's question, "Would you like a glass with that?" was pointed. He waved away the proffered glass with bored annoyance: he didn't give a fuck about her pointedness. Grabbing a bag of unopened Doritos on the counter, he muttered something in Spanish to his sister.

"*En un minute*," she said. "*Tenemos que ser amables con ellos.*"

Chips and cerveza secured, Domingo returned to his perch at the table and went obliviously back to his phone. Everyone else remained standing.

Though her English had improved somewhat, when Martine wanted to be sure to be understood she still used Google Translate: "We start north together, but we get separated. My phone from Honduras was robbed. I only get a new one, with a new number, from Border Patrol. Domingo's phone from Honduras must also be robbed, because when I call a stranger answer. I text, nothing. We do not see each other for many months, do not talk for many months. I do not know if he is even alive. Today is a big, wonderful surprise."

It was a tortuous explanation meant to emphasize, Nico supposed, that the two hadn't been in touch and she'd had no idea until just now that *this Domingo person* was awaiting her here. But even limited acquaintance with the man suggested that Domingo could take care of himself, and Nico wouldn't envy anyone who tried to separate the guy from his phone.

"So how did your brother know where to find you?" Nico asked.

"I think Human Resource Administration," Martine replied smoothly. "They make 'family reunification.'"

"So, ah . . . ," his mother addressed Martine. "Is your brother joining us for dinner, or does he have other plans?"

"No, no, no, no, no!" Martine said brightly. "Me *y* Domingo, basement? I cook *para mi hermano*? We need talk. Long no talk. You *y* Nico, nice time, *madre y niño*."

Given his retreat to grumpy teenage remoteness, his mother had no reason to relish the prospect of a one-on-one dinner with her son, but she still looked relieved.

As the brother had thus far proved less than a skillful conversationalist, the siblings soon withdrew downstairs (with eggs, tortillas, cheddar, Frank's hot sauce, two thick-cut pork chops Nico had had his eye on, a frying pan—and the Doritos). For the few minutes after they left, the two people who actually belonged in this house kept their minimal remarks innocuous.

"Chicken breast?" his mother proposed. "I'm craving something light."

Uncharacteristically, Nico followed her to the fridge and volunteered to cut vegetables. Having spent all afternoon in a clench of resentment, he felt vaguely ill. But he also felt a deep need to be physically near his mother, not the person of Gloria Bonaventura, but his *mother*, a sensation he couldn't remember experiencing with such intensity since he was ten years old.

Nico had four-plus years' worth of assurance that, unless someone was shouting, dialogue on the ground floor blurred to a murmur in the basement. Nevertheless, when he and his mother spoke about anything more sensitive than carrots, they kept their voices low.

"Do you suppose," she said while stuffing the chicken with olive tapenade, "that he plans to stay the night?" Her cheerful inflection was unpersuasive.

"Who knows," Nico muttered. "Probably."

"Well, he seems . . ."

"He seems like a thug."

"We shouldn't jump to conclusions," his mother said moderately. "His English may be limited, which can make people appear brusque, when really they're just shy and self-conscious. Besides, he's Martine's brother, and Martine is delightful."

"Therefore, by the transitive sibling property, Domingo is delightful. The same principle, since I'm Vanessa's brother, makes me the nicest person on earth."

She placed a warm hand on his cheek and rose on tiptoe to kiss his forehead. "You're not as bad as you think."

When they sat down to eat, Nico asked, "So what's up with our 'newest New Yorkers'?"

"Well, they've built a shelter in Marine Park," his mother said, "which could mean way less commuting for Martine and me. These big tents will house twenty-five hundred migrants!"

"Drop in the bucket," Nico said. "That's four days' worth."

"Honey . . . Ever wonder why you're so involved in this issue? It'd be one thing if you wanted to help us give out diapers, shavers, and tampons. Instead, you watch videos. I can't help but notice your questionable sources. Really, Nico. Fox News?"

"Does it matter if I read that six hundred migrants are arriving in New York every day in the *Guardian*? Facts don't have politics."

"They're useful to certain politics. And I repeat. Why do you care so much?"

"It's my city, too."

"I mean emotionally," she pressed. "What does it mean to you?"

He wasn't supposed to say this. "They're taking over."

"Oh, come on, that's absurd," she said, putting down her fork. "In a city of eight and a half million people, a hundred and twenty thousand is nothing."

"It won't stay a hundred and twenty thousand, and it's not nothing. You asked me how I felt. The taking-over-ness is a feeling."

"Or is that taking-over-osity?" It was a relief when she lightened up.

"Hey, I like this olive junk in the chicken," he noted as her reward.

"You could say the same of the wave that included your great-grandfather from Hamburg, you know," she added, gesturing to their expensively fake-old kitchen. "Look around you. We've taken over, too."

He let her have the last word. They strayed into a ritual discussion of why on earth Saint Vanessa still hadn't found a partner, when she was just the sort of unstinting woman that most men were ostensibly looking for. His mother claimed (again) that Vanessa would make a wonderful mother, but her younger daughter had only three more years before her fertility would start to decline. Nico noted that both his sisters' situations were way worse than that. Forget the mid-thirties. Female fertility peaked between the ages of eighteen and twenty-two. Everyone forgot that not that long ago, girls had babies at fourteen and were grandmothers by twenty-eight. Even now, the chances of an American woman having any children after the age of thirty were only 50 percent, and Vanessa and Palermo were thirty-two and thirty-five.

"How do you know all that?" asked his mother, sounding both impressed and suspicious. "Did you take a course in genetics I didn't know about?"

"Nah," Nico said. "YouTube. It's not a total waste of time."

"It's also not reliable."

"All you mean is you want my sisters to have kids, and I just told you something you don't want to hear."

"Palermo is probably a lost cause. She may not have the temperament, and I'm not sure she could physically carry a child to term without spending nine months in bed. But Vanessa does have the temperament. I can hold out hope, even if she's no longer *fourteen*."

Only on their second glass of wine did she loop back to the evening's red-button topic. "You know, that 'feeling' you mentioned? The sense that migrants are making an incursion—"

"I think the word you're looking for is *invasion*."

She rapped his knee. "Too much Fox! Don't you *ever* use that word."

His mother and her ilk tended to erect linguistic taboos around the truth. You couldn't call a "trans woman" a man because that's what he was. You couldn't call an unprecedented influx of foreigners an "invasion" because that's what it was. If it weren't an invasion, the word wouldn't upset them so much.

"Anyway, that feeling?" his mother resumed, trying to be warm, convivial, and onside. "It's *hostility to the Other*. It comes from a part of you—not just you personally, it's in all of us—that's ugly. It can disguise itself as national pride, but what fires it up is meanness. It's a primitive, tribal emotion that refuses to regard outsiders as fully human. I see it when locals pass migrants waiting outside hotels all the time. A look of pure hatred—even of babies!"

Nico reminded himself that this was his mother, for whom election night of 2008 constituted the peak high of her entire life. Given the websites he visited, he was prone to get careless. Even his goofy formulation of "taking-over-ness" had been poorly judged. He did *not* say, then, that the immigrants in this onslaught being "fully human" was the problem, since few Americans would have objected to the sudden arrival of ten million butterflies. Much less did he propose that maybe the *babies* in those hotel lines were most deserving of hostility, because it was with babies more than bazookas that you enduringly appropriated someone else's territory.

With Martine underfoot, Nico never lent a hand in the kitchen; competition over who could make it to the dishwasher first would have been undignified. Tonight, on a lark, he cleared the table and even wiped down the stove, though he feared setting a precedent he'd regret.

Martine poked her head in when they were almost finished. "Gloria Ador*able*! Is dark, is late. Okay Domingo stay?"

"I suppose," his mother said with detectable brittleness. "Shall I make up a guest room?"

"No, no go trouble. Domingo stay with me, sleep on sofa, *sí*? *Buenas noches, y gracias*."

Unlike the throngs pouring in from Mexico, this time at least someone *asked* if a visitor could stay, but she also hadn't specified for how long.

As it happened, that request was the last of its kind, though Domingo remained. Nico wondered whether Martine herself was exactly thrilled that her brother was sticking around. In the guy's vicinity, her habitual eagerness to please displayed a different texture. She'd always tried to get the Bonaventuras to like her and rely on her, the better to perpetuate this cushy setup. With Domingo, she seemed focused on not making him mad.

Somehow, although Nico never witnessed their arrival, Domingo's possessions manifested themselves, for on day five a large pile of alien male clothing suddenly mounded atop the washing machine. Because Martine did the laundry, the additional items didn't put anyone else out, but their profusion seemed to indicate more than a few days' catch-up with a sister.

"Has that guy *moved in*?" Nico asked his mother quietly after about a week.

"How do I know?" she replied helplessly.

"But it's your house."

"You would think," she said.

"He's not here through the aegis of the city sponsorship program, is he? So you're not getting any cash for your, um, hospitality."

"I don't think Martine has any other family in New York. I'd feel terribly awkward asking him to leave."

That was an awkwardness the interloper deployed to his advantage, and its power only intensified. The longer he stayed, the more his long-term residence became a fait accompli, and the more the prospect of an eviction presented itself as an outrage—writ large, precisely the dynamic that guaranteed all these so-called asylum seekers would never go home. Gloria Bonaventura wasn't usually a pushover, as she'd demonstrated in spades during the divorce, hiring a ruthless lawyer and winning the house along with its accoutrements, not to mention custody of her remaining minor child. But she had that fatal weakness: *people of color*, who triggered an obsequious, apologetic shit-eatery and effectively functioned as her kryptonite.

Like most impoverished refugees fleeing political persecution, Domingo had an Apple MacBook Pro. His external Bluetooth speaker was impressively belting. Thus, whenever Domingo was "home," what Martine had proudly identified as *punta* music pounded throughout the house: perky drumbeats, brass, cheesy strings, and spritely Spanish vocals. For Nico, *punta*'s putative African and indigenous elements failed to distinguish it from standard mariachi. They might as well have been living above a Mexican restaurant. He took back anything disparaging he'd ever said about the Arctic Monkeys. He came to especially detest a number called "Tickita Tickita," apparently a favorite downstairs, as the song would often repeat. It had a swaying, mincing, bouncy beat whose manic gaiety made Nico want to kill himself.

Blessed periods of *punta* reprieve marked the days at a time when Domingo was clearly away. It was obscure enough what he did when here; it was doubly obscure what he got up to when he disappeared. When Nico asked, Martine claimed that during her brother's absences he was looking for work. While privately curious just how many food deliverymen on illegal mopeds even a city the size of New York could absorb, Nico mentioned that many of Martine's recently arrived compatriots had signed up with Grubhub and Uber Eats. She seemed to find the suggestion amusing. "I think no. Domingo, he have more high ideas. In Rivera Hernandez, my brother get big respect."

Nico was too poorly acquainted with Honduran culture to discern whether Domingo's air of entitlement was typical or particular to their new guest. In any event, the brother was proving the Anti-Martine. The guy ignored the homeowner as if disregarding something that simply wasn't there. His obliviousness in Nico's presence was flavored with disdain. Though they must have been close in age, Domingo treated Nico Niñito like a pesky, wet-nosed kid. The guy never made small talk. Although by custom he didn't (thankfully) join them upstairs for dinner, he did silently serve himself substantial helpings of whatever Martine had prepared, taking more than his share of meat, then shuffling back to the basement; his sister would return the plate. Per his first day in this de facto hotel, he continued to grab whatever foodstuffs he fancied, and his English was good enough to ask *Mother, may I.* He left the milk out. He left bags of fresh bread agape and dribbled toast crumbs all over the floor. He stared obliviously for minutes into the refrigerator, sometimes walking away with his booty and leaving the door ajar. Martine was forever trailing after him, putting his empty beer bottles in the recycling bag or washing up the knife with which he'd hacked off a six-ounce chunk of cheddar, the mauled remains of which she would carefully rewrap and restore to the refrigerator's cheese drawer. He often grazed on the homeowner's groceries in the usual long-sleeved, turtlenecked shirt but wearing only boxers below the waist, wang shamelessly flickering at the flap.

Worst of all for Nico were the days Domingo was in the house and, Martine in tow, his mother was out do-gooding—as if installing the huddled masses yearning to breathe free in her own home hadn't bestowed sanctity enough. Inevitably, this meant putting up with the pounding, infantile jollity of *punta* for hours on end. Just knowing the brother was here introduced an atmospheric doughiness, the mood equivalent of a dumpling, in comparison to which Martine's company was angel food cake. Barricaded in his childhood bedroom, Nico dreaded creeping down to the kitchen, lest he intersect with Domingo's simultaneous desire for lunch. Why was he so anxious to avoid getting in the fellow's way, when this was his house and surely those roles should have been reversed? Moreover, in a display of the very resourcefulness that his mother admired in these "natural problem solvers," once Brooklyn's Indian summer had subsided to a biting chill, the brother located the thermostat. After the two women left, he cranked up the 60°F setting by almost twenty degrees. Before his mother returned, Nico would scurry down to turn it back to sixty, though she'd surely notice walking in that the house was bizarrely toasty, and she'd *definitely* notice when she got the bill.

Meanwhile, a parallel drama had been unspooling that for the most part Nico was willing to discount as far away and none of his business, though the few details that managed to penetrate his determined indifference were unquestionably gross.

He'd already cataloged a curious selectivity when it came to which news stories super exercised his mother and elder sister. Neither would-be activist ever seemed especially upset by the Chinese persecution of Uighurs, for example, or by the Iranian theocracy's repression of women, although you'd think that anyone obsessed with "social justice" would care about modern-day concentration camps, and self-avowed feminists would logically find distressing stories of young women murdered by morality police for not wearing headscarves. Nevertheless, a few days after Domingo graced them with his enchanting presence, both women's initial horror when news broke about a terrorist rampage through southern Israel seemed both genuine and spontaneous. Something like 1,200 people were murdered, among them a bunch of young people blissed out on E at a music festival, geezers, biddies, and little kids, while over 250 Israelis were abducted. The Palestinians', how would we say, *violations of social norms* included beheadings, plain old rapes along with more inventive penetrations with blunt objects and knives, eviscerations, amateur caesarians, and the throat-slitting of babies. It was as if these Hamas guys had sat around working out beforehand, "Okay, what's the most animalistic, universally repulsive stuff we could do that should alienate the sympathies of the entire world? Here's an idea! Stab women in the pussy while they're still alive and pull their entrails out through their vaginas!" Himself, Nico was broadly of the view that getting worked up in Ditmas

Park about any news story halfway around the planet didn't do anybody any good, and that included armchair handwringing over Uighurs and Iranian morality police. At least his *neutrality* was consistent.

Palermo and his mother were not consistent. Their spontaneous horror was short-lived. Way before Israel hit back with shock and awe, it was as if everyone in their informal membership had been sent a memo. Suddenly on a dime all those two fulminated about was the poor Palestinians. They went on marches in Manhattan, chanting catchy couplets like "From the river to the sea, Palestine will be free!" Not that Nico was invested either way, but the dizzyingly abrupt switcheroo was clinically interesting.

Though it was getting nippy, Nico resumed his long walkabouts across the city, the better to keep mercifully away from Domingo all day. Leaving that chancy character alone in the house was idiotic, and maybe one day they'd return to find that the TVs, laptops, and his grandmother's heirloom silver had magically vanished. But letting yourself be taken advantage of dependably encouraged folks to take even more advantage of you, and his mother would have asked for it.

Nico would first tool past the Brooklyn Vybe, a red-brick hotel on Flatbush whose reviews on Trip Advisor were scathing: drug dealing in the lobby and no shower gel! The Vybe was listed online as "permanently closed," but it was not closed. The owners had redeemed their investment without splurging on shower gel. Block-booked by the city, the building was now home to guess-who.

From the Vybe, he'd hike up to Prospect Park, which was none-too-subtly self-segregated into discrete ethnic enclaves, their boundaries especially apparent during mass picnics on weekends. Hispanics clustered in the south, though the upper perimeter of the Spanish-speaking domain was steadily expanding northward. Fond of thickly iced commemorative sheet cakes and metallic helium balloons, the Latinos claimed their turf by blaring banda, *ranchero*, norteño, corridos, *grupero*, salsa, bossa nova, tango, *cumbia*, or bachata (thank you, Wikipedia, but every style of Latin-American music sounded the same to Nico, who hated all of it). The whole eastern side of the park was black, with a few pockets of families who were born here, but more predominantly Africans and Afro-Caribbeans, who were partial to steel pan drum bands and enormous aluminum trays of spicy chicken. The north was mixed, with an area just south of the bandshell unofficially reserved for native-born white people, whose territory shrank every year.

As he headed north along the western edge, the "bike lane" alongside would be whizzing with heavy electrified two-wheelers whose city-mandated 15 mph speed limiters had been disabled, mopeds without license plates, and not a few proper motorcycles. Their overwhelmingly Hispanic riders didn't glance over their shoulders before overtaking or signal when making a turn. Their facial expressions were habitually blank, as if the doings of the indigenous were an irrelevancy conducted behind glass. Nico sometimes played a game with himself, Spot the Actual Bicycle, seldom counting more than two or three bikers churning on their own power, reliably of the pale-skinned variety keen to get their precious *exercise*. To the battery brigade, the obsolete cyclists were so slow as to constitute stationary objects, an annoyingly obstructive form of litter.

Strolling down Flatbush Avenue, he'd reach the sloping, mud-brown Barclays Center stadium, across whose plaza camped dozens of migrants and sometimes whole families, often parked beside their luggage and propping signs (SEKURITE, DIGNITE, RESPET). Blankets on the paving tiles might offer up down-at-the-heel leatherette boots, a pilled watch cap, a rusty pair of scissors—the dregs of some local's trash bin—for a dollar or two. A couple of years back, this plaza would have been clean and uncluttered.

Atlantic Avenue would at least sport the comfortingly familiar host of delivery vans from Amazon, FedEx, and UPS backing up traffic for blocks on one side and the trailers of a television production company commandeering a whole lane all the way from Nevins to Smith on the other: dysfunctional business as usual. Nico was nostalgic for the days when Brooklyn was way too unhip to attract film crews. Nowadays, this borough was crisscrossed with open-topped double-deckers, from which Midwestern sightseers would rubberneck at *real* Brooklyn cannabis outlets and take pics of *real* Brooklyn dry cleaners.

Since he'd been undertaking these marathon treks, the situation on the pedestrian ramp of the Brooklyn Bridge had steadily deteriorated. The dwindling ranks of American out-of-towners crossing the landmark off their bucket list had been replaced by novice tradesmen from every corner of the globe hawking plastic cups of spiced mango slices or malformed Statue of Liberty trinkets to the few passersby who weren't selling something themselves. When he finally struggled to the Manhattan side, the park across from City Hall would also be jam-packed with foreign merchants selling bric-a-brac that no one in their right minds would want for free.

By this point Nico would be on the weary side, though a seven-mile hike to Chambers Street was no big deal for a healthy young man of twenty-six. What would really be fatiguing him, then, was cumulative incredulity. The Covid lockdowns had been stupid enough, destroying small retailers and restaurants and marring the streets with plywood and padlocked shutters. But on top of all that economic self-harm, the city of his birth was being transformed over a mere eighteen months into an unrecognizable third-world hellscape.

This was the point at which, when talking to the likes of his mother, he'd have to hastily underscore his searing sympathy with all these innocent, well-meaning intrepids who understandably yearned for "a better life." He'd be forced to clarify as well that he had nothing *personally* against any of these strivers; that, were their circumstances reversed, he'd have hightailed it to America himself; that, whenever he encountered a migrant one-on-one, he flushed with an intense recognition of their *common humanity*.

While there would have been some truth to these defensive declarations, the whole "common humanity" schtick was wearing thin. Were he totally honest with himself, lately when laying eyes on yet another pack of brooding young men—loitering with hooded eyes and five words of English between them—he felt the initial inklings of *personal* animosity. A cascade of strangers had thrown themselves on the mercy of people like his parents who had no rational motivation to assume such a burden and who were therefore being taken for chumps. So for the first time since the fiasco began, this fall he found himself not simply disliking illegal *migration*, but also *disliking the migrants themselves*. Yes, *Mom*, this "hostility to the Other" hailed from a place in himself that was "ugly." But all these interlopers forcing him to feel something ugly merely slathered on an extra layer of resentment.

If he were really, really honest, then, the root purpose of these urban hiking trips was to work himself into a rage. Accordingly, he would proceed onward—launching up Center Street, jigging over to Lafayette, merging onto Fourth Avenue, crossing Fourteenth Street, cruising up Park, and swinging around Grand Central Station, until he finally hit 45 East Forty-Fifth: an easy-to-remember address whose once-elegant nineteen-floor Italian Renaissance Revival structure formerly sponsored Guy Lombardo's iconic radio rendition of "Auld Lang Syne" on New Year's Eve but had now been rechristened "the new Ellis Island": the Roosevelt Hotel.

Its commercial profitability also a victim of Covid lockdowns, the Roosevelt still presented a formidable edifice, occupying an entire city block. But the gleaming jut of its boxy marquee now meant something very different than the promise of Old World luxury accommodation. The line from that main entrance sometimes stretched down East Forty-Fifth, around the corner to Vanderbilt, then back across East Forty-Sixth. The extent of the supplicants was enough to make you curse the inscription on the Statue of Liberty about giving us your tired, poor, hungry, homeless "refuse of your teeming shore." The hackneyed American exhortation was merely a *poem*, which Nico's thicko compatriots fatally mistook for statutory immigration policy.

On his walkabout a week after Veterans Day, that long line wasn't moving. The whole area reeked of urine even from across the street. Trash was everywhere: takeout containers, potato chip bags, soda and coffee cups, but also dropped socks, broken toys, trodden panties, soiled diapers, and sodden Spanish comic books. Many of the foreigners slumped against the hotel were wearing surgical masks, though they were in the open air and New York's Covid mask mandate even for indoor public spaces had lapsed a good year and a half before. Did the superstitious prophylactics signal genuine fear of disease, genuine concern about spreading disease, confusion about current CDC regulations, or a brown-nosing desire to please?

As for the motley line overall, it was the progressives' collapse of a population with all the diversity of a post–George Floyd television ad into an undifferentiated, universally benevolent and deserving mass that was really dehumanizing. Maybe the kids didn't have a choice, but all these adults had decided of their own accord to barge into someone else's country and to demand, if they were huddled outside the Roosevelt, free accommodation in a foreign city with exorbitant housing costs. It seemed fair, then, to hold the grown-ups individually accountable, and therefore as justifiably subject to *individual dislike*. After all, this crowd included a surprisingly large proportion of Africans, who having started out on the other side of the planet would have gone to stupendous trouble and expense to arrive on East Forty-Fifth Street. This line was the consequence of calculated, premeditated welching, and in Nico's book that made its components *personally unattractive*. Doubtless in the terms of this town's gullible, weak-kneed collective judgment, his finding the supplicants personally unattractive designated Nico himself as personally unattractive. Yet there was surely an element of courage—a more substantive courage than the kind required to select a controversial paint color—in sticking to an unpopular perspective even at the price of appearing despicable.

Thus, still from across the street, Nico experimented with singling out particular *asylum seekers* and catching their eyes, loading his gaze with aforesaid *dislike*. Most of the women looked away. But several men met his look head-on. The eyes of the black guys and Latinos filled with a returning dislike, whose ferocity knocked him back like a flamethrower.

Maybe there were exceptions, but the general feel from these folks wasn't beseeching humility and gratitude. They were bored to death. They were under-slept. They were hungry, after having been assured on TikTok they'd get lots of free food a damned sight more "culturally relevant" than periodically distributed egg salad sandwiches and bruised bananas. They wanted to know where, after all this dead time, was their fucking free hotel room, and they were *pissed off*. So, yeah, with nothing else to do, several of the men got a load of the American dude gooning at them from across the street—with his cozy waterproof Patagonia puffer coat in a flash designer color ("oxblood"), his $175 Nikes, his smug, lazy, unearned native-born citizenship, his fat wallet and full stomach, his spacious hang to go home to, and his sniffy, superior attitude written all over his self-satisfied white face. To Nico's surprise, the guys slouched in that sluggish line resented Nico way more than Nico resented them.

His hadj complete, he wasn't up for a ten-mile slog back and headed for the B train at Rockefeller Center. It was a straight shoot down to Newkirk Plaza, and in the olden days he might have zoned out en route, lulled into a doze by the familiar rumbling, juddering, and screech of brakes.

No such luck. The carriage was perpetually traversed by women with two or three kids in tow who should have been in school. These mothers were mostly peddling midget packets of M&Ms and miniature Mars Bars for a considerable markup at two bucks apiece. The MTA subway trade in tooth decay had been cornered by stocky South and Central Americans; Nico newly appreciated Martine Salgado's comparative good looks.

The first tout was torpid. Scrawled with the heavily overwritten GOD BLESS USA! GOOD CANDEE HEP ME, the sign looped around her neck swayed over a cardboard box rustling with a standard Halloween haul. Hawking cups of cubed watermelon whose hygienic preparation hadn't likely been given the Health Department's seal of approval, the next one was more assertive, shoving her phone at Nico's chest as it translated, "Please help feed my family." This enterprise was halfway between commerce and blackmail; the passengers who capitulated were largely paying the women to go away. But the market was saturated. By the fourth entourage to shake down the car, the hearts of the riders who'd already purchased candy bars they didn't want had hardened.

By the time the B train pulled into the Atlantic Avenue–Barclays Center station and picked up still more touts, Nico had had enough. When yet another phone was pushed in his face demanding he feed yet another family, he'd loaded Google Translate.

"I already pay taxes to feed your family," he entered clearly in English. "You should go back to your own country, because we don't want you here."

At the Spanish translation, she spat back, *"Puta!"*

Nico refused to believe that he was the sole New Yorker to harbor such go-home hostility. Yet most of this ridership could also have been foreign born, and their expressions were horrified. Yeah, yeah, of course what he said was "ugly." But the main problem with his token pushback was that he'd lied. It was his mother who paid taxes to feed that woman's family, and his mother didn't mind in the slightest.

5

Ostensibly to confer on the best approach to Thanksgiving, Nico cajoled both his sisters into a powwow at Manchego.

"Can't we ditch the whole soup-to-nuts schmear for once?" Palermo pleaded after they'd put in their tapas order; privately, Nico thought the kale and quinoa salad was a waste of thirteen bucks. "I'd happily downsize to a turkey crown, a pot of peas, and a commercial pie."

Vanessa biffed her sister's shoulder. "Killjoy! Make your usual cranberry sauce with port. Or just show up. Mom, Martine, and I will do everything. Meanwhile, I was wondering whether we should invite some migrants from the Brooklyn Vybe. They'll be lonely and a long way from home, while everyone else is stuffing themselves with friends and family."

"Aren't we doing our bit?" Nico said. "Two of these people live in our mother's house."

"So?" Vanessa said. "Martine's the best thing that's ever happened to Mom."

"Martine will try to assume responsibility for the whole shebang," Palermo said. "And Martine's turkey will be *fried*."

"That's not as crazy as you think," Vanessa said. "There's a Cajun technique for deep-fat-frying a whole turkey in only forty-five minutes—"

"Here's what I really wanted to talk to you guys about," Nico interrupted, keen to skip the recipe and cut to the chase. "Do we have to invite Domingo?"

"Terrifying," Vanessa said. "And totally dangerous."

"Domingo is terrifying and dangerous?" Palermo said.

"Who knows," Nico said.

"Deep-frying a whole turkey," Vanessa said. "But why wouldn't we invite Domingo?"

"If experience serves?" Nico said. "He'll march into the dining room and hack off both turkey legs with a cleaver. He'll slurp Palermo's cranberry sauce straight from the bowl, throw five bottles of wine in a sack, and disappear downstairs. Cue *punta* music."

"Yeah, Thanksgiving *gratitude* isn't the guy's forte," Palermo said.

"So he's the strong, silent type," Vanessa said. "He's pretty hot, honestly. And maybe he keeps to himself because he's uncomfortable imposing on someone else's family."

"You kidding?" Nico said. "He couldn't be more comfortable. *I'm* uncomfortable."

"You're not big on Migrant Number Two," Palermo said.

"No," he said. "I don't think Mom's big on him, either."

"But you're also not big on Migrant Number One," Palermo said.

"*What?*" Vanessa said.

"Never mind Martine," he said. "Right at first, Mom said she was uneasy about sponsoring a single man. Now that's just what she's doing, and he's a total jerk."

"Mom also said she'd be open to housing more than one migrant if the first one worked out," Vanessa said. "Martine's more than worked out."

"There's something sketchy about him," Nico said. "The backs of his hands are covered in tattoos."

"Most of my friends have tattoos," Vanessa said.

"I have tattoos," Palermo said.

His sisters were infuriating. "Not like these you don't."

"Has he done anything?" Palermo asked. "Filched anything, for example?"

"Like, an object, as opposed to anything I might have my eye on for lunch? So far the pewter-and-crystal coasters haven't caught his fancy."

"You mean the answer is no," Vanessa said.

Their tapas arrived. Personally, Nico preferred ordering exactly what he wanted and eating all of it. Maybe this whole migrant palaver was all about learning to share: his basement, his mother, his city, his country. What was the World Economic Forum's master game plan again? "You will own nothing and be happy."

Vanessa was busy shoveling the high-value dishes onto his and Palermo's plates—the garlic shrimp, tuna ceviche, and grilled octopus—while tossing a few balsamic brussels sprouts on her own. He forced her to take two more shrimp.

"Is Mom unhappy about the situation?" Vanessa asked.

"I guess she's made her peace with it," he said. "That's not the same as liking it."

"I don't think Domingo has much time for women," Palermo hazarded. "He never talks to me or looks me in the eye. He doesn't engage with Mom, either. And Martine waits on him hand and foot. Which is a little strange for a sister. But, Nico, are you just blowing off steam? Or proposing something?"

"I'm making an observation. That is, even if we decide he should find somewhere else to stay, I'm not sure we could get him to go. I hate to sound like a pussy—"

"Please don't use female genitalia as a pejorative," Palermo said.

"I hate to sound like a *kitty cat*," Nico revised sourly. "But if I picture myself announcing to Domingo that in *x* number of days he has to move out, I feel sick. IRL, I'd probably throw up." "In real life" now meriting an initialism meant something, though he wasn't sure what.

"You can get super hotheaded behind people's backs," Palermo told him. "You're not great about confronting people with your uncharitable opinions face-to-face."

"Oh, who is?" Nico said.

"Like, some of the stuff you've said about Martine—"

"*What* has he said about Martine?" Vanessa said in alarm.

"He thinks she's a scheming, manipulative opportunist." So much for sibling confidentiality.

"That's insane!" Vanessa exclaimed. "She's the sweetest, most good-hearted person I've ever met! If you can look into a pure soul like that and see only conniving and treachery, there's something wrong with *you*."

"Vanessa's right," Palermo said. "There's something dark going on in that head of yours, and you're projecting it onto other people. Mom says she's caught you watching anti-immigrant hate videos. That far-right stuff gets inside."

"I was trying to talk about Domingo," Nico said. "Who even if his sister is the second coming doesn't seem to be made of sugar and spice and everything nice."

"Okay," Palermo said, "I admit the guy hasn't been to charm school."

"Are you honestly worried he *is* dangerous?" Vanessa asked.

"It's the same with all these people!" Nico exclaimed. "Sure, most of them are probably harmless. Better than harmless! A valuable contribution to the glorious multicultural quilt of the United States! An addition to our labor market and a boost to our GDP! Future taxpayers! Patriots in waiting, who still believe in the American dream, now that the people born here think it's a moral cesspit! Harder workers than our own slackers—slackers like your own brother!"

"Nico, pipe down," Palermo shushed. "Our waitress can hear you, and she's Latinx."

"*But,*" Nico said, "a percentage of any large group of people is *not* harmless, and we can't tell who they are."

"We can't kick him out unless Mom wants to," Palermo said. "And Mom hasn't put her foot down."

Swap "Mom" for "US federal government" and you had the last three years' policy paralysis in a nutshell.

When Nico got home, his mother had gone to bed, but Martine was still cleaning the kitchen. The beer at dinner had mostly made him tired, though he wasn't keen to decamp to his confining childhood bedroom just yet. When he parked at the kitchen table to idle a few minutes on his phone, Martine wiped her hands on a dish towel and set a bottle of a caramel-colored liquid called Flor de Caña before him, along with two shot glasses.

"Nico Niñito," she said, sliding into an adjacent chair and pouring them both measures. "You no like me, do you?"

Which quite took him aback. Martine had shed the exhausting effervescence she conjured for his mother and sisters. Her manner tonight was cool, matter of fact, and direct.

"I never said that," he said.

"You no have to." She nodded at his wrist. "You no wear watch I give you."

"Sorry, I . . ." He lifted his phone with a shrug. "I'm saving it for special occasions."

"You no good liar. Go on. Try. Is rum, from my country."

A little sweet, fiery, high proof.

"So, you say, Nico—why you no like me."

"It's not personal," he lied. "I don't like you as a phenomenon." He used the app to find *fenómeno*, but they seemed tacitly to agree to using Google Translate only when they had to.

"You no like *inmigrantes*."

"I like some *inmigrantes*. But there are too many of you."

"USA is big country. Big space everywhere."

"But you didn't come to the big spaces. You came to New York. Where it's very crowded and expensive. The people who live here have to pay for you."

"You pay?"

"Not me exactly. My mother pays."

"Gloria get money for me be here."

"She pays very high taxes." *Impuestos*. "The city is paying her with her own money."

"America is rich."

"America is broke—thirty-three trillion dollars in debt, and a couple trill more every year."

"*Los inmigrantes* take small money."

"Small money adds up."

"*You* is crowded? This house, three bedroom with nobody. In Honduras, thirty, forty people live here, *no hay problema*."

"Okay, no, I'm not personally crowded."

"*You* no pay. *You* no crowded. Why big feeling?"

"The 'big feeling' has to do with *home*. Home isn't only a place; home is a *big feeling*. That you belong. That you can understand the people around you, and they can understand you, because you're mostly the same." Nico was struggling for a definition that didn't stray into the tar pit of race. He resorted to Google's conversation mode. "It's about feeling comfortable and welcome and not having to try very hard. It's a place where people laugh at your jokes, and you laugh at their jokes. You can sing some of the same songs. You watch some of the same TV programs. You know you can trust most people, and you know how to recognize the people you can't trust. When your home fills up with people from somewhere else. Who speak different languages so you can't understand each other. Who think different things. Who have no deep connection to your home, no 'big feelings' for your home. No history there. Who often . . ." Here he hesitated; this was awkward face-to-face, but he remembered Palermo's unflattering characterization of her brother as only braving negative sentiments about people behind their backs. "Who often come to your home to take advantage, to see how much they can take. Well, then your home doesn't seem like a home anymore. It seems like anywhere. It makes you sad."

"Nico Niñito. I think you sad before I come here."

To the contrary, I was happy as Larry before you and especially your fucking brother arrived, and now the experience of coming back to this house as I did tonight is totally different and not in a good way. Ditto living in this city, which is now glutted with beggars and touts selling disgusting candy and fruit cups.

"How would you know?" Nico said. "You can't know what I was like before you got here." That was his best stab at expressing *the observer effect*. Back to Google. "The point is, think of being back in Honduras, and suddenly lots and lots of Americans move there. Every time you leave your house, you see more and more Americans. They only speak English, and they mostly speak to each other. There are so many Americans, humming the 'Star-Spangled Banner'"—not that Americans ever did that—"and discussing the finale of *Friends*, that there are even Americans in your own basement. Does it feel like your home anymore?"

Martine's laughter was unusually rich and relaxed. "I see *Friends*. In Honduras, *en español*."

"You didn't answer my question."

"You no want change," she said. "But everything change. Is life."

"There's slow, small change, sure, that's life. And there's sudden, big change because other people did something to you without asking your permission." *Permiso.*

"How I hurt you, Nico? What I take from you? Why new *inmigrantes* no just extra big party? Make extra big country. Where is hurt? I see you, every day angry. Why angry? I make you huevos rancheros. Where is bad? What you have before you no have now?"

Well, all that "home" shit had got him nowhere. "I hear you talk about 'my country.' This rum, you said, 'is from my country.'"

At which point Martine poured them another shot.

"Well, this is *my* country," he continued. "If I go to Honduras"—though God knows why he'd ever do that—"and I want to stay forever, I need *permiso* from your government."

"*Sí*. Asylum is *permiso*."

"You don't have asylum yet. Most *inmigrantes* don't qualify. They stay forever anyway."

"Vanessa promise I get asylum."

Only because you've researched how to game the system. "Asylum is not for people unhappy with where they live. The asylum system is stupid. It's a great big loophole." *Escapatoria*.

"I no make *sistema estúpido*. You angry at your government."

At last, a breakthrough. "Yes. I am very, very angry at my government."

"So why you make angry to me?"

"I'm angry that you and so many millions of people from all over the world all think you have a right to come here."

"USA no only for Americans. USA for every people. Any people can be American. America is 'land of opportunity,' *sí*?"

"It's supposed to be a land of opportunity for *me*."

Here she, too, resorted to Google: "You don't seem to be taking much advantage of opportunities. You sit with your phone. You sit with your computer."

Nico's cheeks burned. "One of the opportunities I can take advantage of if I want to is the opportunity to do nothing."

"You no help your mother. No clean, no shop, no cook. Why I call you 'Nico Niñito'? You act like little boy."

"Maybe the problem isn't that I don't like you, then," Nico said, drawing up and crossing his arms. "Maybe you don't like me."

"Gloria say you go *universidade*. Big money. For what? Gloria say four, soon five years you 'sit on ass.' Throw *universidade* in trash. In Spanish, we have word, *encaminado*. This mean 'go in one same direction.' When we say this about *niños*, this mean they on path for be grown-up. When mama say her son is *encaminado*, she proud. He be man soon. You, Nico. You no *encaminado*. You no go in any direction. No walk down path for be man."

"If you don't mind, that's my business. You say you're not hurting anybody. Well, I'm not hurting anybody, either."

"In shelter, before I come Ditmas. We all say Americans, how lazy. No work hard. Americans no *merecen*"—she entered some text—"no 'deserve' America. And no *inmigrantes*? USA *desmoronarse*"—she entered more text—"'crumble.' Whole country *crumble*. You need *inmigrantes* for you sit all day *con tu computadora*."

"You've come out of the goodness of your hearts to replace us with a better-quality population." He said this quickly and she didn't quite get it, which was fine. He added more slowly and clearly, "Palermo and Vanessa work very hard."

"*Sí*. And Gloria make toys for small money. This house, *su padre* buy. You, do *nada*. Two good, two *nada*." She waggled her hand with her thumb and little finger extended in a gesture of dubiety that she must have picked up north of the border. The mathematical implication was that two toilers and two spongers canceled each other out.

"You haven't met him, but my father works pretty damned hard, too. He's even sort of famous." Nico thumb typed. "*Mi padre es famoso.* Three out of five ain't bad."

Martine poured them another shot. He was losing track of their consumption, though the bottle was noticeably depleted.

"Palermo, I like," she said. "Vanessa, I like. But Palermo, no *bebés*. Vanessa, no *bebés*. For be mother, your sisters old. Palermo marry mucho years, no make *bebés*. Vanessa, no *hombre*. You, Nico? Is *bebé*. No *señorita*."

"Okay, so far none of us has continued the distinguished Bonaventura family line. What of it?" In truth, Nico found fatherhood somewhere between alien and petrifying.

"Soon, *tu familia?*" She made an exploding expression with both hands. "No *familia.*"

He gestured with his shot glass at the ripe swell of her presumably fertile belly. "What about you, then?"

"I make *bebés,*" she said flatly.

"That a proposition?"

"'Propa' . . . ?"

"Skip it."

"You say crowded. You say *los inmigrantes*—too many. But someday this house—nobody live here. You say big love for your 'home.' But love home, love *bebés.* No love *bebés,* no love anything. No love *bebés,* this house, this country, just be home *para los inmigrantes.*"

The last thing he expected tonight was a deep dive into below-replacement American fertility rates. "Well, you can have it, then." The flippancy flagged that he was getting plastered. "The house and the country both. But only after I'm gone. Like, seventy years from now. I'll leave you a set of keys."

"'Bonaventura'?" she continued, as if mentally ticking down a list. "*Su padre es Italiano.* Before marry, your mama name 'Gloria Feldhaus.' *Su familia es de Alemania.* America '*nación de inmigrantes,*' *sí?*"

Oh, Jesus, that old saw. "So? Both the German and Italian sides of our family have lived here for generations."

"No *inmigrantes,* you no be here."

"*Just* because we can trace our lineage back to somewhere else shouldn't mean we can't ever enforce our borders and that we have to let fucking everybody in. That would mean we don't deserve to have a country because of what our ancestors did, since if you let everyone in you're not a country, you're just an outline on a map. Some of the people who feel this most strongly are *other immigrants,* who came here before you, and who don't want you to take their jobs for lower wages. Who don't want their taxes to pay for your healthcare. Who actually *liked* the halfway orderly, halfway coherent, predominantly European country they emigrated to in the first place and don't want it to turn into the kind of dog-eat-dog shitholes they left behind."

This time he hadn't enlisted Google. Yet rather than look baffled, Martine looked strangely victorious, as if she'd successfully goaded him into so losing his cool that he ceased to communicate. Leaving his intemperate and pointless diatribe untranslated, she took a different tack. "You born here. Grow up in nice big house. No hungry. ¿Eres especial? You earn born here? I no born here because God no like me? I bad señora. So God born me in 'shithole.'" She'd at least recognized one word.

"If you mean being born American is lucky, okay, yes. I'm lucky." Rather clumsy thumb typing. "*Yo afortunado.*"

"Americans think born here, they better."

"I don't think I'm better than you or anyone else who wants to live here. Okay, maybe it's not fair. Some people are born in bad countries; some people are born in good countries. It's pure chance."

However fogged his concentration, Nico's internal bullshit alarm still went off. Had he the cogency and presence of mind, he'd have liked to insert here that, actually, "good countries" were the cumulative consequence of diligence, social cooperation, and innovation over many years, whereas "bad countries" were the result of tyranny, social indiscipline, and corruption, so in an intergenerational sense the fashioning of a desirable place to live had precious little to do with luck. Hence Martine and her ilk were trying to cash in on civilizational benefits their forbears hadn't amassed; their attempted shortcut to prosperity was effectively a kind of cheating, mooching, or theft. But that argument might have proved a bit much for his impaired lucidity and Google Translate both.

"Still, total fairness, everyone gets the same, means we'd *all* live in shitholes," he wrapped up. "Besides, what good is luck if you throw it away?"

The question didn't seem to compute.

He rephrased. "I want to *stay* lucky."

"I *make* me lucky," Martine countered. "I take *mi fortuna*. I no sit *con computadora*. Who is better person, Nico? Who is better *American*? Everything from where I come is fight. You fight for what is yours or what should be yours. Because you no fight? Someone take it from you. Is no so different here, even if you no see it. You no fight, you lose. You think you have nice country, nice soft life. But you only lie around? Other people take your nice country, they take your nice soft life. Because you no fight."

On the Tuesday before the holiday, Nico's father texted, **Hey, pal. Rita w family I don't get on w for Thanksgiving. Just checking, dinner out w me on Thurs? But you probably plan to eat w your Mom.** Rita was, of course, his father's new wife, who didn't really qualify as "new" anymore but would doubtless enjoy that designation until the end of time, and whom Nico duly detested as a matter of family obligation. Consensus dictated that his father's remarriage had been too soon and was therefore unseemly and suspicious.

The last-minute invitation transparently anticipated refusal. Ordinarily, Nico would have indeed declined, and not only out of kneejerk loyalty to his mother, but because his father did not subscribe to his mother's kid gloves approach to their only son's career inertia. Yet now even the family's adoptive mascot was hectoring, "You go *universidade*. Big money. For what?" Might as well opt for being badgered in complete, grammatical English sentences—especially if it got him out of Thanksgiving with *Domingo*.

Nico located his mother in the kitchen around noon on the holiday itself—okay, not much advance notice, but it turned out he'd put off his announcement for good reason. Because when he told her he was deserting the traditional family spread to join Evil Dad at a bloodless commercial restaurant, his mother defied all the conventional therapeutic homilies about how divorced parents should never subject the children to a tug-of-war.

"WHAT?" she cried, withdrawing her hand from the raw turkey's cavity fast enough that a big wodge of stuffing scattered on the floor. "Your sisters, Martine, and I have been cooking nonstop while you watch YouTube, and your thanks are to waltz out of here the moment your father crooks his finger? I go to *huge* effort to maintain a semblance of our old traditions—not just Thanksgiving with all the trappings, but *Christmas* and *birthdays, lamb* on Easter, and Fourth of July picnics in

Prospect Park! I still find time to decorate the house for Halloween, which in this neighborhood has become a demanding competition! I do everything I can to give you kids a consoling sense that you still have a history, and a family, and you're still part of a culture! What does your father do? When not publishing callous opinion pieces that taint his children's good name? Takes you out to dinner, capriciously, on the rare occasions he remembers he has a son, like discovering some gift certificate in the bottom of a drawer." Clanging the pot of peeled potatoes in cold water with a serving spoon, she scoffed, "But God forbid he should *make* anything. He *buys* it. And he has some nerve to ask you out on Thanksgiving, of all days! The only thing worse is your saying yes! I've read about how the parent who's less 'available,' who makes less effort, who's emotionally stinting, is *always* the favorite! Everyone responds to scarcity! While the parent who's constantly there, who takes care of business, who's the one person you can rely on, who's generous, and considerate, and solicitous, and *cooks from morning to night*, gets treated like shit! Well, I've had it! I quit! As for all these repetitive, exhausting, formulaic holidays, you kids are now officially on your own!"

With that, she hefted the stuffed twenty-something-pound turkey from its roasting pan and thunked it in the pedal bin.

Carlin Bonaventura had been an established fixture on New York's intellectual scene forever, or that's the way it had always seemed to Nico: his father was a big-wig journalist, documentary filmmaker, and political commentator, period. The few classmates at Fordham who consumed legacy media recognized his father's byline, which Nico rather liked, though he didn't like himself for liking it. Kids who rode the coattails of accomplished parents were pathetic.

Yet now that Nico was plodding through his own twenties, it occurred to him that his father had also, once, been twenty-six. As the guy's professional bed wouldn't have been feathered by a father who sold light bulbs on the Lower East Side, presumably he wasn't "an established fixture on New York's intellectual scene" straight out of the starting gate, and on his graduation from Bennington "Carlin Bonaventura" wouldn't have rung with the lilting musicality of the household name but must have sounded like just anybody. As the youngest kid, Nico was hazy on his father's early career, but Mr. Authority on Everything would presumably have *ended up* on the staff of the New Republic while getting regular commissions from the New Yorker and Harper's and doing guest appearances on the PBS Newshour; he couldn't have simply waltzed in the front door of the fourth estate on Day One. But Nico had no inkling how all this A-to-B-ing was accomplished. In his limited experience, people got crap jobs with low pay, and then they continued to work in crap jobs with low pay. The process of career ascension was as mysterious as the rise to the right hand of God the Father. Alas, Nico was insufficiently enthralled by what was popularly known as adult life to even attempt to decipher its rituals of self-promotion.

His father was a competent grown-up of a sort they didn't apparently make anymore. And Nico wasn't envious. Not in the least. Dad was eternally busy, and busyness seemed a plainly unpalatable state. (How interesting, that the word *business* really meant busyness, which made employment in the mercantile sector sound like frantic, purposeless make-work, just as an "occupation" suggested that merely being *occupied*, never mind with what, was the point.) All that rushing to catch taxis to the airport, the worrying about tight connections in O'Hare, the hotel reservations, the constant checking of your watch (little wonder that he didn't wear the one from Martine). Busy people were always late and always anxious and there was always something they hadn't done. All through high school and college, Nico hated that feeling of somethingorother being *due*, and as soon as you met the one obligation somethingorother else was *due*. That's what graduation from Fordham had meant to him: nothing was due. This perfect absence of temporal encumbrance induced an exhilarating sensation of expanse, of boundlessness, of lightness, of cleanness, of purity even, of total self-possession and full inhabitation of the present, with no nagging future imposition dragging him forward, and he was pledged to avoid at all costs putting himself in a position ever again where anything else was *due*.

Owing to said busyness, father and son had never been close, though Dad had done his mighty best to be "supportive" during Nico's schooling, clapping his kid on the back in a near-parody of the "proud father" and in fact repeating specifically how "proud he was" over and over as Nico consistently churned out the expected high grades and test scores—as if Dad were trying to talk himself into something. That is, Nico suspected that his father wasn't proud. Not actively, inwardly proud. Dad wanted to feel proud, and he aped being proud pretty convincingly, but "I'm so proud of you, son" was a mantra, and it was too verbal, too prescribed, too much of a parental recitative. Nico had a feeling that real pride, even on someone else's account, was quiet. It expressed itself in an upright bearing, a low burn in the eye, or a slight smile, and as soon as it became spoken, a statement, it was outside you, something you gestured toward, or aspired to, and it became an artifice, a conceit. That tacit little warmth in your chest, the real thing: that was the kind of pride that Carlin Bonaventura felt in *himself*.

Nowadays, the situation was a great deal worse than the subtle distance between naming an emotion and wanting to feel that way versus actually feeling it and keeping your mouth shut. Nico had solved the problem of that hollow-sounding "I'm so proud of you" line by latterly failing to furnish any accomplishments of which his father might conceivably claim to be proud. The poor guy couldn't comprehend why his own son would graduate from college and then do absolutely nothing for four and a half years (much less five, to which Nico would soon eagerly round up, as the duration of his neglecting to achieve anything whatsoever amounted to a form of achievement). There was no way Nico could have successfully explained himself, either, even if declining to explain himself were not company policy. He felt sorry for his father, who wasn't so much ashamed as stymied. Before his son's "stall," the man had never imputed complexity to his youngest, who'd presented as what-you-see-is-what-you-get: a bright, diligent youngster who didn't take drugs (or not that many) and turned in his papers on time. Dad wasn't interested in engineering, but the one thing he grasped about studying engineering is that people who did that became: engineers. Overnight, his only son had converted from a standard-issue "promising young man" to an opaque black box. Dad had tried everything to crack that safe: cajolery, bribery, flattery, criticism, inquisition, and expressions of despair. Not, however, anger—because Nico's contented inertness didn't seem to make anyone mad, exactly. It made them feel helpless, a weakening sensation that drained away all the energy required for fury.

While being subject to all that fruitless hacking at the walls of his enclosure was sometimes unpleasant—he could sense the vibration from inside—Nico remained confident that the impenetrability of his personal Portakabin would hold, and he took a guilty enjoyment in his father's frustration. He quite liked being bewildering. Having registered with delight that you didn't have to return voicemail if you didn't feel like it, that you wouldn't get arrested if you didn't respond to emails or texts, and that even in your family when someone asked you a question it was possible to take the Fifth, he'd discovered the imperviousness of being flat-out unavailable. It had been boring as fuck to be the good son and conscientious student. While he wasn't persuaded that he'd become genuinely complicated—subjectively, having fuck-all ambition was supremely straightforward—he did relish having conjured the appearance of complexity. It turned out that being unfathomable was a great deal more fun than being drearily understood.

What Nico himself had thus far failed to understand was his parents' divorce, though he was torn less over which account of the marital breakdown rang true than over whether he cared.

One version of the estrangement ran like this: starting around 2012, when Nico was fifteen, after having seen politically eye to eye for the whole of their marriage, his parents began to diverge. When a societal obsession with transgenderism came out of nowhere and went from zero to sixty faster than a Ferrari, his mother was engrossed, watching every one of the documentaries about little boys wearing dresses that showed almost back-to-back during this period, while to his father the trend was warped and decadent. During the relentless cable news coverage of the killing of Trayvon Martin in a Florida gated community by a neighborhood watch "vigilante" named George Zimmerman, his mother grew outraged, while his father continually objected that the unthreatening, childlike picture of the seventeen-year-old victim used exclusively on CNN was clearly taken when the kid was twelve. Over the following couple of years, his mother's "progressive" left grew increasingly strange.

That was a detached summary with which Nico was satisfied because the details didn't interest him in the slightest.

When his father announced he was leaving the *New Republic*, where he'd grown at odds with the staff, his mother assumed the new online magazine her husband aimed to establish next would naturally align with cozily Democratic websites like *Politico, HuffPost,* and *Slate.* When she learned the inflammatory authors he was bringing on board, she accused him of constructing a "far-right" bastion of "bigotry and hate." His father countered that, because the "far-left" was headed for la-la land, he was breaking ranks with the fanatics and getting in on the ground floor of the resistance. In hindsight, *Sanity.com* was ahead of its time. It was "anti-woke" even before the word *woke* became fashionable in lefty activist circles, and well before the term was co-opted by the opposition as an object of derision.

His parents' doctrinal conflicts spoiled many a family dinner and apparently spilled into social occasions, during which the couple's mutual sniping spoiled other people's dinners, too. To use an adjective latterly flung at everything from deficits to fossil fuels, the situation was *unsustainable,* and unlike everything else that was supposedly unsustainable, this one, as you would think anything unsustainable would be, was not sustained.

So there you go: a long-standing marriage fatally cleaved by the political passions of the era. Nico didn't buy it.

As for version two: In 2013, a fetching young intern at the *New Republic* accused his father of sexual harassment. In this respect as well, Carlin Bonaventura was ahead of his time, as this was over four years in advance of the #MeToo hullabaloo. (His mother's rage when the story broke was epic: a proper two-floor, five-hour job.) The magazine did an internal investigation and eventually cleared him of the charge, but his mother still didn't believe in her husband's oft-declared innocence. His father walked out because she didn't believe him.

While nothing stopped observers from accepting scenarios one and two as simultaneously true, Nico suspected they were both poppycock. Pieces of the puzzle didn't fit into either jigsaw—like the fact that his mother had once cultivated aspirations of her own and had never pictured herself married to a big swinging dick. Toys & Trinkets hadn't developed much beyond a hobby that covered its costs. While garnering the odd modest exhibition, her fabric art never broke out; most of the few shaggy pieces she sold were hanging in the houses of friends. Infuriatingly for a self-proclaimed feminist, she'd done the abundance of the parental heavy lifting, just as her mother had. Given a choice, Gloria née Feldhaus would probably have preferred marriage to a nonentity over basking in any man's reflected glory.

Of course, a divorce would neither improve her business's prospects nor retrieve all that time squandered on raising her children, but it was only when you threw in loads of irrationality when explaining relationships between men and women that your rendition would start to sound plausible. His mother was irked when *Sanity.com* not only took off, thriving even after it switched to a subscription paywall, but also accrued a reputation among centrists and more than a few classical liberals as well written, well researched, and data driven, although among her own coterie it grew only more heinously "far-right." To this day, nothing enraged his mother more than being identified as "Carlin Bonaventura's ex-wife."

In his father's telling, the *New Republic* intern had a crush on him; when he didn't return the favor, she took revenge. As the maître d' led Nico to the corner banquette of the chichi Upper West Side restaurant called Autopsy, that squared-off, oversize head and thick black hair, whose touches of gray suggested sagacity more than decay, helped explain why the flattering story about the smitten intern hadn't seemed far-fetched. At sixty-four, the guy still looked a catch. He could have stood to lose a few pounds, but the modest excess advertised his credentials as a bon vivant: yes, he would spring for another should-we-or-shouldn't-we bottle of wine and, no, he'd never order a single measly dessert for the whole table and ask for six spoons. He had status, and he exuded a restless energy that many women found irresistible. Nico's mother remained "attractive," but lately she could only qualify as pretty in low light. Maybe it was a male thing, but his father would still pass for "tall, dark, and handsome" under neon.

Their hug was hearty; Dad didn't suffer from the physical embarrassment of so many white people. "Hey, thanks for defecting to El Diablo for the holiday," he said, gesturing for Nico to have a seat. "I hope the betrayal didn't cost you too much in Ditmas."

"My hearing may have suffered a temporary threshold shift. And she threw the turkey in the trash can."

His father chuckled. "You know, I asked for *one thing* from the house when we split, just *one thing*: the desk in my study. Maybe you remember it: that massive oak rolltop—"

"With lots of little drawers and cubbies."

"That's the one. So she immediately had the desk picked up by some junk removal outfit. I probably shouldn't say this, but everyone thinks your mother's biggest problem is being too soft-hearted. What's really wrong with her is that she's spiteful."

Quite. She hadn't pulled down the shelves, hung bland travel posters, and installed another double bed in his father's once book-lined, award-plastered study just to accommodate more visitors. To fill up all those guest rooms, she'd have had to go out and make loads more out-of-town friends.

"Never fear," Nico said, "when she cools off, she'll haul the turkey out and wash off the coffee grounds. If only because she has so many mouths to feed. She and Vanessa have been trying to entice even more migrants to come to Thanksgiving dinner."

"Oh, yes, all that suffocating *goodness*. Like breathing this summer's Canadian wildfire smoke year-round."

They consulted the menu, both opting for the "deconstructed" traditional Thanksgiving dinner, since the constructed kind wasn't on offer.

"So," his father began, after ordering a cabernet/petite Syrah/Mourvèdre blend. "Made any progress on your next move?"

"Seriously?" Nico said. "You want to start in on that before the appetizer?"

"If I didn't 'start in on that' right away, I'd only be putting it off, and anything else I said would be disingenuous."

"All right, let's get it over with, then. No-I-have-not-made-any-progress-on-my-next-move. Satisfied?"

"Anything but. I'd think with this transition to electric-everything, an electrical engineer would be in demand. What about getting involved in the installation of EV chargers?"

"Electric vehicles," Nico said, "aren't ready for prime time. The batteries keep bursting into flames."

"But the next generation will have increased range . . ." Dad already sensed the inevitability of his defeat, as his son's expression would have been all too familiar: impregnable blankness, salted with a hint of pity and stirred by a twitch around the mouth, since it was always difficult not to smile. There was a less-than-remote possibility that Nico was a sadist.

"I don't want to install EV chargers," Nico said, with the greatest of sincerity.

"What *do* you want to do?" At this point, Nico often wondered if his father might cry.

To reply "absolutely nothing" might erode his precious veneer of complexity, so Nico settled for a microshrug as they accepted their amuse-bouche: a porcelain espresso cup of warm green foam. The mysteriousness of the goop's ingredients made it an apt prop for an enigma.

"Are you afraid of failure?" his father asked, not for the first time.

Nico wiped the foam from his upper lip, the edible shaving cream leaving an algal stain on the linen napkin. "Not especially." Contemplating failure would entail contemplating doing something that one might fail *at*.

"Is the future so bleak that there's no point in trying? I hear this all the time. Because of the eco lunacy. Young people don't want kids or careers because we're all going to die."

"Well, aren't we?" In truth, Nico's imagination simply cut out circa 2030, beyond which he envisioned a last pure white page in a book that leaves off midsentence. Maybe it was no coincidence that the generation his birth year demarcated, Z, was the last letter of the alphabet.

"In due course," his father was saying. "That doesn't preclude profitably occupying yourself in the meantime."

"I guess it's a question of what 'profitable' means. And profitable for who."

"For *whom*," his father corrected reflexively. "Don't you get bored?"

"No," Nico returned readily. "I like *observing* things. So far I haven't run out of stuff to observe."

"Reality is obliging on that front," his father begrudged. "But observation is so passive."

"It doesn't feel that way. It feels very active. After all, plenty of professions are nothing but observation. Marine biology. Astronomy."

"Then why not go into one of those fields?" his father exclaimed in frustration.

"Maybe I'd wake up and not feel like looking at jellyfish or a black hole. Besides, when you're forced to scrutinize something instead of choosing to, it's heavier. It's not the same."

"So you *aspire* to be a lightweight amateur. The autodidact in the attic getting cobwebs in his hair."

"Yes. That's nicely put. If I'd known myself better when adults asked me as a kid what I wanted to be when I grew up, that's exactly what I'd have told them. How did you put it? 'I want to grow up to be a *lightweight amateur.*'"

Speaking of observation, the wonky power dynamic of this conversation was fascinating. Nico clearly had the upper hand. Our layabout twenty-six-year-old was *toying with* his famous, credentialed, sixty-four-year-old dad, who not only had less power; he had no power. Wow. Super cool.

"Do you think you lack confidence?" his father asked, returning to the well-plowed psychic furrow.

"I'm exceedingly confident," Nico replied pleasantly. "I've been told since kindergarten that I'm a special person—that I was a perfectly baked bun straight out of the oven. That whatever I make or say or write is amazing. That I should bask in 'self-esteem' regardless of whether I've accomplished anything."

"So all this . . . torpor. Stasis. Which if you don't mind my saying so comes across as almost self-congratulatory. Your teachers and parents were invariably encouraging, and the result is . . . lethargy?"

"You people asked for it."

"Do you regard yourself as depressed?"

"Not clinically. For a while, girls in college could get out of being plain old white people by claiming to have been sexually assaulted. But the guys usually went for a diagnosis—anxiety, depression, PTSD, ADHD, bipolar. Maybe there's something wrong with me, but I seemed to be the only kid at Fordham who wasn't trying to get everyone else to feel sorry for them."

"So you *don't* feel sorry for yourself."

"Why should I?"

"But do you *feel* depressed?"

"Not you, too. They asked us how we *feel* ten times a day in high school. Like, junior year we were required to do 'mood journaling'—"

"There's no such gerund as *journaling,* because *journal* isn't a verb."

"It is now! Most of us hadn't a clue what we felt or felt nothing to speak of. But keep saying you feel fine? You're a disappointment. So we made shit up. Then after shoveling all this junk about your 'trauma' to make them happy, you start buying your own sob story."

"To clarify: you're *not* traumatized?"

Nico had had his fun and was ready to move on. "Honestly, having my own home turned into a migrant shelter has been a little traumatizing. And I may not need Zoloft, but I still find certain externals depressing. Like, are you aware Mom has taken in a second 'asylum seeker'?"

"You're joking."

Voilà, Nico deftly transferred his father's disgust to an absent party. "It's this Martine person's brother. Though Mom didn't apply to the city for another sponsorship. He just showed up, and she can't muster the chops to tell him to leave."

"She sure had no problem telling me to leave."

"I thought you marched out because you were indignant she didn't trust you."

His father sighed. "As the late Queen Elizabeth would say, *recollections vary*. What's this fellow like?"

"Keeps to himself. Doesn't say *please* and *thank you*. He's an animal, and I hate him."

"Is he dangerous?"

Vanessa had asked the same thing. This time, Nico supposed, "Maybe. But you only find out people are definitely dangerous when it's too late."

"I don't know what possessed your mother to take part in that foolhardy program," his father launched in vigorously, perhaps as relieved to have dispatched the obligatory item on the evening's agenda as Nico was. "The take-up's been way lower than expected—since it's one thing to get sanctimonious about your 'sanctuary city,' quite another to pick migrant pubic hairs from your own drain. So Big Apple, Big Heart—a saccharine tag I detest—isn't making any appreciable difference to the burden on the city. With one high-profile case where some Somali rapes a gullible sponsor like your mother, the whole program will draw to an ignominious close."

"I've never understood why Mom feels so guilty for living."

"Guilt is in fashion. I know I'm not meant to speak ill of your mother, but she's never been an original thinker, and she falls for ideological fads. Besides, it's not real guilt. Real guilt isn't something you parade in front of other people; it makes you want to crawl down a sewer drain and pull the manhole cover over your head. This is guilt as display, guilt as moral one-upmanship. Gloria's putting up migrants in *my house* is a form of showing off."

The first course arrived: served with a graffiti tag of piped pea puree, a terrine of pureed yam layered with thin stripes of what, no matter what the waiter called it, could only have been Marshmallow Fluff. However traditional, the combination was sickening. "Sorry to sound ungrateful," Nico said. "But this is, like, baby food."

"Lots of upscale restaurant fare is basically baby food. They never just serve you an artichoke. They have to put it in a blender." His father took one bite and shoved it aside. "You figure this young woman who's staying with you in Ditmas is planning to little by little bring in her whole family? Most of these people have form in that respect."

"I have a hard time reading Martine. I don't know what to make of people who pretend to be dumber than they are. I honestly don't know what her game is, or if she has a game. Mom, Palermo, and Vanessa all think the sun shines out of her ass. But I pick up an element of . . . an element of predation." It was the first time he'd reached for that word.

"Son, this whole flood over the border is predatory. They want what we have, and they're helping themselves to it. *None* of them are saying *please* or *thank you*. I'd never say this in print; it's just an impression. But the last big wave, in the nineties and early aughts, overwhelmingly Mexican, well—they seemed to keep their heads down, and they used their own networks to get by. The, uh, how do I put it? The *emotional texture* of this inundation is different. More aggressive. More, if you will, entitled. They don't try to evade detection, but line up to throw themselves on the mercy of the Border Patrol, and if they don't see an agent they go looking for one. That process of plunking themselves in the authorities' lap, it's not an entreaty. It's a shakedown."

"The problem's the cell phone," Nico said. "Friends and relatives who got here first have told them what to expect, including free transport to anywhere in the country. They already know that nobody's going to deport them—not right away, and not ever."

"And the court dates for asylum claims are now up to eight, even ten years out!" For once, his father paused his wineglass midway during its busy commute from the table. "All these people are assured before embarking on their $10,000 package holiday that even if they deign to show up in court, losing the case won't mean getting kicked out. The whole legal procedure is theater—expensive theater, for us. Meanwhile, government agencies and NGOs are doling out all these freebies—"

"When migrants arrive at Port Authority? They're not bused to the Roosevelt anymore but put in prepaid Ubers. That drove the comment section in the *New York Post* insane."

"But the weird thing is?" His father took a grateful gulp of his Australian blend. "The more we pile on the goodies, the more disappointed they seem to get. I've come across multiple migrants on the streets who're vocally pissed off. The food sucks. They want an apartment."

Nico always paid a price with that ritual face-off over his future, but one advantage of an evening with his father was finally having a conversation about the subject that was consuming him without having to pull his punches. It was such a relief to be away from all those *women*. Nevertheless, he was mindful of where he was—the Upper West Side surely had the largest concentration of the "be kind" contingent in the country—so he kept his voice down.

"There're all these videos online of migrants hauling out and punching some stray passerby in the face," Nico said. "Out of nowhere, for no reason. They seem to be, like you said, disappointed, or worse than that: *disgruntled*. It's like they bought a car—or someone gave them a car—that doesn't turn out to come with heated seats."

"Surprise," his father said. "A new country won't solve all your problems. It creates new ones."

"But at home, I can't ever say anything. You know what Mom and my sisters are like."

"That word *existential*?" His father used a breadstick as a pointer. "It's so overused that it's almost meaningless. But it's supposed to mean something that puts your very *existence* at stake. Well, the scale of this stampede is genuinely *existential*. Eight million 'encounters' at the border during this administration that we know about. But no one knows how many aliens are really crossing into this country, since a certain dodgy element *doesn't* go looking for a border agent. I gather there're probably as many visa overstayers, who fly in as tourists or students and disappear, as there are border crossers. And no one has any idea how many illegals are already here. One especially meticulous study came up with a range whose upper limit was thirty-five million, and that was several years ago. Those researchers at Yale were floored. As of this year, easily add another ten million to that."

"But we do have a labor shortage," Nico returned moderately, using his own breadstick to make contemplative jabs at his unappetizing first course. "The real free riders are millions of Americans, mostly men, who've opted out of the labor force. They're not even counted in the unemployment figures. Agriculture, restaurants, hotels, construction—all dependent on the *undocumented*. Less immigration would mean higher prices and a smaller GDP. We need immigrants in the care sector, because the native-born won't change their grandparents' diapers.

Immigrants *take jobs that Americans don't want*—like in meatpacking plants."

Nico's father had appeared bored at first and now looked put out. *And the night had been going so well!*

"This country's huge," Nico spooled away, "with enough empty space to absorb tens of millions more people, if not hundreds of millions. That book from a while back, *One Billion Americans*—it was hortatory, not a scare story. Immigration increases the tax base. With an aging population, we need more young people to prop up Medicare and Social Security. Big deal, immigration as the solution to a top-heavy age structure is a Ponzi scheme. That shouldn't bother your generation. You'll be long gone by the time the immigrants get old, too."

By now, his father had clued up. Crossing his arms, he leaned back in the green leather banquette to enjoy the show.

"After all," Nico continued, "if Americans can't be bothered to have enough children to replace themselves, they ought to make way for foreigners who still believe in their own lineage, in their own culture, and in humanity in general. Only people willing to make the sacrifice of bearing and raising children have a right to inherit the earth. We're *privileged*, so we owe it to the *vulnerable* to be generous. We don't deserve this country anyway, because we *stole it from indigenous peoples*. American citizens have no more of a moral right to the advantages of the United States than anyone else; everyone on the planet should be able to seek out a *better life* for their families. Sick, evil white folks owe opportunity to *marginalized peoples* to make up for *centuries of oppression*. This is a *land of immigrants*, so we have no business *pulling up the drawbridge*. We fucked up Central America with fruit companies and the CIA, so it's only fair we accept the migration that's a direct result of *our own interference*. Most migration is due to *climate change*, for which industrialized countries are totally to blame; so again, we're just reaping what we sowed. *Diversity* adds vitality and energy, and diversity is *our greatest strength*. We have all these great restaurants and ethnic food stores. Oh, sorry it took me so long: to ever oppose *people of color* coming into the country is *racist and xenophobic*.

"Practically, we can't defend a two-thousand-mile border, which would take too much money and personnel, and walls can be climbed or tunneled under. Anyone really determined to get into the US will find a way. We can't keep them out. There are too many of them. *Demography is destiny*, and all the population growth now is in Africa and the Middle East. People of European descent are dying out. We're dwindling into irrelevance even in what we used to think of as our own countries. We'll succumb to being outnumbered eventually, so we might as well give up now. Right-wing conspiracy theorists think Democrats want open borders to bring in more future Democratic voters and so create a one-party state. But the real reason the feds don't control the situation is they don't know how." A slight, droll smile, the facial equivalent of a curtsey, indicated that he was finished.

Bursting out laughing, his father defied the stuffiness of the venue with a round of applause. For the first time in years if not ever, Nico detected in the man across from him that glowing coal of tacit paternal pride. "Have to say, son, your mother's been working overtime."

"Especially since Martine showed up, I have to listen to this stuff all day."

"Could you also rattle off the talking points on the other side?"

"I don't get much practice. In Ditmas, putting opposing arguments is pissing in the wind."

"Go on, give it a go."

"US, population one billion? *Water*," Nico summarized succinctly. "Tax base? In New York, hardly any of these migrants are applying for work permits, even after they qualify, because they'll only work for cash. Gotta give them credit for being quick studies. Labor shortage? Besides depressing wages, low-skilled immigrants extract way more wealth than they generate. The industries they work in for peanuts are heavily subsidized by taxpayers through education, healthcare, and tax credits. They may increase GDP, but they reduce GDP per capita, which is what ordinary people really care about. Besides, even GDP growth from increased consumption is minimal, because they send massive remittances back home. In Honduras, the money wired by its US diaspora makes up a third of the economy."

Nico nipped his oratory in the bud. Their waiter was finally delivering their main course. That is, their Latino waiter.

Presumably, a crustless piece of toast topped with two fried sage leaves, a pickled onion, and a diagonal of stewed celery was deconstructed stuffing. The mashed potatoes were un-mashed: an uncannily perfect cube of boiled spud supported a sculpted pyramid of cold butter; alongside, an ice cup threaded with chives contained a tablespoon of cream. The vegetables comprised one diamond of carrot, one thinly sliced raw sprout splayed like a hand of cards, and two crossed green beans, leaving the plate resembling a canvas by Joan Miró. As for the holiday's centerpiece bird, it was somewhere in a croquette, or what the waiter called a "quenelle," a fried football whose interior proved ominously smooth.

"Dad, you were right," Nico said once the waiter had departed. "They put the turkey in a blender! What do you see in this place?"

"Rita likes it. I couldn't come up with anywhere else that was open. Sorry."

As they poked at their abstract expressionist montage—at least the football was edible—Nico noted, "Now I see how they got the boiled potato to have such sharp corners. It's practically raw."

"Hey, how do you know all this stuff?" his father asked. "Like, remittances in Honduras."

"Everyone assumes all the time I'm online I'm playing Super Mario Brothers."

"You know, the chaos on the border could swing next year's election."

"Mom thinks you're a Trump supporter."

"Your mother is quite wrong, and she simply betrays that she never reads my work."

"But if it really does come down to Biden and you-know-who, who will you vote for?"

"I have no idea."

Nico put down his fork. "Wow. And you're a pundit. Don't you have to take a side?"

"I keep waiting for a deus ex machina. A stroke? I don't even care which candidate has one. But I'd settle for an invasion from outer space. What about you? You're over eighteen."

"I probably won't vote." Who was he kidding? He totally wouldn't vote. Go *neutrality*.

"You even registered?"

"Nope."

"It's your sheer consistency I find chilling, Nico. That business you cited about labor participation? You're right. Over forty-four million mostly male, native-born Americans of working age aren't working and aren't looking for work. I always picture discouraged guys in their forties and fifties with at best a high school diploma who lost manufacturing jobs from globalization." His father waited a beat. "But you're one of them."

"Yeah, well," Nico said. "I've always been precocious."

After their "pumpkin pie"—a crescent of baked, skin-on squash with a caramel glaze, a tiny scoop of ice cream that "deconstructed" by melting on arrival, and an empty tartlet shell that prompted Nico to suppose, "I guess we're lucky they didn't just give us a bowl of flour"—his father was loath to entrust his only son to the subway late at night, so offered to drive Nico back to Brooklyn. Down the West Side Highway, Nico went quiet, leaving his father to fill the void.

"I bet you take it for granted that you're surrounded by people who barely speak English," his father began as Nico gazed at the lights from New Jersey glimmering in the Hudson.

"Sure," Nico said to the window.

"After all, by the time you were born, New York was only about forty-five percent white. I only know that because I had to look up the stats for a piece I was editing a couple of days ago. When you've lived through big but gradual changes the way I have, it's easy to project the present onto the past. I tend to misremember this city myself as always having been a tower of Babel. But it turns out that when *I* was born, New York City was *ninety percent white*. Lots of Ashkenazi Jews, Irish, Poles, and Italians, obviously, but Europeans. Those were the kids I went to school with, and our ethnic origins were already irrelevant. Thanks to the near moratorium on immigration between the 1920s and the 1960s, most of my classmates' parents not only spoke English, but spoke only English, and the differences in accent were mostly due to social class. There was already lots of intermarriage, and where one side of the family hailed from was mostly a point of curiosity—later to become a point of vanity, since for us boring white folks, any non-Anglo heritage now bestows cache. When I was growing up, my family may have eaten more pasta, but pretty much everyone drank Tang, lived on tuna casseroles topped with potato chips, and had Jell-O with Cool Whip for dessert.

"Anyway, turns out that by 1980, around the time I came back here after college, the proportion of whites in New York was down to sixty percent. Plenty of that decrease was crime-driven white flight. Still, nowadays? This city is *thirty-four percent white*. But the population has barely increased. I don't want to sound like some paranoid French reactionary, but that's not Great Replacement *Theory*; it's just replacement. These days, thirty-five . . . no, it's thirty-seven. *Thirty-seven percent of New York City was born in another country.* We have the highest concentration of foreign-born residents in the world."

"But that's supposed to be fucking wonderful."

"Well, maybe it is fucking wonderful," his father said. "In any case, if you say a single discouraging word about this town's fabulous 'multiculturalism,' you'll get your head cut off."

"You don't ever write about that, do you?"

"Oh, no, no, no, no, no," his father said, tapping the wheel. "I most certainly do not."

6

When his father dropped him off—the prospect of El Diablo popping in to say hello was so preposterous that Nico didn't bother to suggest it—he expected to walk in the side door to find his sisters polishing the last of the kitchen counters and arguing ritually over whether Palermo would take home the rest of Vanessa's pecan pie.

Instead he entered pandemonium. No one had done anything about the dishes, which were piled, unrinsed, on every conceivable surface. The leftovers were congealing on serving platters, rather than neatly sealed in Glasslock containers and stacked in the fridge. At least Vanessa was stripping the meat from the turkey carcass and packing it into Ziploc bags. Yet his mother, Palermo, and her husband, Byron, weren't pitching in with the cleanup as usual but were gathered at the kitchen table in various postures of helpless concern. Martine was hunched head-in-hands over her phone, and she was crying.

Adding to the hysterical ambience, Vanessa's dog, Kumquat, a small, blindingly white American Eskimo, was running about unsupervised and began yapping nonstop the moment Nico came in. Everyone claimed to love Kumquat, but the excitable fluff wad always seemed to uniquely dislike Nico; its bark was loud, shrill, and hostile. Through the open door to the dining room, he could see an entire family of total strangers seated at one end of the curly-maple table, at last cleared of unread *New Yorker*s but now covered in a riot of dirty wineglasses and soiled serving spoons; to seat a dozen fucking people, they'd have had to expand the table with both inserts. Four young kids were engrossed in their phones, while the unoccupied Latino parents did their level best to appear patient and as if they belonged here—which they didn't. Still and silent, the couple exuded a long-suffering vibe. Honestly, they looked trapped. They also looked as if they were used to feeling trapped.

Nico sidled up to Vanessa, who exclaimed, "Hi, honey!" and threw her arms around his shoulders while keeping her greasy hands in the air. "Happy Thanksgiving."

"It doesn't look especially happy on this end," he said, barely audible above the yapping.

"Kumquat!" Vanessa reprimanded. "Shush, now!" The dog settled down to an inimical growl. "I've never understood what that dog has against you. Maybe you've snowed the rest of us into believing you're a sweetie pie, and only Kumquat senses the darkness of your nature."

"Listen, who are those people?" he asked quietly, nodding at the dining room.

"The Ortegas. They're from Ecuador."

"Don't tell me. You dragged them in for Thanksgiving off the street."

"Something like that." She handed her brother a Ziploc. "Here, seal that. I want to send the Ortegas home with some turkey. And stuffing, and potatoes, and sprouts."

"Do they speak any English?"

"Only Spanish"—Vanessa gestured to the kitchen table—"so they probably know what's going on over there better than I do. Martine has been screaming a streak, and when you're upset you don't usually practice your foreign language skills."

As if to illustrate, Martine let fly with a rapid-fire keen in Spanish. She arose from her chair, clutched her hair, did a circuit around the breakfast room, then plunked back down in front of the phone in seeming despair. Both precious lifeline and object of horror, the phone itself took on the quality of The Ring in Tolkien, with powers to enhance or corrupt. He'd seen Martine bubbly and hyperactive; he'd seen her cut the bimbo act cold and be directly confrontational. He'd never seen her distraught.

"Hey," Nico said as the carcass grew denuded. "Leave a little turkey for me?"

"I thought you had dinner with Dad."

"Yeah. Lots of *bonding*, if that doesn't sound too traitorous. But it was nouvelle whatever. I'm starving."

Nothing made Vanessa happier than meeting someone else's needs, so she hustled to assemble a piled-up plate for the microwave. Before the ding, he overheard his mother murmur, "Oh, *mi amiga*, what are you going to do?"

Standing at the counter, Nico hoovered the warmed-up leftovers, while Vanessa packed up a sturdy flat-bottomed tote bag from Whole Foods with bulging baggies for "the Ortegas."

He asked his sister quietly between mouthfuls, "So what's Martine so fucked-up about?"

"Her children have been kidnapped in San Pedro Sula."

"Sorry," he said, trying not to choke. "What children?"

"Her three children back in Honduras. Honestly, if I were that poor girl, I'd have cracked in two by now."

"I feel like we skipped a step here. Has she ever said anything to you or Palermo about having three kids? Any kids?"

"Well—no."

"She's lived here for six months. You'd think they'd have, like, come up in conversation."

"My best guess? She didn't want to seem like too much of a burden. Since, you know, most normal mothers would be planning to reunite with their kids."

"No wonder she's had an eye on those three empty bedrooms," Nico muttered.

"They're not occupying any bedrooms if she doesn't get them back."

"What, were they staying with the husband?"

"With her mother. They had guns. She couldn't stop them."

Having thumped upstairs, Domingo sauntered into the kitchen. Kumquat immediately trotted up and began licking the brother's bare feet. That dog had lousy emotional instincts.

"*Hola*," Domingo said begrudgingly. Kicking the dog away, he reached casually into the Ortegas' goodie bag to retrieve one of the turkey parcels, whose contents he proceeded to selectively munch. Apparently, he preferred dark meat.

Nico rarely saw Vanessa annoyed, but she whisked the Whole Foods bag from the floor with more than a touch of irritation. She bustled to the dining room to deliver her care package to the Ortegas, who, after having been held hostage for leftovers for God knows how long, looked greatly relieved. But if these folks were housed at a shelter or hotel, they wouldn't have access to a fridge or microwave, in which case Vanessa's bounty could be destined for a dumpster. Mumbling *¡Muchas gracias!*, the family trailed to the side door and unhooked their thin jackets from the coatrack. Glancing around the strange dirty kitchen, the children tugged at their parents, making no effort to disguise their desperation to leave. They had no idea what they were doing in this big house. If they'd trekked from Ecuador, those kids had suffered no end of menacing strangers and improvised lodgings; their current accommodation would at least have grown familiar, and they yearned to return to it.

Vanessa grabbed a bulging black garbage bag sitting by the door and foisted it into the father's arms. "Here. Please. You guys don't have nearly warm enough gear for New York. You have no idea. It's gonna get super cold."

As the father couldn't have understood what Vanessa said, he poked into the open bag to reveal the garment on top: Nico's distinctively colored oxblood puffer coat.

While Vanessa saw the Ortegas out with a lavish embrace for each, Nico was forced to make conversation with Domingo.

"So what do the kidnappers want?"

"Are you *estupido*?" Domingo said, hacking the tip off the triangle of pie remaining in a tart pan, thereby ensuring it could no longer be cut into coherent wedges. "They want money."

"Thirty thousand dollar!" Martine wailed from the table.

"How would Martine ever get her hands on thirty grand?" Nico wondered.

"They know she is in America," Domingo said. "*Land of plenty*."

"What happens if they don't get the money?"

Again, Domingo looked at Nico Niñito as if he were thick even for a kid. "They shoot the children. You don't keep your word, nobody take you serious. You make example. Neighbors hear, so next time? The mother get the money. You don't mess with these people, *chico*."

Nico was starting to feel queasy. However combatively he and Martine had squared off after he came home from Manchego, they had at least, with seasonal seemliness, talked turkey. They had appeared to make some progress, even if you could hardly call their interests aligned. Why, that was precisely what the conversation over Flor de Caña had formally established: their interests were not aligned, and mutual recognition of that fact constituted a narrow common ground. So while he had no reason to wish her ill, her present plight had nothing to do with him. Or to rephrase, her plight should have had nothing to do with him. But a glance at his mother stroking Martine's shuddering shoulder confirmed that this kidnapping would have altogether to do with him.

As the night wore on, Martine collected herself sufficiently to explain in English that kidnapping in Honduras had developed into a lucrative industry, which anyone who kept up even passingly with Central America already knew. His sisters filled in a few narrative gaps for Nico. Thanksgiving dinner had imploded early in the final course, when Martine got a weepy call from her mother, followed by a couple of gritty text messages confirming the woman's story. That explained why so many of the dessert plates on the counters sported big chunks of unfinished pie in pools of melted ice cream, when Vanessa's pastry was top-drawer: everyone had stopped eating.

Having knocked herself out preparing the meal, even Vanessa couldn't disguise her exhaustion. Byron was ready to go home; Kumquat expressed a similar sentiment by pooping on the kitchen floor. Their mother was shattered, since she'd gladly invited a nice, needy migrant *looking for a better life* into her household, for whom she'd willingly invested in additional dispensers of liquid soap. But for a standard liberal Democrat, contending with a $30K kidnapping ransom was benevolence simply on the wrong scale.

So everyone went home or to bed, leaving the encrusted pots and dirty dishes piled in the sink and strewn over the kitchen island. The remaining leftovers, which Vanessa would traditionally have wrapped into neatly sealed foil parcels so that each guest would have the makings for a reprise the following night, were abandoned to spoil. Nico was no neat freak, but his mother never even left a water glass out on the counter overnight, and this unprecedented culinary chaos betokened havoc on a larger scale.

By the time Nico arose the next morning, Martine was unloading the dishwasher in preparation for another cycle.

"Hey, listen, about your kids. I'm sorry," he told her limply.

"*Sí*," she said bitterly, draining water from the lip of a pan lid. "Everyone is *sorry*."

Because this was officially a crisis and the Friday was a holiday, both Palermo and Vanessa showed up pronto. Their mother came down later than usual, because, she said, she'd lain awake in bed for hours. "Is okay," Martine said, when the sisters expressed their chagrin that they hadn't helped clean up. "I need keep busy."

Nico quietly collared Vanessa before the confab came to order. "Did you have to give the Ecuadorians my oxblood puffer coat?"

"I'm sorry, honey," she said with a pat on his arm. "We'd already scoured this house top to bottom for neglected clothes during the last donation drive. All that was left last night was the stuff people actually wear. If it makes you feel better, I also gave them Mom's black wool car coat and the shearling bomber jacket I'd worn on the way here."

"The dark brown one? But you love that jacket."

"Winter's coming. We can always buy new coats, and they can't."

"I'm not sure I can get a puffer in oxblood anymore." He sounded peevish.

She pinched his cheeks a little too hard. "Then you'll get a different color, poochie. Martine could lose her children. Puts losing a style statement in perspective."

After he'd been duly shamed, it would have been uncool to creep away, so Nico joined the coven at the round table with a pot of Martine's battery-acid coffee. They must have spent half an hour passing around Martine's phone and cooing over pictures of her kids, who had so confoundingly failed to feature in gatherings previous. The fact that her progeny also comprised two older sisters and a little boy made her children's perilous circumstances only more resonant, though the age spread was tighter than the Bonaventuras': eight, five, and three. Not usually a sucker for kiddie pics, even Nico had to admit they were cute. The oldest was fated to become a hottie; the middle one had a devious gleam in her eyes that resembled Martine's expression when she thought no one was looking; the youngest was watchful and bizarrely serious for a three-year-old. In over half the shots, Domingo was at least in the background, causing Nico to remark that the kids certainly had an attentive uncle. But where was their father?

"He no like photo," Martine explained. "Most time, he away drinking with *hombres*."

Once show-and-tell wrapped up, Martine bowed her head. "They give me till *día de Año Nuevo*. I no know how I get thirty thousand dollar in one month."

"Why would they demand such a large amount of money?" their mother asked. "You say this happens all the time. They must have some sense, then, of how big a ransom someone in your position could raise. Why's it in their interest to ask for the impossible?"

"They force you use all friends, all family, all you save, all you have."

"Would it do any good," Vanessa said, "to contact the Honduran police?"

Martine snorted. "Half time, kidnappers is police."

"You told me Domingo is respected in your neighborhood," Nico said. "Can't he apply pressure? Isn't kidnapping his nieces and nephew a form of disrespect?"

"Domingo have respect from one *pandilla*." Martine seemed put out that Nico imagined he had any grasp of shithole politics. "This boys, different one."

"Will your children be all right in the meantime?" their mother asked. "A month is a long time for men to take care of small children, and I should know. Carlin never took responsibility for these three for more than a weekend."

"The *pandillas*, they have *señoras* also. The kidnap, *muy organizado*."

"But how can you be sure the kidnappers will release your children," Palermo asked, "even if you come up with the money? I'm sorry to be brutal, but how can you even be sure they're still alive?"

Martine said hotly, "If your children? You think, oh, *no hay problema*, they dead already?"

"No, sorry," Palermo backed off. "Obviously, you've no choice but to assume they're still okay. But do they always let their hostages go if you pay?"

"No get *niñitos* back? Next time, kidnap no work." Ergo, truth-in-advertising policies pertained even to extortion.

Martine stood and paced, raking her hair. "How I get money? I only think, maybe *prostitución*. How much dollar *hombre* pay for fuck Martine?"

"Here we call it 'sex work,'" Palermo corrected. "There's nothing wrong with it. It's a legitimate way to make a living."

"You fuck for money?" Martine charged.

"Well, no," Palermo said. "It's not my job."

"Fuck for money no *my* job." She was clearly offended. That's what you got for trying too hard not to offend anybody.

Vanessa shot an eye roll at her sister. "No one wants you to sell your body, and Palermo doesn't want you to do that, either."

"I take *productos* from store? Sell black market."

"Stealing is a terrible idea," his mother admonished. "If you were caught, your asylum application could be endangered."

Of course, Nico considered silently, police in a sanctuary city would be statutorily forbidden from reporting Martine to the coldhearted meanies in ICE, and even a criminal conviction would never get her deported. Besides, thanks to concerns about "disparate impact"—meaning, the law had an impact on the people committing the crimes—shoplifting goods worth under $1,000 in New York had been downgraded to a misdemeanor. Martine could walk brazenly out of Target with armfuls of the high-value products popular with the light-fingered crowd—printer cartridges, razors, jeans, makeup, and (believe it or not) replacement electric toothbrush heads—and the cops would let her go, in the doubtful instance that they bothered to show up. In other words, Martine's plan to thieve her way to her children's liberation was superbly doable. If the Catholic merely borrowed a diligent Protestant work ethic, she'd clear $30,000 in fenced goods before the end of the year with days to spare.

But Martine had already moved on. "Or maybe I work for *la pandilla*. Smuggle *contrabando* over border, till I pay off debt. This is how many *inmigrantes* pay snakeheads."

"Oh, great," Palermo said. "That's the answer: modern slavery."

"No, no. I get better idea!" Martine said, suddenly excited. "I know what I sell! Make *muchos dolores*!" She quickly entered text in Google Translate. "'Kidney'!"

"Don't even think about it!" Vanessa cried. "You don't want to sell your kidney!"

"She's right," Palermo said. "You want nothing to do with the illegal organ trade."

"But I hear this," Martine said. "Two kidney, no need two. Sell kidney, I make big, big money!"

"Forget it," their mother said firmly. "We won't allow you to sell your kidney."

That was the first time in this ludicrous discussion anyone in the family had used the word "we."

Accordingly, Martine excused herself to pick up groceries for dinner, when the fridge was still full from the big pre-Thanksgiving haul of three days before. Clearly, their damsel in distress was leaving the Bonaventuras to confer among themselves over how best to come to her rescue—not that The Women acknowledged the calculation behind Martine's departure. Despite their outsize esteem for "black and brown peoples," the family's female contingent never gave Martine any credit. Only Nico allowed for the possibility that the Honduran was a mastermind.

"So, what are we going to do?" their mother said.

"I don't suppose involving the police on this end would do much good," Vanessa said.

"No jurisdiction," their mother said.

"Why do we have to do anything?" Nico said. "Why is this our problem?"

His mother shook her head. "Where did I go wrong with you, Nico? How could you ask that? Martine is a part of our family now."

"We haven't seen the ransom note," he said. "Which anybody could write anyway. This is all hearsay."

"You weren't here when her mother called," Palermo said. "It was pretty dramatic. That's not hearsay."

Yes, it was, too, but Nico let it go. "Doesn't it bother you guys that she never said anything before now about having kids?"

"It's a little weird," Palermo said. "Maybe she didn't want to send for them until she got settled."

"According to Mom here, she's settled as could be," Nico said. *"Part of the family.* Besides, if she's been secretive about the kids, what else do we not know?"

"Martine's three beautiful children have been kidnapped," Vanessa said passionately. "She's sick with worry, and this is no time to vent your baseless suspicions."

It was exactly the time to vent suspicions—like the moment in cold-call solicitations when they ask for your credit card number.

"I'm afraid we have no choice but to pay the ransom," their mother said (surprise!). "That's why kidnapping works. The stakes are too high to entertain puristic notions about how rewarding kidnapping only asks for more of the same. I hate the idea of handing over that much money to such awful people as much as you do, but I can't see any other way forward."

She was employing the same "we" that had gotten them into this fix in the first place: "we" had to welcome uninvited interlopers and all the chaos they brought with them into our home because "we" were so terribly glad "there's somewhere for them to go."

"Do you even have thirty grand in cash on hand?" Palermo asked their mother.

"I have . . . some cash on hand," she replied carefully. "But I've thought about this; it's one of the things that kept me up last night. I was hoping we might discuss the possibility of all of us putting something into the pot. I think it would be good for you three, spiritually, politically, and emotionally, to participate in this shared trauma and to make a personal sacrifice for our friend. After all, you've all benefited from an inheritance from my father. A contribution wouldn't make that big a dent in a nest egg of seventy-five K."

As anyone with an engineering degree had a background in math, it took Nico a microsecond to divide $30,000 by four: $7,500 apiece. At his miserly rate of expenditure, that represented at least a year—if not two, should he eliminate takeout and stick to Molson—of serene hovercraft repose. The subjective value of a whole year or two as a *lightweight amateur* was priceless.

"I thought that was a gift, not a loan," Nico said. "I don't remember Granddad's will including the caveat 'until your mother wants it back.'"

"Unfortunately, Byron and I plowed that whole inheritance into the business." Palermo's readjustment in her chair to indicate that her back was killing her was pointed. "You know, it went to a second van, a new compressor. Everyone thinks construction is larcenous, but we operate with a narrow profit margin. Other players who use cheap materials and do shoddy work are always undercutting us."

Palermo was acting like a proper grown-up. She was thirty-five. So faced with keeping her money versus sucking up to her mother, she picked the money.

"Isn't much of your workforce undocumented?" their mother asked. "In a way, this is an opportunity to say thank you."

"Um—I like to think we say thank you every day," Palermo said. "We give them jobs."

Out of curiosity, Nico asked, "Yeah, are your workmen on the books? Social Security numbers, New York and federal withholding, all that?"

"Um," Palermo said again, and she wasn't generally an *um* person. "Usually."

Punching at his mental translation app, Nico got his answer: never.

"I mean, I could see what we could do . . ." Palermo said. "But it would be very, very difficult for Byron and me to part with thousands of dollars right now."

"I said I was asking you to make a personal sacrifice," their mother said. "If it's not difficult, it's not a sacrifice."

"This whole thing with Martine wasn't my idea," Nico said. "Palermo and Vanessa thought it was great. I thought it was dumb. You didn't seem eager to solicit my opinion, but I thought at the time this sponsorship thing was asking for trouble, and now it turns out I was right. Now you want me to pay, not just pay by giving up my basement and putting up with all that sucky music"—Domingo had just begun to furnish their soundtrack—"but pay actual money for—I'm sorry, I'll just say it—for your mistake."

"I don't think it's been a mistake," his mother said, affronted. "I think it's been one of the most enriching experiences of our lives."

"I totally agree," Vanessa said. "Martine's a wonderful person, and I'm super grateful to have gotten to know her."

Right. Your best friend who has three kids you'd never heard of until last night.

"Nico," his mother said, "you're the one who can most easily afford to help Martine out."

"I'm also the one who argued against getting into this mess in the first place," he said. "I've got nothing against her, but I could have lived without ever having met Martine Salgado, and I could definitely have lived without having met"—Nico lowered his voice—"her brother."

"Maybe I should put it differently," his mother said. "I'm asking you to help *me* out."

Now, that was awkward.

"I've been able to save a portion of the sponsorship payments from the city," she continued. "But next year my alimony runs out. It's time-limited in New York, and I was awarded what the courts call 'spousal maintenance' for forty percent of the length of my marriage. Aside from this Big Apple, Big Heart arrangement, I'll soon have almost no income. I'm just old enough to start collecting Social Security, but I'd be much better off waiting another five years, because the earlier I sign on, the lower my monthly payments. They'll be low anyway, because my contributions have been sporadic. This is a very bad time for me to drop thirty thousand dollars on a crime syndicate."

Unlike all the other times when paying gangsters a packet would have been just swell. As this session was throwing up endless opportunities for *observation*, Nico found it noteworthy that neither he, Vanessa, nor Palermo ever pointed out that their mother was sitting on a $2.5 mil property. They didn't want her to sell the house.

"What about Dad?" Palermo suggested. "What if you laid out the situation to him? He could probably afford thirty grand."

"The fact that your father wouldn't contemplate financing this ransom for a New York minute," their mother said, "is one of the explanations for why we're divorced."

For Nico, that was it. He'd found a fragile solidarity with his father toward the end of their dinner the night before, and if Dad would remain perfectly unmoved by his mother's appeal, then Nico could remain unmoved as well. With the simple clarity of his seminal epiphany, *I don't want to be an engineer*, the resolution seemed to run in neon across the cornice of the breakfast room: *I won't contribute to any ransom.* The whole business was sordid, corrupt, and not part of his world; he didn't want it to become part of his world, either.

"You know I used that inheritance from Granddad as a down payment on my apartment," Vanessa said, having been awfully quiet ever since their mother had proposed picking all their pockets. "So that's just not available."

Their mother wore a tired expression. With three strikes, she was out. It must have been crushing to discover that the once-omnipotent scythe of parental disappointment couldn't cut butter anymore.

"But I do have some rainy-day savings," Vanessa went on; her voice had gone small, and the offer obviously pained her. "Not quite five thousand? You could have it. I couldn't live with myself if Martine's children were murdered because I was too stingy to help."

Of the four, Vanessa could least afford to part with any cash. She kept a tight lid on her salary at Peanuts to prevent the poorly funded outfit from going under. Though her apartment was tiny, the mortgage was stiff. He'd no idea how she ever saved ten cents after constantly shelling out for flowers, ingredients for fruit breads, and affectionately quirky presents when it wasn't even anybody's birthday. Given his younger sister's costly donation, he should probably feel ashamed of himself. He didn't.

The bottom line? They were all three adults in law, but when it came to mutual family expenses their assumption was still one of juveniles: parents pay for everything. (No wonder Nico didn't want kids.) The concept of chipping in, even to spring three young children from the clutches of violent gangbangers, seemed foreign and unfair—which is why even Vanessa had taken a long time to volunteer her meager savings and clearly found the forfeiture nearly a bridge too far. They didn't want to hear about Gloria Bonaventura's coming crisis of income or about some "forty percent of the length of her marriage" limitation on her alimony payments, because she was not some fellow grown-up with money problems; she was Their Mother, who along with Their Father had always made sure they needn't worry their pretty heads about family finances.

Surveying her brood with a sigh, Their Mother, too, seemed to take in this rock-solid fact of middle-class life. "No, Vanessa, I can't accept your savings if your brother and sister won't also make a contribution. I suppose I can claw together the thirty grand from somewhere."

There. Order had been restored. Though their mother shot a glare at the two grasping black sheep, they were impervious to her rebuke. Were Nico and Palermo monsters who, the better to retain their six-packs and compressors, were ready to send three innocents to their deaths? Nah. They simply knew full well that their mother would cover the shortfall.

When Martine returned with a sack of food they didn't need, their mother announced with no fanfare that "we"—for once her first-person plural was too kind—had decided that "we" would pay the children's ransom. Martine immediately threw her arms around her savior while proclaiming her utter amazement, as if this solution to her troubles had never entered her head. Uh-huh. The outpouring of gratitude, relief, and abashed astonishment was convincing, but just because a performance was very well done didn't mean it couldn't still be a performance.

For the following week, Nico was genuinely tortured, and not because up against it he'd proved himself to be criminally selfish, and not because he was worried about whether Martine's abducted children would be safe, and not because ever since the family conclave over the ransom his mother's demeanor around her only son had grown distinctly frosty. He felt burdened, indeed uniquely burdened, by a question that he shouldn't, in terms of his own self-interest, even consider posing. Obviously, to raise this point of doubt would do untold damage to his relationship to his mother and sisters while accomplishing absolutely nothing. Nevertheless, putting this question front and center was his responsibility, because it had to be put, because he would have contempt for himself if he didn't put it, and no one else was going to. The psychic turbulence of this week confirmed that the experience of responsibility was altogether odious, and he'd been hitherto wise to avoid assuming such a millstone by any means necessary.

Thus every day he rehearsed the sentence under his breath—in the mirror, to the ceiling while lying in bed, on the way to the bodega for shaving gel. Pronouncing it full voice to his mother would be an act of naked self-immolation. Frosty? He hadn't seen real frosty, not truly glacial frosty yet. His commitment to this ruinous course of action pushed Nico to consider whether he wasn't, after all, a parsimonious parasite but might have the makings of a martyr.

Continuing in this roiling vein promised only insomnia and indigestion. So he set himself a deadline. He awoke that Thursday with his gut in a leaden clench.

His mother was out during the day waving placards in a counter-protest outside Floyd Bennett Field, where a large demonstration was opposing the tented shelter for migrants recently opened in Marine Park. The neighborhood was up in arms because people in tents didn't *stay* in tents. Throughout southern Brooklyn, there'd been reports of shoplifting, drug taking, thieving of Amazon deliveries, begging, scamming, and prostitution (just in case his mother failed to "claw together" the whole of that ransom payment, Nico could now inform Martine that the best place to wear fishnets was around Kings Plaza). His mother was certain that their racist, tiny-minded neighbors' accounts of rampant panhandling and criminality were vastly overblown.

In an obliging illustration of what those neighbors objected to, the doorbell rang that afternoon while his mother was still counter-protesting, and there on the front porch stood Exhibit A: wearing the standard knit watch caps, rumpled sweaters, jeans, and smart-looking athletic shoes, two young men who looked African, one of whom foisted a smartphone in Nico's nonplussed face. As ever, the translation app was proving an invaluable tool for scroungers.

"Please, we are starving," the device asserted stoically. "Can you please give us money so we can please buy food. Please, we love America, please."

In retrospect, this might have been an ideal opportunity to inform these gentlemen that this municipality had already extended to them and their many fellows its considerable largesse. Why, to cover the expenses of this unexpected surge of out-of-towners, the mayor had already been forced to cut the budget of all the city's major departments by 5 percent. Nico might have observed to his doorsteppers that this belt tightening, which cut the hours of public libraries and reduced the ranks of the police, facilitated three meals a day at shelters such as the one for which his own mother this very afternoon was advocating. As Nico had it on good authority that nutritious snacks, even hard-boiled eggs, were available night and day, these supplicants' submission that they were "starving" seemed, at the very least, exaggerated. True, the third-party catering for which the city had contracted at $33 per person per day might not have been serving the customary roasted goat, corn meal *ugali*, and *peri-peri* sauce of their native land. Were "culturally inappropriate" fare an issue, then, this was an apt juncture at which Nico, as a volunteer *life coach*, could repeat the helpful recommendation he'd shared with that candy seller on the B train: perhaps these two might reconsider the viability of their long-term goals and, not to put too fine a point on it, go home.

Alas, Nico was so tormented by his looming encounter with his mother and so unprepared in that moment for opening the front door to a couple of Africans that he simply stared dumbly at the beggars in disbelief. He cared solely about making these extraneous elements standing on his porch go away. Expedience being paramount, he reached in his jeans for the change from the shaving gel, stuffed a five in an extended palm, and shut the door.

When he returned to the kitchen, Martine asked who'd rung the bell.

"*Inmigrantes*," he said. "I gave them five bucks."

"You no give them money," she admonished. "They only come back for more. And begging make *inmigrantes* look like lowlife."

"I thought you'd be glad I was generous."

"They do this everywhere, ring people doors, drive people crazy. Make people mad. Enough people in Brooklyn hate us already."

"Hate you? That's a little strong."

"Hate us," she repeated. "For good reason, sometime. I talk *inmigrantes* on street. They no want work. They very happy with selfs. Make hundred fifty dollar in one day by ask people money and make people feel bad. Free money, no taxes. They . . . *rifi-rafe*."

Nico was surprised Martine exhibited such a sense of rectitude. For a moment, he reconsidered raising that question with his mother.

When the woman of the house returned, she propped her placard by the side door. It was professionally printed in green and black: a silhouette of a mother holding her child's hand below the slogan IMMIGRANTS ARE NEW YORK.

"There were fewer of us," she said. "But our signs were way better. Some of theirs were handwritten in *crayon*. Often misspelled, with lots of childish underlining, exclamation points, and capital letters. They'd run out of space and have to finish their nasty accusations about 'illegals' in tiny print. Oh, and naturally Helen Levitt was there." The olive trench coat she hung up was thin for the season, but her heavy wool car coat now belonged to the fine peoples of Ecuador. "Screeching 'close the border!' and 'Americans first!' and 'this is a national emergency!' Honestly, I wish I'd never brought her that batch of muffins when she moved in."

Martine began to rustle up dinner, and for once his mother didn't raise a token objection. While technically she hadn't taken in a servant, his mother would soon be out every penny the city had paid her and then some, so she might as well get something for her thirty grand. Instead of helping chop onions as usual, then, she spoke quietly to Nico at the table, not wanting to embarrass their lodger. "I spoke to my accountant this morning," she said stiffly. "About an *unanticipated expense*. She suggested I draw down my IRA. Fortunately, because I'm over fifty-nine and a half, I won't have to pay the ten percent tax penalty for early withdrawal. There are a few advantages to turning into a hag."

"Oh, cut it out," Nico said. "You're a fine specimen for your age."

"Hardly every woman's dream," she said, seeming to soften toward him and to resist softening at the same time. "I'll still have to pay income tax on the lump sum, meaning it will cost me almost half again as much, not that I expect our friend there to understand that."

"What do you think," he supposed. "Are ransoms to Honduran hoodlums tax deductible?"

Though determined to remain pissed off at him, she couldn't suppress a smile. "I can see the 1040 now: *1a, retirement distributions. 1b, Central American ransom payments. Subtract 1b from 1a . . .*"

Of course, Martine would never wonder how her patron raised the cash. After years of wringing out her neighbors' laundry by hand for chump change, the insouciance was understandable, too. Comparatively, their family really was rich, and the R-word induced money blindness—conferring the impression of resources both unearned and inexhaustible. Any nitty-gritty regarding the extent of his mother's liquid assets would constitute nothing but noise. Had those kidnappers demanded $60,000, or $600,000, or maybe even $600 million, Martine would never have questioned her benefactor's ability to pay. She might regard the forfeiture as nice, but she'd be unlikely to perceive it as painful, much less as the sacrifice of a limited pot that would no longer be available to cover emergencies in her sponsor's own family. Nico made a note to self that accruing any appreciable financial wherewithal marked you a target and a patsy—although in view of his current career trajectory, predation on his titanic wealth should probably feature low on his list of pressing fears.

After dinner, Nico loitered in the living room with his phone, because he wanted to catch his mother the moment she excused herself to bed. That said, he willed her to stay up as late as possible, the better to delay his senseless confrontation. Meanwhile, the two women returned to their knitting. As part of her Making Martine Indispensable program, the Honduran had learned to crochet donkeys, cats, and rabbits for Toys & Trinkets in brightly colored yarn. This lead-up to Christmas was his mother's annual opportunity to move stock, and Martine claimed that crafting handmade playthings was a welcome distraction from her anguish.

Nico had a soft spot for his mother's handicrafts, which took so long to fashion that unless she rated her labor as worthless she always operated at a loss. Each one-of-a-kind creation exuded a distinctive character. When he'd moved upstairs from the basement, he'd been sure to scoop up the woebegone giraffe, bashful tiger, lost-looking sheepdog, and pugnacious piglet that had peeked from the Christmas stockings of his childhood. He kept the menagerie on his desk upstairs as rare but precious totems of healthy filial tenderness.

Martine had broadened the range to include wildlife from her country—

armadillos, jaguars—and was presently working on an anteater, which American children would mistake for a smashed elephant. His mother's latest handiwork in baby-blue yarn looked almost complete: two squash-ball-size orbs joined to a round column with a little hat on it.

Martine tee-heed. "Gloria Ador*a*ble. That look like *chico*'s pee-pee."

"I should hope so," his mother said. "That's what it is."

Martine looked at a loss.

"It's a 'packer,'" his mother explained. "For girls who are really boys and were born in the wrong body. It fits in a pouch in specialized underwear. My cashmere packers are soft and especially comfortable. They're the one new product line so popular that it's murder to keep up with demand. If all I cared about was profit, I'd knit packers all day."

Martine simply said, "Oh." She was surely horrified, but the ransom hadn't been paid yet, and she would keep her outmoded opinions to herself.

As his mother at last went upstairs to bed, Nico followed heavily a few steps behind. Appointment Wank would have to wait, and for once he wasn't in the mood. When she said good night and turned toward the master bedroom, he touched her arm.

"Can I talk to you in private for a second?"

She looked surprised but ushered him into the inner sanctum. Nico closed the door behind them. He was hardly ever in here. She kept it fanatically neat, and any sign of his father, even the books he'd left behind, had been expunged. On the wall behind the bed, there was still a faint rectangular ghost, where once hung a classily framed print of the Brooklyn Bridge in fog—*which she had loved*. But the print was an anniversary present and therefore tainted. The very day his father left, she'd yanked it down and dragged it to the curb, kicking in the glass so the hanging couldn't even be salvaged by a passerby. That white-on-white phantom on the wall was a reminder that his mission was perilous.

She sat on the edge of the bed. "Okay, what is it?"

He perched on the adjoining chair. "Do you know yet where you're supposed to transfer that money?"

She shrugged. "There's an account. Not in Honduras, but probably in the Cayman Islands or something. Martine showed me the details, and it's some shell company. I don't think it's very complicated so long as I give my approval to my bank."

"The thing is—you have no idea where that money is going really, or who to."

"I don't see any way around that. It's frustrating, but I didn't make the rules here. We won't get a receipt. Or a money-back guarantee."

"But we don't really know Martine that well. I know you think we do. But a week ago, we'd no idea she had three kids. All we really know is that she has pictures of herself and her brother with three kids."

"Why on earth would her phone be full of pictures of someone else's children?"

"She said her phone was stolen in Mexico. The one she has now she got from the Border Patrol. Why would it be full of family pictures?"

"There's iCloud. Or her mother could've sent them by WeTransfer."

"None of us ever talked to the mother after the kids were supposedly abducted—"

"*Supposedly?*"

"And even if we had, we'd have no way of knowing it really was her mother. It could be anybody. Or even if it was her mother, we don't know anything about her mother, either."

"What are you getting at?"

"This whole story is happening off camera. We have no firsthand evidence of any gang, any abduction—just a couple of text messages that anybody could have written and a phone call you guys heard one side of in Spanish. Does Martine really have three children in Honduras? Maybe, maybe not. Were they really kidnapped? Maybe, maybe not. We totally have to take other people's word for everything—people like Domingo, who we also know nothing about. If that guy 'gets respect' from a local gang, who's to say he's not *in* the gang? The only part of this setup I'm betting is definitely real is that bank account number. So I just have to wonder . . . It would be irresponsible not to raise the question . . . What if Martine is in on it?"

7

"Nico, how could you say such a thing?" his mother exclaimed, standing abruptly from the mattress. "How could you even think such a thing? That's beyond cynical. It's almost . . . wicked."

Well, no surprise there. He'd done his familial duty yet reaped no credit for his sacrifice. All around, it was a very Jesus-y juncture, moving Nico to speculate that maybe he should have paid more attention to the World Religions unit in high school. He hazily recalled that all that taking on the sins of the world stuff didn't end well.

"Thirty grand is a lot of money," he said, leaning back, slack, in the bedside armchair. "I thought you needed to consider more than one angle, that's all."

"But what you just said isn't an 'angle.' It's an accusation. A terrible accusation. Whose implication is that Martine is an ungrateful, scheming liar, and she's a thief."

"Yeah, that's the angle, all right," he granted glumly.

"You said last week you have nothing against her. I have to wonder about that. Has she done or said anything to make you nurse a grudge?"

"Not really."

"Then why would you slander her like that? Is this a case of sibling rivalry once removed? You're competing for my love and attention? I don't understand why you'd be jealous, when before Martine got here I couldn't pay you to spend any time with me."

"I'm not jealous," he recited dully, not for the first time.

"You haven't been on board with this sponsorship from the beginning. Is this your I-told-you-so moment? Do you have a misguided notion that, if you raise enough doubts about Martine's probity, then our household can return to some fantasy version of our incredible happiness, before Martine came along and ruined it? Is that it? You want your basement back."

"I'm not trying to get you to kick her out." Nico's tone was mournful with a touch of boredom. This conversation was so predictable.

"If I took your accusation seriously, why wouldn't I kick her out? I'd be insane not to."

"I guess."

"You watch those rancorous videos," she said, glaring down at him as he shrank into the upholstery. "I've seen snatches. Demonizing migrants as all criminals and drug runners and rapists. Cultivating resentment. Decrying all the money wasted on them. Just like Trump, claiming that all these foreigners are 'poisoning the blood' of our country—which, if you don't mind my saying so, because I know the analogy is overused, is overtly eugenicist and straight out of the Nazi playbook. Tell me, are you a Trump supporter now?"

Nico wasn't quite sure how they got from putting a teensy question mark over whether Martine was entirely on the up-and-up to Donald J. Trump in less than two minutes, but his mother and her friends were never more than five seconds away from their fat blowhard nemesis. Being mistaken for a Trumpster didn't faze him; in isolation, the label was merely incorrect. But impugning him as an ally of her bête noir was, in his mother's terms, the very worst insult she could fling at him. It was the intent to wound that was wounding.

"I don't care about the election," he said honestly.

"Well, that's appalling in itself."

Huddled morosely in the armchair, Nico had no idea how he was going to get out of here. And he kicked himself. He'd anticipated his mother's reaction, but he may have underestimated its scale. He should have shown up for this encounter in body armor.

She'd started to pace. "I've no idea why you've become so involved in the migration issue, which for reasons beyond me you seem to take personally."

"I'm interested. I thought you liked it when I'm interested in something."

"This is unhealthy interest. That whole 'close the borders' crowd I faced down this afternoon—they draw out poison like a poultice. The emotions they stir up . . . suspicion, hostility, selfishness, bigotry, and hate. That's what you're steeping in. That's what you're allowing other people to bring out in you."

All was lost anyway, so he made a stab at not being a total wuss.

"Somebody's got to defend the interests of the people who were born here, even if sticking up for regular Americans makes us look bad."

"Makes 'us' look bad? I'm afraid your 'us' may be my 'them.'"

"No problem. Just put your preferred pronouns at the bottom of your emails."

She wasn't amused. "You do realize you're also indicting your mother, don't you. If Martine is a Machiavellian con artist, then your mother is a fool. A gullible fool who invited a devious manipulator into her home because she's such a poor judge of character."

"I only raised the *question*. I thought it might be a good idea to get some sort of external verification that the story is legit."

"How? What would persuade you? Texts, letters—you'd just claim they 'could have been written by anyone.' Photographs of her children with guns to their heads? You'd say they could have been posed. There's no way to release those children without proceeding on *trust*."

"I guess," he said again.

"I'm sorry to reach for Psych 101 truisms, but what we see in other people is often a projection of ourselves. Which makes me worry about you profoundly. Are *you* deceitful? Do *you* steal? Do you routinely use other people's best qualities against them—their generosity, their goodwill, their decency? When people are nice to you, do you see that as an opportunity to extract even more benefit for yourself? Are the people in your life merely pawns, to be moved coldly around a chessboard and exploited until you get what you want? Because that's a functional definition of a sociopath."

Maybe that's what the clouds parting on Edwards Parade had really meant to reveal. Not *I don't want to be an engineer* but *I am a sociopath*.

"You're my mother," he said. "If I was that fucked-up, you'd know that already."

"I'm not so sure. The newspaper is full of pleasant-seeming if withdrawn young men who spend too much time online and suddenly kill fourteen people."

"I try to protect you, and now I'm a mass murderer."

"Maybe you're protecting yourself. If this kidnapping is really an elaborate swindle, then you don't have to feel guilty about not helping pay the ransom. After all, you haven't volunteered to throw in even a few hundred dollars. This way not only do you economize, but you also get to play the hero, who's saved the family from an awful, expensive mistake."

"This is about your money, not mine."

"You keep harping on our lack of hard evidence that this abduction in Honduras is 'legit.' Let's turn it around. Do you have *any* hard evidence, even a scrap, that it's fraudulent?"

Nico dropped his head. "I just have this feeling . . . an uneasiness—"

"Answer me."

". . . No."

"In that case, you're going to have to promise me: to never, ever suggest to Martine herself that you think there's anything dubious about the dreadful circumstance in which she finds herself. Never. She'd be devastated. This is hard enough for her. On top of handling the daily terror of her children's fate lying in the hands of thugs, she has to endure the embarrassment of accepting my financial help. Though she's beside herself with worry over those kids, she still manages to make us dinner and knit stock for my company. If you so much as open your mouth, you'll make things immeasurably worse. You'll grievously hurt her feelings. Your relationship to her, such as it is, would effectively be over, and I can't imagine how awkward the atmosphere in this house could become."

"Don't worry, I won't say anything." At last, he sensed he was excused. He rose from the armchair as if he were ninety-five.

"I'm tempted to say let's pretend this conversation never happened," she said to his back. "But I don't like pretending."

Over the following few days, when Nico and his mother crossed paths, she was at best civil. Yet when Martine was also around, his mother assumed a forced cordiality, as presumably she didn't want to appear to cold shoulder her son to a degree that might demand explanation. After all, Martine had become his mother's go-to confidante, to whom she poured out concerns about how Vanessa simply wasn't made for dating apps, whose stick-figure profiles could never capture what made her younger daughter special, but this was apparently the only mating ritual in which that generation engaged; or about her wistfulness regarding Palermo's foregone artistry in gymnastics, which had exhibited a spiritual if not sublime aspect that keeping the books for a construction company simply couldn't duplicate. Nico wasn't sure how long he'd been sentenced to the doghouse, and for all he knew he'd altered his mother's estimation of his character for keeps. Still, he didn't regret what he'd said. Someone had to say it; he was the only one who could have said it; saying it had therefore been his job. The disagreeable aftermath merely confirmed what he knew already: having a job sucked.

Besides, his perceived perfidy might have accomplished something after all. He had planted a seed of doubt. No amount of his mother's indignation could make her unhear the question he had raised. While his father dismissed his ex as an unoriginal thinker, anyone with even a middling imagination listened to a version of events at odds with their own, and then that alternative reality, especially one spiced with the intrigue and duplicity of an airport thriller, sprang into being. Nico had surgically inserted in his mother's head a depraved parallel universe certain to contaminate the innocent universe she preferred. Like it or not, she'd be watchful for any sign that the kidnapping story didn't quite add up. She might hate herself for it, but now she wouldn't look at Martine in quite the same way. He had split his mother in two. She would continue to be affectionate and unguarded toward her new Best Friend Forever, but a fractional shard of her psyche had been sheared off, and the shard would be wary. In retrospect, given that he never expected her to give his airport thriller plot any credence, evoking that wariness had been his true purpose.

Vanessa helped their mother sell off some equities in her Schwab IRA, not at the most profitable of junctures, alas, and showed her how to arrange a one-time withdrawal from the account. Having grown up with analogue banking, their mother was always anxious making sizable transfers online. So she waited for Vanessa to return so that her daughter could also hold her hand when she wired the ransom payment.

Earlier in the evening that Vanessa was to perform these dodgy honors, Nico was cruising through back-to-back Douglas Murray interviews when his mother came home flustered. He slipped off his headphones to hear her mutter, "It would have to be today!" as she wrenched off her trench coat. "That was the last thing I needed."

"Everything okay?" This of all nights, Martine had reason to be attentive.

"I was driving up Flatbush and slowing for the light at Avenue U—"

"You go Floyd Bennett Field, *sí*? Sorry I am so anxious I no go, too."

"That's totally understandable, sweetie. This time I mostly gave a family a hand moving their stuff to another tent. The mother and a woman in the next unit kept getting into fights. *Physical* fights. You know, the usual." The women shared a look.

"So," his mother continued. "On the way home I hadn't come to a stop yet, when I heard this thunderous whomp on the right-hand side of the car. I hit the brake, got out, and came around to find a young man lying in the road beside my right front tire, clutching his knee and writhing in agony. He said something like, 'Lady, you hit me! You watch where you drive!'"

"What sort 'young man'?" Martine asked.

"Well. He was black," she said carefully. "Not that that has to do with anything."

"American?"

His mother shrugged. "I had no means of knowing his citizenship status. Though I'd venture, from his accent, that he was born elsewhere."

"*Inmigrante*." Better that Martine said it.

"I was terrified he was seriously hurt. At the same time, I confess I was irked. I wasn't in a crosswalk, and I'd had no reason to be watching for pedestrians. All this jaywalking. I realize newcomers don't know our customs. I know the motorist always has to be on the defensive, and in any accidents with pedestrians the driver is likely to get the blame. Still. It did seem to me that he was partially at fault.

"Anyway, after I helped him hop to the curb, I pulled over. I offered to call an ambulance. Though I was dreading having to call the police. I can't afford for my insurance to go up again, and if it went to court . . . Well, the time, the hassle . . . So I was relieved when he said he'd go to a doctor on his own if I gave him money for it. Maybe it was shabby of me to just pay him off and abscond. Technically, despite the fact I stopped, if I didn't call the cops it was hit-and-run. But I gave him two hundred and thirty dollars. He wanted five hundred, but that was all I had on me in cash, and the ATM he kept pointing at wasn't for Citibank. At least if he's one of ours at Floyd Bennett, he can get seen to at the facility. Still, the whole business did my head in. I was shaking for the rest of the drive home."

This time it was Martine and Nico who shared a look.

"That was a setup," Nico said. "You were scammed."

"Oh, of course you would think that!" his mother exploded furiously. "You always think the worst of people! All you ever see around you is deceit and corruption!"

Even Martine seemed to find her sponsor's blowback oddly unbefitting. She tsked. "No, no, Gloria, no so hard on Nico Niñito."

"That's okay," he said. "My mother is under a lot of stress."

"Nico is right, *mi querida*. Is trick they play, for money. At Floyd Bennett, they think is very funny. You no notice? They practice throwing selfs at cars in parking lot and laugh and laugh."

"So I've been had?" his mother said. "He wasn't really hurt."

Martine patted his mother's arm. "You pay two hundred thirty dollar to learn lesson. Is cheap. Better than five hundred."

When Vanessa arrived, their mother retold the story, but more ruefully.

Although the payment itself may have had dramatic implications, any online monetary transfer is brief and mundane. Their mother repeated the swift code, routing number, and account number so Vanessa could triple-check it. When the bank sent a security code to their mother's phone and his sister entered the six digits, even Vanessa's hand trembled. It was a large transfer to an account Gloria Bonaventura hadn't paid into before, so the website advised that the wire was put on hold pending confirmation. Sure enough, the landline rang shortly thereafter.

Their mother panicked. "I don't have to tell them what it's for, do I?"

"Of course not," Vanessa said. "Just pick up the phone."

"Hello?" Their mother's voice was quavering. "Yes, this is she. . . . Yes, thirty thousand dollars, that's correct . . . Seven five four seven. No, that's not right! I mean seven *four five* seven. Sorry, I'm just a bit rattled. I mean, no, I'm not rattled really, just, you know, absentminded . . . My mother's maiden name was Bauer, that's B-A-U-E-R . . . April sixteenth, 1961 . . . What's it for?" Her eyes widened in frantic appeal to Vanessa, who mouthed a sensibly vague reply. "A friend. A very good friend—a friend in need . . . Tomorrow? Thank you. Thank you so much." When she hung up, she looked gray. "My heart is beating so hard I feel a little sick."

Martine wrapped her benefactor in her arms and rocked her back and forth. "*Gracias, gracias, gracias, muchas gracias,*" she said. "And now, *mi querida*, we pray."

Undercutting the pathos of the occasion, Nico belched, and Vanessa swatted his shoulder in reproof. It's just that his mother wasn't the only one feeling a little sick.

Two days later, Nico was diluting his coffee with boiled water when Martine squealed. Her phone, over which she had hovered obsessively for the previous twenty-four hours, had come alive. Ever since their rum-soaked head-to-head, she'd changed her Google Meet ringtone to the theme tune of *Friends*.

"*Por favor, madre de Dios, que estén bien,*" she whispered before picking up. "*Mamá, ¡dime que las niñas están de vuelta en casa!*" A torrent of Spanish poured from the phone, during which Martine began to whoop, literally jumping up and down, causing his mother to rush to the kitchen from upstairs. "*¡Jesús, María y José, gracias a Dios! Mamá, por favor pon a los niños al teléfono!*"

Laying a hand on Martine's shoulder, his mother whispered, "Are they all right? Were they released?"

Martine clasped one of his mother's hands and led her in a leaping, swirling dance into the breakfast room. "They every three home! All thank for you!"

"Oh, Martine, what a relief! I'm so happy for you! I'd have paid anything for your children to be safe!"

"Come, come here, you say hello *mi niños*!"

Nico gathered reluctantly around Martine's screen, hanging back while his mother leaned in. He wished she hadn't said she'd have "paid anything," which in the darker version of this tale might have given Martine ideas.

The three kids were gathered into the same shot, the two girls waving and shouting greetings to their mother, while the little boy was quiet; they looked unharmed and not especially traumatized, though Nico couldn't say what appearing traumatized on Google Meet would have looked like. After excited back-and-forth Spanish for several minutes, Martine said, "Lucia, Renata, Felipe? *Esta es* Gloria Ado*rab*le. *Alla es su salvadora!*"

"*¡Hola*, Lucia!" his mother said, waving. "*¡Hola*, Renata! *¡Hola*, Felipe!"

"*¿Le dirás a Gloria gracias?*" Martine said.

The two girls chimed, "Gracias, Gloria!" while the boy stayed silent.

"*¿Puedes decirle a Gloria gracias en inglés?*" Martine prodded. "'Thank you, Gloria!' *Todos ustedes pueden hacerlo*. 'Thank you, Gloria!'"

Again the two girls recited, "Tank you, Gloria!"

"You're very welcome, *niños!*" his mother cried gaily, while Nico experienced a reprise of adolescent chagrin.

"You say, *de nada*," Martine instructed.

"Of course," his mother said, beaming. "*De nada, niños!*" My, my. Practically fluent.

Pulling Nico into the range of the camera, Martine introduced, "*Y este es* Nico Niñito!" at which point the girls giggled.

"*Hola, niños*," he said flatly, feeling obscurely humiliated.

At last, with an immoderate smacking of kisses, Martine sorrowfully wrapped up the group conversation, which had been streaked with so many implied exclamation marks that a transcript would have looked rained on. She then set about preparing an elaborate celebratory breakfast for which Nico had no appetite, while his mother phoned to tell Vanessa and then Palermo about this sunny turn of events. He wasn't sure what about the histrionic song and dance of the previous twenty minutes he'd found nauseating; maybe he really was the "wicked," "jealous," and "cynical" sociopath his mother thought he was, since he couldn't simply feel glad that three blameless kids in Honduras were all right. Still—and maybe he missed something; maybe amid all the hugging and hand squeezing right after that first phone call Martine had indeed tripped hurriedly downstairs while his mind was wandering elsewhere—but he couldn't remember her rushing to tell Domingo the good news. As if the guy knew already.

Once he'd eaten enough of the breakfast that he wouldn't seem to be boycotting the joyous occasion, Martine loaded the dishwasher while jigging around the kitchen and singing "Tickita Tickita." His mother raised her eyebrows at Nico with a glare and under her breath said, "*See?*" Presumably, the theatrical return of children they had no evidence ever disappeared in the first place demonstrated that his misgivings were unfounded. Of course, it proved nothing of the kind.

After a divorce, apparently the most valuable assets to be divvied up weren't the fine furnishings but the friends. When the Bonaventuras split, their pals faced picking Gloria, who was nicer, versus Carlin, who was more important. Ergo, Carlin won out almost every time.

However adept Nico had grown at fending off social come-hithers, and despite the proposed gathering's inclusion of his presently glacial mother, in the run-up to Christmas he received an invitation difficult to refuse. Longstanding Friends of the Family, Vernon and Colleen Carmichael had unusually resolved to maintain ties with both spouses independently. Supposedly, then, Vernon and Colleen saw each of his parents every other occasion, though Nico suspected that even the Carmichaels had dinner with his father a smidgen more often. Dad was more fun. Vernon and his buddy Carlin were big drinkers, and they both had subversive streaks that grew only wider with booze. By contrast, the ardent sincerity of Carlin's ex had pooped many a party. Oscar Wilde notwithstanding, Nico had learned from his mother's negative example the importance of not being earnest.

Had this dinner invitation involved only Vernon and Colleen, Nico might still have been tempted to make an exception to keeping a diary so superbly blank that he'd deleted the Calendar app on his phone. They were the one couple from the olden days whom he actively liked. A large, animated guy, Vernon was a bundle of appetites. His weight was forever yo-yoing, because his desire for magnetic virility took turns with his desire for Black Forest cake. His vitality lent any old weeknight a sense of occasion, and he told good stories. Vernon didn't compete with his friend Carlin exactly; it was more that they played off against each other, each taunting the other to go one step further in some outlandish top-this taboo-breaker. While his father had undertaken single video projects, Vernon was a full-time documentary filmmaker, who'd worked on episodes of *Frontline* and *American Experience* and now ran his own production company. The two powerhouses first got acquainted in the 1990s while working together on a television special about recovered memory syndrome.

One of the only of his father's docs that Nico had watched. Therapists all over the country managed to convince a plethora of their needy, attention-seeking patients that one of their relatives, usually a parent, had diddled them, often when they were only babies. The reasoning was exquisite: being unable to remember being assaulted was sure proof that you'd been assaulted. Warning signs of having repressed memories of sexual abuse included joint pain, failing to trust your intuition, and neglecting your teeth—among sixty to seventy other symptoms collectively guaranteeing that 100 percent of the American population had been incestuously interfered with as children. Aggrieved filial accusations arising from this professional exorcism of evil spirits nuked a slew of families to smithereens. For several years, repressed memories were accepted as factual testimony in court. And people wondered why Nico might opt for conscientious objector status rather than join the phantasmagorical world of grown-ups.

Having met Vernon in film school at Columbia, Colleen was a freelance film editor who edited her husband's work—an arrangement not nearly as cozy and subtly subjugating as it sounded. Wiry, willful, and every bit as opinionated as her spouse, Colleen and her husband had conducted many a battle in Ditmas over what slant to emphasize and what footage to keep or cut, which was entertaining to watch. By contrast, for most of their marriage Nico's parents hardly ever fought, so when they did fight, they split up. They hadn't had enough practice.

Still, what clinched his obligation to show up at the Carmichaels' Park Slope brownstone for dinner was their son Tyler's return from Chicago for the holidays. The same age, he and Tyler had been friends through high school and had continued to get together on semester breaks when Nico was at Fordham. While they'd mysteriously lost touch during the hovercraft years, nothing had happened to sever the relationship, so everyone assumed they'd enjoy reconnecting. Nico refrained from formulating the reason he'd just as soon skip seeing Tyler, even to himself. The guy had been a fuck-up in high school—drugs, drink, the works. Crap grades (and by then you really had to outdo yourself to get less than an A minus), poor prospects, big parental disappointment—while Nico was a poster boy. Then Tyler got his act together, humbled himself by going to Georgia Tech, and now had, according to this most recent email from Vernon: a "good" job. A "nice" girlfriend. A "stunning" apartment on the lake. The role reversal was . . . disconcerting. Nico would never be able to fashion a respectable excuse for getting out of this reunion, but the truth was that he and Tyler had nothing to say to each other.

"Hey, ho!" Vernon hailed them as Colleen led Nico and his mother into the big open-plan kitchen. Vernon was on the heavy side of his yo-yo, and considering he popped two cheese thingies before washing his hands to say hello, he was probably on the upswing. His clothes were loose, sloppy, flopping, and a touch sweaty; thankfully, you never had to dress up for dinner at the Carmichaels'. The enormous leg of lamb, spikey with garlic and rosemary sprigs, resting on the counter looked propitious.

The embrace was enveloping; Nico rarely got a hug from someone as tall as he was. "Skinny as ever!" Vernon said. "I don't know what makes you luckier, handsome, taking after your father or your mother."

Typically, the glasses of red wine the guy poured for his two guests killed most of the bottle. "So what are you up to, Nico?"

"Eh? *Nada.*"

"Always code for getting up to no good. Here, take the Parmesan crisps to the living room before I polish off the batch." On the way, he shouted up the stairs, "Tyler! Nico's here!"

The foursome settled with their drinks in the living room, where an open fire flickered on decor that took its cue from Vernon's dress sense:

sagging oversize pillows, slumping sofas, worn armchairs covered in cat scratches, and tangles of woolen throws. Messy, comfortable, relaxed—thus implicitly permissive, like the quality of the Carmichaels' conversation. Nico settled on the rug by the fire and slipped off his shoes.

"So, Gloria," Colleen said. "How's that migrant sponsorship working out?"

"For the most part, splendidly," his mother said. "It's shut my obnoxious neighbor across the street right up. After all her 'if you think these people are so great, why don't you invite them to *your* house?' she's had to put a lid on it. Which didn't stop her from circulating a Facebook petition objecting to housing migrants in private residences in Ditmas."

News to Nico.

"And how's the girl?" Vernon asked, turning to Nico. "Do you like her?"

"I think she's more complicated than she seems at first," Nico said carefully.

"But do you like her?" Vernon repeated.

"She's smart," Nico said. "I'm the only one who gives her credit for having a brain."

"Hardly!" his mother exclaimed. Oh, here we go. "Martine is a jewel. Helps with the cooking, does *all* our laundry, and brightens up the whole atmosphere . . ."

Mercifully, the Song of Praise was interrupted when Tyler thumped downstairs. Like a gentleman, he greeted Gloria with a kiss on the cheek first, while Nico clambered to a stand.

"Hey, man, great to see you," Tyler said, clasping Nico in a hand hug and clapping him on the shoulder. "Come on into the kitchen with me. I need to get a drink and catch up with these guys. Might as well catch up with you, too."

Nico had forgotten, but there'd always been something winning about Tyler, even in his fuck-up days—if not especially then, when Nico could flirt with the dark side while also benefiting from the comparison. Tyler was the rare sort whom others liked *right away*. It was partly the wry skew of his face, the soft, amicable flop of his hair, and back then a hapless gentleness, now turned straight-up gentleness, since in this incarnation there was nothing hapless about him. Having inherited his mother's build, the kid was still lanky, but he'd filled out across the shoulders; presumably, all those "good" and "nice" and "stunning" assets came with a gym membership. He seemed older, and not merely older than when last they met, but older than Nico himself, and they were born a month apart. Tyler's air of authority was easy and unforced. More *observation*: young people in their twenties who tried too hard to seem like mature adults failed. You needn't try to be what you already are.

As Tyler opened a cabernet in the kitchen, Nico asked dutifully, "So what's the job?"

"Information security analyst," Tyler said with parodic pomposity as the cork popped. "I'm an antihacker. Which, when all is said and done, isn't any different from being a hacker."

"Tech."

"We go through companies' systems and look for vulnerabilities. You have to learn to think like a criminal. Maybe it was my misspent youth, but it turns out I'm good at that."

"Zeros and ones. You don't find it dreary?"

"Nah," Tyler said, pouring himself a glass. "It's a game. Very detailed, line of code by line of code, but it's kind of fun."

"So is it like, clock-in-at-nine-a.m. type of crap?"

"I get up when I want. Since Covid, lots of these jobs are work-from-home. If I'm onto something, I can keep going till midnight. I'd never have thought way back when I'd have cared about such a thing, but, hey—the work's useful. I keep your credit card company's database secure. I keep your bank account from being drained from Uzbekistan. Best of all, my parents find this stuff unfathomable. Finally, my dad can't lecture me on my own work. You have a know-it-all father, too, so you know what I mean."

"I drive my father crazy."

"On purpose?"

"Yeah, maybe." Nico wasn't ready to be confiding, even if he could have come up with something to confide. "Your dad mentioned you have a girlfriend."

"Lyla's ambitious and pragmatic, and these days that's a rare combination. All the other girls I met wanted to be *influencers* or something.

Lyla's almost finished qualifying as a nurse practitioner. There's a shortage of nurse practitioners, and the demand for cybersecurity is through the roof. For both jobs, pay's great. We'll be able to write our own tickets, live wherever we want. Like, not Chicago. Fucking weather!"

"That's how you guys decided what to go into?" Nico might have been interviewing a Martian. "Demand?"

"Sure, partly."

"Sounds like you and Lyla are a long-term item. Isn't that kind of fast?"

"Been together over a year. I'm almost twenty-seven. Why's that fast?"

"I don't know. Still pretty young."

"I'll tell you what's fast. Life's fast. And if we want to have kids—"

"Whoa! You're joking."

Tyler laughed. "You find that fantastical? This is where my dad opines that our generation's 'low natality intentions' are why the whole country's coming to a dead halt."

"What's wrong with coming to a dead halt?" Nico supposed idly.

"You would say that." Peeling a surreptitious shred of lamb off the roast, Tyler side-eyed his old friend. "And you, Nico? What's up?"

This was what he was dreading. He'd had a sixth sense that he wouldn't be able to toy with Tyler in the same way he had dicked his father around at Autopsy. "Not much."

Conversational silence thereafter spoke volumes.

". . . You're still living at your mom's," Tyler said. "In the basement."

"No, I got kicked out of the basement to make way for my mother's very own real-life migrant. I'm back in my old bedroom." He'd struck a note of defiance.

"Do you even have, like, a part-time job?"

"Don't need one. I have resources."

"Don't you get lonely?"

"It's other people I have a problem with. I get a buzz from being by myself."

"But you do see friends."

"Some," Nico said vaguely.

"You know, I sent you three or four how's-tricks emails over the last few years, and I never heard back. Tried texting, too. No reply."

"Yeah, well, email . . . I get lots of Substack newsletters and everything. Stuff gets lost in the shuffle." Nico remembered getting those emails, and Tyler knew it.

"Can't even throw back a 'Yo, bro!' to a text?"

"I go through periods of keeping the phone off," Nico said. "Digital fasting. So I can concentrate."

"On what?"

"My *spheres of concern*. My private observations."

"But in high school, you used to hang with tons of people. In fact, you were fucking popular."

"Not as popular as you were."

"That's just because everyone likes to hang with bad boys," Tyler said. "Adjacency to degeneracy means you get most of the fun without having to accept the consequences."

"I don't think that was the reason." The modesty. That bafflingly open, undefended face. Tyler had been what the girls called "cute"; along with other transitions that had eluded Nico, he'd now segued to attractive.

"And you—no girlfriend."

"No, I do not have an *ambitious yet pragmatic* girlfriend. Think of it this way. Now *I* make *you* look good."

Nico was losing control of this script. That hint of bitterness: out of order. The forces arrayed against him were perpetually attempting to impose shame. He refused to accept the charge, as if declining a 20 percent automated tip. They could not make you feel something that you did not feel and did not want to feel without your complicity. They could not shame you unless you volunteered to generate an interior sense of dishonor at their behest. Thus your emotions had to be fenced, and more fiercely than any sad-ass Trumpian border wall. Indeed, this was a *border issue*. His feelings were in his domain. They could not and should not be lobbed into his territory from the outside. Any psychic projectiles that successfully sailed over his defenses were to be thrown back.

"But . . ." Tyler scrambled. "*Why?*"

"Why what?"

"Don't fuck with me. Why have you come to a 'dead halt'?"

"Maybe because I . . . can." Tyler wouldn't have realized it, but that was a higher quality answer than usual.

"What are you waiting for?"

"I'm not waiting for anything. Everyone keeps trying to convince me that I must be so miserable. I'm not. I'm fine. You said you were glad to feel useful. Good, I'm happy for you. But I don't care about being useful."

"Do you care about anything?"

"What is this, psychoanalysis?" Nico exploded, with more vehemence than he'd expressed in months. "I care about being left alone. I care about quiet, which I never get now this asshole Domingo person has moved in. I care about not being grilled all the time. I know this sounds weird, but I care about the millions of low-rent-seeking foreigners flooding this country—"

"Ha! *Low-rent-seeking foreigners* is a new one on me," Tyler said. "Maybe you should write Republican ad copy."

"No, I'd probably be better off not caring that we're being colonized and taken advantage of, either, and I should work on not giving a shit about a lost cause. Because otherwise, I have no desires. This is a culture of wanting and getting. Of chasing and buying. A culture of envy and dissatisfaction. Of goals you only meet so you can set yourself more *goals*. So I get why everyone seems to find me incomprehensible. But in Buddhism, having no desires is nirvana."

"Okay." Tyler seemed to let up after having given the interrogation his best shot. "You were always the philosophical one."

Nico did not remember himself in high school or college as philosophical in the slightest.

When the two young men rejoined their parents in the living room, Colleen was saying with an air of atypical restraint, "Well, that's unbelievably generous. But can you afford generosity on that scale?"

Nico's mother was backed into the corner of a sofa hugging her arms. "Not easily."

"Just . . . some account number," Vernon said.

"Put yourself in my shoes," his mother said. "What else could I do?"

"But weren't you feeding the beast?" Vernon said. "I hate to point the finger at Israelis at this harrowing time. But all those hostages taken on October seventh—the Israelis asked for it. They keep rewarding abduction. Ten, fifteen years ago? They traded a *thousand* Palestinian prisoners for one weakling IDF soldier. So, of course, Hamas takes more hostages. They'd be stupid not to."

"I'm familiar with the moral hazard argument," his mother said. "But in this situation, refusing to 'reward abduction' wouldn't have accomplished anything but heartache. I couldn't stand idly by while a beloved member of my household suffered an unimaginable loss when I had the means to help her."

"What's this about, if you don't mind?" Tyler asked, refilling everyone's glasses.

Though the Carmichaels were close friends, Nico was still intrigued that his mother had spilled the beans tonight about the kidnapping. She must have been torn over sharing the saga, if only because the sordid business put a cloud over her jolly migrant sponsorship. Sure, the story further enhanced her reputation as "a good person." Yet her recap for Tyler's benefit sounded less boastful than tinged with unease.

"Wow," Tyler said. "That's, uh. Disturbing."

"I worry about the kind of people you're getting mixed up with, my dear," Colleen said.

"They're at least at arm's length and anonymous," his mother said. "Besides, I didn't engage with unsavory elements by choice."

"The whole Martine thing was a choice," Nico mumbled.

"Not really," she said. "All these people have come to our city seeking our help, seeking shelter. If you have a conscience, rising to that occasion isn't a choice."

Vernon indulged in an eye roll. It seemed his friend Gloria's vocabulary was *triggering*.

"The right to shelter," Vernon launched in, "has been a disaster. We may be the only city in the world that guarantees free housing to anyone who asks for it, at mind-blowing expense. That half-baked 'right' is the *reason* so many of these people are coming here. The mayor's office is frantically trying to get that idiotic ruling from 1979 revised, but they're tinkering around the edges. If the courts don't remove that onus completely, now that it applies not to eight million but eight *billion* potential supplicants, this city is finished."

"I didn't say anything about the right to shelter, Vernon," his mother said coolly. "Though I do think the commitment is laudable, even if the current numbers are challenging. There'd be an unholy local uprising if the city reneged."

"There may be an unholy local uprising," Vernon returned, "if this ceaseless stream of foreign panhandlers isn't stanched."

This could be fascinating. Since his father walked out, Nico had only seen his mother in social circumstances where everyone else agreed with her on everything.

"I thought you were a Democrat," she said. "Capital *D*."

"We're independents. Little *I*," Vernon said. "But this issue isn't partisan. It's existential."

"You sound like my father," Nico said.

"It's more likely your father sounds like me, pal," Vernon said.

"I used to feel real proud of the way New York is a mosaic of people from everywhere," Tyler said. "I'd look down the streets at shops selling clothes from Bangladesh and food from Indonesia, while the people walking around spoke all different languages and were from, like, Somalia, and Argentina, and Bulgaria. I thought it was cool. I thought it meant we were sophisticated, you know, *worldly*. And I thought it made this city unique. But I travel a lot for this cybersecurity job. Atlanta, Houston, Denver, but also abroad—Toronto, London, Brussels. They're all the same. They all look exactly like New York. They all have people from everywhere and shops from everywhere and languages from everywhere. When I come back here, New York doesn't seem special anymore. It's like we're all living in the same city."

"Maybe we're all living in the same wonderful city," Nico's mother said.

Tyler didn't get annoyed; he just ignored her. "In Chicago," he continued, "busloads from the border are also arriving every day. It's the black community that's getting hacked off. The migrants are dumped in their neighborhoods and housed in tents in their parks. And the imports get way more benefits than black Chicagoans ever do: laundry service, daycare, *fifteen thousand bucks* in rent support *per person*."

"I'm sure the wealthy white folks are NIMBYs," Nico's mother said.

"Oh, suburban white folks are getting a fair whack of them," Tyler said pleasantly. "So don't worry. There's enough imposition to go around for everybody."

"Don't forget, Tyler," Nico's mother admonished. "We're talking about real people—"

"Good grief, Gloria," Colleen said. "You've been around the block. So you know there's nothing more horrific than *real people*." With that token injection of levity, she stood up. "Vernon, the lamb has rested long enough. We don't want it to get cold."

She might have been referring to the descending temperature of the conversation.

Vernon was the cook, and he did everything at scale. The enormous salad on the sideboard had such an abundance of pita chips, olives, feta, and pancetta that he might as well have skipped the insipid bits of lettuce altogether. There was rice pilaf studded with currents and pine nuts *and* potatoes au gratin covered in half an inch of melted cheddar *and* a towering platter of homemade onion focaccia. Drowning in olive oil, the green beans were mostly smoked almonds. When he carved at the head of the table, the lamb proved not a cautious, middle-class pink but raw around the bone; the roast pooled in a marinade strewn with stewed figs. The profusion expressed such a sheer zest for life that Nico briefly questioned whether absence of desire qualified as nirvana after all.

All the serving and passing helped restore a metaphorical give-and-take. Swooning over the food eased the company into the benign, the neutral, the mutual. The only shadows over this groaning board were cast by the four open bottles of cabernet placed equidistant down the table. Nico's mother was a trace fearful of alcohol; Tyler was now a committed moderate; it was okay, but fancy wine was wasted on Nico, who was more of a beer man. But Vernon was already growing more voluble, and he was a momentum drinker. Colleen could put away more than you might expect, so what likely kept her consumption in check was keeping an eye on her husband.

Inevitably, they couldn't coo about the focaccia forever.

"So what are you working on now, Vernon?" his mother inquired, once the company was down to fishing stray cubes of pancetta from their host's mountainous servings of salad.

Vernon and Colleen locked eyes. Were Nico to hazard a guess, Colleen's expression said *You'd better watch it*, while Vernon's said *What do you mean? She asked.*

"By coincidence," he said, "the doc we're wrapping up is about the southern border."

"Now that the Oscars have racial quotas," Colleen said, "Vernon finally found a subject that wouldn't have any problem with *diversity*."

"What's it called?" Nico's mother asked.

"*Guests of the Nation*," Vernon said.

"That's the *working title*," Colleen said.

"It's the title," Vernon said.

"It's too sarcastic," Colleen said.

"It hits just the right note for our target audience," Vernon said.

"For the viewership, maybe," Colleen said. "But our initial target audience is streaming companies, and Apple TV is not going to buy a documentary about the border crisis called *Guests of the Nation*. If we can't sell it, there goes your viewership."

"We shall take this up another time," Vernon said.

"We've taken it up before," his wife countered. "We settled on *A Better Life*."

"But that's even more sarcastic. Like, better for whom?" Vernon drained his glass and poured a refill. "Gloria, we went down to the infamous Darién Gap, which used to be a treacherous, virtually trackless jungle between Colombia and Panama where small, incidental parties heading north often got lost and perished. The pathway across the mountains is now so well-trod by hundreds of thousands of our add-water-and-stir Americans that it's become a migrant superhighway. The litter is worse than Coney Island."

"I know something about that crossing point," Nico's mother said. "Though I assume you and your camera crew were equipped with camping stoves, waterproof tents, and Patagonia hiking gear. Most of the subjects of your film slog through that undergrowth in wet sneakers if not flip-flops, and they're continually robbed and raped. As you know."

"As I know," Vernon granted. "But bear with me. All the pilgrims we interviewed told the same few stories. Their father was murdered by the government, so they might be next—not that American immigration judges will ever be able to confirm the veracity of that account. They're gay or lesbian, and their country is homophobic. They're trans. They're Muslims who've converted to Christianity. The women are fleeing abusive husbands or gang violence. They've obviously been schooled to tailor their bios to conform to 'credible fear of persecution'—all the Spanish speakers recited *temor creíble*—and they're good students. We never caught them saying something un-asylum-worthy like 'I just want to make more money.'"

"What makes you so sure they weren't telling the truth?" she said.

"Because these stories slot too neatly into the categories of US asylum law," Vernon said. "Life isn't like that. Truth is, the whole asylum system should be shit-canned. It was designed for a handful of legitimate World War Two–type refugees, not several billion job seekers and welfare shoppers in an age of cheap transportation and smartphones."

"So we shouldn't offer safe harbor to anybody," she said.

"Yup," Vernon said. "Better a few sob stories than be taken for a ride en masse—"

"But we have international treaty obligations."

"Which can be revised, rescinded, or ignored. That's the whole point of being a sovereign nation: you make the rules."

"My dear, would you stop being so dogmatic and domineering?" Colleen said. "You *always*—"

"Yes, I *always*." Vernon turned to Nico. "Women are prone to punish you for the very qualities they fell for to begin with."

"I'm not sure I was charmed because you're a bully and you never shut up," Colleen said.

"Horseshit," Vernon said. "You loved that I never shut up. You still do."

She smiled. "True." They had a thing. Nico admitted that he enjoyed being around the thing.

"But back to story hour!" Vernon said. "The real eye-opener was at the northern end of the trail. The UN, fat-cat international charities, and a shitload of American NGOs have set up huge camps to provide our pilgrims everything they need for their righteous journey: food, water, medical care, clothing, provisions for the road, and rest for the weary. Cash. New phones. Legal advice. Maps of established routes north. These outfits are veritable travel agencies. It's an industry. The atmosphere is carnival-like. The worthies are cheerful and convinced they're doing God's work. We tend to imagine this illicit traffic is on the QT, secretively organized by unscrupulous people smugglers. But the do-gooders and the smugglers are in cahoots. No one's hiding anything. It's all out in the open and terribly well organized. Most people assume that all these migrants are doggedly trooping up through Mexico on foot, too. Not so. There's now a whole migrant bus and van service with more frequent departures than Greyhound. The cops in the countries en route wave the buses through, no questions asked, because nobody wants to get stuck with the passengers. This whole charity-slash-smuggling network now extends not just from Venezuela and Brazil, but from China, Mali, Turkmenistan, you name it. Mind you, despite the 'Non-Governmental' tag, American NGOs are massively funded by public money. We're paying to invade ourselves."

"Come on, Vernon," Nico's mother said. "You know better than to use that word."

"Funny you should object to that verb," Vernon said, taking out his phone. "Because I've started writing the voice-over script, I took a screenshot of my faithful *Webster's Seventh*. I don't trust online dictionaries, which change definitions on a dime for devious political purposes. Any day now the online Oxford will spell out, '*invade*: seize territory militarily.' Syntactically, migrants cannot "invade," and this misusage constitutes a hate crime.'"

"I'd have no problem with that definition, either." Her voice unsteady, Nico's mother must have clocked by now that in this gathering she was solely responsible for defending the Progressive American Way. She was used to singing in a chorus; suddenly she was alone onstage. Nico occupied the same isolated minority position in Ditmas. For his mother to also experience unassisted sink-or-swim was only fair, and he gave himself permission to enjoy this.

"Ready?" Vernon began.

"Honey, why don't you skip it," Colleen said.

"'*Invade*,'" Vernon proceeded. "'One: to enter for conquest or plunder. Two: to encroach upon: *infringe*. Three-A-one: to spread over or into: *permeate*. Three-A-two: to affect injuriously and progressively. Three-B: *penetrate*. See *raid, assault*. Synonym, see: *trespass*.' I'd say every variation of that definition applies to the current incursion in spades."

"Plunder?" Nico's mother said. "Don't be ridiculous. And there's nothing 'injurious' about arriving in a country you hope to contribute to. They just want to participate in our democracy, work hard, and raise a new generation of Americans—"

"You asked what I was working on, and I'm telling you," Vernon overrode. "So! We get to the Texas border. Where the Border Patrol doesn't require proof of any vaccinations or even ID. Just recite *temor creíble* like *open sesame* and you're in, presumably forever. As for what's so credibly terrifying, you don't need a shred of evidence. And get this: they're herding migrants onto commercial flights along with regular passengers, and the migrants *can travel with no ID on airplanes*."

"Wow," Tyler said. "Next time a flight attendant asks for my passport, I'll just recite *temor* . . . ?"

"*Creíble*," Vernon provided. "On the US side, the same treasonous NGOs are busy shipping our Guests of the Nation all over the country."

"Lucky for us, too," Nico's mother said staunchly.

"Walking around New York right now doesn't make me feel lucky," Vernon said.

"It'll take time to integrate the latest surge," she conceded. "But this city has thrived on wave after wave of immigrants: Italians like Fiorello La Guardia; the Irish, Germans, Poles—"

"Notice the countries you mentioned," Vernon said, who having polished off the nearest bottle reached for the next nearest, which was almost full. "Boys, you've been to college. Tell me. What do Italy, Ireland, Germany, and Poland have in common? Or for that matter, England, Scotland, and Wales? Denmark, Norway, and Sweden? Holland? Portugal? Greece? Go on, take a guess."

"Europe," Tyler said quietly.

"Head of the class!" Vernon bestowed. "Sure, all those nationalities you mentioned, Gloria, were once shunned as inferior peoples carrying diseases who were going to pollute our pure native population with deficient stock. In due course, and without any 'asylum seekers' allowances' or 'right to shelter,' those arrivals got with the program. Along with the Jews, thank God for the Jews. But this melting pot nonsense was only possible because if you take a *half* step back, they all shared the same larger civilizational heritage. They were all Europeans."

For Nico, the look on his mother's face was all too familiar: icy and self-righteous. "You mean they were all white," she said.

"That's just a word," Vernon said. "An abstract political category that covers complexions from the porcelain to the swarthy. The point is, this country's been successful not because it's so 'diverse,' but because it is, or it used to be, relatively homogeneous. The big exception being blacks, who hardly immigrated voluntarily. But look what a shitshow that's been. Look at what a shitshow it still is. You could plausibly argue that the descendants of the Africans who were dragged here against their will have still not fully assimilated into the United States a hundred and fifty years after emancipation."

"Vernon," Nico's mother said shakily, "I'm starting to find this conversation unpleasant."

"Oh, ditch the touchy liberal grandstanding over race for a second," Vernon said (and there was little chance of that). "I put to you: we think we've been everyone-but-the-kitchen-sink forever, and we've proved to the world that an atomized, polyglot mishmash can still function smoothly as a unified whole. I'm afraid we've proved quite the opposite. Until that calamitous immigration bill of 1965—which advocates in Congress *promised* wouldn't alter the country's demographics—all we'd proved was that having even one visually and culturally distinct minority brings you a host of problems, especially if they have a cracking good reason to bear a grudge. But now we really are a melting pot—or more like a slot machine readout fixed so that no one ever wins a bucket of quarters. We're building massive and *genuinely* foreign subpopulations. This is a *new* experiment. We've no idea how it ends. Historically, polities with serious ethnic divisions suffer from constant conflict and often fail. Jesus, look what's happened to peaceable, please-tax-me-more Sweden. One in five mostly Muslim foreign-born. Now Sweden has the highest incidence of *grenade attacks* in the world."

Nico's mother folded her napkin and placed it on the table. "Vernon, I'd like to thank you for a lovely meal. But I'm afraid we'll have to be on our way." She stood up. "Nico?"

It was only 10:30 p.m. Whether he always acted like it, Nico was well beyond the age of majority, and he had volition. "Mm, I think I'll stay a little longer. You know, I haven't seen Tyler in ages. I can always get an Uber home."

However stoic, her expression still conveyed that his remaining behind was traitorous. Colleen rose to fetch the guest's coat and see her out. At the sound of the front door closing, the three men around the table exhaled in unison.

"I guess walking out," Tyler said, "beats pulling a pistol from her purse."

"My mom," Nico told Vernon, "isn't used to flak. Especially since my dad left. She's only around people who agree with her, so tonight would have been kind of traumatizing. I think you made her feel *unsafe*."

At the lefty university buzzword, the trio shared a smirk.

On return, Colleen seemed torn between affection and disgust. "You went to all this trouble," she told her husband, gesturing to the leftovers. "Why spoil your own dinner party?"

"I didn't spoil anything!" Vernon protested. "We were conducting a lively discussion about a leading issue of the day."

"You know she feels strongly enough to board a migrant in her own home—"

"Two migrants," Nico said. "I guess she didn't mention the brother."

"Even worse," Colleen said.

"Totally worse," Nico said.

"And to top it all off, she shelled out *thirty grand* for that creepy kidnapping thing. So, my dear, how'd you expect her to react to that rant?"

"Your mother," Vernon told Nico, "is a fine woman, and we've been grateful to count her as a friend. But it's naivete of her sort that's digging this country's grave. Our demented president babbles on about 'the threat to our democracy.' But a wide-open southern border is a far bigger threat than that clown Donald Trump."

"Maybe it's good for you to get this gonzo stuff out of your system behind closed doors," Colleen said. "But you can't put anything in the documentary about how much better off the US would be if it only contained white people."

"I didn't say that," Vernon said, splashing another glass of cabernet.

"You came pretty close," Colleen said.

"It's possible to put what I was saying more diplomatically," he said.

"It's possible to not say it at all," Colleen said.

"I never used to care much about the whole immigration whatever," Tyler said. "But everyone in Chicago is getting sick of it. The tents. The shit on the sidewalk. The begging. We already had a huge shoplifting problem. Now it's worse."

"When even the *Times* admits New Yorkers' generosity is 'under strain,'" Vernon said, "the feeling on the street is homicidal."

"That statistic they're always pulling out," Nico said, "about how the immigrant crime rate is lower than the native population's? Turns out to be bullshit. See, the studies dilute illegals with Indian IT guys and French grad students. But eight of the Top Ten Most Wanted in Texas are Latino immigrants. In California and New York, illegals are twice as likely to be in prison than regular residents. In New Jersey? Four times. Arizona? Five times."

"You have a link to those figures?" Vernon asked eagerly. Nico swelled with a sense of public service.

After pouring everyone another round, Vernon brought out the flourless chocolate cake he'd forgotten to serve in the heat of the "lively discussion." With whipped cream and a raspberry sauce, the cake was killing. Over tequila shots, Vernon launched into a set piece about how, while populations in the West were heading into gradual decline, Africa was the exception, certain to rise from 1.4 billion this year to 2.5 billion by midcentury and almost guaranteed to reach four billion or more by

2100. Way before then, he said, the pressure on European borders from their neighbors to the south would be fantastic; as for all the overloaded dinghies crossing the Mediterranean now, "they haven't seen anything yet." That was because the "dark continent" was still too poor, arid, and politically dysfunctional to support twice or even three times its current population. Since meager education budgets already couldn't keep up with rising demand for schooling, most of these sojourners would have little to no education, making them a net drain on European social resources and likely leading to the complete collapse of the welfare state. The obvious, *ahem*, racial element was bound to make these mass flotillas, "shall we say, *awkward*," he noted, which alone would make muscular policy responses politically untenable before total reverse colonization was a fait accompli.

"My mother would say," Nico countered—in her absence, someone had to do the honors—"what's wrong with a bunch of Africans in Europe?"

"Have you ever been to Africa?" Vernon asked.

"No."

"Well, take a trip and then get back to me."

Even now, Vernon continued, the real problem, if you could call it that, was that Africans had more money than they used to, and so they'd "discovered the airplane." That was bad news for the United States. On his second tequila, Vernon avowed that in due course when the West was faced with, not millions, but billions of Africans who understandably want the hell out of a pretty disagreeable continent, migration was sure to become a military matter.

"What," Tyler scoffed, "you mean we're going to start shooting people?"

"Maybe," Vernon said. "But the situation will escalate to a Border Patrol with AKs only once it's way too late. You know, horse. Stable door."

"Okay, let's talk turkey," Colleen said, clearing off their dessert plates. "*None* of this is going in the doc, you hear me? I suggest not even mentioning Africa, all right? Because it's full of you-know-who. You will never, ever say anything in the script about the military shooting migrants even as a fanciful decades-off scenario. We'll also bring in the likes of Gloria Bonaventura to testify to the many wonderful aspects of immigration; in fact, we might have used Gloria herself if you hadn't just drastically reduced the likelihood she'll ever speak to us again. If you do say anything even vaguely portentous about the distant future, you'll also promote the alternative theory: about how, when our native populations are shrinking, Western countries will all be *fighting* among themselves over who gets to take in the remaining working-age migrants, who really will be 'guests of the nation.'"

"Oh, all that evenhandedness sounds so dreary," Vernon moaned.

"Better a drearily evenhanded doc on Netflix," she said, "than a racist, Trumpy diatribe in the trash can."

8

Nico had to give his mother credit: despite her terrifying capacity for losing her rag, she hadn't made a big flouncy scene at the Carmichaels' but had executed a simple, dignified departure in quiet protest. She hadn't called the couple names. Thereafter, she didn't, as far as he knew, send an intemperate email renouncing a friendship of over thirty years. Well, good for her. That combative evening, all these mere opinions had varoomed and collided blindly about with the inconsequent entertainment of bumper cars. Nothing had been at stake. Neither Vernon Carmichael's feverish fulminations nor Gloria Bonaventura's puristic posturing made the faintest difference to American immigration rates. Even if it did hit Netflix, Vernon's documentary wouldn't influence the real world a jot, either. For his mother to have sacrificed an abiding friendship over a dinner party gab fest would have been retarded.

Formally, then, all ties remained intact. But amid the crumbs of plum pudding at the family's Christmas dinner, their mother staged a theatrical rendition of Vernon's appalling views (what a relief she missed the really out-there stuff once she left—like Border Patrol of the future mowing down hordes of invading Africans with AKs, an image that Vernon appeared to rather relish). His sisters were aghast; Martine acted aloof. Informally, then, the chances of their mother getting together with the Carmichaels again anytime soon were dim.

The second week of January furnished still more opportunity for communal disgust, not that The Women ever seemed to run dry in this department. In the face of an impending winter storm with dangerously high winds, Martine and his mother joined a cadre of city workers in moving the entire population of Floyd Bennett Field's tented encampment to overnight in James Madison High School. The fact that Nico and his sisters were Madison alumnae facilitated a funny sense of intimacy with the story. The local ruckus over evicting the students to make way for "illegals"—a word that shoved an electric cattle prod right up his mother's behind—when Brooklyn residents had *paid property taxes* to *educate their children* made successive newscasts on NY1. The school received hate mail and even a bomb threat.

Nico's mother found the whole huffy to-do "embarrassing," "disproportionate," "opportunistic," and "confected." These were the same parents, she noted, frantic to close all New York City schools in virtual perpetuity during Covid. "So in 2020, no problem, little Jayson and Tanya can stay home for months. Until suddenly when it's to keep twenty-five hundred so-called aliens from dying of hypothermia, two days of Zoom classes are an abomination." Nico sided with his mother on this one. The furloughed students themselves would have been happy as larks.

That January's Ruckus #2 was a tad more difficult for The Women to dismiss. The video filmed on a bystander's phone went national: in Times Square, a gang of Venezuelans from the nearby migrant shelter viciously kicked and pummeled two policemen who'd tried to keep them from congregating on the sidewalk. Though eight of the attackers were subsequently arrested, all but one were released on their own recognizance, while the single culprit detained was also let go, once a pious pastor posted his $15,000 bail. (Good luck ever getting that back, pal.) "Out of 170,000 newcomers, you're bound to get a few bad apples," his mother said. "It's just math."

Other than the Venezuelans' obliviousness to the little matter that they weren't beating up plain old anybody but the NYPD, what may have been most incendiary about that news story was that, when one of them was released from the courthouse, he flipped a bird at awaiting reporters. The taunting gesture of contempt wildly violated the popular version of "our newest New Yorkers" as humble supplicants who were shit-eatingly grateful for free sandwiches.

The assault in late January having become something of a milestone, it must have been one morning in early February when Nico came downstairs to find another total stranger sitting at the kitchen table. Given the signature grilled tomato, the man in his mid-twenties was finishing up one of Martine's rib-sticking breakfasts. Martine herself was not in evidence. In rumpled jeans riding down his buttocks and a sleeveless fleece vest (it was too comfortable in here by half; Domingo must have cranked up the central heating again), this gentleman was on the heavy side and wore an expression of beaming benevolence. As these things went, the tattoos snaking around both his arms were tasteful, and the tribal artwork was articulated cleanly enough that it didn't look to be the work of a *colleague* with a great deal of time on his hands, a dull straight pin, baby oil, and soot.

"Ah, you must be Nico!" the man exclaimed, wiping his hand on a napkin and extending it. Nico's handshake was flaccid. "I am Alonso."

The functional English was a relief, insofar as anything was a relief about a man who wasn't supposed to be in your house. "Don't take this wrong," Nico said. "But what are you doing here?"

"Me and Elijah—Domingo for you—we are business partners."

"What kind of business?"

"Many fingers in pies," the guy declared, wiggling his hand. It was up for grabs whether his palpable satisfaction regarded his command of American idiom or his evasion of a straight answer. "Please, sit, sit!" he said, gesturing to a chair. "You like coffee?"

Accustomed by now to foreigners offering him hospitality in his own home, Nico took a seat.

After bringing his putative host a mug and himself a refill, Alonso returned to his reading. Aside from the fellow's very presence, what made this morning's tableau extraordinary was the physical *New York Post* by his plate—printed words on paper being no less anachronistic than a chamber pot.

"These Venezuelans," Alonso tsked, tapping the paper. "What they get from punch police? Money? No. Fancy Nike sport shoes? No. Trouble and only trouble? Yes. They are stupid boys."

"It was an assertion of power," Nico said.

"Okay, but what good is show off *power* when you no get nothing for it?" the jovial guest proposed. "You go to jail, they take your power away."

"They didn't expect to go to jail. They may still not go to jail, because the courts in this town are feeble. Those guys aren't afraid of the police. That was the point: *we can do whatever we want*. Everyone got the message, too. That's why it's such a big story."

"Even you send message?" Alonso took a slurp of coffee. "You get something for your message. This punch police in front of peoples. Is *very bad discipline.*"

While Domingo was sullen and tight-lipped, this character was chatty and high-spirited—although he exhibited the same perfect lack of self-consciousness about having popped up without explanation in someone else's property. Nico might sensibly have insisted stiffly that the visitor justify his presence or leave. But Alonso's affability was seductive, and Nico had nothing better to do than shoot the breeze.

"Three of them almost got away with it," Nico said. "Some NGO bleeding hearts bundled them into a bus, and they weren't arrested until they'd gotten to Arizona."

"This is what I say!" Alonso declared. "They almost get away with what? You get away with shoplift? You have sweatshirts, you have iPhones. You get away with punch police, you have sore hands. This boys, they are little children."

"*Niñitos,*" Nico said.

"*Sí, sí, niñitos!* Also. For migrants, in your city. Very good thing here, yes? Hotel room, bathroom, sheet and blanket—even toilet roll! Meanwhile, *mucho* opportunity for, what you say, 'side hustles.' The peoples live here, they are suckers."

Nico laughed. "I find it telling you know that word."

"For English, I know all the words I need," Alonso said. "When I come here, first words I need translate are *los idiotas, los crédulos.* Americans, they give clothings, they give doctors, they give money. Your mama, she even give her house. Best of all, they give their country! You think you, Nico, you come to Honduras and we give you our country? You try take our country, *this* is when we punch you in your face."

"Martine—I assume you know Martine?"

"*Sí, sí,* everyone know Martine. Very shrewd lady."

"*Shrewd.* You know the word shrewd."

"Like I say, I know all the words—"

"Yes, got it, but I just mean it's interesting to me that you *need* the word shrewd," Nico said. "See, Martine claims the whole world is entitled to help themselves to the United States—which you've graciously called 'my country,' but which Martine basically calls 'everybody's country.' She thinks immigration to America is a *human right*."

"Like I say, Martine is *shrewd*. She think this, and say this, is her advantage."

"But lots of Americans think the same thing. That a 'nation of immigrants' has to welcome anyone else who wants to live here with open arms."

"*Sí*, I know this sad, stupid story you tell your peoples," Alonso said lightly. "Is like suicide. 'We let everyone come here and take what they want.' This is . . ."

"Pathetic," Nico provided.

"Just the word I try to think! *Pathetic*. I tell you: I have country? I run country? Is my country? You cross my border without my permission? I shoot you. Then your friends, who think maybe they also cross my border without my permission? They decide they stay home. Bingo. No more 'migrant crisis.'"

Nico chuckled. "I have a friend in Park Slope you'd get on with like a house on fire."

"The *niñitos*, they punch police and mess up good thing for everyone else. New Yorkers, they believe their silly story and they give their country away. They say this is 'sanctuary city' like giant church, and nobody ever call *La Migra*—you say 'ICE'—even if you hit and steal them. They say everyone have 'right to shelter'—so I don't understand why *any* New Yorkers pay rent for apartment. Okay, *maybe* they keep give away their things and money even if you punch their police. But you don't take the risk New Yorkers stop give migrants things and money because you make them mad."

"The people the attack on the cops pissed off?" Nico said. "They were already mad. I mean, you must realize that lots of New Yorkers want you to go back where you came from."

"*Sí, sí*," Alonso said with a shrug. "But the mad peoples, they do nothing. Some Americans pass shelters and squeeze eyes tight and make mouth like prune. Other mad peoples poke the air with signs. Why I care about mean look or sign poke? Is no skin off my toes."

"Nose," Nico said. "No skin off my *nose*."

"Thank you. I glad for help with English. Funny language. Toes, nose, make no sense either way. English is very idio . . . idio . . . *idiomatic*," Alonso finished triumphantly.

"English is very idiotic," Nico returned, and they both laughed.

Getting up to throw some bread in the toaster, Nico resumed, "But after two years of this crap, the New Yorkers who aren't mad by now will never get mad. My mother and older sister will only get angry if the city stops giving migrants free hotels, free food, and free medical care. Then they'd go *loco*."

"You make one more toast, Nico?" Alonso asked. "I like with strawberry jam. Now, I know these nicey-softy peoples. They, how you say, 'don't get it.' Americans, you think we come here, we kiss the ground, we kiss your feet, maybe we cry. We say thank you, thank you. We promise, we do anything so we stay. You give clothings, we say thank you, thank you. We embarrass for take your nicey-softy presents. We promise some day we pay you back. We never stop with thank you, thank you, with kiss-kiss and cry and be small. This is stupid idea."

Why, the conversation was getting interesting. "Why stupid?"

"Migrants, they just peoples. You know something about peoples? You give free-everything, we think: is only right I get free-everything."

"You mean, they immediately assume they deserve it."

"*Sí, sí!* They take your free-everything with granite."

"They take it *for granted*," Nico corrected helpfully.

"*For granted*. Also, after free-everything? We think: this is not *enough* free-everything. We are cheat, this is no fair. Look at Americans with their cars. Where is *my* car? See, I go in shelters. I am businessman; I look for staff—"

"You're a recruiter," Nico picked up sharply.

"Alonso is in *HR*," he corrected. "So in shelters, all I hear is complain. They hate the food. Is cold, or is no taste, or is mashy. Almost all this meals they throw in garbage—"

"Maybe the caterers sometimes forget the parsley garnish, but those meals cost taxpayers a bomb."

"You think we will eat not-nice food because we are so grateful for you feed us at all? No, no, this is what I explain you! What I *don't* hear, never, in many shelter visits? *Thank you, thank you.* Like, I see big fight with two boys. They both have nice jacket. But one jacket is North Face. Many zippers and pockets. So the boy with nice jacket hit the boy with *very* nice jacket, because he don't want only nice jacket, he want North Face jacket. You see? All migrants want North Face jacket."

"To wear in their free cars," Nico said.

"*Sí!* So, you try take free-everything away? You think we say, *Oh, but I so lucky I have free-everything before, so thank you, thank you, never mind*? No, no. We get mad. We deserve free-everything. You take away free-everything, we hate you. Don't give us free-everything, we *take* free-everything."

"You mean you become criminals," Nico said, handing Alonso a plate of buttered toast and the strawberry jam.

"Sometime," Alonso said innocently. "You hear new rule? Single adults, they now have leave shelter after thirty days. Family, have leave shelter after sixty days. *This* is take-free-everything-away. You think migrants say, *I very lucky I already get free shelter months and months, so thank you, thank you?* No, no. We say, *You steal me! This shelter is my shelter! You give my free shelter back now!*"

As Alonso slathered his toast until the snack was more jam than bread, Nico supposed, "You said migrants are 'peoples, too.' I think everyone's like that. Like, whatever they have, and whatever you give them, is the least they can expect. Whatever they have, they've earned. Take anything they have away, including gifts or welfare, it's an outrage."

"And you, Nico?" Alonso said through sticky crumbs. "Live in big house. Dry and nice. Food in fridge. Clothings. You think you earn all this also?"

Lest he contradict his own psychic universal, Nico said mildly, "Of course."

"And you work for job?"

After his parents, his sisters, his mother's destitute boarder, and his Model Young Man long-lost friend, now Nico had to explain himself to a cheerful Honduran thug. Besides, he sensed Alonso had been briefed and knew full well that the homeowner's son was a slacker. "Not at the moment."

"But you think you earn this big house."

"It's my home. I grew up here."

"You are skinny, but grown man." He licked his fingers. "And you live with Mama."

Nico had to stop himself from again blithering about how his quiet, unassuming, inexpensive existence did no one any harm. "I don't think that's any of your business."

"Nico, Nico! We only talk. I joking you. Beside, your mama. She work for job?"

Nico was suddenly wary about giving anything away, though he wasn't sure what he'd be wise to conceal. "She runs a small company."

"Is good money?"

". . . No, not really."

"So you and Mama both. Big, big house, *very* nice strawberry jam. No big work. This is how we think of Americans in Honduras. Nice life, no work. Americans all lazy and weak."

"You calling me lazy?" Nico said, careful to keep any edge off; he used the same tonality he'd have employed for "Would you like more toast?"

"*Are* you lazy?" Alonso returned with the same geniality.

". . . Probably."

"Ha! I lazy, then no lazy. Lazy, no lazy. Today? Lazy."

"Still, you and your compatriots all seem to think it'll be easy here. But it's expensive. Lots of Americans work two or three jobs and barely survive. My father worked hard to buy this house, and when my parents moved in, the place was a wreck."

For the first time, Nico was clearly boring the guy, since Alonso changed the subject. "On Mexico side of the border, the dirt is soft with passports and ID cards, like leaves on the ground in fall. So all the peoples, including those Venezuelans—they can be anyone, like magic. The names they give Border Patrol are from the sky. This mean you get arrested? Always you give police wrong name. They let you go. You get arrested again, give police different wrong name, there is no 'record.' They let you go. This don't work in Honduras. We have national ID. But it work in New York, over and over. I tell you, this city is very good place to do business."

Alonso obligingly took his dishes to the sink. "You know this say, 'land of opportunity'? Is true. Even this thirty-day limit is opportunity. Migrants kick out of shelters are new customers. So you find store that close. Nico, why so many store with boards? This is New York! City never sleep!"

"Covid lockdowns," Nico said. "Lots of small businesses went broke."

"But this is more *opportunity*! Break in close store, buy cheap cots, rent to migrant one month for three hundred dollar. Cheap for migrants, but three hundred dollar with forty peoples is twelve thousand dollar." Alonso did the math with striking alacrity.

"Are you doing that?" Nico asked cautiously. "Breaking into vacant commercial property and running illegal dormitories?"

Alonso shrugged. "I hear about. Also, more opportunity with *squatting*. Is crazy, but you live in other peoples house? Police, they no do nothing! Is now *your* house! Also, also! You shoplift, walk out store with arms full? Nobody stop. You sell shoplift stuff right in front of shoplift store! Small prices. Peoples don't buy from store. Only in America!"

Martine bustled in the side door with a load of groceries in canvas NPR totes. Nico made a show of relieving her of the totes and putting the food away, like a useful person who pulled his weight and didn't take his big house "with granite."

"So you meet Alonso," she said, looking with surprise at Mr. Helpful.

"Yes," Nico said, storing the whole wheat tortillas under the cheese drawer. "We've been having an extensive conversation about American immigration policy."

"You no believe a word he say," Martine said. "Alonso is the bullshitter. He in love with sound of his voice."

"No fair," Alonso protested, taking advantage of the open refrigerator to graduate to Nico's Brooklyn Lager. "I tell Nico about life for migrant from inside. Like, in Roosevelt Hotel during 'processing': we all say, go red, white, and blue! Go USA! God bless America! Land of the free! Star-Spangled Banner! *Estados Unidos*, most greatest country in world! McDonald's! Pizza Hut! Statue of Liberty! Empire State Building! Bruce Springsteen! We the Peoples! Patriot missiles! Air Force One! Apple pie!

Fourth of July! President Biden! Stars and stripes! I pledge to flag! Is joke, see. We think is very funny."

"You mean you shovel a lot of shit," Nico said. "And the paper pushers eat it up?"

"They love hear how wonderful, wonderful is the USA and how more wonderful than stupid old poor countries. At shelters, migrants laugh and laugh—"

"Some migrants really think America is wonderful," Martine said sharply, shelving the cans of black beans. "Everyone is no so dark like Alonso."

"Martine, Nico want to know *the real deal*." Alfonso took a swig of "his" beer. "Because you Americans think we admire you. You think we look up to nicey-softy peoples, who let us in your nicey-softy country. Your Border Patrol reach to help us through the hole in your wall. We break your law? They give us water bottle and tuna sandwich. You think we are all amaze by kind and good police? No, no. We think *you* have the stupid country. You have no control. You let peoples take from you. That don't make us admire you. That make us contempt you."

"This is *totally jive*." Martine had picked up the expression from Palermo. "Some Americans no appreciate what they have, this is all. This is what most migrants think: is better here than Americans have any idea."

"*I* tell you what migrants think." The two seemed to have a competition going. "We do DoorDash. We cook food in restaurant, we clean dishes and floor. We drive vans, we clean your office. We mow your lawn, we cut your chicken in factory, we clean your toilet, we build your house. We make country go. We not here, country stop. New York stop. We not here, Americans starve. *Where is my pad Thai? Where is my housekeeper, I don't know how I turn on my vacuum?* Nico, you don't even do your own crime! We think maybe you need us more than we need you. Migrants do all the work? Then USA belong to migrants. Maybe you Americans are the freeloaders." Another word that Alonso *needed*.

"It's not only crap jobs that make this country 'go,'" Nico said, for the first time in this cautious discourse allowing a note of annoyance in his voice. "And once robotics and artificial intelligence take off, you people will be shit out of luck. DoorDash will use unmanned drones, and all the electric bicycles with insulated plastic handlebar bags will be piled in landfill."

"*Sí*, this is why I don't do DoorDash," their latest guest explained, still maintaining his bonhomie. "Alonso is *businessman*."

"Is your name really Alonso?" Nico asked.

"*Sí*, you call me Alonso." Didn't answer the question.

After Martine spoke to her friend, or acquaintance, whatever he was, in Spanish, the guy heaved to a stand and polished off the beer. "Nico, so good to meet you. I sure we talk more." He shouldered a small duffel sitting at his feet and lurched to the main stairs.

"What was that about?" Nico asked.

"I tell him I make up bed upstairs, in room across from your one."

"You mean he's staying here."

"For now." Martine carefully folded the NPR totes, not looking Nico in the eye.

"Does my mother know about this?"

"I tell her," Martine said lightly. Sometimes she used broken English to her advantage. It was unclear whether she meant *I told her* or *I will tell her*—though she did say "tell" rather than "ask."

Quietly texting his mother about the new arrival, Nico reviewed the vocabulary that Alonso "needed": *sucker, shrewd, advantage, suicide, pathetic, squatting, shoplift,* and *freeloader*. An evocative lingual montage.

When Nico's mother returned from volunteering at Floyd Bennett Field around 6 p.m., Martine was already cooking up a storm. Apprised that Domingo and Alonso would be joining the Honduran feast underway, his mother called to ask Palermo and Vanessa to dinner as well. Unable to speak to his mother candidly with Martine around, Nico could only infer that she'd invited his sisters either for an extra layer of protection—from what or from whom?—or to achieve a numerical majority: this way there would still be more of *us* than of *them*. He wasn't supposed to think of the Hondurans as the Other, but that's what they were.

It was a weird evening. Alonso emerged in a flowing tropical shirt covered in birds of paradise that was jarring for February, and it wasn't only his shirt that was loud. The party atmosphere conjured by Domingo's Bluetooth speaker on the kitchen counter felt forced; underneath a thin veneer of multicultural enthusiasm, four of the seven diners disliked the music. The blaring *punta* had the same effect as pounding hiphop pulsing from passing sports cars: it claimed territory. Thus even before they sat down, the Bonaventuras seemed like the guests, whose demeanor was consequently muted. As the two "business partners" glugged Flor de Caña into pineapple juice, Martine rushed about ensuring that the men had everything they needed—"the men," mind, did not include Nico—straws, ice, napkins, hot off the griddle *pupusas* stuffed with stringy cheese. Her eagerness to please had an anxious edge.

Once the meal proper commenced, the Hondurans still spoke only in Spanish, and in his native tongue Alonso was even more verbose than he'd been at noon. The guy took up a lot of space. The family was left to mumble among themselves. Seated beside Alonso and thus having to give the man's sweeping hand gestures wide berth, Palermo was unusually reserved. Having typically arrived with a generous dessert, a twelve-inch Junior's cheesecake, Vanessa had been delighted to meet Alonso at first. But she soon grew overwhelmed, and her smile through dinner was dazed. Their mother wore an expression Nico recognized from the tense period right before their father moved out. No doubt she was trying to assume a sociable look of openness and good fellowship, but the artifice was such a strain that all the fine muscles in her face crumpled into a six-car pileup, and the dominant feeling they conveyed was pain.

When Martine brought the cheesecake, Domingo troweled a wodge from the middle and plopped it on his plate. The guy failed to grasp the concept of *slices*. Cowed, the women all asked for "a small spoonful."

With no thanks to their hostess or the cook, Domingo and Alonso lurched drunkenly to bed. Nico's mother insisted that Martine also call it a night. His mother wasn't likely in the mood to clean the kitchen, either, but she'd at last secured the privacy to talk.

"I don't think Martine invited him exactly," she said quietly, after the family had collected dishes for a good five minutes in shell-shocked silence. "But she doesn't seem comfortable, for now, asking him to leave."

"*Comfortable*," Palermo repeated. "For *now*. Does that mean showing him the door just seems sort of awkward?"

"Who is that man, anyway?" Vanessa asked.

"Some associate," their mother said.

"In what enterprise?" Nico asked.

"Heaven knows," their mother said.

"When he deigns to speak English, he can be entertaining," Nico said, putting the remains of the mauled cheesecake back in its box. "He's more honest than a lot of these people, who all claim they only want to live in the 'land of liberty' and pay taxes."

"He treated me to this whole 'we demand free-everything' spiel," Palermo said. "He feels under no compunction to put a respectable gloss on his base motivations."

"I don't understand Martine," Vanessa puzzled. "She seems so strong and independent. Except around those guys, when she's weirdly servile and apologetic."

"They make her nervous," their mother said.

"Her own brother?" Palermo said.

"The point is," Nico said, "is Alonso staying?"

"I guess that's up to him," their mother said.

"It shouldn't be," Palermo said.

"I'm not sure what to do," their mother said. "I have to think. In the meantime, he's at least . . . amiable."

They were talking around something—something heavy, a big, fat cheesecake of unsaid that just sat there, oblivious to their avoidance.

Tossing in bed that night, Nico was tortured by a question that he hadn't marshaled the nerve to pose when Martine came home with the groceries: "Is your name really Martine?" It was completely irrational, but if the answer was no—not that she'd ever admit as much—the whole construct on which this household was currently built seemed to collapse. "All the peoples," Alonso had said. "They can be anyone, like magic."

Like Domingo, Alonso disappeared without explanation from time to time. But at least when resident Domingo preferred to hole up antisocially in the basement. By contrast, their new Guest of the Nation made even freer with the house than Martine ever had. He took his meals in the main kitchen, assuming that Martine would provide. He snoozed on the couches in the living room (and he snored). He leafed through books picked idly from the shelves and discarded them on the curly-maple dining table. He left behind the peels from his oranges, the empties from his beers, and the scatter of reddish salt from his chili peanuts wherever he happened to settle, complacent in his surety that someone else would tidy up. He thought nothing of lumbering into the den where the homeowner was watching *Dear White People* on Netflix and switching the channel to ¡Hola! TV in Spanish. When she got her February Visa bill, said homeowner discovered that a certain unidentified someone had been merrily purchasing multiple films from Amazon and using the account's default credit card. He never turned off lights. Once Alonso was installed, Nico's mother gave up on keeping the thermostat at sixty, because their newest resident had shared sternly that Hondurans were accustomed to a tropical climate, and chill air put them at risk of pneumonia.

Alas, Alonso and Nico shared the same bathroom upstairs, where the visitor made no effort to close the shower stall properly and got water all over the floor—on which he also discarded his towels, as if he were an ecologically oblivious guest at a five-star hotel. Those showers ran to twenty minutes. He left gnarly toenail clippings on the lid of the toilet, whose bowl was perpetually smeared and splattered from his explosive bowels. He blithely availed himself of Nico's razor and shaving gel.

Yet the latest arrival's presumption may have reached its apotheosis when Nico went into the kitchen late one afternoon to locate the source of a low churning hum, to find Alonso at the table with his jeans rolled up and his feet in a bucket of water.

"Very soothing!" Alonso declared brightly. "This massage machine keep water nice and hot for Alonso's achy feet. I tell you, Nico, today was a no-lazy day, and I am poop."

"That's not a massage machine. It's my mother's *sous vide* wand," Nico said with undisguised horror.

"Shoe heat pond?" Alonso puzzled. "I must keep shoes on?"

"No, it's for cooking food in a plastic bag. Don't ask! Just turn it off!"

Nico rinsed and stored the appliance, resolving to keep its misuse to himself. His mother was infernally attached to the stupid thing, and if she knew it had been sharing a bath with Alonso's smelly feet she'd never again come near it.

The pally fellow took to providing Nico career counseling free of charge. A young man had to display entrepreneurial gumption! The secret to capitalism, he said, is spotting what people need. "What migrants need, more than anything?" Alonso proposed. "Money." Newly issued to these destitute arrivals straight off the bus, Mastercards preloaded with $350 per week for food and baby supplies only worked in supermarkets and bodegas. Yet shelters confiscated microwaves and hot plates, meaning the migrants could only buy food edible off the shelf. "They get sick of Cheetos fast," Alonso advised. They'd soon want to turn the restricted cards into money. A resourceful middleman could offer the migrants, say, $150 cash for each preload of the debit card, and the migrants would happily take it. The card would buy $350 worth of goods, which could either be peddled on the street at a discount or sold back at wholesale prices to the supermarkets. Voilà. Scaled up, so long as you'd done your sums right, a nice little profit.

"I'm getting a feel for how you think," Nico said.

There was no question, however, that still another resident, who was also not bringing in $110/night through the aegis of Big Apple, Big Heart, put a detectable strain on Gloria Bonaventura's short of boundless hospitality. (Martine's total monthly payments from the city had still not quite compensated for the $30,000 ransom payment, accountancy that both parties had surely tabulated, though only the benefactor was sure to add nearly half again as much in taxes to the debt.) Nico's mother was a neat freak, and Alonso's slovenly habits rankled. Sensing this, Martine frantically tidied the new guest's messes minutes after he made them. Between meals, she kept the kitchen spotless. She put in overtime crocheting for Toys & Trinkets, even stooping to craft the ever-popular packers, which she clearly found repulsive. She made up for Alonso's lack of *boundaries* by scrupulously observing her sponsor's, no longer lounging sociably in the den to slum it with *Emily in Paris* unless expressly invited to do so and keeping otherwise to the basement after dinner. She no longer sang and chattered through her chores, but kept her mouth shut. She assumed responsibility for the considerable extra laundry and food shopping that Alonso's presence imposed. She seemed keenly conscious of skating on thin ice. Three hangers-on for the price of one wasn't in the contract.

Thus in March, with an eye to springtime, Little Miss Helpful supposed that she might have been so aggressive with the hedge trimmer last summer because the blade was dull and volunteered to take the tool to the Home Depot in Marine Park to have its teeth sharpened. When the trimmer was ready a few days later, she reminded her sponsor that they needed a range of hardware essentials and proposed the two of them make an afternoon outing of its retrieval. This was the kind of boring household shit to which Nico was ordinarily oblivious. He hadn't even noticed his mother and her sidekick had left on their errand until they returned.

In quite a state. While Martine had a resolute, almost marshal air, his mother no sooner burst in the side door than flopped into a kitchen chair. Her color was high, her hair in disarray, her breath rapid. Curious, Nico slid his headphones off an ear.

"My heart is still jumping out of my mouth," his mother told Martine.

Martine placed the trimmer on the counter. It was missing its protective plastic sheath. She put a hand on his mother's shoulder. "I make you Sleepy Time chamomile."

"Honestly, I'd rather have a cognac."

That got Nico's attention, even during Cash Jordan's video "Migrants Get Luxury Apartments in NYC." His mother almost never drank spirits, much less at 4 p.m.

"What's up?" he asked.

"We'd just gotten off the B41 on Flatbush—you know, it runs all the way from Avenue U, and after my encounter with that scammer in the car I prefer taking the bus," his mother began, when Martine returned from the dining room.

"Sorry, Gloria." One benefit of Martine's lower-profile manifestation was her dropping of that compulsive "Ador*a*ble," which Nico detested. "There is no cognac."

"But I've had nearly a full bottle on hand forever. But never mind. Bourbon, then."

"There is no bourbon. Only cassis." She mispronounced it *cass*is, but it was still pancake syrup.

Nico hopped up to confirm his suspicions: the liquor cabinet in the living room had been cleaned out. But then, it had been stocked largely for *guests*.

Meanwhile, Martine was plying his mother with an oversize glass of white wine. "You have shock. You sit back and relax."

"I'm the one who should pour you a drink." His mother took a slug. "I've never seen a display of such raw courage in my life. Martine, you were a tiger! And so resourceful, so quick thinking. It would never have occurred to me . . . On my own, I'd have just given them everything and cried."

"I was one carry it," Martine demurred. "You carry, you think also you use same way. Beside, this thieves, they make me so angry. They walk like they so important. So big, so scary men. But only big men in group. Alone, they are *niñitos*. That little skinny one. I am much taller and stronger. He should be scare of me."

"I think he was!" Nico's mother said. "I think they all were! I think they were terrified!"

The two women laughed.

"Going to let me in on the joke?" Nico asked.

"It was no joke," his mother said. "This gang of five or six young toughs—"

"Was only five," Martine said.

"They sidled up on either side of us," his mother continued. "It took me a minute to realize what was happening, because for pity's sake, it was broad daylight, in the middle of the afternoon! You'd think it was still back in the early nineties, when Carlin and I first bought this place. Back then, you assumed you were a target. If you absolutely had to leave the house, you kept your wits about you—"

"And then what happened?" Nico had no patience for long, dragged-out stories that in real time probably lasted, like, sixty seconds.

"Well, it also took me way too long to notice that the bigger, especially thick-looking one had a knife—"

"A small knife," Martine said.

"A six-inch blade is not a small knife!" his mother said. "Though of course Martine spotted it right away and pulled me over until we were facing them. In fact, she put herself between me and the boys. They mumbled something about phones and wallets. I'd already started checking which pocket I'd slipped the phone in—"

"What *ethnicity* were these guys?" Nico asked.

"Why would you care?" his mother said. "For goodness' sake, Nico, you always—"

"They all from Honduras," Martine said with authority.

"And then I heard this juddering electric buzz," his mother resumed. "I wasn't thinking straight, so at first I didn't understand where it was coming from. It was the hedge trimmer! Martine had whipped the sheath off, and she had one hand on the power switch and the other on the red handle. She jabbed it toward the kid with the knife, and didn't he leap back! Never mind a six-inch blade, that trimmer's blade is half a yard long! Then she starts swishing it back and forth"—their narrator got up to demonstrate, lunging and slashing the mimed garden tool in the air— "zzzzzzzz, zzzzzzz, zzzzzzz! Zzzzzzzz, zzzzzzz! It was like a scene out of Marvel comics! Like a superhero, with a sword of vengeance! Like Luke Skywalker in *Star Wars* with his light saber! Those kids scattered every which way! I've never seen anything like it!"

"Well, well," Nico said. "Isn't it lucky we bought the cordless kind."

"Oh, don't be so droll and underwhelmed," his mother said. "We were just mugged at knifepoint. We're always hearing about 'strong women' in the movies. Thank God there's such a thing in real life."

"Anyone do same," Martine said modestly.

"I beg to differ," his mother said. "Most people would have handed over the phones, all their credit cards, their watch, the bag of weather stripping and LED light bulbs, and probably the trimmer, too. It takes a quick wit to realize you're already wearing the ruby slippers."

Nico had no idea what she was talking about. Maybe the encounter on Flatbush really had messed with her head.

"Did you draw any blood?" Nico asked Martine. "Lop off any limbs? Last summer, you sure amputated the hydrangeas."

Martine got the squared-off look that he remembered from when they met. "I am no sure," she said coolly. "Maybe I cut one or two boys. They no stay around long for me see."

Nico drifted to the power tool on the counter. The teeth of the blade were clean and shiny. "Doesn't look like it."

"Gloria, I sorry I drop the cover thing," Martine said. "I go back and find on sidewalk?"

"The sheath?" his mother said. "Oh, forget it. Besides, that trimmer is now iconic. I should have it mounted on the wall as a museum exhibit, like a Civil War musket. The truth is, that thing has always frightened me, even doing the landscaping. Thank heavens you didn't end up striking any of them. There'd have been blood everywhere, like *The Texas Chain Saw Massacre*. *The Brooklyn Hedge Trimmer Massacre* could have been quite a sequel."

His mother was a little giddy. She'd finished the wine.

The disquiet that haunted Nico the rest of the afternoon was disturbingly familiar. Being saddled with an odious obligation he hadn't signed up for was familiar. The dread was familiar. The sense of hopelessness and self-destruction was horribly familiar. Even the venue for his futile sacrifice was familiar, once later that night he'd rapped on his mother's bedroom door. After nearly four frigid months, his mother had thawed somewhat; why, by his twenty-seventh birthday in February, she actually wished him many happy returns (albeit with no present, and in tandem with the announcement that, having aged out of her less expensive family policy a year ago, he was now obliged to pay for his own health insurance—larcenous coverage that he blithely allowed to lapse). So naturally he had to send their moderately improved relations back to Go.

"Hi, sweetie," she said, removing her earrings in the mirror. "I hope whatever this is about won't take too long. When you go through something traumatic, there's a funny delay. It only hits you after the fact. It's starting to hit. I feel positively run over. I tried to make that mugging into an amusing anecdote, but it wasn't amusing at the time. It was petrifying."

He had prepared an icebreaker. "I wasn't just being nosy, because we don't know much about Alonso. So the last time he was out, I slipped into his room to look around. I found, like, a pack of about fifty Social Security cards on the dresser. I assume they were fake, but if so they were good ones. Maybe he sells them. It's probably one of his 'fingers in pies.'"

She sighed. "Could be worse. With a fake Social Security number, you pay into the system and don't get anything back when you're old or sick. I think payroll deductions on fake and borrowed numbers significantly bolster the system's income. The party really getting scammed is the migrants."

"It's still illegal, and we don't know what other pies he has fingers in. But I guess you admire it when migrants are 'resourceful.'"

"I do, as a matter of fact. Though I have to say, you didn't seem very impressed by Martine's derring-do this afternoon. She really was extraordinary."

"I don't think it was supposed to impress *me*."

However weary, she suddenly looked alert. "What do you mean, supposed to?"

Nico glanced at the bedside armchair, which had an emotional stink on it, and decided this time to remain standing. "You were there, and so obviously you know better than me, but . . . Is there any chance, any chance at all, that Martine's rescue on Flatbush was staged?"

His mother's face hardened. There went that trace of restored amicability that he'd stifled so many insensitive remarks to kindle. "How could it conceivably have been 'staged'?"

"It's just, from the outside, the whole story stacks up as awfully convenient. It was Martine's idea to sharpen the hedge trimmer to begin with. Even after sitting all winter, the lithium-ion battery was charged. The battery was also connected, when it's the heaviest part of the tool, and if I were bringing the trimmer in for sharpening I'd have left the battery home. She didn't actually hurt anybody. And it wouldn't have been that hard to hire a few of her compatriots to follow you two off that bus."

"To what purpose?" Mothers really weren't supposed to use that tone of voice with their own sons, ever. It was awful.

"Your gratitude," he said.

"Then it worked. I'm very, very grateful."

"I thought you might just, you know, rerun it in your head . . ."

"Maybe I wouldn't go so far as to say that Martine saved my life today." The suppressed quality of her fury made it seem more potentially combustible. "Still, her heroics were in that ballpark. But you have so much time on your hands that you've nothing better to do than to sit around concocting conspiracy theories. Because that's what you just put together. A far-fetched conspiracy theory that impugns a woman who's shown me unflagging loyalty. To such an extent that she put herself in physical peril today on my behalf. If one of those boys had wrestled the trimmer away from her, that scene could have turned to carnage."

"Well, there you go," he said. "You said there were five of them, all young men. They probably could have overpowered her, if they'd really wanted to."

His mother sat down on her stool and placed both hands flat on the dressing table, looking down. "I don't know what to do with you. Or about you. I don't have much faith in psychotherapy. I never thought I'd ever say this about one of my own children. I'm starting to feel that you're simply not a nice person."

9

Nico had calmly taken the hit when his mother called her only son a sociopath. Yet her assessment that he was "simply not a nice person" cut him to the quick. The earlier aspersion was over the top; this latest charge was on a regular-life level. It was the kind of reluctant conclusion you drew when a difficult friend whose shortcomings you'd overlooked for years just wasn't worth the grief, and what you'd always labeled to yourself as "ambivalence" toward this ball and chain tipped over into plain dislike. But surely you weren't meant to wash your hands of your own kid. Nico wasn't sentimental, or he didn't think he was, but he'd always hazily conceived of family as The People You Couldn't Get Rid Of, or even as the people who, if push came to shove, you didn't especially want to get rid of. Their mother might have tried to jettison their father, but once you'd had children there was only so divorced you could get.

That was the only explanation he could contrive for his disconcerting implosion circa 2 a.m., at which time presumably sweeping repudiation of her son's very soul had not impeded his mother's descent into untroubled slumber. Admittedly, he'd had three or four beers—Molsons, and they were warm, because stashing a six-pack under his bed had proved the sole guarantee that they'd not be pillaged by Central American parasites within twenty-four hours. He'd ended up sobbing, curled atop his bedspread clutching the woebegone giraffe, the bashful tiger, the lost-looking sheepdog, and the pugnacious piglet—the stocking stuffers of yore he was now too old for by a good fifteen years.

From the slightest remove, this mucus-stringed blubbering was excessive, bathetic, and embarrassing, albeit embarrassing in a particular sense. It was one thing to be embarrassed in public—over smashing a jar of *passata* in a supermarket or leaving your fly open on the street. It was quite another thing to be embarrassed in front of yourself, which was way worse. While eccentric public embarrassment could be slyly repurposed into attractively self-deprecating anecdotes, private embarrassment never saw the light of day.

By returning home coming up on five years, maybe he'd become a mama's boy, for he was surely at an age that whatever his mother thought of him shouldn't have kept him up nights. Nevertheless, he refused to believe that most other grown children confronted their own mothers' wholesale character assassination with utter indifference. So even after whimpering himself to sleep like a two-year-old, he woke the next morning still smarting from a burning sense of injustice. She should have understood that her son was only looking out for her, even if his suspicions proved unfounded. Any respectable mother would give her own kid the benefit of the doubt, rather than eagerly surmise that her youngest was a paranoid, far-right white supremacist and therefore a write-off.

When he crawled out of bed, his face was swollen and his eyes were red, what little he could see of them in the mirror, since they were squeezed to slits. He struggled to concoct a story that would explain why he looked like the loser in a bar fight that would improve on "I bawled like a baby for hours, because my mommy doesn't like me anymore." But he needn't have scrambled for a cover story, as his mother didn't seem to be downstairs, though the Prius was still in the drive. He finally located her off the laundry room, because the door to her cramped office, originally the maid's quarters, was, unusually, shut. Perhaps its atmosphere retained an off-putting taint of servitude, since she mostly used the hideaway for storage of yarns and Priority Mail boxes for Toys & Trinkets. As he crept past the dryer, he could hear her typing at a clip on her laptop, though she might have composed whatever she was writing more comfortably at the kitchen table, where she commonly answered emails. Was she confiding in some private journal? Maybe their harsh encounter the night before had messed her up, too. Like, maybe there was hope for a halting reconciliation or forgiveness—though in Nico's mind, any forgiveness should be two-way.

Yet when she finally emerged at about one thirty that afternoon, her demeanor suggested no hint of softening or regret. Her motions were jagged; her face was set in a mask of obscure purpose. With just the two of them in the kitchen, neither spoke. When he dropped the lid of the mustard on the floor, the tiny clatter sounded clamorous.

Then his mother announced briskly that she had "an appointment" and would return in a few hours. Something about the syntax was punishing. Had Alonso or Domingo been underfoot, fine; whomever she needed to meet was none of their business. But with your own family, you had "a *dental* appointment" or "an appointment *with your accountant*" or "an appointment *to get your hair done*." The privacy was pointed. She was freezing him out. The side door might not have precisely slammed, but her departure didn't merit even a cursory "bye."

Might she evict him from the house? She wouldn't fear throwing him onto the street, because his small inheritance would keep him from being homeless for a while. Yet what distressed Nico about this plausible prospect wasn't depleting his precious nest egg in a matter of months, locating a shitty apartment with a bathtub in the kitchen, and engaging in all the tedium of the much-vaunted "adulthood" that this half-decade hiatus had spared him: his own telecom contract, tax returns, not to mention a job. No, what most alarmed him was leaving his mother with no one to look out for her.

Thereafter, when his mother abruptly scheduled a visit to her sister in Phoenix, Nico told himself it was absurd to take the trip personally, which didn't keep him from taking the trip personally. Yes, normal women in their sixties did sometimes have a normal impulse to visit siblings from a normal desire to fortify normal ties, but he couldn't help but suspect that, in lieu of kicking him out, for now she was removing herself from the house instead. Honestly, she couldn't stand the sight of him. In the run-up to hopping her taxi to JFK, she unerringly walked out of a room within seconds of Nico having entered it.

As it happened, the visit with his aunt Lauren—even crazier than his mother and unlikely to exert a mollifying influence with all her "neo-Nazi Israeli settler colonialism" guff—coincided with a period during which Domingo and Alonso disappeared without explanation. Nico was able to verify their absence by experimentally placing one of his Molsons in the refrigerator door, where it remained. In other words, for the time being he and Martine—or whatever her name was—were the sole residents of the house.

It wasn't fair to say that he disliked her, though the temperature of his feelings depended on which version of Martine he designated as authentic. He effectively lived with twins. One of the duo was vivacious, physically brave, uncomplainingly industrious, and so constitutionally generous that she was susceptible to exploitation by sexist pricks like Alonso and her brother—if not also by Nico himself, who'd likewise grown accustomed to a chef, house cleaner, and personal shopper on call. This was a mother painfully separated from her children and hoping to reunite the family once she'd established herself in the new country that would facilitate a more prosperous future for them all. Plucky, determined, affectionate, and faithful, this Martine had formed abiding attachments to his mother and sisters, and if she had not quite bonded with Gloria Ador*able*'s youngest, that was surely his fault. From the start, Nico had been remote. While this Martine was perplexed by his distance, she would wait patiently for the boy to come around. He was, after all, troubled in her view, uneasy in himself. He held back from the household's new resident because he resisted change of any kind, and that included growing from boy to man. Meanwhile, she had overcome untold adversity—poverty, domestic abuse, spousal alcoholism, gang violence, extortion, a perilous journey to America—and had miraculously managed to preserve her indomitably joyful spirit.

Then there was the effervescent innocent's doppelgänger: scheming, duplicitous, dangerous, and very smart. So tiresome did Nico find the blander edition, and so much more compelling did he find the resentful, secretly raging, lying-sack-of-shit Martine, that it was not inconceivable, if only to keep himself entertained, that he had made the second woman up.

She had at least learned to drop the bubbly "Tickita Tickita" routine when no one else was here. This didn't imply that the more sober, no-nonsense, lay-her-cards-on-the-table persona she adopted in his presence was necessarily the "real" Martine; it merely betokened her accurate appraisal that this was the persona Nico preferred. Yet her dialing back of the life-of-the-party song and dance didn't alter the fact that he was uncomfortable around her, as he had been from day one. Negotiating a house with just the two of them made the discomfort more intense. The exact source of that discomfort he'd shied from identifying, aside from feeling fairly certain that their having little to nothing in common wasn't it.

This March was unseasonably warm, leading strangers waiting at the local ATM to grumble about the "climate emergency," since in the progressive worldview you could now be despondent even about nice weather. Thus Martine had returned to the clinging muscle Ts, snug jeans, and heeled sandals she'd favored over the summer. Whether by hoisting groceries and buckets of soapy water or via a covert regime of push-ups in the basement, the woman had preserved those strapping, striated arms—becomingly hard and sinewy rather than bulging and bulked-up. Her breasts didn't grab his attention—about a handful apiece—because he'd grown accustomed to the water-baby-about-to-burst knockers online. But something about the way those jeans settled on her hips just so was riveting. She sometimes turned to find him staring at her ass—two bigger handfuls, though still tight and reminiscent of his mother's comely buttocks before they flattened during menopause. He usually dropped his gaze when caught, but once in a while met her eyes instead, which was far more interesting.

Martine had announced with authority that Domingo and Alonso were attending to "a job" out of town for a good ten days. Nico assured her at the outset of this honeymoon that she was welcome to take a breather from cooking; he could order takeout and give all those migrants on unlicensed scooters something to do apart from running down pedestrians on the sidewalk to steal their handbags and phones. Ha ha, she said. But she'd make meals for herself anyway and claimed it was just as easy to cook for two, so they ended up having dinners together, no stinting on the cheese.

The first night, when Nico was prepared to bolt his food in silence over his phone, Martine formally introduced a talking point: surely Gloria's absence provided an excellent opportunity to plan a surprise party for her upcoming birthday.

"Oh, I'd forgotten about that," he said, sawing at another bean-and-pepper-jack concoction on a corn tortilla glistening with lard.

"You so very busy you no remember your mama's birthday?" A better question was why Martine remembered it—or knew his mother's date of birth in the first place.

"As a matter of fact, I have plenty of things on my mind, so *yes*. But especially since she turned sixty, my mother hasn't been big on birthdays."

"Your mama be sixty-three, party or no party. Better sixty-three with party."

He'd been about to say that his mother would interpret any party he helped throw as a clumsy, overobvious attempt to make nice, then stopped himself. He hardly wanted to explain why his mother was so angry at him to Martine of all people.

"I don't know how to contact most of her friends," he said.

"Email."

"But I don't have access—"

"I have access."

"You know my mother's passwords?" Jesus, this woman's genius for inveigling herself into his family's business continually exceeded expectations.

"Gloria get over hundred trash emails every day. Companies, ads, newsletters. I clean up her inbox in mornings. Is my job."

"*I* don't have access to her inbox."

Martine leaned back and crossed her arms—her shapely, rippling arms—with a distinct air of self-congratulation. "So? Maybe your mother no trust you."

"But she trusts *you*."

"*Sí*." A slight smile. If an opponent, a formidable one.

Nico was tempted to ask if she also had the passwords to his mother's financial accounts, but the prospect was so horrifying that he almost didn't want to know.

"But is lucky I have access," Martine noted. "We get friend addresses. Like in CC: of Gloria's book club."

Nothing interested him less than organizing some flipping party, but maybe it would do his mother good to feel appreciated. Besides, even at the risk of his seeming like an apologetic suck-up, if there were to be such an occasion, maybe it was better that he be seen to have played a part in it, rather than letting Martine get all the credit. "Can we at least keep it low-key? Not too many people. Though I guess we'd still need a cake or something."

"Of course. And mucho food, mucho drink, mucho *punta*."

"My mother hates *punta* music."

"She say me she love *punta*!"

"Yeah, well she's fucking lying."

"Gloria *learn* to love *punta*. She no hear enough."

"In this house? She's heard plenty. Face it, it's freaking awful. Mincing and mindlessly perky and cheap." Nico performed the refrain of "Tickita Tickita" with exaggerated peppiness and moronic cheer, employing the lobotomized hand gestures you saw in nursing home sing-alongs when the residents were especially far gone. At least he made her laugh.

"*Muy bueno!* You have future in Honduras!"

"God forbid."

"We no play Mozart at party."

"I think she used to like the Eagles. The Police. Talking Heads. Steely Dan. Just get 1980s mixes off Spotify and keep them on repeat. Most of that generation never even graduated to grunge. She hates hiphop almost as much as *punta*."

"We tell Gloria's friends keep secret. On birthday, you and your sisters take Gloria for birthday drink. You take her to bar, somewhere terrible. Ugly place, ugly people, bad drink. You make disappointment. Gloria pretend very nice, but in secret Gloria sad. And Gloria still hungry! You take your mama home. She walk in, *surprise*! We string up sign, sing birthday song. No disappointment."

Well, you had to hand it to her for getting with the cultural program; that was the standard surprise party protocol, all right. "So aside from finding the most depressing bar in the neighborhood, what do I do?"

"You make video. Happy times. Family pictures. Friends and family no can come, they send happy birthday videos. You put all together. Plug laptop in TV, play for party."

It sounded like more work than he'd bargained for. "I guess. And you're making the food?"

"Tres leches cake. *Baleadas*, enchiladas, *pupusas, pastelitos, tajadas* . . ."

"How about making some stuff that my mother wants to eat? She can't stand when everything's fried."

"She no say me she no like fried!"

"She's too polite."

"Everyone like fried."

"I know they do. But try some, like, baked chicken. Shrimp with cocktail sauce. *Salad*. Because my mother doesn't really care that much about food. She cares about being skinny. You've been here ten months. You should have picked that up by now."

Finally he'd struck home. She looked unsettled. He had impugned her ingratiation skills.

She nodded at his plate. "*You* like fried?"

For some reason he was inclined in that moment toward a bit of ingratiation of his own. "I like fried."

"One more *catracha*?"

"Sure, why not." She may have been a double agent or even a thief. But she was still a woman, and they were all the same in one respect: they wanted you to like their cooking.

The second night, Nico offered her a beer, since she was the only interloper in the household who wouldn't simply help herself. If he wasn't mistaken, that was the same clinging, fire engine–red muscle T she'd worn when she arrived. The color suited her.

He liked fried, he got fried: a mighty mound of cracked up deep-fat-fried wheat tortillas, strips of sauteed beef, their token vegetable (a few shreds of cabbage), and cheese, cheese, cheese. Honduran nachos, basically.

As for the topic de jour, she wasn't shy. "So, Nico Niñito. Why you no have girlfriend?"

"Why would a 'little boy' have a girlfriend?"

"You no like 'Nico Niñito'?"

"Of course I don't. Who would? I thought the whole reason you use that insulting nickname is you know I can't stand it."

"But it has happy sound. *Nico* and *niñito*—they go together. If words can fall in love, this words get married."

"What's more important to you, poetry, or my feelings?"

"*Nico, Gran Hombre.*"

"Even worse. Sounds sarcastic."

"But you no answer my question. Your face, no so bad. You tall. You no so fat, like most Americans. But no *señorita*. Or you like boys?"

"You think I'm gay."

She shrugged. "Seem everyone in New York is gay."

"Being gay is totally yesterday," he filled her in. "Now that even the churchy people aren't denouncing homosexuality I doubt it's even much fun. It's not risqué."

"Risky?"

"Risqué, meaning 'dangerously abnormal,' so it's not 'risky,' either. Hell, it's not even sexy. Those guys used to get up to some sick shit, and now they just bicker about the napkin rings for their wedding receptions and scour the internet for surrogates to have their babies. I'm not even sure they bother to take it up the ass anymore. So no thanks. I'm not gay. It would be too passé."

"You have girlfriend in *universidad*?"

"Yeah, sure." He almost added "sort of," except it was past time that he lived down this "little boy" crap.

"You like fucking with her?"

"It was okay."

"*Okay.* Maybe you no do it right."

"I think sex is overrated."

Though her English was coming along nicely, the adjective required Google Translate.

"You mean she break your heart," Martine surmised.

"I think the last time my heart was broken was in fifth grade. I was ten." A lie, but it sounded slick. It might have been worth asking why he was trying to impress her.

"Is good for you, break your heart. Every time break, it grow back stronger. Like muscle—you no use, it get small and weak."

"You'd know something about that," he said, nodding at her bare shoulders.

"You like muscle?" she said.

"You mean muscles on women? Yeah, I do." He added with more honesty than he'd planned, "Though they make me nervous."

"I think is woman make you nervous."

Got that right. Nico had stopped eating.

"So all time I here," she said, "I no see you with lady. Why?"

"Too much trouble," he said, getting up for another beer. "Too complicated."

She reached to arrest him. "I think maybe you need complicated."

The hand on his forearm sent his pulse racing, and the blood went straight south. When he met her eyes, they conveyed as clearly as the digital readout in Times Square: this was a dare. He could break the contact and continue to the fridge. Nothing would have happened, there'd be no consequences, and she'd laugh it off if she acknowledged the moment at all. Or he could do something else. He wasn't used to making decisions of any kind, and all the synapses in his brain, with which one presumably made decisions, promptly shorted out. But then, decisions themselves were instantaneous. It was dithering that took all the time.

Before the dithering could get underway, then, he reached both hands under her arms and lifted her in a single motion over his head and settled each of her thighs on either hip. The squeeze of her quads at his waist and the hooking of her high heels behind his back more than sufficed for "consent." This was the most he had felt like a man in years. Despite his having run from the experience for most of his life, the sensation was surprisingly pleasant.

They ended up on the living room's cream-colored oriental rug, and Nico had forgotten how annoying it was getting all your clothes off—though slipping a hand up under that little red T satisfied an impulse he hadn't realized he'd been suppressing for ten months. When they'd finally wrestled down to the essentials, he noted that she had a bush on her. Although he flirted with Ruskinesque revulsion, even the men on Pornhub shaved every last follicle; pubic hair was the sole kink only available IRL.

She was unbelievably aggressive. In fact, she was a fucking animal. At Fordham, Kayla was technically uninhibited—there was little she wouldn't agree to—but she always seemed to be checking off a set of tips she'd read in a magazine. Martine heeded only raw, unmediated appetite. It was a battle to maintain the lead, but he wasn't about to cede the initiative and let her do as she pleased with him. The contest was bracing, because she was so infernally strong; when she rolled on top and pinned his wrists to the carpet, he was astounded by the force he had to marshal to release his arms. That said, he may have boycotted the bench press, but Nico was a male, just then feeling very male to boot, against whom even a lusty female specimen didn't have a chance in the long run. Once he'd established summarily who was boss, she seemed to savor her own defeat. What woman really wanted a man she could overpower?

The failings of awkward, hasty fumbling in high school were a coming-of-age mainstay. But once better familiar with the protocol in college, Nico had still found sex in the flesh disappointing. He wasn't sure what he'd expected. If nothing else, maybe he expected something he couldn't have expected, and the real deal proved all too imaginable. And he'd only been "transported" in the wrong sense. That is, the grappling by custom known as "intimacy" hadn't made him feel closer to Kayla but further away. They seemed to become different people, or not quite people, and he never knew what she was thinking. Lying in bed afterward was nicer. Little wonder that ensconced in the basement back home he hadn't gone out of his way to repeat the dispiriting exercise. He honestly hadn't missed it. Rather, as with so many other things in his life that he was apparently meant to be doing, he'd been relieved to opt out of any healthy young man's implicit obligation, if not to have sex, then at least to pursue it. Celibacy had thus far not felt like a deprivation but more like another sly evasion of anything that might be *due*.

Martine was not disappointing. There was none of that separating off and hovering overhead and looking down on it all. He was right there, aware of every fiber of the rug as it chafed his ass. The sole distraction was a vague, irksome recollection that he should probably have offered to use a condom, but he put the thought aside. Surely it was her job to raise the issue of protection. After all, she was the one so keen on making *bebés*. Off-loading the onus on the girl was totally irresponsible, but Nico *was* irresponsible, and this was the ideal occasion on which to embrace that identity with open arms.

What struck him most powerfully was that he felt like himself. He didn't lose his sense of humor, and he didn't forget for a minute that his dick was up a woman who was either the innocent victim of gang criminality or a coconspirator in an extortion racket that had cost his mother $30,000. Why, the notion of fucking the woman behind door number two was positively thrilling.

Because he had felt like himself the while, there was no coming to his senses once the proceedings concluded. They both dressed slowly and methodically and without a trace of chagrin.

"You want we finish dinner?" she asked, zipping up her jeans. "I put plates in microwave, *chilaquiles* get little soft. But I still hungry."

"Me, too, come to think of it. Yeah. Warm it up."

After the leftovers, they retired to the den to watch TV with more beers. When he propped his legs on the coffee table, Martine extended on the couch and put her own legs in his lap. The weight on his groin was enjoyable, and as he flicked through the Netflix watchlist he idly stroked her calves and massaged her insteps. At the end of the evening, Martine pecked his cheek and departed downstairs, while Nico returned to his childhood bedroom in a state of both amazement and curiosity. To his surprise, after he'd turned off his light, the door opened. "I brush teeth," Martine explained, disrobing without ceremony and crawling in beside him.

"One thing," she mumbled into his shoulder. "Maybe you no tell Domingo."

Fair enough, the whole don't-you-dare-touch-my-sister palaver was a cliché. "Okay," he agreed. "And let's not tell my mother, either."

"Okay."

They didn't do anything more, but the sensation of her naked body against his as he dropped to sleep challenged the proposition that what he'd been feeling for the last five years had truly qualified as contentment.

Nico and Martine continued to play house for the next five days. They went shopping for groceries together, and they went for walks in Prospect Park. Nico taught her how to make his signature tuna melt with chopped fresh chilis and olives, one of the only meals he knew how to make when his mother was out. They designed the menu for the surprise party, not quite all of which was deep-fat-fried. They compiled the invitation list by consulting his mother's inbox, in which he was surprised to spot more than one email from a law firm. But he was presently so oblivious to anything that didn't concern how he and Martine would capitalize on their window of privacy—whose texture was timeless, apart, indefinite, even if in the back of his mind a clock was ticking—that he couldn't have cared less what the correspondence was about. They watched *One Day* on Netflix. The series proved so schlocky that halfway through Nico insisted on switching to *3 Body Problem*, though Martine found it harder to follow. Without calling attention to it, he started wearing the watch she'd given him, to which she added a few other modest presents: a cheesy "Yo-heart-NY" baseball cap, whose Spanish pronoun gestured toward a purely perfunctory assimilation; a teasing Los Roland's CD that included "Tickita Tickita," making him grateful that he didn't own a CD player; a cashmere "packer" in a discordant pink that she'd knitted herself, which gave them both a good laugh over how creepy all this trans shit was. The more recent gratuities didn't make him feel unwillingly indebted but touched. And they had sex—in the den, against the kitchen counter, in his childhood bedroom—during which the Honduran continued to not disappoint. In fact, while he wasn't about to share this with Martine, lest she be tempted to put on airs—that is, fall prey to condescension and demote him back to Nico Niñito again—it was arguable that he'd never really fucked a woman before, not the way you were supposed to, and he finally had an inkling why other people seemed to make such a big deal of it.

They didn't talk about American immigration policy. They also didn't talk about what they were doing, whatever that was. For example, they didn't talk about the fact that, according to Martine way back when, she was, strictly speaking, married. But if the woman's confidences were to be taken at face value—while Nico wasn't relinquishing any of his suspicions, accepting the veracity of these details currently suited him—her husband in Honduras was a violent, drunken, unemployed lout. It was not unreasonable to infer that when she hightailed it to El Norte, she also walked out on the marriage. He saw no cause to worry about cuckolding some loser de facto ex.

In contrast to his hovercraft repose, Nico's floating sensation across these few days evoked less skimming just above the surface of the ocean than drifting in a helium balloon a mile high. This period was disconnected to anything or anyone else, and to subject the tryst to analysis of any kind would have brought it soughing down to earth.

Which didn't preclude the odd inquiry. "So what do you want here?" Nico asked, lying on his back while they rested from their exertions the fourth night. "In this country."

"I don't know. House?" she said, trailing a finger down his sternum. "Nice kitchen. Full fridge."

"Sounds like you want what you've already got. That's my problem, too. I'm fine."

"Fine is problem?"

"That's what everyone keeps telling me."

"I think I want bicycle," Martine decided.

Nico chuckled. "Aren't you demanding. I don't even want a bicycle."

Nevertheless, the dates on the upper-right-hand corner of his laptop screen continued to progress, and his mother's looming return from Phoenix pressed the question of what they would do when she got back. Presumably, too, Alonso and Domingo would reappear at some point, and he and Martine would no longer have the run of five empty bedrooms.

Languidly, frivolously, fancifully even, Nico considered whether an alternative to protecting his mother from the depredations of unconscionable foreign grifters was to stop fighting fate. His mother might have initiated this Big Apple, Big Heart lark merely to bolster her moral standing, but maybe she'd also serendipitously unlocked the door to maturity that her son had hitherto refused to walk through. Granted, he'd instinctively resolved to keep his mother in the dark about just how much the mice had been playing while the cat was away. She'd probably think he was taking advantage of Martine somehow, due to the *power imbalance*, as if he'd been schtupping the maid. But the relationship wasn't incestuous. He and Martine were close in age. She might not be well educated, but she was smart; look at how quickly she was picking up English.

So why *couldn't* she be his girlfriend? The truth was he'd never had one, certainly not a girlfriend who would say aloud "I am your girlfriend." The delectable tension between them had grown more playful but hadn't dissipated, which was promising. He liked that both in and out of bed she was combative—she demanded that they go back to finish *One Day* to find out what happened, and though he ridiculed her typically Hispanic appetite for soap opera he complied—because he didn't want to hang with a doormat. In time, he could make more of an effort to learn some Spanish. If on return Domingo didn't like the household's astonishing social realignment, the guy wasn't his sister's keeper, and she didn't need his permission; maybe they'd be lucky and the dickhead would clear off in a huff, at which point Nico could resume his rightful place on the basement's king-size, its comforts furthered by all the pillows with which his sisters had girlified the bed. Speaking of whom, Palermo and Vanessa wouldn't care for his trumping their courtship of Martine either, and they'd regard his deployment of certain genital equipment they lacked as cheating—but they'd be obliged to act incredibly happy for the new sweethearts all the same. In due course, his mother wouldn't merely drop her objections; she'd be thrilled to pieces. Her own son, hooked up with a *person of color*! That would see an end, too, to her consternation over his hostility to the wholesale invasion of their country by an army of calculating moochers determined to bleed the place dry in healthcare costs alone. He wasn't sufficiently supportive of *diversity, equity,* and *inclusion*? Why, the calisthenics of the last few days couldn't have been more *inclusive*. If their houseguest of nearly a year really had extorted $30,000 from his mother, Martine could add her cut to his inheritance, thereby extending the period during which they could afford takeout from Uber Eats. Nico was admittedly lukewarm on suddenly inheriting three kids, assuming Martine sent for them in due course—and assuming she did have three kids—but that was a matter for later, and who knows, maybe an inflatable family would be just the ticket. There were always those three unused bedrooms upstairs, one for each urchin, which would give his mother a good excuse for evicting Alonso. Instant children would at least mean skipping all that getting fat and throwing up.

Fine, fine, worse than jumping the gun; more like running five times around the track before the guy with the starter pistol has gotten out of bed. But the mind was a regular fun fair where you could go on all the loop-de-loops you liked with no one the wiser, and too few people seemed to capitalize on the free mental merry-go-rounds eternally at your disposal even when you were awake. Besides, this implausible weeklong vacation from reality had one palpable consequence. A hard perpendicular turn off his predictable linear plot line had imbued Nico's future with a tingle of possibility. For the first time in ages, he didn't know what came next.

Yet the glorious week every summer of his childhood when his family rented a cottage on the beach in Margate, New Jersey, had never seemed to last a full seven days. The first day was squandered on travel, hauling luggage, and squabbling with his sisters over who got the bedroom facing the shore. The second half of the week was tainted by mournfulness that it would soon be time to go home. Contaminated with dismay that the getaway was basically over, the last full day before they packed up the car was always a write-off.

In kind, the day before Nico's mother was due back from Phoenix assumed a dolorous cast. Until that point, their mutual disinclination to address what on earth they were up to had felt liberating. This tacit embargo on parsing their "feelings" induced in Nico, for one, a sense of serene superiority to all the over-therapized pygmies who couldn't leave well enough alone, and who, gifted with something enigmatic yet exquisite, compulsively picked it apart, until their bird of a thing lay in a heap of feathers and guts on the lawn like cat kill. Still, by the last day on their own, Nico was nagged by one of the few truisms he'd garnered about relationships: you refrain from asking questions when you already know the answers and you don't care for them one bit.

That evening, they didn't finish the episode they'd resumed of 3 *Body Problem*, a title that resonated uncomfortably with his mother's imminent arrival, and it seemed unlikely now that they'd ever finish the series. When he took Martine up to his bedroom, he wrapped around her back and cupped one perfect-handful breast, but made no move to have sex. He couldn't explain it, but he simply didn't want to.

The next day, Martine fixed him huevos rancheros, but he only stirred it around his plate. They didn't talk much, and finally their silences did feel like avoidance. When she loaded their breakfast dishes in the dishwasher, the dynamic was no longer ironically spousal, but once more like the ministrations of a foreign visitor intent on seeming helpful and no trouble. The kitchen cleaned, she slipped downstairs, leaving Nico both forlorn and relieved. Maybe she should have stuck around to give him practice at acting normal, even if the definition of *normal* was something you didn't have to act. How was he supposed to behave around her now?

His mother's plane would land at 3 p.m. It was a Saturday, with light traffic on the Belt, so she'd probably return from JFK by about four thirty. Earlier that afternoon, Palermo texted that she'd like to drop by, so that she could nail their plans for misleading their mother before the surprise party and say hello when their mother got home. He couldn't think of a reason to discourage the visit. The hiatus of floating far above the clouds was already over. The helium balloon had deflated, its frayed basket toppled on tarmac.

"So have you got enough acceptances for a quorum?" Palermo asked, settling at the kitchen table. "Too few well-wishers is depressing."

"Most of the book club can come," Nico said. "A couple of other volunteers at Floyd Bennett Field. Two neighbors who stuck their necks out on Facebook about refusing to sign that petition to keep migrants out of Ditmas. That's enough." Expressing these practicalities was effortful. He worried that something in his demeanor might betray the nature of the last few days' extracurricular activities. He felt changed.

"What did you decide about Vernon and Colleen?"

"Asking for trouble," he said. "Especially with Martine here. Vernon might have one drink too many—"

"Or five," Palermo said.

"And then he might say something uncool about immigration, and it could get awkward."

"Nico. You yourself do nothing but say uncool things about immigration."

She had a point. Had he switched sides?

"Mostly," he said, "I didn't want to ask so many people that we burdened Martine with too much cooking." He liked bringing up Martine, but at the same time felt proprietary about her even as a subject of discussion. Martine didn't belong to Palermo any longer.

"Oh, I don't think she minds. In fact, she seems to love concocting ginormous batches of whatever. She always makes too much food. Is it all going to be Honduran?"

"No. We decided to add some lighter stuff." He wasn't sure he'd ever referred to Martine and him to anyone else as *we*.

"But here's what I don't get," Palermo said. "I loved Martine's idea of taking Mom to a terrible bar—like, big downer birthday, is this what my life is coming to. But how are we going to field her inevitable interest in getting something to eat? I don't want Martine's spread to be wasted on a birthday girl who's already full."

Oh, God, he didn't care. "Tell her we already have takeout sushi back at the house."

"Let's not get her hopes up, because she'd way prefer to have sushi," Palermo said, lowering her voice. "You know she's secretly sick of all these cheesy, beany things, but she doesn't want to hurt Martine's feelings."

"Martine has seen a lot of American TV. She says surprise parties always have a banner." It was a little nutty, but they seemed to be fighting over her.

"Martine could pick one up at a party supply store. I bet they even have happy birthday streamers in Spanish. That might be a nice touch: *feliz cumpleaños*."

"Touché." Show-off.

"Hey, where *is* Martine? I never congratulated her for *The Brooklyn Hedge Trimmer Massacre*." Their mother had clearly shared her witticism on the phone. "Wasn't that wild? I mean, when she needs to be, that woman is an animal!"

Nico thought, *You have no idea.*

He directed Palermo to the basement, where Martine had remained since cleaning up after breakfast, though she could probably hear that someone was visiting. After the heady tactility of the last week, she might not trust herself to come upstairs. How could she keep from idly smoothing a hand over his ass and giving the game away?

Nico wasn't used to feeling this estranged from his older sister. So far their conversation had been boring, although he had the means at his immediate disposal to plug their small talk straight into a live socket. He could just hear her: *You did WHAT?* Palermo was the one member of his family in whom he was most inclined to confide. But he'd a gut sense that she'd disapprove, and not only from irrational jealousy. Byron had earned an exemption; otherwise, Palermo's default assumption was that men were callous, shallow, and ruled by their dicks, a cliché that would easily extend to her own brother. Instinctively protective of Martine, Palermo would rebuke him for trifling with a "vulnerable" young woman's affections. It would never occur to her to wonder which party was trifling with whom.

Palermo emerged from the basement too quickly, and she had a funny look on her face.

"I didn't realize Domingo was back," she said.

Nico looked up sharply. "I didn't either. Shit."

"You must have liked not having him around," she said quietly.

"Can say that again," Nico muttered. "Didn't see the prick. Must have come in the outside entrance. So you didn't get to talk to Martine?"

"Um, no. Seems those two have some catching up to do . . . Listen, can we—?"

Just then, their mother pushed her luggage through the kitchen door. "Hi! Palermo, how nice to see you! My plane was early, believe it or not. How about a cup of tea?"

They sat around hearing about the trip to Phoenix, his sister's presence helping to insulate Nico from whatever grudge against her son their mother had continued to nurse in Arizona. But now it was Palermo who seemed distracted and not especially engaged by stories of their ne'er-do-well cousins. Given that Layla, the cousin closest to her in age, had taken up gymnastics immediately following Palermo's car accident, his older sister would usually listen avidly to reports that Layla had gained still another hundred pounds. Oddly, too, Palermo begged off sticking around for dinner. As she hugged their mother goodbye at the door, she met Nico's eyes significantly, though he had no idea what was so significant about what.

Palermo's text came in twenty minutes later: **Can you make an excuse and meet me in Manchego as soon as you can get away? I'm there now**

Mumbling something about needing to stretch his legs, Nico was more than happy to escape a house peopled by an aggrieved parent, a young woman to whom he now had a torturously ambiguous relationship, including, possibly, no relationship, and her unambiguously obnoxious brother. As for this hugger-mugger assignation with a sibling from whom he'd just parted, he was immediately certain that either Martine had whispered something about their escapades to Palermo in the basement or he'd done or said something despite himself to tip his carnal hand. His sister must have been intent on grilling him about what in God's name was going on between him and the sexy Honduran mother-of-three.

Well, damned if he knew what was going on. Though maybe it was a relief that Palermo was now in on the fling, or whatever it had been, or whatever it was still. He surprised himself on this point, but he wasn't greatly enjoying keeping the secret, and it might be useful to confide in his sister after all. On the walk over, he reflected that he hadn't even had an opportunity to consult himself on what the last week had meant. He now wished he and Martine had talked at least briefly about what they were up to and whether in some form or another it would continue. He felt suspended, but not in a good way.

He could tell by Palermo's crooked posture at the table in the corner that her back hurt. It was early for her, but she'd ordered a glass of wine. He wasn't sure whether to prepare an expression of innocence or sheepishness, and he wondered if he might avoid landing in Palermo's doghouse by confessing without being prodded. Best play it by ear.

"So what's this about?" Which was exactly what he should have asked Martine.

"I don't think Domingo is Martine's brother," Palermo said.

"Why?"

"Well, unless they're into some seriously warped . . . When I went downstairs, Martine's jeans were unzipped, and Domingo's hand was down her pants."

Nico's ears started ringing. He didn't know what to say. For the moment, he decided to say nothing, because this news was affecting him more than it should have.

"I've seen a couple of other interactions before that were less *glaring* but that also seemed slightly off," Palermo went on. "I think Domingo is the husband."

Nico cleared his throat. "If so, why pretend he's her brother?"

"Hard to say. If he is the husband, he's not the person she described. I've never seen any sign that she's been beaten up. No bruises or marks. He drinks, but he sobers up if he has something to do. In fact, he's always seemed almost military to me. He's in good shape, and he keeps his mouth shut. He's no slugabed alcoholic."

"I guess he could be just a boyfriend. But why lie about that?"

"I don't know. Maybe a 'brother' who comes and goes seemed like less of an imposition on Mom than a couple. Couples are full-time. And when he first showed up, no one said anything about his moving in forever, did they?"

"No." But these were not the questions that Nico wanted answered. Whether the creep was a boyfriend or a spouse, either way why did she sleep with the kid upstairs for a week? Just for the hell of it? Because she couldn't contain her desire? (And why was that scenario so preposterous?) To get back at asshole for some reason? Or to achieve some other purpose? Was Domingo one of those vengeful Latinate types, and if he got wind of the affair, was Nico in physical danger? Or was the guy blithely up to speed, having given her permission in the interest of some new plan they were hatching, and the two were at this moment laughing about it, comparing Nico Niñito's sad little wiener to the mighty schlong of a *gran hombre*?

"I don't like the feel of this," Palermo said. "Along with not saying anything for months about having three kids. It's just weird."

"When you went downstairs—did they see you?"

"I don't think so. They were *otherwise engaged*. The stairs are carpeted. I just crept back up."

"Are you going to tell Mom?"

"Martine has become, like, her best friend. I don't want to mess that up by creating distrust. Maybe we should keep this to ourselves for now."

The last week's tacit moratorium on discussing the nature of Martine's and his relations and whether the involvement would continue suddenly appeared in a different light. "They" hadn't resolved not to talk about it; *Martine* hadn't wanted to talk about it. While he'd known that technically she was still married, having an abandoned spouse two thousand miles away was a very different matter from having a husband—or boyfriend, it hardly mattered—downstairs. Okay, she hadn't promised Nico anything, much less had she made any rash declarations of undying love. He had no right to feel wounded. Still, emotions weren't subject to the Constitution, so presumably he could feel as wounded as he liked. And he felt like a fool. The disagreeable sensation was a reminder of why he'd been wise to avoid any such entanglement for over five years. Now he had sabotaged the one thing that was most important to him: his equilibrium, his neutrality, his secure status as an *observer*.

Nico didn't know why or to what end, but Martine seemed to have been toying with him, and he was offended. However little he cared to dissect the matter with Palermo or anyone else, the shenanigans of the last seven days had within minutes in Manchego foreshortened to something silly, trivial, and humiliating. Once again, however well protected from the ridicule of outsiders so long as he kept his own counsel, he had embarrassed himself in front of himself.

"I think we should also not let on to Domingo and Martine that we know," he proposed. It would be the one thing he had over on her.

"Agreed," Palermo said. "Calling her out on the lie would be super awkward."

Hesitantly, Nico shared his misgivings about the kidnapping, and even about the hedge trimmer episode. For a few minutes, he seemed to have won a tentative ally. In contrast to their mother, Palermo didn't recoil in indignation or denounce him for projecting onto the innocent the nature of his own dark heart. She asked dispassionate questions. The possibility of comradery was tantalizing, and for once not being scorned as evil or crazy was a relief.

"I don't know, Nico," she said once she'd heard him out; he could feel her slipping away again. "Isn't that awfully far-fetched? What I see is a woman in precarious circumstances who has a family. She gets an opportunity to stay in a wonderful house with nice people and all the trappings of middle-class American life. But the opportunity is only for her. So she slips her man into the picture under false pretenses, trying to make him seem like a temporary addition and hoping over time her sponsor gets used to him. What you suspect is devious and criminal."

"I'm not making accusations. I'm only raising questions."

"Semantics. I think what Martine probably hopes for in the long run is that we'll take in her whole family, or at least provide for them. That must be the source of the dissembling, since to begin with Mom only agreed to put up one single woman. I bet she plans to have her kids sent up here sometime soon, and ideally we'll help them get settled—if not in Mom's house, then somewhere else that's safe, pleasant, and affordable."

"There being no such place in New York," Nico said. Three Honduran children installed in his mother's empty bedrooms had featured in his whimsical (and *obviously* parodic) daydream two days earlier. The same scenario credibly featured in Martine's fantasies with more sincerity.

"People from the developing world often think Americans have infinite resources," Palermo said. "So Martine might imagine we can help her more than we can. But she's grabbed the only lifeline she's been thrown, and she's hanging on to it like a motherfucker. That's the only devious scheme I can discern. It's a far cry from extortion. She fibbed about Domingo, and I do find that disturbing. If he is the husband and not just a new boyfriend, she may have concocted a sob story about her abusive homelife in San Pedro Sula. But that's what we force migrants to do: shove the round peg of their genuine, complicated stories into the square hole of an asylum application. She could still have had to pay gangbangers a portion of her laundry income—that part rings true. And while she might have mentioned her kids earlier, I totally understand that she didn't want to frighten Mom into backing off, like, 'Whoa! Hold on here! I never said anything about taking on a whole family!' On balance, I still think Martine Salgado is a nice person."

Which was more than Nico's own mother said of him.

10

tell you great story," Alonso promised, sitting down to another of Martine's big hot breakfasts later that week. For shortly after Domingo had returned to stimulate his "sister's" genitals, their newest freeloader had also reappeared, oblivious to the homeowner's displeasure. Plotting how to be rid of Alonso doubtless occupied a goodly proportion of Gloria Bonaventura's waking hours.

While Nico usually enjoyed the very festive cynicism that put his mother off the guy, just this morning it was tempting to slip off to the porch—the mosquitoes hadn't hatched yet—to sip his coffee in peace. He didn't want to seem to be avoiding Martine, but he did want to avoid Martine, and that was a tricky line to walk. Now he was stuck listening to a "great story."

"There is some 'special status' for migrant when he is victim of serious crime," Alonso continued. "You testify for police, you get green card! You get in whole family! Parents! Children! Wife! Your immigration law, it is full of holes, like fine Spanish lace."

"Full of holes?" Nico said. "It's one big hole. Through which Americans get fucked."

"But I continue!" Alonso said cheerfully; he was impossible to offend. "In Chicago now, migrants make pretend robbings, so they get this 'special status.'"

"You mean like insurance fraud," Nico said. "Staging an accident to get the money."

"*Sí*, same idea. You get gun, make play holdup, and witnesses are all 'serious crime victims.' Bingo, green card. Except some fake robbings, they go wrong."

"What a shock," Nico said. "They haven't watched enough movies."

"Yes! What is this . . . Philip Seymour Hoffman, yes? You remember?"

Nico punched at his phone. *Before the Devil Knows You're Dead.* No one can ever remember the name of that film."

"The brothers, they steal their parents' jewelry store, right?" Alonso recalled excitedly. "Then—total disaster, right?"

"That's the one," Nico confirmed.

"Is perfect compare."

"Perfect comparison," Nico corrected.

"*Comparison.*" Priding himself on his English, Alonso appreciated help with the fine-tuning. "See, these idiot migrants in Chicago stage fake robbing for special status, but they end up killing real people! No green card, only jail time! It is the joke on them! Or in another time, one fake liquor store robbing—"

"Robbery," Nico said.

"In one liquor store *robbery*, migrants pretend a holdup, but then some goody-goody from the public come in and shoot them!" Alonso laughed heartily. "Is so funny! Someone should tell Quentin Tarantino! It make such good movie! Though he never do better than *Reservoir Dogs*. Everyone fuck up. Everyone shoot everyone. This is my favorite."

"You'll make a great American, then," Nico said in all sincerity.

"With *La Migra*," Martine contributed from the kitchen, "you say you like *Sound of Music.*"

"Wrong generation," Nico said coolly. "Totally suspicious. You're better off touting more recent dreck. Like *One Day.*" The mention was the closest he'd come to alluding to last week, and he'd dropped the name of the show as flatly and insignificantly as he knew how.

Waiting a seemly beat or two, Nico rose to dilute another cup of coffee, though he didn't quite trust himself to meet Martine's eyes with the casualness the moment required.

"Also, more story!" Alonso said. "You know these border agents, in Arizona and Texas. They are train to be big scary police. Now they are like nursery teachers. They hand out diapers. They give children sippy cups with apple juice."

"That's catch-and-release for you," Nico said. "All they do is process. They hardly detain anybody. Welcome Wagon could do the same job."

"*Sí*, this is my point!" Alonso said, slathering the usual half cup of strawberry jam on his toast. "This poor border agents, they are depress. Nico, the agents are killing their selfs! I tell you, by the dozen!"

"You think that is funny?" Martine said as Alonso chuckled.

"So serious, Martine," Alonso said. "But okay, maybe not so funny. *Interesting.*"

Leaving them to it, Nico slipped off with his coffee to the side porch, though it was nippy without a sweatshirt and the Wi-Fi cut out here.

He had no desire to reflect on that weird period of walking in Prospect Park hand in hand and deciding what to buy for dinner together and fucking against the kitchen counter, but it tortured him anyway, since the most challenging if not impossible form of discipline was controlling your own thoughts. He couldn't stop chewing on whatever had driven her to release that fateful initial button of her jeans, for while technically he'd been the one to make the first move, it seemed in retrospect that she had seduced him. After their hanky-panky—a dated expression, but pleasingly a word that made the hookup seem cheap and piddling—he felt at a disadvantage, though he couldn't say why. Did she imagine she now had something over on him? *Did* she have something over on him? If she blabbed, sure, maybe Domingo would bear a grudge or even have a go at him, but wouldn't Martine herself be in at least as much trouble with her asshole inamorato? Unless they'd cooked up the hookup together. But how could an affair with the kid upstairs have advanced their cause? What *was* their cause? He wondered whether Martine had somehow divined his suspicions about the kidnapping and hedge trimmer rescue. But even if she'd discerned that he had her number, how was fucking him a checkmate? While she could always spill the beans to his mother, that would only do so much damage to a filial reputation already in tatters *unless* she cried rape. Yet Martine prided herself on being a tough cookie, and the whole weepy, wussy he-forced-me routine didn't seem like her bag.

He was angry and he hated being angry; he hated feeling anything about that woman. Yet he continued to feel toyed with, and he was still unable to build a convincing case that he had equally toyed with her.

Obviously, he'd stopped wearing that stupid watch, and while he'd been indifferent to whether she noticed when he'd started wearing it, it was important to him, too important when nothing to do with Martine should be important, that she noticed he had stopped wearing it. He'd kicked the Yo-heart-NY baseball cap, taunting "Tickita Tickita" CD, and absurd pink packer to dust-bunny under his bed, but he could have and should have chucked all these meaningless trinkets in the trash. Meanwhile, since last Saturday he had spent more time in his room or on walkabouts through his colonized city, the better to reduce intersections with the household's original charity case. But he shouldn't have changed his routines one whit, and he shouldn't have cared about running into her in his own fucking house (or sort of his house). When they had intersected, he'd assumed a cultivated blitheness, but he shouldn't have had to "assume" any attitude at all. He shouldn't have *acted* blithe. He should have *felt* blithe, and when you feel blithe presumably you act blithe without having to think about it.

In the spring bite, the last of his coffee was getting cold. But before he retreated inside, he took a minute to consider what most struck him about this discombobulating aftermath. Martine herself didn't appear to have any problem running into Nico, and she never evidenced the slightest awkwardness in his presence. She met his eyes easily, and her clear, untroubled glance never conveyed mischief, remorse, or collusion. For moments at a go, he would question whether he had made the whole thing up, so perfectly did her demeanor fail to reflect that either of them had ever put a hand on the other's knee. It would never hold up in court, but as far as Nico was concerned this flawless performance of amnesia was the best evidence yet that the real Martine lurked behind door number two: a lying sack of shit.

At least he had a task to distract him, though completing a sentimental video montage by his mother's birthday did entail taking on a project that was *due*. He had wish-I-could-be-there-to-help-you-celebrate videos from her sister and long-distance friends in DC, Portland, and LA, which he'd solicited during the week-that-never-really-happened. He had a fair whack of still family photos on his laptop. (He'd never figured out what it was about still photographs that evoked so much more emotion than those same walking, talking people In Real Life.) He could lift clips from the family videos of his childhood in which his mother featured. Yet honestly. Why did people anywhere near his mother's age ever mark birthdays? Beyond a midpoint, you weren't measuring from your birth but counting down to you-know-what. "Let's raise a glass! I'm 365 days closer to terminal brain cancer!"

Being at odds with his mother, Nico was in no mood for this mission. Still, he begrudgingly appreciated that when younger his mother was pretty hot. She might have come to resent her husband's gathering professional preeminence, but it was clear from the pics that for most of the marriage she adored the guy. You had to wonder what she reaped from her late-life independence. She'd hardly dated. She had less money, and her retarded answer to a nearly empty house was to fill it up with Central American spongers. Sure, she hadn't liked being a nobody married to a somebody, but after jettisoning the somebody, now she was just a nobody married to nobody.

The sole upside of her divorce was the boundless opportunity to go on at great length about heteronormativity and neurodiversity and systemic racism and marginalized peoples (or was it "minoritized peoples," which didn't make any sense) and ableism and Islamophobia and white adjacency and why their country was obliged to take in millions if not billions of the world's riffraff, and no one would tell her to put a sock in it. Which wasn't a gain but a loss. One of the few videos that moved him to genuine nostalgia was the one around the kitchen table after dinner, when Palermo filmed their parents right before the couple's playful tit-for-tat banter degenerated to bitter combat. Their mother was on her usual progressive high horse, this time about "gender identity," and their father was making fun of her ("What if I felt in my mind that I was a chair? Could I surgically demand four legs to be 'congruent' with my inner being?") until finally he got her to laugh, to laugh with him at herself. Across all this footage, these were the few minutes in which she was at her most appealing.

Fortunately, their mother's birthday landed on a Tuesday, when she regularly volunteered at Floyd Bennett Field. That morning, Martine begged off coming with; her claim to feeling under the weather would also excuse her from the family's early evening celebratory drink. After wishing his mother a perfunctory happy birthday, Nico added casually that turning sixty-three in a society obsessed with base ten was no biggie. The aim was to reduce their mother's expectations to below zero.

Given the all-clear after their mother left to catch the bus, Vanessa swung in the drive to unload the groceries and lend a hand with the prep before her after-school shift at Peanuts. Nico hung the FELIZ CUMPLEAÑOS! banner over the curly-maple dining table. For his video tribute, he moved the den's TV to the living room and plugged his Mac into the HDMI input; with the same hookup, they could play those shopworn Spotify playlists from back when their mother never imagined turning sixty-three and "Every Breath You Take" still sounded catchy and fresh.

Nico got the charm of the surprise-party format. It granted unlimited permission for gleeful duplicity and guaranteed that the mark would enjoy having been deceived. His discomfort, then, regarded the lack of contrast. The household already felt thick with lies. Despite himself, he continually pictured Domingo with his hand in Martine's crotch. He and Martine had organized this party during a week that in hindsight had only grown more incongruous—a lemon in a slot machine's solid lineup of limes, the captcha square that doesn't contain a traffic light, the wrong answer that elicits a reproachful *WHAAA!* on *The Price Is Right*. Ever since, their limited interactions had been false. She'd left him feeling like some pubertal kid who'd just lost his cherry to a more experienced older woman in an act of intergenerational charity. Which was absurd. He hadn't been a virgin, she was only two years his senior, and he'd been in no need of sexual compassion.

Cutting her workday short, Palermo pulled in the drive at five to retrieve Nico en route to picking up their mother at Floyd Bennett Field.

"Guests arrive at eight thirty, but Martine says we shouldn't show up at the house until nine," Nico said as they drove toward the shelter. "That gives us too much time in the bar. We'll end up getting shit-faced way before the big reveal."

"Did you locate a really rank dive?" Palermo asked.

"Ugly colored lights. Hokey, arbitrary cowboy theme. I bet they have terrible wine."

"Good show!"

"Think she'll really get off on this surprise thing?"

"Parties are mostly fun as something to plan and to idiotically look forward to," Palermo said. "The real thing is almost always flat, and the moment you get there you start calculating how soon you can leave. Face it: we just want her to be touched we went to so much trouble."

Bustling into the backseat, their mother seemed in a ratty humor. "Everyone in Floyd Bennett is freaking out," she exploded even before fastening her seat belt. "Families are coming up against that new sixty-day limit on how long they can stay, and they have nowhere to go. It makes no sense. You kick people out of homeless shelters and so make more homeless people, so you can put other homeless people in the same shelters, whom you're also planning to make homeless in sixty days. I mean, it's absurd."

"Can't they reapply?" Nico said.

"Well, yes. But for several intervening days, some of these people *with children* will be out on the street. And the whole process-as-punishment is underhanded. The city's hoping that a proportion of qualified reapplicants won't figure out how to do it. Or they'll assume that no functional bureaucracy would go through the arduous business of kicking them out only to let them right back in. In other words, they're hoping the migrants will infer rationality where none exists. I'm simply livid."

"They have to do *something*," Nico said. "The city's taken in almost two hundred thousand migrants. The numbers will only keep going up, if Biden gets reelected—"

"You'd be hoping for anyone else?" their mother said in horror.

"But New York has a chronic housing shortage—"

"Let it go, Nico," Palermo intervened. "Birthday Girl gets to win the argument. Or maybe, just today, *not have one*."

They would get less drunk because it took so long for Palermo to find a place to park. Having beaten them to the rendezvous, Vanessa waved from the bar.

Nico may have overdone the disagreeableness factor, since in no time their mother was chafing to go. "It's awfully loud here, and it smells weird." She sniffed her white wine. "Even the wine smells weird. Can't we go home, open a bottle, and order that meze you mentioned?"

"Aw, you hardly ever go out on the town," Vanessa said.

"And you don't turn sixty-three every day," Palermo said.

"Thank God for that," their mother muttered.

Nico ordered the guest of honor another glass, but she wasn't a heavy drinker and the ploy wouldn't last. It was indeed difficult to carry a conversation over the hiphop that she detested. By seven thirty, she'd had enough.

"It's terribly sweet of you to take me out," she shouted, "but can we please go home?"

The foursome slipped outside among the smokers. "What a relief," their mother said.

"Would you like to go somewhere else?" Palermo proposed.

"The patrons of bars around here are a third my age. If you three want to stay out and carouse, I can meet you back at the house. It's a short walk from here, so you can keep the car."

"You can get a second wind, can't you?" Vanessa implored.

"Spending all afternoon with mothers hysterical about suddenly having no roof over their children's heads . . . I'm pooped. You kids have a lovely time." She kissed all three briefly on the cheek and turned heel.

The siblings met one another's eyes. This was a fail. "Mom!" Palermo shouted. "Come back a second! Please!"

Reluctantly, their mother returned, eyebrows raised.

"You can't go home yet," Vanessa said. "We're throwing you a surprise party."

"At nine," Palermo said.

"Oh?" their mother said blankly. What a pity that she found being thrown a surprise party so incomprehensible. "Oh." The info landed. "Well, how sweet of you. I just messed everything up, then."

"No, I messed up," Nico said. "We wanted to take you to a really awful place, so it would seem like your worst birthday ever. But I found a place that was too awful."

"Listen, Martine's been cooking all afternoon," Palermo said. "Can we go for a walk? My back could handle it if we take it slow. Then we can show at nine, and you can pretend to be surprised. No one else will have to know we've already blown the secret."

"Sure, I think I could pull that off," their mother said. "Why don't we stroll toward the park, and I can practice." They did just that, all four taking turns staging increasingly over-the-top versions of pop-eyed astonishment, including a feigned heart attack. For a brief while, then, the family felt almost intact, warmhearted, and jovial. Why, they very nearly had *fun*.

Yet midevening sponsored a proper surprise after all.

From inside the car with the windows up Nico could detect the jounce of *punta* music while they remained a block away. When Palermo pulled in the drive, glasses clinked from inside. The harsh tenor of the laughter piercing the twilight air didn't resemble the muffled titter of a small crowd trying to keep quiet. Warily, Nico got out as Vanessa pulled up in her Fiat Panda behind them.

Nico went first through the side door. The deserted kitchen toppled with unwashed pots and pans. A sheet cake on the kitchen table was gouged. Shattered glass crunched underfoot as he led their party toward the *punta* pounding from the dining room. Yet no eager greeting committee crowded around the banner hooting "Sur*priiiise!*"—so their mother's budding talents as a thespian would no longer be required. No one segued into a cheesy, off-key rendition of "Happy Birthday to You," either. The platters on the dining table were ravaged. Multiple bottles of wine on the sideboard were open and empty. The FELIZ CUMPLEAÑOS banner had dropped on one side and now draped illegibly over the upright piano. In addition to the excitable lyrics maxing out on the familiar Bluetooth speaker, the dominant social chatter was in Spanish.

More to the point: the gathering appeared larger than he and Martine had planned. Domingo and Alonso were slumped in armchairs with highball glasses brimming with red wine. Nico counted four strapping young men he'd never seen before: muscular, on the short side, in jeans and shirtless. Their heads were shaved. Tattoos crawled up their necks, across their scalps, and over their faces. Nico had no wish to be critical, but the tats didn't look like professional work.

Meanwhile, on the far opposite side of the living room, the surprise-party guests proper cowered around the leather sofa; the ensemble might have been posing for a veterans' poster about the importance of asking for help if you had PTSD. Instantly grasping that the heavily scriven well-wishers hadn't been included on the original guest list, their mother rushed to her friends and hugged them in turn. But her embraces didn't have the congenial vibe of "Oh, weren't you so sweet to help celebrate my birthday!"; they were more like the ferocious hugs Israeli relatives gave newly released Hamas hostages on CNN. "Oh, dear!" she declared over the din. "Things seem to have gotten rather out of hand."

Palermo whispered at Nico's elbow, "We'll hear from the neighbors about this music. And the whole ground floor is already a wreck. We've got to get these people out of here."

He muttered in her ear, "Easier said than done."

"Elijah!" the guy with "XVIII" inked across his forehead shouted to Domingo. *"Toca Ococity!"*

"Nico Niñito!" Domingo cried from the armchair, as he switched the music on his laptop to another hyperactive tune. "You come drink with us!"

"*Sí, sí,* Nico, join the party!" Alonso seconded. "Martine's *pupusas* are top door!"

"Not now, thanks." Nico picked his way across two of their unexpected visitors sprawled on the floor. Martine hovered over the table, dismally arranging the remaining food into a semblance of culinary comeliness, while one of the walking art exhibits scooped up the last of the shrimp. Though Nico hadn't touched her since that doughy Saturday his mother came home from Phoenix, he pulled Martine by the arm and urged her into the kitchen.

"What the fuck," he said.

She looked miserably at the floor. "I am sorry."

"Did you invite these people?"

"No, no, no. Of course, no."

"Will we be able to get rid of them?"

"I am honest. I am no so sure."

"And who are they?"

"Domingo . . . business partners."

"If he's their *partner*, or more like their *boss*, he can tell them to get the fuck out."

"*Sí*. But maybe he no feel like. And I am no boss of Domingo."

No, you're the bitch of Domingo, Nico did not say.

"My mother must be freaked," he said.

"Is no so happy birthday," Martine conceded.

"It's sure happy for those guys! And aren't you glad you cooked all day."

"There is still mucho salad," she said dryly. "*Los hombres*—they never touch the salad."

Nico surveyed the dining and living rooms from the doorway. Eliciting caustic laughter on the Latino end of the big double room, Alonso was holding court. But while Alonso was the jester, none of the new foursome ever laughed at Domingo. Rather, they brought over a bottle when his glass was still half full and placed the last of Martine's *pupusas* on the arm of his chair.

Though the attendees divided by a strict apartheid, one of the book club members was sufficiently in need of a drink (for understandable reasons) that she braved edging to the sideboard to pour herself a brimming measure. She took a hefty slug and topped the glass back up before rejoining her terrified brethren. Having quite a tale to tell their Facebook group and perhaps already regretting her refusal to sign the petition to keep migrants from boarding in houses like this one, one of their Ditmas neighbors sidled to the dining table, assembled a plate of what little the Hondurans had yet to ransack, and brought it back to the American camp—displaying the daring stealth of World War I soldiers who braved live fire in No Man's Land to retrieve the bodies of their fallen comrades.

By his count, the fourteen *non-Hispanic whites*, in the terms of the U.S. Census Bureau, well outnumbered the gate-crashers, but most of the native-born partygoers were pretty old and pretty weak (which might have been said of the country at large). Nico should probably have invited Vernon after all—a big guy at home in tough circles who might have helped roust these hoodlums out. Because otherwise: oh, boy, his mother did yoga.

Palermo was a pistol in high school, but now could barely walk, and Vanessa was terminally nice. Himself excepted, all the gringos were women—and in the context of the opposition, Nico felt like an honorary girl. For of the six Honduran men, five were in unnervingly good shape, and the four new arrivals were testosterone-jacked sidemen no older than twenty. As for which camp Martine belonged in, that had been a puzzle for nearly a year.

Overwhelmed and disoriented, their mother had initially withdrawn timidly to her friends collected around the black leather Chesterfield. Still, one young man whose complexion was exploding with self-expression kindled her courage.

"Excuse me!" Nico's mother shouted, striding aggressively toward the malefactor lounging on the floor. "There is no smoking in this house! If you have to do that, you absolutely must go outside, and I mean out on the sidewalk, not simply on the porch!"

The fellow stared indifferently up and exhaled smoke into her face. "Elijah!" he said. "*¿Cuál es el problema de esta anciana?*"

"*Un insecto atrapado en su coño de la vieja por culpa de tu cigarrillo,*" Domingo said.

"*Oh, lo siento mucho, vieja bruja,*" the guy told the homeowner in a tone of exaggerated consideration. He took his time finishing his unfiltered ciggy, tapping the ashes into the pewter-and-crystal coaster on the coffee table, then extinguishing the butt in the fibers of the cream-colored oriental rug. Nico could smell the acrid whiff from the doorway.

Ominously, his mother's complexion was turning the same purple as it had when, at twelve, he'd broken one of her beloved Depression-era tumblers with ruby-red Art Deco crosshatching—the very purple she'd turned when plunking an enormous and enormously expensive free-range turkey in the trash can. Nico swept in with an arm around her waist and steered her back to her own delegation. "For once, take my advice," he murmured. "Let it go."

The Hondurans seemed to find the brief interaction with the local wildlife amusing, and it inspired more than one of the young men who were enlivening the country with the vibrant customs of their homeland to light up cigs and spliffs as well. But witnessing exactly how much influence their friend Gloria exerted on these earnest would-be Americans yearning to make a "contribution" to their adoptive nation, the guests around the Chesterfield quietly filtered to the kitchen. Sullenly, Nico's mother followed in their wake.

Though it was barely 10 p.m., one by one the guests took their leave. One book club member voiced a cautious concern that perhaps their friend Gloria's generosity toward "the newest New Yorkers" had gone a bit too far. When they told the honoree at the side door to "take care of herself," they seemed to mean it.

In no time, then, the numerical advantage reversed. The music grew louder. Though the buffet was pillaged, the legitimate guests had added bottles of wine to the case that Martine had laid in, so the *hombres* wouldn't run dry anytime soon. The family remained in the kitchen, where Martine served her shell-shocked sponsor an apologetic slice from the mauled tres leches cake.

"Any point in calling the cops?" Palermo muttered to her brother.

"With a party that's gotten out of hand," Nico said under his breath, "at most the cops will urge everyone to disperse. What if everyone didn't go—or came back?"

"We can't leave you here like this," Vanessa told their mother. "We don't know who these people are—"

"We sort of do," Nico said. "That's the problem."

"It doesn't seem safe," Vanessa said.

"They no hurt you, I think," Martine said. "You just . . . no bother them. Let them drink and drink. They get tired, they pass out."

"No, Vanessa's right," said Palermo. "Mom, why don't you come back with me to Corona. We can make up the sofa."

"I'm not abandoning my own house to a bunch of . . . to ill-behaved strangers," their mother said. "After all, I have Nico here."

So: at long last he was formally offered his rightful role as his mother's protector. But as with most jobs he'd contemplated, his immediate impulse was to pass it up.

The three children helped Martine clean the kitchen, insisting their mother mustn't do dishes on her birthday. No one dared a return to the dining room to retrieve the platters, so Nico foraged the odd crust left behind in the baking pans. He cursed the fact that his laptop was still hooked up to the TV in the living room. Meanwhile, the party to which they had uninvited themselves got into full swing, with frantic drumbeats, the thump of clumsy dancing, and the occasional crash of crockery.

"Do you think," their mother submitted hopefully from the table, "that maybe they'll just go away?"

The clean-up crew left the wistful supposition unanswered. Nico thought grimly: Domingo didn't go away. Alonso didn't go away. Even Martine, whom his mother hadn't necessarily expected to put up for nearly a year, had not gone away. For that matter, ten million illegal immigrants tossed to the interior during this administration—and that was only the people the Border Patrol knew about—were not going away.

Wiping the counters, his sisters proposed staying over "to help hold down the fort."

"Adding two good-looking young women to a house full of shit-faced . . . 'ill-behaved strangers'?" Nico said. "I don't see how that improves anything."

"Gloria, I no want make you nervous," Martine said. "But you lock your bedroom door."

"Do you know those boys?" their mother asked.

"I no know this boys," Martine said. "But I know those boys."

Martine pressed care packages of tres leches cake on both sisters as rather marginal compensation for their mother's altogether too surprising surprise party. Insisting on an immediate update the next day on whether the dubious elements had cleared off, Vanessa and Palermo reluctantly departed.

"I doubt I'll sleep with that racket," Nico's mother said. "But I'm not going to stay down here while those young men get only drunker. Martine, we'll talk about this tomorrow." With that, she rescued her handbag and took the long way around to the staircase.

"You follow your mother," Martine told Nico. She didn't exude any of her usual muscularity or bravado, and her aspect was contrite. "You no leave her alone upstairs."

For a few days, she'd made him feel male. The effect had worn off.

"I may be tall, but there's only one of me. How much can I defend her, really? Or my sisters, or even you? Martine"—he leaned over and slid his hand forward on the counter for emphasis—"*what have you done?*"

She didn't answer but slipped her hand on top of his. Nico stared down at it. After a few seconds, she pulled it away. He didn't understand her.

Ears pricked for Hondurans headed upstairs, Nico hardly slept, remaining fully dressed atop the spread in case his fearsome masculine energies were required. That said, his only qualification as his mother's security guard was having a dick, which as a weapon was overrated; the appendage was more a point of vulnerability than the source of superpowers, and every gate-crasher downstairs had one, too. His most recent victory as a Real Man had involved wrestling a five-foot-five young woman into a sexually receptive position when she wanted nothing better, or so it appeared, than her own defeat. Hardly like winning the Battle of Waterloo. Nico rehearsed what objects within reach could double as ordnance. Maybe the curtain rail, though he'd need to loosen the fixing screws, and all the tools were in the basement.

When he woke from a fitful doze the next morning, *punta* still pulsed from below. As he crept down the hall, familiar snoring emitted from what, like it or not, was no longer known as "your father's study" but as "Alonso's room." He padded downstairs to find Martine and his mother in the kitchen. "Are they all still here?" he whispered.

"Probably," his mother said, also keeping her voice low. "We haven't been up long, and we're afraid to check."

Pulse racing—which was ridiculous—Nico eased through the creaking swing door to the dining room. Two of the newest arrivals were passed out on couches, the two others sprawled comatose on the floor. He tiptoed to the speaker on the dining table and hit the kill switch.

When he retreated to the kitchen, his mother said, "That's such a relief I could cry."

"I should warn you," Nico mumbled, "the living and dining rooms are trashed."

"I clean them, no worry, Gloria," Martine said. "I make everything same."

"'Make everything same' means buying new rugs and refinishing the dining table," Nico said.

In due course, Domingo emerged from the basement and demanded Martine make breakfast. His henchmen had stirred, because the TV in the living room was blaring a Spanish language soap opera. One by one, the young men groggily shuffled into the kitchen, poking in the fridge for orange juice and helping themselves to cake. When the fourth guy emerged, Nico finally felt free to retrieve his laptop. It had disappeared. The wire from the HTML plug dangled from the back of the TV set. In retaliation, Nico had half a mind to swipe the MacBook Pro that Domingo had left to blast *punta*. But he thought better of it.

At no point did any of these men acknowledge the existence of the household's residents, whom they ambled past as if negotiating the ground floor in a parallel dimension where the *non-Hispanic whites* were invisible. Meanwhile, Martine fired up the stove for eggs, bacon, sausage, and tortillas; the men treated her like a fry cook. She'd often acted so forceful—sticking up for her people in the face of his own criminally "nativist" attitudes, taking vengeance on his mother's hydrangeas, at least pretending to rescue her sponsor with a hedge trimmer. So it was curious to see her behaving so submissively, keeping her head down and plating up whatever the men ordered—and *ordered* was the word.

Both sisters called, but their mother stressed she couldn't talk and begged them to stay away. Nico and his mother stood at a distance while the men assumed all the chairs. There was no English. When they'd eaten their fill, they lounged on their phones, lighting cigarettes and extinguishing the butts in cold scrambled eggs. One of them left, but not out the door; given the clank of the pipes, he'd sauntered upstairs to shower. Another approached Martine rubbing his thumb and forefinger; she fished in her bag for a twenty. The guy waved come-come, until she'd emptied her wallet of cash. This one did leave the house, only to return with two cold six-packs. Shockingly, the fellow hadn't shopped with the environmentally friendly NPR totes by the door. On top of the yammering TV, someone turned the Bluetooth speaker back on. More *punta*.

On Nico's brief recce to the shambles of the dining room, far more disturbing than the white rings on the table had been a pile of dirty duffels by the piano. Slipping beside Martine as she cleaned the kitchen—again—he mumbled in her ear, "They're not leaving."

"No," she said.

"Are they ever leaving?"

"I no sure. Maybe no."

"This is not cool," he said.

"No," she conceded. "But cool or no cool, no matter."

"My mother never agreed—"

"Nico." Martine grabbed his wrist and looked him in the eye. "You no be hero," she said in a harsh whisper. "You no cross these people. You leave them alone. You no make them mad. They want anything, you let them take it. You no say *nothing* to them. Understand me?"

"Nico, Nico!" Alonso cried, having finally come downstairs. "You miss our great party! Why you go to bed so early? Next time, you stay and drink with the *hombres*."

Next time. No less so than if the Nazis had billeted in their farmhouse in France, the Bonaventuras were under occupation.

11

Regarding many a medical matter, a laissez-faire approach did the trick. The chronic rash on Nico's shin in high school cleared up on its own. Senior year at Fordham, the muscle spasm in his back that kept him from turning his head to the right for weeks eased at last with the application of mere patience. A mysterious abdominal pain of two summers past remained mysterious but nonetheless vanished as inexplicably as it had come on. Voilà, problem solved, with no appointments, ointments, prescriptions, or abstinence from alcohol for fourteen days.

Yet the same wait-and-see passivity failed to ameliorate the abrupt overcrowding of the Bonaventuras' house in Ditmas Park. Supposing that perhaps this new contingent had merely arrived for a spot of carousing with *amigos* before moving on to ruin someone else's life, Nico and his mother held their breaths for another day or so, but their newest visitors did not, as his mother had idiotically hoped, simply go away.

On the third day, one and then another of the young men did filter off elsewhere in the afternoon, but when they reassembled that evening the strapping younger cadre no longer numbered four but five. Nico hadn't distinguished among them much; they varied in how heavily scribbled they were—one of them was so inked up that he was almost black, reminiscent of Nico's old secondhand paperback of Ray Bradbury's *The Illustrated Man*; a couple of others still had patches of virgin skin left, which must have exhilarated the fellows with a sense of possibility. One was shorter and chunkier, but no less muscled. They had a uniform air of easy insolence and the kind of cold eyes that require cultivation. As they'd all breezily slung their duffels upstairs—and Alonso objected to having to share—at least Nico's mother could stop feeling guilty about her many empty bedrooms.

That evening the chunky one poked his phone at the kitchen table while his *colleagues* necking Corona Extras called out proposals; given the recurrence of *burrito* and *tostada*, they must have been ordering takeout from a nearby Mexican joint. The number of dishes soon became immoderate.

Having scavenged two stools from around the kitchen island, Nico and his mother had set up wary watch in the far corner of the breakfast room. "The whole house is beginning to reek," his mother grumbled, gesturing at the haze of cigarette smoke over the table. "Much longer, and I'll have to get the drapes dry cleaned and the furniture reupholstered."

"That's assuming," Nico mumbled, "some sunny future in which these pricks clear off."

The evening's organizer looked up. "*Tarjeta de crédito,*" he said, and then more sharply, "*¡Señora! ¡Tarjeta de crédito!*"

Martine intervened from the kitchen. "Gloria. He need your credit card number."

"What do you mean?" His mother knew full well.

"Your Visa," Marine said firmly. "The expiration date and CVC on the back."

"But I haven't ordered anything," she said.

"Yes, you have," Martine warned.

"It isn't safe—"

"It isn't safe *not to.*"

"This is like being—"

"Yes," Martine cut her sponsor off. "Yes, it is."

"I'm afraid the card is upstairs," his mother said.

Martine told the stocky one, "*La tarjeta de crédito está arriba.* Go ahead. They wait."

Her expression burning with resentment, his mother slid slowly off the stool. Taking her handbag and wallet with her when she went to bed had been wise but nevertheless proved unavailing. When she returned with the one card, she tried haltingly to read the number aloud in Spanish. "*Quatro . . . uno . . . seis . . . nuevo . . .* I'm sorry, I don't remember Spanish for zero—"

With annoyance, the guy grabbed for the card, but Nico's mother pulled it out of his reach. The two did a little dance, a lunge here, a recoil there, a lunge again. The fellow seemed to enjoy the game for a moment, but once he tired of it he clutched the homeowner's arm none too gently and plucked the plastic from her fingers with his other hand. "*Dile a la vieja: no seas tan estúpida la próxima vez*," he told Martine, entering the numbers on the website.

"Is best," Martine interpreted, "do what they say."

Even at a beanery, those guys must have run up a tab of two or three hundred bucks. When the prodigious order from Los Mariachis arrived, the gringos weren't invited to the feast.

At least the men were absorbed for now. Nico's upward nod to Martine and his mother suggested they convene upstairs.

His mother closed her bedroom door behind them. "So should I cancel that card?"

"They only make you give them another one," Martine said morosely.

"And don't tell me," Nico said. "If the card is rejected it might make them mad."

"*Sí.*"

"And whatever we do, we don't want to make them mad," Nico said sourly. "First your kids are kidnapped, and now we are."

For Nico, the full-tilt home invasion had one upside. His mother had softened. In fact, she clung to him, physically just then, clutching his upper arm. Oh, she hadn't converted wholesale to the view that Martine was a two-faced collaborator, but she'd have conceded by now that the Big Apple, Big Heart palaver had gone summarily south. He might have better relished the moral high ground had his mother's sudden faith in her manly offspring seemed well placed. Um, no. He was just as stymied as she was by how to rid their home of these marauders, and those rippling hieroglyphs downstairs scared the shit out of him.

"Martine, I'm sorry to put you on the spot," his mother said. "But this . . . this is unacceptable."

"It no matter you no accept it. Now you see what was like for me, in Rivera Hernandez. The *pandilleros*, you can no say no to them."

"But you left Honduras," his mother said. "And now Honduras has followed you here."

"I worry, the ransom . . ." Martine speculated. "I was so grateful, Gloria. But maybe it call attention to your house. This nice house. To me being in place where people have money."

"No good deed—" His mother stopped to answer her phone. It was doubtless one of her daughters—for the fourth time that day. "No, of course they're still here. In fact, I just bought them dinner with all the trimmings . . . No, I haven't eaten a thing all day. On my birthday, I only had that piece of cake. Yesterday, Martine was cooking for these people morning to night, and she barely managed to slip me a sandwich. Apparently being under siege is slimming . . . We'll have to powwow. Come up with, well . . . something. Can you and Vanessa get away? We're holed up in my bedroom. . . . *Why* won't Byron let you? . . . Of course they're dangerous. That's why we have to talk . . . No, you can tell Byron that I refuse to leave my house and all my things to a bunch of thugs. Martine is here, and Nico is here. We're trying to give them a wide berth. But you tell him this is a crisis, which we have to resolve as a family . . . Okay, but they're in the kitchen, so come in the front. Bye-bye."

Living nearer by, Vanessa rapped lightly on the locked bedroom door first, though a yeasty aroma preceded her. "Quick, give me a hand. The cardboard's starting to sog."

"Oh, my God," their mother said. "Honey, you're a lifesaver."

"Palermo said you guys aren't eating," Vanessa said as Nico relieved her of the boxes. "Honestly, those people are animals. Even POWs get rations. I went for two Vesuvios: tomato, mozzarella, pepperoni, sausage, mushrooms, peppers, and onions. It's a neighborhood staple. I hope that's all right."

"All right? I'd settle for the crusts in Vesuvio's dumpster." At least home invasion had cured their mother's horror of cheese.

Even in these fraught circumstances, Vanessa had packed a tote full of paper plates, napkins, and canisters of chili flakes, oregano, and Parmesan. Yet the three captives fell on the pies without remembering the condiments. A year earlier, it was Vesuvio's legendary pizza that their mother and the crusading members of her book club had distributed to migrants queuing around the Roosevelt Hotel. Now their mother needed rescue from the people she'd fed.

Once Nico was on his third slice, Palermo and Byron tapped the door for admission.

"Look, I was against our coming over and just putting more of us at risk," Byron said, locking the door again—though those little tab locks were Tinkertoy. "But maybe I can be more persuasive in person. My wife isn't prone to exaggeration, and she's allergic to any form of racial stereotyping. So if the guys who've taken over this house are anything like the way she describes them, you're all in over your heads. You have no idea who you're dealing with. I mean, Gloria—none of these gangbangers *asked* if they could stay here, right?"

"They come with Domingo," Martine said. "These boys, they never ask nobody."

"Okay, finish eating," Byron continued. "But then we should all get out of here. Grab your phones, your passports if you can lay hands on them, and cut your losses. Deal with this situation from a safe distance and leave reclaiming the property to the police."

Granted, Byron was a decade his senior, old enough to have developed a classic construction worker's potbelly and thinning hair, but Nico still found it annoying that his brother-in-law reflexively took charge. While the guy's arrival doubled the men on their side, his advice to tuck tail between legs and flee seemed a pretty low-testosterone solution.

"They could ransack this place," their mother said. "They could burn the house down. All this smoking . . ."

"A house is just a thing," Byron said. "Keep a sense of perspective. Do we know if these lowlifes are armed?"

"They at least have knives," Nico said. "They prefer their bowies to Mom's Wüsthofs for cutting chorizo."

"Why can't we call the police now?" Vanessa said.

"To report them for what?" Nico said. "Our *resident aliens* let them in, so they didn't break and enter. They haven't stabbed or shot anybody, and you can't arrest people because they *look* like criminals."

"Trespassing," their mother said. "Credit card fraud."

"You gave them the number," Martine said.

"Because you *told me to*," their mother said.

"I try to protect you," Martine said.

"Well, a fine job you've done of that!" It was the first time Nico had seen his mother direct her anger at the origin of their travails.

"I think one of them stole my laptop," Nico said. "But I can't prove it."

"In my country," Martine said, "the police are bad like the *pandilleros*. They are on the same side. They take money."

"Well, you're not in Honduras," Palermo said. "Here, the police aren't all in the back pocket of mobsters." This was the same sister who'd marched with the Black Lives Matter loonies demanding that the police whose honor she'd just defended be "defunded."

"But if you call police," Martine reasoned, "they have to arrest the boys. All the boys. They only give the boys warning? Then the *pandilleros* get mad. They get mad at Gloria."

"Why wouldn't the police arrest all of them?" Palermo said.

"With the no-bail laws, they'll get thrown right back on the street anyway," Nico said. Palermo had been all in with scrapping bail in New York, too. "Look at what happened to the Venezuelans in Times Square in January: nothing, or not until the case became a big media black eye. And those guys didn't crash a surprise party, but beat up NYPD cops."

"There's no way the police will let four toughs take over—" Palermo began.

"It's five now," Nico said. "And that's not counting Alonso." Or Domingo. Or Martine.

"Five, six, who cares!" Palermo said. "The police aren't going to let a bunch of uninvited, knife-packing hoodlums take over an elderly taxpayer's home—"

"'Elderly' may be jumping the gun," their mother objected.

"The boys out from jail? They come back here," Martine said. "You cross them, you pay. I see this in San Pedro Sula. Gloria, they can kill you. And even if they stay in jail, all *pandilleros* have friends. They get their friends take revenge."

"I can't believe this is happening," their mother said. "I feel like one of those kids in *Stranger Things* who's been sucked into The Upside Down."

"I'm amazed you watch that schlocky show," Nico said.

"I repeat," Byron said. "We should all get out of here. We can deal with reporting the situation to the police later."

"No," their mother said. "I'll stay out of their way and try not to provoke them. It's true they've been sleeping in my beds and eating my porridge. Even so, I don't think Goldilocks got gobbled by the three bears."

"It's Little Red Riding Hood who's gobbled up," Vanessa said. "It's Goldilocks who eats the porridge—"

"Oh, never mind! I was just trying to say that, okay, they obviously have no respect for other people's things. But so far those yobs haven't hurt anyone or directly threatened us. Byron, I'm not abandoning my home to barbarians." This was the same intransigence she'd displayed when wresting the property from her soon-to-be-ex-husband.

"Then I'm at least taking my wife out of harm's way," Byron said.

"There's safety in numbers," Palermo said. "Maybe I should stay."

"I mean this in the nicest possible way," Byron said. "Absolutely not."

"I'd stay, too," Vanessa said. "But Kumquat's alone in my apartment. He'll be frantic."

"Call it tough love," Byron told his wife. "Unless you and your family are being hysterical and the guys downstairs are castrati choirboys, getting out of this house pronto is a matter of life and death. I'm not leaving without you, and I'm leaving right now."

"All right, all right, I'll go," Palermo said, charmed by the display of chivalry despite herself. "But at least wait and let me have a slice. Vesuvio's, if I'm not mistaken."

So! Nico thought after he'd hugged his sisters goodbye and the visiting party of three had slunk downstairs and ever so quietly opened and closed the front door. After all that conferral, they had exactly: no plan.

Nico had never bought into the mythology of his sex, whose clichéd attributes he'd viewed with ironic detachment. In a feminized era that had pissed all over aggression, the capacity for violence, valor, the desire to dominate, a determination to win, and a proclivity for doing as opposed to thinking or talking, Nico's failure to embody these qualities had never perturbed him. Nor had dwelling amorphously in the androgenous middle of the so-called gender spectrum ever damaged his status among his peers, who lived predominantly in a world of gigabytes and expressed their urge to kill by pressing buttons. He'd accepted without necessarily labeling it as such that they lived in a post-male age. Physical force was irrelevant; everything vital happened on-screen. Even gym rats didn't lift weights with an eye to *doing* something with the strength they gained; the clanging and straining was all about looking pretty, and therefore part and parcel of Girly Land. (In fact, fitness agnostics like Nico looked on these meatheads still sweating it out IRL with pity; in the *real* real world, you could grow all the muscles you liked by clicking a mouse.) Yes, by fixing on having no ambition as his sole ambition, and by operating reactively against what he did not want rather than striving for anything he did, he made a rotten fictional character. But that also meant he made a rotten guy.

Big whoop, right? Yet following the arrival of the coal-eyed quintet, Nico finally appreciated what it meant to feel *emasculated*. Sure, these skinheads were digitally literate; they had phones, which they used to stream porn but which were otherwise, he sensed, instruments for the giving and taking of orders. That is, their phones connected them to the material world, in which something might happen, or be made to happen, other than the delivery of a corn removal kit from Amazon. Out here in the wild, wacky universe of three dimensions, the *pandilleros* did whatever they wanted. They took what they wanted, including a nicely done-up five-bedroom house in Ditmas Park. They weren't big talkers. And they clearly lived in a world of nothing *but* force, physical force, even if the ghost Americans dwelling wholly online were always surprised there was still such a thing. The *bad hombres*, as a certain former president would say, disdained and subjugated women, which Nico shouldn't have admired but sort of did. In the Hondurans' vicinity, he felt childish, weak, and gelded. They were shorter than he was, but every time they sauntered into the room his gut stabbed, spurring Nico to wonder if a single man, woman, or child walked the earth who was afraid of him. A platoon of goons had invaded his mother's home, and what did the only son do about it? *Nada*.

If Martine wasn't at ready hand, they thought nothing of demanding that the gringo kid fetch them a *cerveza* or prepare them *huevos*, and to his own horror, though he'd never scrambled an egg in his life, Nico would find himself obediently bowed over the stove. When, starving, Nico ordered twelve pieces of spicy chicken tenders with biscuits and honey-mustard sauce from Tex's Chicken & Burgers for lunch, the slightly taller, slightly skinnier fellow with XVIII across his forehead intercepted the delivery and ate it himself; Nico didn't say a word. More humiliatingly still, the chunky guy coolly set up shop at the kitchen table with Nico's filched starlight-colored laptop, and even when the thug left the machine unattended to go to the john, its rightful owner couldn't bring himself to snatch it back.

Perhaps it went without saying: he loathed them. The shine had even gone off Alonso, who with his little friends underfoot made less effort to envelop Nico in his loquacious bonhomie. The rest treated Nico like an errand boy, though he was several years their senior. What these punks were probably capable of made them contemptible in "nicey-softy" terms, but an aptitude for atrocity made them highly successful animals. In contrast to his failings as a man, it truly bugged him that he made a rotten animal. Accordingly, Nico was constantly afflicted by violent fantasies: of whacking the wide boys in the jaw with a two-by-four, swiping a borrowed bowie to dispatch their entrails as if gutting fish, or garroting them from behind with his laptop cord. He preferred to envision Domingo, for whom he nurtured a heightened antipathy, duct-taped to a chair, so that Nico could administer tortures at his leisure; see how well the guy liked it when he couldn't flash his cock through the gape of his boxers anymore because he no longer had one. Holed up in his room, Nico got into character by rewatching *Pulp Fiction* and *Django Unchained*. Yet hatred he couldn't vent simply wore him out.

His mother must have felt a female version of the same emasculation. She'd been thrown into a prefeminist if not prehistoric domain, successfully pushed around by men who got their way not, so far, by hurting anybody, but by carrying themselves with an *air* of men who *might* hurt you. None of them having held a gun to their heads or a knife to their throats was strangely demoralizing. Her only resistance took the form of facial expression—a hard glare (but not too hard), a press of the lips—and a rigid marshal gait, arms stiff. Nothing stopped her from going out, really, but her anxiety about abandoning the house to the intruders imprisoned her there. When she'd gone AWOL for three slots in a row, the organizer of volunteers at Floyd Bennett Field called to express concern.

His mother explained in clipped tones, "It seems I'm already helping migrants settle in my own neighborhood."

Had anyone described these circumstances beforehand, Nico would have feared that his mother would explode—thereby putting them both in peril. After all, this was the tumbler-smashing, turkey-chucking hothead who had his father's grand cubby-filled rolltop desk impulsively carted to the dump. You could bet she didn't rescue whatever was in the drawers, either. This was the same harridan-on-a-dime who'd spent ten minutes on the phone viciously laying into the driver in the accident that ended Palermo's gymnastics career, who, though the poor guy had admitted to having had a couple of cocktails, had brought himself to call *her* purely to *apologize*, and *already felt terrible*. So what did that accomplish? This was the same woman whose opening of an exhibit of her fabric art miniatures in an unassuming Brooklyn gallery turned out to fatally coincide with the occasion at which his father would be given a major National Press Club award, a black-tie event he had thoughtlessly decided to attend—moving her to lose her rag so loudly that Helen Levitt knocked nervously on the front door because she worried that someone had died. While as a rule his mother's disproportionate, futile, and/or irrational paroxysms would be followed by prolonged sheepishness, the emotional equivalent of a hangover, it wasn't the subdued phases of shuffling penance that burned themselves into the family's collective memory.

Yet now that venting her temper could be, not just figuratively self-destructive, but literally so, she was able to keep her trap shut—thereby exposing all her previous fits of pique, seemingly the fruit of unmanageable passions, as sheer indulgence. In retrospect, then, she *could* have assured her son that she realized he didn't mean to break that glass, that he couldn't have known how much she loved that set, and that the only thing he'd be punished for was sneaking the gin; she *could* have swallowed her resentment, continued to stuff that turkey, and urged him to have a lovely time on Thanksgiving with a father he saw all too rarely; she *could* have carefully wrapped that desk in moving blankets and hired a Man With Van to haul it to the Upper West Side; she *could* have gently assured the motorist in Palermo's accident that the guilt he'd carry for the rest of his life was punishment enough;

she *could* have congratulated his father on his well-deserved award and cheerfully accepted that he couldn't help the schedule clash with her opening. She just hadn't felt like it.

Once the occupation was two weeks in, any pretense that their latest houseguests would any day now drift off to greener pastures of their own accord had been put to rest. Other interchangeable skinheads were making appearances at the outside entrance to the basement, either to deliver packages or to take packages away. Their body language was purposive, their bearing, like Domingo's, military, and they didn't dally to chat. In all, the house was beginning to teem with entrepreneurial gumption—the very self-starter's fairy dust that Alonso had tried to sprinkle on his unpromising twenty-seven-year-old protégé.

The live-in contingent had commandeered the whole ground floor, so whenever Nico eased into the kitchen to fix a surreptitious sandwich, he fought an impulse to apologize for the interruption. Martine tried mightily to keep order, but her powers of tidiness were no match for the men's powers of chaos, so the place increasingly looked like a dump. A rank perfume hit as soon as you walked in the door—a complex amalgam of sweat, fart, belch, ripe garbage, and fried food. Using the Visa card, the boys installed a case of Flor de Caña, while in the background Martine ensured that the washing machine and dishwasher churned all day.

Nico hadn't previously given the conundrum any thought—he wasn't hard-pressed for problems to solve—but "Elijah" was an awfully Judaic nickname for a Honduran, especially one whose given name was supposedly Domingo. On a hunch that his aural decoding might be off, he played around with Google Translate. So "Elijah" was "Elías" in Spanish anyway. He tried "El ijah" and "el ayzha" and got no hits. But "el acha" triggered "Did you mean *el hacha*"—bingo, as Alonso loved to say. Domingo's handle with his minions was The Hatchet. Oh, great.

In sum, the situation had grown only more *unacceptable*. Thus his mother defied the glaring inefficacy of its seminal gathering and reconvened the What the Fuck Are We Going to Do committee. This time she asked Palermo to come over without telling Byron. Naturally, Vanessa brought a freshly baked batch of brownies, which lent the second summit in their mother's bedroom the atmosphere of a Girl Scout troop meeting.

Martine was able to slip away only after frying up their occupiers a mess of steaks, also courtesy of the homeowner's Visa. That case of rum would keep the conquistadors contented for the time being. Personally, Nico wouldn't have included Martine in their deliberations, but his mother still didn't countenance the possibility that she was inviting a mole.

"Martine, I take your point that calling the police could be risky," their mother began. "Even if I agree with Palermo that the NYPD is likely to take one look at those people and realize they aren't exactly friends of the family. But if the officers don't haul every last one of them away in handcuffs, we could be inviting retribution. Short of taking that step, then . . . Well, one thing that's been torturing me about all these people here without my permission is my own passivity. It finally struck me that I've never, actually, asked, or demanded, that they leave."

Martine squinted. "You think this is good idea?"

"We've just rolled over!" their mother said. "I'm no expert on Honduran culture, but it's obviously very macho. That sensibility admires strength. People who stand up for themselves. Who push back. And instead, we've been timid and cowering, and we do everything they say."

"So what are you suggesting?" Palermo said.

"I thought we could present a united front," their mother said. "Go down as a family and ask them—or tell them—to go, because they've overstayed their welcome."

"What welcome?" Vanessa said.

"And which is it," Nico said. "Ask them, or tell them?"

"I am no sure it make big difference," Martine said glumly.

"Let's not get angry or act unpleasant," their mother said. "We should simply be *firm*. Just say, all right, boys, you've had your fun, but enough is enough. Time to run along."

Their mother had a chronic first-person plural problem. "What's with all the 'we'?" Nico said. "Who's being 'firm'?"

"Would you like me to do it?" Vanessa asked in a small voice.

The image was consummately ridiculous. "God, no," Nico said. "Mom, I don't mean to seem like a pussy—"

"Nico!" Palermo chided.

"This house has been taken over by drug dealers, and you're upset about my language hygiene?" Nico said incredulously. "Mom, I'm not volunteering to deliver your eviction notice—and not because I'm a *pussy*. If you insist on doing this, I don't think it's smart to have the only male here lay down the law. The mano a mano thing, it's a red flag to a bull. The confrontation would escalate. And there're a lot more of them than there are of me."

"So you are a pussy," Martine goaded.

Nico reeled in her direction. "You brought these people here. Watch the mouth. I studied electrical engineering, not domestic pest control."

"So?" she fired back. "You could have study How to Live with Mama. *Electrical engineering?* You never change one light bulb."

"Please stop bickering. I don't understand why you two can't get on." Nico's mother may have misunderstood the source of friction here, and he wasn't about to enlighten her.

"Besides," Vanessa said, "it isn't fair to say Martine *brought* these guys here."

"Isn't it?" Nico said. "She *brought* Domingo here. She didn't make any kind of stink when Alonso showed up. And Domingo *brought* the boy band downstairs. No Martine Salgado, and your only worries are what to wear to watch next month's Pride parade."

"Finger-pointing is a waste of time," their mother said. "As for which of us acts as a spokesperson—it's my house." There was no disguising her dread. "I'm the one who should announce I'd like it back."

"When do you want to do this?" Vanessa asked.

"I'd love to put it off indefinitely," their mother said. "But we're all here. We might as well do it now."

"Oh, shit," Palermo said.

"Should we soften them up first with some brownies?" Vanessa asked.

"I'm not sure that's quite the right look," Nico said.

"Martine, I'll need your help as a translator," their mother said. "Google Translate isn't the right look, either."

As the five of them threaded down the staircase, Nico flashed on the motley, hapless baseball team in *Bad News Bears*. Except their team in

Ditmas comprised: a short, plump children's after-school monitor who gave total strangers on the street twenty dollars because they'd "just been mugged and have no money to get back home"—and had fallen for exactly the same story more than once; a construction company bookkeeper with a bad back; a sixty-three-year-old dilettante who knitted toy animals and whose alimony was running out; a physically underpowered malingerer whose most sacred values were "neutrality" and "observation"; and, the only intimidating member of their posse, a young Honduran laundress whose loyalties were at best divided and at worst allied with the opposing side. Jesus, even in that otherwise formulaic film, the shabby, little-engine-that-could baseball team still loses the championship.

Their mother led them into the kitchen, and they assembled behind the pass-through counter facing the big round kitchen table. They could as well have been a choral group arranging to entertain their guests by lilting into "America the Beautiful."

Domingo, Alonso, and the five henchmen—or was it six now?—paid the petitioners no mind. They were surrounded by plates strewn with slabs of beef fat. As the diners must have cut the steaks with their bowies, multiple unsheathed fighting knives now lay on the table. The men were knocking back glasses of rum, four of them having helped themselves to the remaining Depression-era tumblers with ruby-red Art Deco crosshatching, saved for special occasions. As which maybe this evening qualified at that. The company's rapid-fire Spanish was heated, and though the younger men talked over each other, they never talked over Domingo.

"Excuse me," their mother said over the din, to no effect. "Excuse me!"

The contentious discussion only rose in pitch.

"Domingo!" Martine said more sharply. "*Lo siento. Gloria quiere decir algo.*"

Her "brother" looked wearily over. "*¿De qué se trata esta mierda?*"

"*Esta no es mi idea,*" Martine said. "*Por favor, hazme un favor y al menos finge escucharla.*"

"Okay, *chicos,*" "El Hacha" said, and the rest of the table shut up. "*La vieja bruja quiere hablar. Esto podría resultar entretenido.*"

"I'm sorry to interrupt your evening," their mother began shakily, nodding at Martine, who duly translated this and each proceeding sentence. "And we all hope you've been having a wonderful time here in Ditmas Park. We've been glad to be able to provide you our hospitality."

Nuts, *Get the fuck out of my house, assholes* this was not.

"We've been participating in a New York City program called Big Apple, Big Heart," she went on, "which houses migrants in the local community. I'm very sympathetic with how hard it is for newcomers in a strange, expensive city. So we agreed to take Martine in, and we've come to love her very much. If I had it to do all over again, I'd still welcome her into our family."

In that case, Nico thought, *you are an idiot*. The men around the table were getting restless and already looked bored.

"But this is a family home," their mother said, clutching the edge of the counter with white knuckles. "We're happy to put up Martine, but this is not a shelter. We only agreed to house Martine. I'm afraid the rest of you will have to leave."

The presentation was tremulous, but Nico was proud of his mother; that hadn't been easy. Yet the translation merely roused a few smiles.

"It's all right if you need to spend tonight here," his mother said. "But by tomorrow I would like all of you please to take your things and find somewhere else to live. I've talked this over with my children, and we all agree that it's time for us to get our privacy back. It's been nice to meet you all, and Martine, of course, can stay. But everyone else has to go. That includes you, Domingo, and you also, Alonso . . . Thank you."

When Martine finished the translation, the whole table burst out laughing. The hilarity only accelerated, with backslapping, shoulder punching, and what sounded like puling imitations of their mother's edicts: *¡Pero todos los demás tienen que irse! ¡Por favor tomen sus cosas y busquen otro lugar para vivir!*

"*La pobre está loca*," the chunky one said.

"*La pobre es estúpida*," XVIII Forehead said.

"Come, we get out of here," Martine said, urging their party out the side door.

"I'm not sure that went very well," Nico said beside Vanessa's Fiat Panda. "I didn't see any of them start packing."

"At least I made it clear we want them gone," their mother said, steadying herself against the car.

"I have a funny feeling they knew that already," Nico said.

The homeowner's deadline for the intruders' departure came and went, with no detectable bustling of dirty underwear into duffels upstairs, no frantic combing of Craigslist for apartments to rent, no loading of the Amtrak website for train schedules to upstate, where alternative accommodations would be more affordable. Like the chorus of "America the Beautiful" Nico had envisioned that night, the family's "united front" had merely served as amusing dinner theater for young self-starters who were quite happy staying put, thank you very much. Domingo put in an order for another round of steaks.

A flurry of furtive phone conversations ensued, which their mother conducted from the driver's seat of her car. Martine was still dead set against it, but despite Palermo's previous cynicism about the predatory bigotry that had resulted in the murder of George Floyd, and despite how convincingly their mother could have elucidated Americans' broad loss of faith in their institutions, and despite Vanessa's uncanny ability to see the good even in the most seemingly unsalvageable of humanity's dregs, the other three women were soon in accord on the next step. Aside from scoring an assault weapon and further boning up on Tarantino films, Nico couldn't come up with an alternative himself: it was time to call the police.

Nevertheless, Nico was too up to speed on New York law enforcement to feel juiced about this prospect. The recent no-bail regime entailed same-day release, making you wonder why the constabulary went through the whole handcuff/Miranda folderol in the first place. Yet surely the uninvited houseguests would find the process of arrest, however temporary, an irksome disruption of their affairs, leaving the gentlemen a tad miffed. Martine was right. Why wouldn't they return to a house they now seemed to regard as their own to express this displeasure? The whole situation wasn't well thought out. His mother seemed to realize as much, since for a couple of days she put off making the call.

Then the Toyota Prius disappeared.

"I'm afraid I may have left the key fob on the usual shelf by the door after the last time I talked to Vanessa," his mother admitted to Nico, standing bereft in the empty drive. "Storing it there is automatic. I'm not used to worrying that people staying in my house will steal my car."

"This is a way bigger deal than my Mac," Nico said. "Any point in objecting?"

"'Can I please have my car back?' All we'd get is ha-ha-ha. Though this is the limit. Now we've no choice but to call you-know-who. She's out buying those savages more steaks, but I'll warn Martine what to expect. We'll have to wait for a time they're all here."

They'd wandered to the curb for privacy. "Do you ever stop and think how surreal this shit is?" Nico reflected. "I keep waiting to wake up."

"I'm grateful you've refrained from saying I told you so. I feel maybe, sweetie, I've done you a disservice. I still think you're dead wrong about Martine, and for me at least she really has made the last year so much more stimulating."

"Too stimulating," Nico said.

"Okay, too stimulating," his mother agreed. "But most of the millions of people crossing the border are *nothing like* the bullies in our house. They're families. They're hard workers—"

"Oh, put a lid on it, Mom."

"I just mean, this sponsorship seemed a moral obligation at the time. But in retrospect . . . You were the only one who had reservations."

"I didn't have 'reservations.' I thought the idea was ridiculous."

She laughed. "Okay, yes. And it hasn't worked out great."

"Your talent for understatement is fucking British."

"I may have been too hard on you. I may have been a little unfair."

"I've only been looking out for you. I've only been trying to protect you."

"I can see that now," she said, reaching for his hand.

"And now I can't." To Nico's disgust, he was starting to tear up, and he wiped his eyes with angry annoyance. "I don't have the muscle or the weapons. I don't have the friends with the muscle and the weapons. I don't have the strategic mindset—like, I don't know what people do when their house is taken over by thugs. Those guys aren't afraid of me. They think I'm a joke. And I am a joke. All I do is step 'n' fetch it. I'm like that kid in *GoodFellas*, the one Joe Pesci shoots in the foot. Who just limps around and keeps bringing the wise guys their drinks. I don't know what to do, and I can't help you. I'm a shit son. You might as well not have one."

His mother gave the hand a squeeze. "That's not true, and don't think like that. You're not a joke. I wouldn't want a son who knew what to do right now, because that would mean you'd be just like those callous boys. It doesn't take strategic genius. Gangs solve territorial disputes by shooting people. I'm no anthropologist, but I know that much."

"Know the truth, I have had fantasies."

"Forget it. What gives those people power is not caring about anything or anybody."

"On that score I sometimes come close."

"Nonsense. Those boys are hard, and that takes practice. Having no feelings isn't natural, it's learned. You have a heart. You haven't carved it out with a bowie knife."

"I'm just trying to say I'm sorry. I'm sorry I'm so useless."

"But that's what I'm trying to say—that I'm sorry, too. I'm sorry I put us in this awful situation. I still can't work out how we got from taking in one lovely young woman to . . . to this. Still, it's obviously my fault. And . . . well, I did something. I did something rash. I was very, I don't know, exercised. You know I have a bit of a temper—"

Nico guffawed.

"It was an extreme reaction," she said. "I just want you to know that I'll fix it as soon as I can. I'll take it back."

His mother refused to explain what the hell she was talking about, and they shuffled hand in hand back to the house. "You know, I made a video for your birthday," Nico mentioned on the way. "Like, the Bonaventuras' greatest hits. It's on the laptop they swiped. I'm sorry you never got to see the show. It was kind of cool. In some of those old vids—well, you look great."

Once his mother forced herself to place her fateful phone call from that front sidewalk, she might have expected sirens to immediately wail in the distance, so that within minutes multiple cars would careen around corners and descend on her property from all directions. To the contrary, nothing happened. The popular hostility of the Black Lives Matter riots and a dispiriting refusal to prosecute at the top had led to early retirements and unmet recruiting targets. The cops were overstretched and undermanned.

So Nico and his mother patiently assumed the stools they'd dragged to the corner of the breakfast room. Loath to betray to their *guests* that anything was up, they'd urged Palermo and Vanessa to stay away. Nico watched muted Dave Rubin podcasts with closed captions, keeping his headphones off in case the doorbell rang. His mother browsed the *New York Times* app, doubtless digesting nothing. Martine took out her anxiety on cleaning the oven. Their enterprising homesteaders had made themselves unusually scarce and for once weren't harassing her for lunch. But it was impossible to remain on tenterhooks for hours, so when the doorbell finally rang in the late afternoon Nico happened to be in the john and his mother had slipped upstairs for another Xanax.

"Good afternoon, officers! How can I help you?"

While Nico was drip-drying, Alonso had beaten him to the front entrance.

"Sir, could we speak to Gloria . . . Bondaventure? We've had a complaint."

"But, of course, officers, right away. Won't you come in? And can I get you officers a refreshment? Coffee, Coca-Cola?"

"That won't be necessary, thanks."

"Right this way," Alonso said. "Why don't we go into the sitting room, where you'll be more comfortable. *Gloooriaaaa!*" he called in a lilting falsetto. "It's the *poliiiiiice*! They'd like to *speeeeeeak* with *yoooooou!*"

When Nico made it to the foyer, Alonso was already leading the two men in blue to the *sitting room*—and it was anyone's guess what BBC series the guy had snarfed that expression from. Notably, Alonso had tucked in his shirt—a long-sleeved button-down, rather than the fleece vest he commonly preferred, so that his boxers and ass crack were no longer showing, and neither were most of his tattoos.

Nico trailed the procession, hanging back to wait for his mother just long enough to take in the tableau. The spacious living and dining rooms were immaculate, with none of the usual beer bottles leaving rings, decorative bowls abused as ashtrays and overflowing with butts, open baggies of weed, fast-food wrappers, and plates of crusting burrito. More signally still, Domingo and his six flunkies—they definitely numbered half a dozen now—were all arranged in various poses of profitable employ as if positioned in a Renaissance canvas. One was gazing in fascination at the latest *New Yorker*. Two were buried in the dated tomes *I'm OK—You're OK* and *The Power Broker*—and none of these guys could read English. Speaking of which, XVIII Forehead had Alonso's *Easy English Step by Step* spread in his lap, with the cover raised for any onlooker's ready appreciation. Another hood had his eyes closed while resting his hands on his knees, as if lost in rapt meditation. Domingo himself was tailing and snapping green beans into a colander, which was the most help he had given Martine in preparing dinner since his surly, presumptuous arrival in October. The last of Domingo's seven dwarves was pretending to knit with the homeowner's crochet needles and had managed to produce a perfect replica of a plate of spaghetti.

They were all sitting up straight. They were all wearing trousers for once, and even shirts—long-sleeved, buttoned to the chin. If they'd only worn gloves and bags over their heads, no one would ever have known they were stenciled top to toe with gang insignia.

"I introduce," Alonso said grandly, pointing. "Luis, Carlo, Juan, Miguel, Xavier, Pedro, and Domingo. I am Alonso."

Finally, his mother brought up the rear. "Officers," she said, extending her hand. "I'm Gloria Bonaventura, this is my son, Nico, who also lives here, and this is my house. Oh, and here is the young woman we're sponsoring through the mayor's Big Apple, Big Heart program, Martine Salgado."

Having hustled from the kitchen entrance, Martine was still wiping her hands on a dish towel. She extended her hand, cuticles black. "Good to meet you, officers."

"Ms. Bondaventure, what seems to be the problem?"

To Nico's eye, this white cop, whose metal name tag said BOWER, was just old enough to verge on retirement. He'd gone jowly, and his expression was permanently tired. Beefy arms bulging from his short sleeves were covered in heavy reddish arm hair. Younger and slimmer, his black partner ("PATTERSON") looked a little less jaded, but only by comparison. Their belts were weighted down with tasers, handcuffs, pepper sprays, radios, batons, and pistols, which must have been a pain in the ass to walk around with all day. Nico had always instinctively regarded the police as a threat. It was weird to feel grateful for their presence. He felt more protected than he had ever since Domingo Not-Really-From-DoorDash pushed past him through the front door, and he wished he could apologize to these keepers of the peace that he'd ever bristled at the sight of their uniforms.

"We've been glad to host Martine," his mother was saying. "It's important for local New Yorkers to help migrants assimilate. But none of these men were invited to my home. They simply moved in. I told them firmly a few days ago that they had twenty-four hours to vacate the premises, and nothing happened—as you can see. They're trespassing. They've stolen one of my credit cards and have run up outrageous charges. They stole my son's laptop. And they stole my car. I want our things back, I want these people out of my house, and I'm willing to press charges to guarantee that they don't come back."

"You have some proof of ownership, ma'am?" Bower asked.

The complainant had prepared. She drew the last property tax bill from her hip pocket. "The tax keeps shooting up," she said. "I'd appreciate some help in return."

"Any breaking and entering?" Patterson asked.

"Not exactly. Domingo there is Martine's brother. He let the rest of them in."

"This brother—he have your permission to reside here?"

"I never gave him permission, but I guess I never expressly told him to leave until a few days ago. Martine seemed to cherish the company of a family member."

"He's not her brother," Nico said—and his mother looked over sharply.

"What is he, then?" Patterson asked.

"Boyfriend, maybe husband," Nico said, careful to not look at Martine.

"Martine part of the problem, then?"

"Personally," Nico said, "I think so."

"Ma'am, why didn't you cancel the credit card?" Bower asked.

"I was afraid to make them angry," his mother said. "Martine warned me that they'd just demand another one. We're effectively being held hostage."

"You still have a phone?" Patterson asked.

"Well, yes. They all have their own, which must explain why they haven't stolen our phones, too."

"You held against your will," Patterson said, "what took you so long to call 911?"

"We're not precisely kidnapped," she said. "It's more that they've kidnapped my house."

"This a squatting situation, then," Bower said.

"Basically," she said. "Although I'm also concerned that these men are . . . unsavory."

"Officers, officers!" Alonso intruded, having stood back and allowed their accuser to say her piece. "I am afraid we have misunderstanding here. The credit card. Mrs. Gloria provide the numbers for a takeout order, when we have a house party. She read the numbers to Miguel herself—in Spanish. We joke that she get very good at Spanish!"

"Is that true?" Bower asked.

"Up to a point, but I was bullied," his mother said. "These men are very intimidating."

"The laptop," Alonso continued, nodding at XVIII Forehead, at which point the young man interrupted his earnest English language studies to pull Nico's distinctively starlight-colored MacBook Air from underneath the sofa. "Mister Nico, he misplace under the furniture, and we find it for him. I would think he be happy, yes?"

"Never mind the computer," his mother said. "You people stole my car!"

"This is mistake, Mrs. Gloria," Alonso said. "We borrow, remember? To go to grocery store. To make contribution to the household. But it is right back."

"You want to check, Gary?" Bower said to his partner.

Patterson went out the front and soon returned. "Your car a Toyota Prius?"

"Well, yes," his mother said.

"Looks like it's okay," Patterson said.

"But there is bigger misunderstanding, officers," Alonso said. "We are *tenants*. Mrs. Gloria seem to change her mind. It is true we are humble asylum seekers, just looking for a better life. But we know our rights, officers. Mrs. Gloria cannot just change her mind."

At the mention of *tenants*, Nico's heart fell. It was the magic word, much like *credible fear* at the southern border.

"You have some documentation of this, sir?" Bower asked.

"*Sí, sí*, officers!" Alonso said, reaching for a sheaf of papers on the pink marble coffee table. "These are our leases."

As Bower shuffled through the papers with little evident interest, his mother objected, "That's ludicrous! I never signed any leases! Those are forgeries!"

"Afraid we're not handwriting experts," Bower said.

It was a cinch to download generic leases from the internet. They could easily have printed the documents in his mother's office.

"So how long you been living here as *tenants*?" Patterson asked. The sarcastic pronunciation engendered a glimmer of hope.

"Domingo live here since October," Alonso said. "I live here since February. All our friends live here more than thirty days."

"They have not," Nico said quickly, all too aware that thirty days of "tenancy" spelled any property owner's doom. As for when the pond scum arrived, it was their word against the intruders', and Alonso was smart enough to have backdated the paperwork. "Martine, these new guys haven't been here for a full month, have they?"

Martine had been hanging back, as if she wished she could disappear. She threw a quick glance at Domingo. "I do not know. I do not remember."

"None of these men has paid me a red cent of rent," his mother said. "I could show you my bank statements—"

"Legally," Bower said, "you're still a tenant even if you've never paid a sous. Real sorry about that, ma'am. I don't make the laws in New York City."

"I don't believe this," his mother said (though Nico did). "We've been invaded. These people come and go as if they own the place. They aren't welcome here. We're afraid for our safety. We need your help."

This was the same appeal Nico would have liked to make to the current administration in DC regarding the whole country.

"If you don't feel safe, ma'am," Bower said, "you can always move out yourself."

"Of my *own house*?" his mother said. "Move out. Of *my own house*."

"Any of these *tenants*," Patterson said, "assault you or your son? Make threats? Injure your person? Make unwanted sexual advances?"

"Their very presence is an assault," his mother said. "Their very presence is threatening."

The two officers looked at each other.

"Look," Bower said, and his perpetual expression of exhaustion deepened. "You can start eviction proceedings in housing court. Though I'd advise you to use an attorney."

"Housing court," Nico said, "is backed up over a year."

"That's what I heard," Bower said.

"My mother would have to pay for her attorney," Nico said. "Long as these guys claim to make less than two hundred percent of the poverty rate, they get free representation from the city. Those pro bono lawyers are notorious for filing nuisance motions to delay, so the case could last way longer than a year. Meanwhile, these guys get to live here rent free. And housing court is civil. It can't levy any punishment for co-opting someone else's property. You rarely get back rent. They can even trash the place, and you'll never get restitution. The best you can do is get rid of the fuckers, after all kinds of aggravation."

"Someone's been reading up," Patterson said. "So you must know the shortcut."

"*Cash for keys*," Nico said.

"What on earth is that?" his mother said.

"You pay them to go away," Nico said. "Sometimes tens of thousands of dollars."

"I won't pay these crooks a dime!" his mother said. "They've run up thousands in steak and booze! Ruined my dining table! Stank up my soft furnishings with cigarette smoke! I mean, look at those boys. They may be wearing shirts for once, but they're covered in tattoos!"

Patterson's plaintive tone implied that he was hip to the nature of their *tenants*: "Nothin' illegal about tattoos."

"They've no right to be here," his mother said. "Respect for property rights is the cornerstone of America's social order! It's a big reason so many people immigrate here!"

"New York statutes are heavily weighted against landlords," Bower said. "Write your city councilman. Um, councilperson."

"But I'm not a landlord!" his mother said. "One look at those worthless papers and you know they're fake!"

"Not our purview," Bower said sadly. "You prove that in court. Like your son said, this is a civil dispute. Our hands are full with the criminal kind. This is, like, not our problem."

"Ma'am, I feel you," Patterson said. "But we arrest anyone turns out a lawful tenant, we get sued up the wazoo. We seen it. Not pretty. And my wife's expecting our third."

The cops turned to go. Heedless of sounding pathetic, his mother called after them, "Please don't leave me!"

The lesson here might have been utile for America's commander in chief: once you let people into your home, it can be legally labyrinthine and larcenously expensive if not downright impossible to get them out. But at present, Nico was less captivated than usual by such a reflection. He and his mother pivoted in horror to face their new boarders. Domingo had finished snapping the beans.

12

"Gloria, Gloria," Alonso admonished as the rest of the men relaxed, high-fived each other, and unbuttoned their uncomfortable shirts. "That was not so nice. And here I am thinking we are become friends. I am so hurt you do not enjoy our company."

"You must be awfully pleased with yourself," Nico's mother said.

"I must say, yes, very pleased," Alonso agreed. "This is game. You are at disadvantage because you think you can rely on your official peoples. In Honduras, we know better. We do not rely on official peoples. We use them, but we are never so stupid we *ask* them for anything. We buy them instead. In Honduras, these officers you bring here—it would be easy. You pay them money, enough money, and you win: all your visitors arrested. You pay big, big money, and, Gloria, they come here and they shoot us! Every single one! No more *tenants*."

"That would do in my cream carpet for keeps," his mother said, deadpan.

"You could have try, you know," Alonso suggested. "You hand those police a fat paper bag full of dollars. Then maybe they say: these peoples in your house, we make them leave."

"Our cops aren't that corrupt," she said.

"You do not test them! Who is to say? Remember, the black one: a third baby on the way. Maybe you lose the game because you are too cheap."

Alonso collected his pile of "leases" and stacked them neatly. "I must say, I am disappointed in your country. Before I come here, I hear how great is America. Everyone in Honduras want to come here. But now I am here, I find it is silly country. Weak country. Very good place to do business, certain business. Follow the right rules, is easy do very well here. But you, Gloria, you follow the wrong rules. The official peoples rules.

"And you know what is so funny? The official peoples, they can make whatever rules they want! They can say, 'You live in old lady's house and she don't want you there, you go to jail.' But no. I do my reading. They say instead, 'Old lady try and make peoples who pay nothing leave her house, *she* go to jail.' Is true! This is rules in New York, and your own 'representatives' make them! This is what you call 'democracy'! Taxpayers vote for their own houses be take away by peoples who pay them no money! Gloria, Gloria, you could not make this stuff up! Because you tell such stupid story in Honduras, no one believe you!

"Gloria, if you think even a small time, you understand everything you do not like now you ask for. How hard for Alonso to live in your house? I walk in. Bingo, Alonso live in your house. Same at the border: I walk over, bingo, Alonso live in your country. This is what I talk about with Nico. You are—I learn this word, because Alonso learn every English word he need, and this is most important word in America—you and your country are *pushovers*. I am thinking also that I do business here and I make my money very fast and then maybe I go. Because USA, soon it is finished. Weak, foolish country cannot last very longer. Even your president—he is shaky, babbling old man. You know how Americans say: *it is not a good look.*"

"Shut up, *y deja de decir tonterías,*" Domingo said. "*Estoy hambriento.*"

"*Sí, sí,*" Alonso said. "But tonight is special night. Tonight I think we order dinner more 'upmarket.' Nico, this restaurant Manchego. It is good, yes?"

"It is good, yes," Nico said flatly.

Alonso poked at his phone and solicited votes for tapas from the online menu. Naturally, the Polpo a la Gallega and Croquetas de Queso would be covered by the woman however nominally still the homeowner, so why not also get five orders of the Jamón Ibérico? Nico looked at Martine and his mother and nodded toward the kitchen. So drastically had the power balance shifted—though "balance" dubiously implied that the home team had any power at all—that he wondered if he should ask Alonso's permission to leave the room.

"So tell me," Nico asked Martine, once the trio had retreated for good measure to the porch. "How'd they know to expect the police? In time for Alonso to bone up and print those generic rental agreements? Did you warn them?"

"Of course not!" she exclaimed, suitably insulted. "Only . . . is possible . . .

I talk with my mother in San Pedro Sula. She worry about me. She no like this boys in the house. I comfort her. I say, tomorrow we call police. She say all police are bad. I say American police are different, they help people. So maybe Domingo hear me on the phone? Or *you* say something they hear, Nico?" she charged defiantly. "Or you, Gloria? Not only I know what we plan."

"What's this about Domingo not being your brother?" his mother said.

"Okay," Martine said, taking a deep breath during which she was probably deciding whether to brazen it out. "Is true. Domingo is my husband."

"Why on earth would you lie about that?" his mother asked.

Martine looked down. "I am shame. I tell you when I come here my husband beat me. I think you no respect me if you know I take him back. I am no so sure I respect myself. But Domingo is much better now than in Honduras. I tell him if he hit me, I tell Gloria, and Gloria know powerful people, and she report him to *La Migra*. But I want you think I am strong woman. Who will not put up with shit. This is a lie. I think maybe I put up with anything."

"In domestic violence cases," his mother said, "the average number of times women take back their abusers is *seven*."

There you go. Martine's instincts were infallible. That was the one explanation guaranteed to work like a charm with his mother.

"I sorry to say," Martine admitted, "I still afraid for him. He do not hit me. But I know what he do if he get angry. I have be careful."

"If you're so mousy," Nico said. "So under his thumb. Wouldn't you rat about our calling the cops to keep on his good side?"

"Everything I do is not for keep on Domingo's good side," she said, meeting Nico's eyes squarely. "Sometimes I do little things to defy him. This is how I keep my self-respect."

"*Little* things," Nico repeated.

Ordinarily, his mother might have detected the oddness of the dynamic, but she was still shaken by their failed rescue. "Skip the blame game. We're in a dilemma."

"No shit," Nico said. "Domingo's gone from beating Martine to beating us. Is this defeat, end of story? Now we live with these dirtbags the rest of our lives."

"There's always the eviction process," his mother said morosely.

"Housing court is a farce," Nico said. "That's because that moronic eviction moratorium for Covid went on for two years. People totally quit paying rent, and finally last year landlords could sue to get the deadbeats out. The backlog is ginormous. Alonso is right. We're playing by the wrong rules. The 'official peoples'' rules. We're prissy goody-goodies who think the nice policemen will save them."

"So what you say we do now?" Martine asked, her delivery a bit sneering, considering that she had to be the source of their tormentors' heads-up.

"Yes, sweetie," his mother said, turning to him as well. "Other than housing court, do you have any ideas?"

Nico threw up his hands. "Like what? Thinking outside the proverbial box is easier said than done. Our family was born in the box. We're so used to it we don't even know there's a box. You're better off asking Martine, honestly—who broke American immigration law and was rewarded with smoked almonds and Cornish-hedgerow bath gel. Now, can we at least use *my* Visa card to order something to eat? I wouldn't count on those guys sharing any of that ham."

Though it got chilly, they remained on the porch to be sure to intercept their order, lest the resident scroungers add it to their feast. His mother used the wait to get Vanessa's bewildered dismay and Palermo's enraged disbelief over with, during the latter eruption holding the phone a distance from her ear. Even once the meze arrived, the mood was sodden. Nico hadn't realized how utterly he'd been counting on the intervention of law enforcement, and he kicked himself for his credulity. Nationwide civil dysfunction got them into this fix, so it was retarded to expect the same dysfunctional mechanisms of due process to get them out.

Alonso wasn't the only one who could do online homework. Apparently, you could hire a private eviction company, but all its employees did was serve notices and file cases in housing court for you; they were *i* dotters and *t* crossers, and the exercise took just as long but cost twice as much. The more creative gambits for ridding your property of a two-legged infestation were problematic for owner-occupiers: blaring loud music throughout the premises, and they could never compete with Domingo's repulsive *punta*. Turning on the sprinkler system that the Ditmas house didn't have. (In the same face-spiting league, Nico could also burn the house down or blow it up.) Jacking up the heat to unendurable levels, which his energy cheapskate mother would never countenance, and Domingo had learned to work the thermostat by his second week. Introducing a pack of rats, which wouldn't necessarily follow the *tenants* out the door as if trailing the pied piper of Hamelin. Otherwise, most of what Nico turned up on eviction how-to sites detailed what not to do. By the inverted logic that Alonso himself had commended, that meant what not to do was what you did.

Switching off the utilities being illegal didn't therefore deter Nico in the slightest, but the prospect of himself having no internet while facing a reeking refrigerator full of spoiled food deterred him entirely. That left changing the locks.

It had not escaped Nico's notice that Martine had keys, therefore The Hatchet had keys, therefore all the intruders had keys. He'd also tracked a pattern. On particular days, the whole platoon marched off together on some unstated mission. The mass exodus always inflamed his imagination. He pictured the arrival of a big shipment of fentanyl and a dodgy exchange of product for money that required an armed security detail. Or, for the people smuggling arm of the operation, another busload who had to be put to work hooking or cooking meth to pay off their debts to the cartels. Or: unaffiliated competition who'd moved in on their territory and had to be taught a gory lesson. Whatever, but he was fairly sure that their houseguests didn't absent themselves as a group to pick up litter along the verges of the Prospect Expressway. What mattered was that when the whole contingent mobilized, they were gone all day.

So the next time the squatters took off as a band, Nico was on it. Thanks to the key fob that had never been restored to its shelf by the side door, for this adventure the Hondurans squeezed brazenly into his mother's Toyota Prius.

Paying through the nose for same-day service, he enlisted a local locksmith to switch out the security for the front door, side door, and external entrance to the basement. Taking a chance, he explained the situation honestly over the phone.

"You sure?" the guy pressed. "Believe it or not, you could go to jail for this."

"I'll take the risk," Nico said. He'd never imagined himself in such a role, but there was growing fury on the ground over migrants claiming unoccupied private property, and right now becoming a popular icon of civil disobedience held some appeal.

Unfortunately, once the locksmith went to work, it was impossible to hide the ploy from his mother, who was already, shall we say, *peeved* that their visitors had again hijacked her car.

"What in God's name is this about?" she challenged the locksmith, who'd just started on the side door.

"Ask your boy there," the guy said. "Though if you're the homeowner and you don't want me to do this, I'll stop right now."

"They're all gone," Nico told his mother. "I'm changing the locks."

"You make them mad," Martine warned.

"And what'll they do if they get mad?" Nico said.

"We no want we find out," Martine said.

"You worried once that our bringing in the police wasn't 'well thought out,'" his mother said. "In retrospect, maybe you were right. But this seems in the same ballpark."

"Okay," he said. "And *you* said you were tired of our being so passive."

"Maybe passivity beats activity that doesn't work," his mother said. "What will they do when their keys don't fit?"

"Only one way to find out," Nico said. "Worth a try, isn't it? We can pack their stuff in their duffels and pile them on the front walkway."

Though he wasn't about to inform her as much, chucking a squatter's possessions from the property was another move that could land you in jail. But in for a penny, in for a pound.

"Even if they can't get in," his mother said, "doesn't that also mean, with them out there, we can't get out?"

"We might need to batten down the hatches for a day or two, yeah," Nico admitted.

"You also keep out my husband?" Martine asked.

"How else will you and I live happily ever after?" Nico taunted, walking on the wild side. His mother didn't pick up. Her social radar was on the fritz. But his own radar was patchy, too. Like, the moment they gave the new keys to Martine, this whole exercise was probably pointless.

Early that evening, the three were hunkered in the kitchen when the Prius returned. Whatever that crowd had gotten up to, it had generated excitement, given the overlapping chatter spilling in the drive as they extricated themselves from the jam-packed car. When a key thrust into the side door jammed, the tonality of consternation required no translation. Through the filmy curtains, he could see one of them walk around toward the front, where the guy would inevitably encounter the duffels of their belongings mounded on the walk. As the man tromped up the front steps, Nico eased into a doorway from which he could peek into the foyer. Obviously, the fellow had no more luck with his old front door key.

That door was inset with vintage glass—beveled and etched in fleur-de-lis—his mother's attachment to which now proved unfortunate. The front walkway was lined with chunks of granite, one of which hurtled through the glass and landed some feet into the foyer. A hand clutching one of the pewter-and-crystal coasters that had disappeared from the living room neatly chipped out the remaining shards edging the pane, then reached down to release the chain and unlock the door with the interior latch. XVIII Forehead, aka Miguel, kicked the door open, then tripped back down the porch steps to retrieve his duffel. The guy didn't even seem mad. He was laughing. Nico was still thinking inside the box.

Without seeking his mother's blessing, Nico tried one last, desperate gambit. When that, too, failed, he turned to the resort most contemporary American men in their twenties would have turned to in the first place: Dad.

They met in a conventional restaurant for once, a midtown Italian joint on Sixth Avenue that served two-for-one martinis. They'd need more than one round. Interrupting only to ask simple factual questions, for once Nico's garrulous father shut up and listened.

Nico started where he'd left off at Thanksgiving: the so-called brother who'd moved in had never left and was really the husband. Though Nico's mother had made him promise never to tell her ex about the $30K, he explained about the kidnapped children in Honduras, at which point his father raised a skeptical eyebrow. "Hold it," his father said as Nico put the story on the 1.5X setting he used for podcasts. "She *paid* them? She *paid* the ransom!" Afterward, the freed kids popped back up with the mother—*maybe*. Then this blustery, good-timey guy Alonso appeared, who was kind of hip company but never asked if he could stay; though his mother couldn't bear the guy, she also couldn't stand up to him and tell him to get out. Then came the questionable hedge trimmer "rescue." (As it clouded the narrative rather, Nico judiciously edited out his week of fucking Martine; even if his father might have admired the red-blooded move, Nico still felt he'd been bamboozled, even if he still hadn't figured out exactly how.) But it was when Nico thumbnailed his mother's surprise party that his father really sat up.

"How do you know they're gang members?"

"It's not subtle. They're covered with tattoos. Face, neck, scalp. They don't try to hide it; they advertise it. They're like walking billboards. All the ink—it's to make everyone afraid of them. And it works. They take anything they want. They've turned the place into a flophouse. The feel is Mom and I only stay there at their sufferance."

"Have you called the police?"

Right, that story. Then the locks.

"Why didn't you tell me about all this months ago?" his father asked.

"Some of it happened drip, drip, drip. Everything got out of control only as of Mom's birthday. I was hoping I could handle it. Then I was hoping the police could handle it—which makes me a chump. Oh, and Mom said she did something 'rash' she now feels bad about."

"Like what?"

"No idea. She wouldn't say. But it sticks in my mind. Makes me edgy."

"This whole account makes me worse than edgy," his father said. "This is insane."

"One last thing," Nico said. "After the lock-change fiasco—and I ended up having to just give them all new keys, by the way—"

"Wait a minute. *You* copied the keys?"

"That's right. I personally copied the keys. Took the originals into the same locksmith and paid for the duplicates myself, the better to ensure that foreign ineducates with a likely proclivity for violence could more easily come and go in my own house. That's what it's like now. They love making me feel like a dickless toady with no self-respect. They got a big kick out of watching me supervise the replacement of the front-door glass. Their idea of fun."

"This probably seems like an anathema to you right now. But have you tried—"

"I may be way ahead of you, because I bet the answer is yes. I had Martine set up a meeting with her asshole husband, and I warned her off telling Mom about it. I offered the guy five grand if they'd clear off. You know, what one of the cops suggested: *cash for keys*. Domingo didn't bite. I upped the bid. Still nothing, even once I got to twenty-five Gs. Dad, I went up to sixty-seven K. That's all I had, which I made very clear. He still said no."

"You were offering him your own money?"

"I wasn't going to offer him Mom's money, what little there is of that. Not after the ransom debacle. It's all I have left of Granddad's inheritance."

"That's remarkably selfless, for you."

"Always nice to know my own father holds my character in such high esteem."

"Come on. Tell me the last time you made a sacrifice on someone else's behalf."

"It was on my behalf, too. But I've made a few sacrifices this last year. Not that I've gotten any credit for them."

"I'm worried these people now know you have sixty-seven thousand dollars at your disposal."

"Yeah, I thought of that. Couldn't be helped."

"But I'm especially worried they wouldn't accept such a large amount of money to leave. It may mean there's some other game on."

"Like what?"

"Can't say. But you only pass on that much money when you think there's another way you can make even more. I doubt these guys are just attached to your mother's retro decor."

"If we went any higher, I'd have to tap you for the top-up."

"I doubt that's the answer, and I'm not just being cheap. Even if we rounded up to six figures, something else is going on. I'm also nervous that you and your mother are in danger."

"Maybe. You know, like, after they took her Prius a second time? Mom used her spare key fob to drive it to a parking garage on Coney Island Avenue—out of their reach. I thought that was cool. But then Alonso 'requested' to 'borrow' it again. She stalled with, like, 'I'd rather you didn't.' Then he said, 'I'm afraid I must quite insist'—in that slightly formal show-off English he's started to speak. I mean, what could she do? Test him? Find out exactly what they do to you when you defy them? So, big surprise, she went and got the car. They haven't actually hurt us—yet—but they don't need to, and they know it."

"Even the law operates almost entirely through threat," his father said. "If everyone overnight started doing whatever the hell they wanted, the authorities would be helpless."

"If my *lived experience* is any guide, they're already helpless," Nico said. "I was super uncomfortable leaving Mom alone tonight. I still wonder if Martine might be buttering both sides of her bread, and while I'm not great protection, I hope I'm better than nothing."

"You're way better than nothing, but it sounds as if these people are out of your league."

"There's the play-it-by-the-book route, of course. Mom and I pack a bag and get out, maybe go stay with, like, Aunt Lauren in Phoenix. We hire someone to slap them with a notice and file for eviction in housing court."

"Housing court!" his father said. "That's like throwing a penny in a wishing well."

"After a year, or probably longer? Those guys would trash the place. I was wondering whether you have a better solution. I've run dry."

"I've got great connections with the few top right-of-center intellectuals left in this town. I've got no connections with the police."

"Aw, Dad. I thought Carlin Bonaventura was king of the world."

"Merely a duke," his father said modestly. "Besides, the cops are still a by-the-book route."

"The prosecutors let all the perps go anyway," Nico said.

"There may be a few advantages to my right-of-center connections. They're more likely to have access to . . . certain resources, and more likely to consider . . . certain courses of action."

"That was opaque."

"It was meant to be."

As his father drove him back to Ditmas, Nico reflected on how embarrassing this whole thing had become, and in that worst sense of embarrassment in front of himself. Until recently, he'd have casually described his own disposition as savvy and cynical, a commonplace self-conception that must have been especially seductive when you were young. Sheltered from reality by the comforts of comparative financial security, the previous generation always seemed to have grown up in a time that was unrecognizably simple, innocent, and stupid. You'd come of age in a time when everything was fast, complicated, and dirty. You could see the sordid business of how the world really worked, while Mom and Dad lived blithely in la-la land, blearily sipping their two-for-one martinis.

The flattering self-portrait was a load of horseshit. Just like his gullible mother and sisters, Nico couldn't get his head around the fact that a crowd of criminal illegal aliens had confiscated a New York taxpayer's legal property, and the cops couldn't do a damned thing. The props had been a nice touch, but he was pretty sure that Alonso could even have skipped printing out those fake leases. Had the miscreants merely claimed to be tenants, the police would have been obliged to take their word for it.

But genuine cynics wouldn't find that scenario astonishing in the least. Truly savvy sorts would welcome such rank injustice as satisfying confirmation of their bleak worldview. Instead, Nico was drowning in incredulity. Ergo, being clued-up and streetwise had been a pose, a vanity, a delusion. Imagining that he wasn't naive was proving the ultimate naivete. He'd apparently bought wholesale into the fair, orderly country whose boasting about these sterling qualities had drawn wannabe

Americans from all over the globe. Alonso had mocked all that jive-ass Coca-Cola land-of-the-free twaddle, but it seemed that Nico himself had accepted his country's shameless self-promotion at face value—fatal self-promotion, since scads of equally credulous foreigners now wanted a piece of all that mythical fairness and order, too. As for truly registering "the sordid business of how the world really worked," he was stuck developmentally at the age of four.

"You wouldn't happen to know a goodly handful of guys about your age who maybe grew up in rough neighborhoods?" his father was asking at the wheel. Nico wasn't especially interested in such propriety at present, but his father had no business driving after four martinis. "You know, who hang out with the kind of people mothers tell their kids to avoid?"

"I don't know a goodly handful of anybody," Nico said.

"Never mind, then. Just a thought."

"There's one positive thing to come out of this shitshow in Ditmas," Nico supposed. "This is the only time we've gotten together in the last five years when you didn't grill me about what I wanted to do with my life."

"Yeah, there's that. But now that you've brought it up . . ."

"Don't even think about it."

After pulling in front of the house, his father put a hand on Nico's shoulder. "Listen. If your mother weren't in need of your protection, I'd never let you walk back into that house. You're my only son. Sit tight, don't rub those creeps the wrong way, and I'll be in touch."

As Nico clambered from his father's SUV, he took his flush of warm, childlike trust—his relief in placing his faith in someone older and wiser, who would make the bad men go away; his gratitude for off-loading a crushing responsibility onto broader, more capable shoulders—as yet more proof that his spoiled, ignorant, middle-class head was up his ass.

Nico's wide-eyed filial trust might have been pathetic, but Carlin Bonaventura moved quickly when he needed to. Maybe there was still something to be said for men who embraced those trite markers of masculinity from which Nico had distanced himself since puberty: aggression, strength, confidence, anger, action, and violence capable of being channeled for good as well as ill. Within thirty-six hours, his father texted that Nico should put himself in a position where he couldn't be overheard one hour later to await a FaceTime call.

Yet that thirty-six hours had allowed plenty of time to schedule another tiny tragedy.

"Before you get started," Nico said at the appointed hour, having slipped behind a clump of hydrangeas in the far backyard, "Vanessa's at the vet. It's Kumquat. I think it's hopeless." What's hopeless? "You know how that dog has never liked me. Well, he likes certain Central Americans even less."

"Canine xenophobia." His father was seated in his home office, and Nico could make out titles on the bookshelf behind him: *The Madness of Crowds, The Coddling of the American Mind, The Diversity Delusion*. A couple of days' growth of stubble gave his face the rougher countenance of an outlaw.

"So when Vanessa came by to check on Mom this morning," Nico resumed, "she brought Kumquat, who started yapping at this Miguel guy to beat the band, and Miguel kicked the dog halfway across the kitchen. The dog slammed against the stove. Kumquat's alive but just barely, and I bet they'll have to put him down. Vanessa's totally fucked-up."

"If what I have in mind doesn't work, we can always resort to the ASPCA, then," his father said. "Occupying a family's home doesn't turn a hair on the bureaucratic head, but animal abuse! That could get the powers that be to come out guns blazing."

"So what's up?"

People who rely on force, his father explained, only respond to force. He'd lined up an intervention. But they'd never coerce the invaders into clearing off unless the persuaders arrived in numbers and well-armed.

"Like, with a gun?" Nico said.

"*Like*," his father repeated caustically, "with a whole lot of guns."

"You still own one?"

"Of course I do." Dad had organized a posse of six, including Vernon—not quite a match for an opposition of eight, but they'd have the advantage of surprise. Between them, they had Dad's pistol from Ditmas Park's Wild West days, two revolvers, a double-barrel shotgun, one bolt-action rifle, and, the cherry on the sundae, one proper semiautomatic assault weapon, an "AR-15," which for some reason Dad imagined would sound meaningful to him.

"Wow," Nico said. "Mom's right. You're hanging with reactionary far-right kooks."

"Don't look a gift liberation army in the mouth. Has to be some benefit to living in this crazy country. And these guys are my friends. When I told them about your circumstances, they were apoplectic."

"Don't tell me. They're immigration *restrictionists*."

"You could say that. If it were up to this crowd, the border'd be manned by the military, and anyone who put a toe over the line without permission would be shot on sight."

"They'd get on great with Alonso, then. Though I'm getting a better feel for why you and Mom got divorced."

"More hard-nosed realism on her part, and you and your mother wouldn't be in this fix."

"They're your friends. Don't take this wrong, but doesn't that mean they're . . . old?"

"They're in better shape than most kids your age."

"Vernon isn't, or last I checked. Around Christmas, his weight was on the upswing."

"The sine wave has descended again," his father said. "The other four are hunters and crack marksmen."

"I'm still picturing *The Over-the-Hill Gang* or something. And with all this packing heat, how does this thing not blow up into *Gunfight at the O.K. Corral?*"

"Interesting how for so many people violence is only vivified by movies. Filmmakers get their ideas from the real thing."

"Save the sociology for *Sanity.com*," Nico said. "I'm serious. What if someone gets hurt? New York will sock you in jail if you put a squatter's T-shirts on the lawn."

"There's such a thing as self-defense, even in this state. And we're not planning to shoot anyone. Even the most belligerent douchebags will hop to when they're on the wrong end of a revolver. Considering how obliging your antagonists become 'under the gun,' it's hardly amazing that there are more firearms in this country than there are inhabitants. What's really amazing is that everyone in America doesn't own five."

Nico wasn't about to say as much, but this bold talk was just that: talk. His father's most devastating weapons had always been words. Rather than envision the guy razing a room with bullets, Nico could more easily picture Carlin Bonaventura bursting through the front door with the automatic of his Latinate vocabulary, while Domingo and his pidgin English cowered in terror. *Rat-a-tat-tat! Take that! "Prestidigitation," all six syllables!*

"On the legal front," his father continued, "it should help we'll all be wearing ski masks."

"God, Dad, that's such a cliché."

"I'm not trying for a starred review in *Publishers Weekly*. Disguise is a cliché for good reason. If anything untoward goes down, which it won't, masks make positive identification by any witnesses unlikely. But, son, there's one question I need to settle. This woman Martine—should we be forcing her off the premises, too? You've sent mixed signals about her."

"She's sent *me* mixed signals," Nico said. Presumably, he was now endowed with the power to eliminate the very source of all his mother's troubles, not to mention his own. "Technically, she's legit. The city still pays her rent. And Mom's attached to her, no matter what the woman does. I don't see resolving the question of Martine's divided loyalties at gunpoint."

"But if she does have divided loyalties," his father said, "much less undivided loyalties in the wrong direction, treating her as if she's on our side could be a big mistake. Unless you can really vouch for Martine, we're going to have to treat her as a combatant for the other team."

"Just don't shoot her."

"I told you: we're not shooting anyone." Which was just what Philip Seymour Hoffman had claimed.

"Then why does it matter that your friends are 'crack marksmen'?"

"Well, do you think those bottom feeders in Ditmas are armed?"

"They have knives. I've never seen a gun, and I didn't come across any when I packed up their stuff for the lock-change debacle, but that still doesn't mean anything."

"We'll assume the worst, though I'm hoping if they had assault weapons, you'd have laid eyes on one by now. They're bigger than a bread box. Still, surprise will be crucial."

"Surprise even for Mom? Or should I warn her ahead of time?"

"No. She'd be horrified. She'd try to stop it."

Got that right. "What about letting her know something's up, without mentioning the G-word? I don't want her to have a heart attack. And if you're all in those dopey ski masks, she won't necessarily recognize you at first. She might think you're more bad guys."

"Mm, you've got a point. Just don't say *anything* about weapons. Think you could get your mother to leave the house?"

"Not easily. She hasn't left once since she was bullied into bringing the Prius back. Won't cede the territory. So she's stopped volunteering at Floyd Bennett Field. Doesn't go to yoga. Doesn't participate in pro-Palestinian marches. Won't meet with her book club, and ever since the car-crash birthday party, the book club won't come to our house, either."

"Your mother may be an idiot, but I hope she's canny enough to stay out of the way."

"What about me?" Acting on an unexamined impulse, Nico proposed, "Why don't I join you? Your 'intervention.'"

Nico wasn't sure whether to take his father's long pause as an insult or a welcome reprieve. Optimally, he'd reap credit for offering without getting the shakes and blacking out.

"I don't know," his father said. "You don't have any weapons training. When you don't know what you're doing, carrying can make you a danger to yourself."

"What if I don't carry a gun, then?" Which he didnotdidnotdidnotdidnot want to do anyway. "I could at least bulk up your numbers. Be the one who takes their knives away when you make them empty their pockets."

"Your mother would kill me, but . . ."

"Mom would kill you for this whole caper. If you don't get yourself killed first." The mention was too casual. The whole conversation had achieved a play-acting quality. Mock Nico's compulsive filmic allusions as he might, his father also seemed to be following a script that owed more to *Reservoir Dogs* than to the newspaper. What had Alonso said about Tarantino flicks? *Everyone fuck up. Everyone shoot everyone.*

"All right, I guess you can join us. But hang back."

"When is this supposed to happen?"

"Unless you warn me the targets have gone elsewhere? Tonight."

"Oh, fuck."

"The longer this involuntary house-share of yours carries on, the higher the likelihood something terrible happens, even without our *blandishments* to please go torture a different family. And when you're making a big move, it's better not to think about it very long."

"Are you sure this isn't completely insane?"

"In the days our *public servants* answered to the citizens rather than to the tender feelings of foreign criminals, how'd the police get scumbags out of property that didn't belong to them? By pointing guns in their faces. It ain't rocket science."

When Nico got off FaceTime after promising to bring along a set of the new keys—his father planned to hit all three entrances at once with two men apiece—this time his dazed disbelief didn't seem naive but rational. His father's *blandishments* were more commonly known as vigilantism, with a reputation for being ill-fated. What had possessed him to bid for membership of this superannuated SWAT team? Well, after years of *observation* from the sidelines, maybe he didn't want to be left out. Maybe he was tired of being thrown in with The Women. Maybe he so viscerally detested the desperados who'd taken over his family's house that he was even willing to violate his sacred *neutrality*. And maybe after five solid years of hovercraft steady-state—interrupted by a single week of soaring in a hot-air balloon, which had promptly shriveled to ground—he was ready for something to happen.

That afternoon, drawing his mother aside for a word to the wise was problematized by her constant phone calls with Vanessa over the touch-and-go situation with Kumquat. When the American Eskimo finally went into surgery, Nico confected horticultural alarm and urged her to the distant hydrangeas currently functioning as central command.

"What's this about noticing a disease?" she asked. "These plants are resilient. They've even recovered from Martine's buzz cut."

"I wanted to warn you that something's up tonight. So you don't flip out."

"What 'something'?"

"Dad has organized some sort of rescue. But I don't know the details."

"Is your father about to do something stupid?"

"I have no way of knowing," he said honestly.

"I suppose he finds it gratifying, how after I try to help a single vulnerable person, everything's gone to hell here?"

"I don't think so. He's worried about us."

"That's touching, in a way," she conceded. "With that new wife and everything, I'm impressed he gives any of us a moment's thought."

The "new wife" again. After how many years? "Just stay out of the way, that's all I'm supposed to tell you."

"Why didn't he contact me directly? Why are you the go-between?"

"I've been the go-between since the divorce."

"You see him more often than you tell me, don't you?"

"Only a little more often. It's not always a party. He gives me a hard time."

"Good for him. Someone should."

Nico nodded at the house. "This is a hard time."

"I'm sorry. For everything. I'd tell you to get your father to call off whatever wacky plan he's concocted, except . . . I'm anxious these people with the run of the house have everything they want, except for this one inconvenience underfoot." She met his eyes. "You and me."

Nico wrapped his arms around his mother, alarmed she felt so birdboned. "I've thought of that, too," he said into her hair. "That they might get sick of us. At least you pay the utilities and their takeout bills. I'm expendable."

As he let go, she said, "Not to me."

"So whatever Dad's cooked up, maybe it's worth giving it a go?"

"We can always hide in my room and lock the door," she said, an image Nico found unpalatable. *We* weren't hiding anywhere.

"One last thing," he said. "Don't tell Martine."

"Why?"

"Just don't."

When the two came back in the side door, Alonso said, "All these feelings over your bushes? The leaves have spots, and you cry!" They were being watched.

The strike team "taking the law into their own hands," as they say, was to mobilize at his father's West End apartment at 7 p.m. On the subway up, for once Nico didn't give a shit about migrants selling cups of unsanitary mango slices. When the B train stalled for ten minutes with the usual absence of explanation, he didn't fret, and when the car lurched into motion again, he was disappointed. His anomalous appetite for "something happening" had abruptly waned, because contentment almost definitionally involved nothing happening, and most things that happened were bad. Besides, now that he'd coasted so long in a state of stasis, the prospect of taking action of any sort had come to appear preposterous. Setting an event in motion seemed as remote as generating infinite, free energy from nuclear fusion.

He was so freaked out by his father's ludicrous liberation plan that as the #1 train climbed the Upper West Side he began to disassociate. Stepping from the car and ascending the stairs of the West Seventy-Ninth Street station, he felt robotically controlled by an outside force, as if he were a drone. When he entertained the notion of simply not showing up, only this sensation of unwillingly heeding an external power took the seductive option of absconding to an anonymous small town in the Midwest off the table. After all, if he was afraid of disappointing his father, he'd been disappointing his father for five solid years, and he was good at it.

Nico was the last to arrive at his father's slick, upscale three-bedroom; in perhaps deliberate contrast to his ex-wife's funky throwback taste, everything here was shiny, blank, white, and new. Three long black sacks already cluttered the floor of the foyer. He got bear hugs from his father and Vernon, who was at an age when losing weight made him look older. Introduced to the other four seated on sectionals in the living room, Nico was too dazed to remember their names, registering only that their grips were hearty and dry, whereas his own was anemic and damp. As instructed, everyone wore black. Two had the close beards he associated with outdoorsmen. Three of them were big guys, solid but broad. The fourth was shorter, though he had the pent-up compactness of a man who'd been overcompensating for his stature with a bench press for most of his life.

Himself sick to the back teeth of his associate membership of The Women, Nico might have anticipated that at last joining a company of men, "real" men, would be a relief. But he felt as estranged as he did around the kitchen table with his mother and sisters. Like his father, these guys were grown-ups. All contributors to *Sanity.com*, they were not only intellectual heavyweights, but also the type who could work a table saw, fell trees, and gut large animals. They were every bit as alien as the females prattling about "the patriarchy." No less than the gangbangers the men had convened to frighten off, they made him feel like a kid.

"Sure you want to include Nico in this operation, Carlin?" the bigger guy with a beard said. "Gotta look out for preserving the line."

"It was Nico's idea to come with," his father said. "I'm still of two minds, but his volunteering was courageous."

Not a word that had been applied to Nico in his entire life.

Vernon clapped a hand on Nico's knee. "Think of it as a blooding."

"Only metaphorically," his father said sharply. "The goal here is not to fire a shot. But also to get through to these punks that the family they've imposed themselves on has connections—connections no more constrained by legal niceties than they are. So they have to get the fuck out, and they'd better not come back."

His father distributed the ski masks from an Amazon multipack; in May, the demand from Aspen must had fallen off, but the criminal market for bargain winterwear was surely year-round. They divided up into teams for each entrance; Nico would join Vernon and his father at the side door. Glad to perform some function, Nico distributed the keys he'd copied that afternoon. "So do we let the goons take their stuff when they go?" he asked.

"Hell, no," his father said. "Think of it like a plane crash evacuation, and you're not allowed to grab your carry-on."

In that event, Nico might get his Mac back.

"Luckily, Rita's upstate paying some outfit a small fortune to shove a hose up her ass," his father added. "I shouldn't have to say this, but you will never mention this operation in my wife's presence, got it? It never happened."

Ritually, his father brought out a high-end single malt and seven shot glasses. "Only one," he said, pouring. They all downed the liquor together in one go, as if taking communion. Whiskey on an empty stomach gave Nico acid reflux.

As the group shouldered the armaments in the foyer, Nico fought a rising panic by making conversation. "Hey, Vernon, how's the documentary coming along?"

"In the can," Vernon said. "Colleen took the edge off until it wouldn't cut butter. You know, plenty of the *other side*, with shots of soulful children and wholesome parents. Even watered down? Can't sell it. Topic's too hot to handle. Oh, and I meant to tell you: Tyler's getting married."

"No surprise on either count," Nico said.

Once they'd all piled into his father's Lincoln Navigator, close quarters altered Nico's impression of his stoical companions. The guys with whom he shared the second backseat didn't seem quiet because they were naturally gruff. They were writers, they were talkers. They were keeping their mouths shut because they were wigging out. Their palms were dry ninety minutes earlier, but now their foreheads glistened, and the arm resting against Nico's detectably trembled. Anthropologically, the obligations of masculinity were relatively constant across cultures, but guess what was also constant? Artifice. Brandishing spears at lions, rushing German Gatling guns: the whole schtick was an act. The men in this car varied less in how brave and steely they were than in how talented they were at pretending to be brave and steely. Personally, Nico preferred to be honestly petrified.

Closing on their destination in Brooklyn, his father pulled the SUV over on Ocean Avenue. "I don't mean to insult you, gentlemen," his father said. "But safeties on until the very last minute." After pulling on rubber surgical gloves—and they'd only be taking care to leave no fingerprints if they were worried this operation might go pear-shaped—the men discreetly withdrew the weapons from the bags at their feet. The sheer physical reality of these things was stunning—their weight, their gleam, and the quality they exuded of being one product that American manufacturing still forged to a high standard. Yet these were stage props in someone else's play; they didn't belong in his life. Would it be worth the humiliation to stay behind in the car? When his phone rang, he jumped.

"It's our landline," Nico said. "Which no one ever uses. I'd better get it. Sorry."

"Nico? Wherever you are, you need come home."

"Martine?" He'd barely recognized her voice, whose timbre he hadn't heard before—not bouncy and chirpy in "Tickita Tickita" mode, not combative and taunting in come-fuck-me mode, but deep, and flat, and dead.

"Something happen," she said, as if hoisting the words with a shovel.

"What happened?"

"You come home now." Either she hung up, or the call dropped. Nico tried calling back, but no one picked up.

"Something's up," Nico announced to the car, "but I can't tell you what."

"Should we abort?" Vernon asked.

"That's not enough to go on," his father said at the wheel. "We've come this far. Whatever that's about, just be prepared for the unexpected."

So they proceeded, though the obscure phone call intensified Nico's conviction that movie plots in which plans like this one never played out as they were supposed to took their cue from real life. His father drew quietly in front of the house—for once not pounding with *punta* but silent. Inside, lights were on everywhere, which would usually have driven his mother nuts. Tugging on their ski masks, the men immediately appeared ridiculous; with its round "Oh, no!" mouth hole of cartoonish horror, the garment made anybody look like a moron. Convinced that the household would still recognize his tall, slight build and the same black jeans and sweatshirt he'd left the house in, Nico put on a ski mask, too. It was hot.

The posse opened the car doors on either side, softly-softly. They'd waited long enough that it was dark, so they could slip stealthily to their appointed entrances without attracting attention. Nico crept behind Vernon and his father to the side door. As agreed, Nico slid the key into the lock and very, very gently eased the bolt over. After texting the signal to the basement and front door parties, his father clicked off the safety on his pistol; Vernon readied his revolver. At a nod from his father, Nico pushed open the door, hanging back so that the two men training their weapons could advance first.

"Freeze!" his father said.

Silence. No commotion, no consternated Spanish. Nico eased up behind the two men, who had already lowered their weapons several inches.

Martine was sitting alone at the kitchen table. She didn't look surprised to see two men she'd never met burst into the house pointing guns at her, and she didn't look very interested. Her expression was dulled, her affect phlegmatic. The coils of her hair were matted, and the left side of her face looked dark and sticky. As usual, she was wearing one of his mother's bib aprons, but its Zabar's logo was badly stained. Underneath the apron, her favorite muscle T was less fire engine red than a darker, more inert brick. It was the color of her voice on the phone.

13

"What the fuck happened to your head?" Nico stage-whispered, tearing off the absurd balaclava. "Did Domingo hit you? I'll kill him."

Martine shook her head lifelessly. "No, no Domingo."

Just then, the basement detail came up the inside stairs. As they trained their rifles in a 180 across the kitchen and breakfast room, one of the men said quietly, "All clear down below." Nico could just detect the opening of doors as the third team, after sweeping the living and dining rooms, checked out the den, laundry room, and his mother's office.

"We're not here to hurt you," his father assured Martine quietly. His pistol was still raised, but at least not pointed at her head, which had seen enough damage already. "Where are the punks?"

"They go," she said. She looked at none of them.

"For keeps, or just to do another 'job'?" Nico asked sotto voce. Team #3 was now creaking up the main staircase.

"*For keeps?*"

It was an odd time for an English lesson. "I mean, did they go forever," Nico said.

"They go *for keeps*," she said.

Something nasty had obviously gone down here, during which his mother could presumably have locked herself in her room as she'd planned to. But if "the punks" had truly cut and run, why had she left Martine down here, all by herself, bleeding everywhere?

"Martine," he said. "*Where is my mother?*"

"CARLIN!" came from upstairs.

"Carlin, long as you got any bad guys covered, you better come up here!" his partner shouted down the main stairway. "But tell Nico to stay put!"

As his father told Vernon to keep an eye on Martine, Nico, never the most obedient of sons, was already on his way to the second floor. The shortest, most compact of their soldiers barred his way at the top of the stairs. "Better to stay away for now."

Nico pushed past him. "I have to find my mother."

The doors to the upper floor's spare bedrooms were all flung open, and at a glance as he passed they did seem denuded of the Hondurans' crap. His own room was still padlocked on the outside—his crude security measure. But the door of his mother's bedroom was also wide open.

The bigger guy with a beard stood blocking the doorway, what Nico could only assume was the "AR-15" dropped to his side. "Look, I'm sorry . . ."

Nico barged past him and froze.

"Did you do this?" he shouted. "You fuck! You fucking . . . fuck! Did you actually shoot her? I knew this would go wrong, I knew it!"

"Of course Frank didn't shoot anybody," his father said behind him. "We'd have heard it. . . . Oh, my God."

They both knelt on the slippery floor. Honor demanding the removal of the ridiculous ski mask, his father then went through the motions of checking his ex-wife's pulse, though the exercise was theater, something to do. Nico was pulling up her clothes. He had sometimes seen chance glances of his mother's breasts, even of her narrowly shaved pudenda if she'd stepped out of a shower and didn't know he was home, and while these moments raced with an energy of the hidden, the forbidden, they also felt wrong, and not in a Sunday school sense, but deeply and privately wrong. She was flung in a posture that made it difficult, but still he tugged her dress back over her shoulders and pulled the skirt down over the mysterious place from which he'd emerged twenty-seven years before. Yet even illicit glimpses of the torso he was frantic to cover were preferable to looking at her face—what was left of it.

"I hate to say this, son, but I'm pretty sure this is a crime scene," his father said. "You probably shouldn't—"

"Oh, since when did you care about, what did you call them?" Nico said. "*Legal niceties*. This whole thing was a stupid, crazy, cowboy idea, and I should have followed my gut. I knew it would end in a giant fuck-up, I knew it!"

"Sh-sh-sh," his father soothed, standing and pulling Nico up to wrap him in a suffocating embrace. "You can take it out on me if you want."

"Take *what* out on you?"
"That's what we have to find out."

Because Nico's first response was rage, wrath blocked any emotions that might have been subtler or more tender. His father led his son into the hallway, from which Team #3 had withdrawn to give them privacy.

His father grasped a shoulder in each hand and looked squarely into Nico's hot eyes. "There will be all too much time later for what you feel and why this happened and whom you blame. But for now we have to be very methodical, and very practical, and very steady. So nobody's going to indulge himself in making any kind of scene right now and becoming part of the problem. We're going to act like men."

Nico was already struggling to understand why he blamed his father and the guy's cockamamie "liberation army" for what they'd come home to. Plausibly, pointing the finger at the family's traditional culprit for the last ten years constituted a final filial tribute, because that's what his mother would have done.

Still, Nico shut up. This whole scene didn't make any sense, and ranting wouldn't clarify, much less rectify, a damned thing. With the numb stoniness that apparently made you certifiably male, he trudged behind his father down the stairs to join the rest of the vigilante eviction service in the kitchen. Each was still carrying his weapon, but at an embarrassed droop, like a failing erection. The absurd ski masks gave the scene the flavor of a *Saturday Night Live* skit that had fallen flat. Given the company's stunned sheepishness, Frank and his partner had clearly told the other three about their discovery in the upstairs bedroom. Only Martine was sitting down, having barely moved since they first burst in on her. The oozing left side of her forehead was starting to congeal. Her expression was blank.

"Before we go any further, Martine," his father said, "who did that?"

"I am no sure. It was accident." Then she added, "Sort of."

"Okay, no answer—yet. Next. Have you called the police?"

"I call Nico first. Is for respect."

"So you haven't. That's the next order of business, then, ASAP."

"Carlin," Frank said, touching his friend's sleeve. "We may all be licensed, but New York isn't an open carry state. This, um. Mission. I think it was righteous, but that's not the way the cops will look at it. How about before anyone calls 911, we get out of here?"

"You guys haven't really . . . affected anything, right?"

Frank shrugged. "Opened some doors. One in particular."

"You all did me a huge favor today," his father said. "Even if it didn't work out as we planned. There's no need to drag you guys into this. Martine? I'm Carlin. *That* Carlin. But even after a divorce people can still care about each other. My friends and I were only trying to help Gloria. I'll never forgive myself for arriving too late. But could you not mention to the police that my friends were here? They had nothing to do with what happened upstairs."

"Whatever." Martine's increasingly fluent English now extended to its most crucial vocabulary: words that meant absolutely nothing.

"I'd give you the keys to the Navigator," his father told Frank, "but I'm staying behind, and my not having the car could raise questions. Even an Uber would leave digital fingerprints. I hate to say it, but I think you guys should take the subway."

"Why don't I stick around, too," Vernon said. "Moral support."

"No, this is my family's heartache. Go home and tell Colleen what happened."

"But I have no idea what happened, bro," Vernon said.

"I'll let you know as soon as I do. Here, take my pistol, too; best they don't find it on me. Also"—his father handed Frank his key fob—"take the bags from the backseats. You're not getting on the B train with a naked AR-15 unless you want the car all to yourself."

For Nico, it was up for grabs whether his father's capacity to be "methodical" in these circumstances was admirable or chilling.

Once Frank returned the fob, the five musketeers hugged Nico and his father hard, said how sorry they were about how things had turned out, and offered to help however they could in the coming days. They seemed like solid guys, and Nico was sorry to see them go, because once it was just his dad, himself, and Martine the vibe in the kitchen was raw.

"Okay," his father said, after no one spoke for a long minute. "Time to call the cops."

"I call them," Martine said, dragging herself upright to retrieve the much-neglected landline radio phone. "Like a real American."

Thereafter, Carlin Bonaventura called first Palermo, then Vanessa, like a real father.

By coincidence, the first duo to show up, siren wailing, was Bower and Patterson—who, if they were feeling any sense of culpability after having left the victim at the mercy of eight scumbags who'd invaded her home, did a good job of keeping their remorse to themselves. The pair went briskly upstairs to survey the scene in the homeowner's bedroom, to which Nico couldn't face return. There was no need. The picture of that figure on the floor was recurring in a mental strobe with a frequency that triggered seizures in epileptics.

After cryptic condolences, the policemen instructed the three of them not to touch anything, not upstairs, not anywhere. On establishing that the older gentleman dressed in black was the ex-husband, the cops shared a flickered glance.

"No, this isn't more domestic violence by an 'intimate partner,'" Nico said, heading them off. "And, no, my dad isn't another bitter ex out for revenge. I met him in Manhattan at 7 p.m., and we've been together ever since. He drove me home. I got this weird call from Martine on the way. She said 'something had happened' but didn't say what. So my dad was concerned and came inside with me. My mother was already . . . like that."

The officers would require more convincing. Cops leaped to trite conclusions because they encountered the hackneyed nature of human relations fifty times a week.

"That's correct," his father said, shooting Nico a look. "I don't get to see my son very often—not nearly often enough."

He and his father hadn't compared notes in advance, so Nico had now impressed the man twice in the same day—by volunteering to join the, as it turned out, bizarrely superfluous SWAT team and now by ad-libbing a persuasively simple, pared-down version of events, no guns.

"Ma'am," Bower said to Martine, "that's a nasty head wound you've got. You want me to call an ambulance?"

"Sir, Martine's the only one here who has the faintest clue what went on up there," Nico objected. The prospect of their sole witness being spirited away while he and his father were left in a state of shocked, idiot ignorance for the rest of the night was intolerable.

"I don't care," Martine said lifelessly.

Vanessa burst through the door, sobbing. Nico was envious. He felt physically run over by a truck, but he'd yet to cry. Maybe he had the makings of a man after all. Accepting the part, he held her. Her face was red and swollen. For minutes, she couldn't talk. The officers hung back, as if waiting out a cloudburst under an eave.

"I—I want to see her," Vanessa finally got out.

"No, you don't," Nico said. "You'd never get it out of your head. And she wouldn't want you to see that."

"He's right," their father said. "Preserve the memory of your real mother."

"Oh, Daddy!" She hadn't called him *Daddy* since she was a kid, and she hadn't even laid eyes on the guy since Nico's college graduation. Still, Vanessa threw herself into their father's arms. He was the only parent she had left, and loyally maintaining the sororal boycott would no longer gratify its intended beneficiary. Vanessa was the sole member of their family who was emotionally competent. The aptitude was underrated.

Palermo, however, was temperamentally more akin to her brother. With Byron in tow, she came in crying, all right, but the tears were mean and squeezed. "What the fuck!" she exploded. "What is this, a *murder?* In *Ditmas Park?* You've got to be kidding me! Who did this? Was it one of those dirt birds the cops were too fucking lazy to clear out of here?" Even if she'd known those self-same officers were five feet away, she wouldn't have contained herself.

Meanwhile, the homicide crew had just arrived, in white coveralls, beekeeper-type hoods, and overslippers. The *Ghostbusters* gear not only preserved the forensics, but also protected the detectives from the excitable strangers in the kitchen, for whom the "suspicious death" was more than a case number. The team swished through the side door with cameras and kits and spoke only to one another.

"I mean, Jesus, all she was doing was trying to help people!" Palermo carried on. "And this is her thanks? What, are we supposed to console ourselves with that saccharine bullshit about how she was just 'too good for this world' or something?"

"Kiddo," Byron said gently, stroking her arm. "Railing won't bring her back."

Palermo shook her husband off. "Oh, God, no, we're civilized, we're middle class, we have to keep our voices down and worry about the neighbors and offer all these cops cups of tea, right? Just because of the minor matter that my mother is *dead*, that my mother has been *shot in the head*, there's no reason to get *upset*, there's no reason to be *unseemly*, there's no reason to . . ." She ran out of *no reason to*s.

"Honey," Byron said, "why don't you sit down?"

"I don't want to sit down! I never want to sit down for the rest of my life! Leave me alone and stop trying to . . . to be calm and nice! This is not nice! I mean, what the fuck, what the *fuck* happened? And what is Dad doing here? No one has told me anything! And where are all the little gangbangers? Didn't want to stick around for the fun?"

"No. They didn't." Impassive and motionless, Martine had hitherto said almost nothing. Her sponsor's proclamations to the contrary, the stark fact that she was not a member of the family exiled her to ancillary status, and they'd all been ignoring her. Though that was about to change.

"Can we get this straight, for the record?" Bower said wearily. "Only Ms. Salgado was present. None of you others were here when the incident occurred."

"The *incident*," Palermo spit out. "For pity's sake. You sound like you get your lines from *Law and Order*."

"Palermo, just for now, could you cool it?" Byron said.

"*Cool it?*" Palermo repeated incredulously.

"*Just* for now," Byron said again. "You can go full-tilt King Lear afterward, but these policemen have a job to do."

"That's correct," their father was telling Bower. "Only Martine was here."

"Ms. Salgado," Patterson said. "We could get you some medical attention and take your statement later at the precinct."

"I get it over now," Martine said.

"Only if you sure you up to it," Patterson said. "And you need a translator?"

"I work my English," Martine said. "You say if you no understand."

"Was it just you and Ms. Bondaventure in the house, then?" Bower asked, checking that his bodycam was running.

"Bonaventura," Nico clarified, and spelled the name out. "When it was just you cops not doing shit to help our mother last time"

"When she *begged you* to save her from a bunch of thugs!" Palermo chimed in.

"Then you could call her whatever you wanted," Nico said. "But now I assume this is a murder investigation? You'd better get her name right."

The extremity of the situation was freeing. Nico didn't fear offending these officers or even attracting suspicion that he was somehow implicated in a violent crime. While finger-pointing didn't make him feel any better, these guys deserved more blame than his father did.

"Look, pal," Bower said. "Sorry about your mother, but maybe watch the mouth. I repeat, Ms. Salgado, was it just you and Ms. *Bonaventura* in the house?"

"No," Martine reported. "My husband, Domingo, was here, and his . . . crew."

"And what business is your husband in, ma'am?" Bower asked.

For a moment she displayed a flicker of sour amusement. "How you say—*this and that.*"

"They were day laborers? Handymen?"

"Very handy," she said.

"Can you just tell us, step by step, what happened?" Patterson said. "Take your time."

At last Palermo stopped pacing and raking her fingers through her hair and sat down. Everyone else but the officers sat down. Vanessa never stopped crying, but they were already used to the metronome-steady lurching of her breasts; she might as well have had the hiccoughs. They all pulled their chairs back from the table, as if clearing the stage for a show.

"This morning," Martine said, "Vanessa come see Gloria and bring her dog, Kumquat. Is cute and puffy and very white. Vanessa love this dog. Is like her baby. Because she no have real baby. But Kumquat is loud, and Kumquat no like my husband's *crew*. And this dog really, really no like Miguel. So it bark and bark and bite at Miguel's foots. Miguel get sick of the sound and the biting. He kick it—hard, to other side of the kitchen. Vanessa, she get upset. There is blood on the white dog. Miguel is no sorry. I think he is only sorry that the dog is no dead. Vanessa cry, and I tell her, please get Kumquat out of here—or Miguel will finish what he start."

"That sounds sad, and I'm sorry to interrupt," Bower said. "But is the dog relevant?"

"*Sí*. Is part of story. Vanessa take Kumquat to dog doctor. Gloria is worry, because the dog no be okay, Vanessa have her heart break."

"I thought broken hearts grow back stronger," Nico said, meeting her eyes.

Martine looked down. "I no think dead dog make Vanessa strong."

Vanessa loosed one fuller sob, but that was it; Kumquat's death had been overtaken by events.

"So Gloria talk on the phone to Vanessa every hour," Martine resumed. "While she keep talk all afternoon, I wash laundry."

"Do we really have to do the laundry?" Bower muttered.

"*Sí*," Martine said, shooting the guy a glare. "We 'have to do the laundry.' I wash all laundry in this house before *los pandilleros*. After, I also do laundry of *los pandilleros*. Seem I do laundry all day. I collect from bedrooms. Before I put laundry in the washer, I check pockets. One jacket, made of jeans cloth, is very heavy. I find big lump in pocket. It is gun. Small, for gun. Make easy carry."

Finally, the policemen looked interested. "A handgun, then," Bower said. "Could you tell if it was loaded?"

"In Honduras, a gun is no *ooh-ooh* scary thing. We see guns all the time. So, yes. I know this gun is loaded."

"I doubt you can tell me," Bower said. "But you didn't notice what make it was?"

"SIG 365 nine-millimeter," she returned smoothly.

"So what did you do with it?" Patterson asked.

"I can put back in bedroom. But after Kumquat, I have bad feeling. Or more bad feeling, because I have bad feeling for days. *Los pandilleros*, they no hurt Gloria and Nico. But I see they tired of Gloria and Nico. They start find los gringos *annoying*. So I keep the gun, and put jacket in the wash. Maybe, I think, I put the gun back in the bedroom, but for now, no—because this bad feeling. With the gun I can make Gloria and Nico safe. The Zabar's apron I wear in the house have big pockets. I put the gun in big pocket."

"Did you know how to work the safety?" Bower asked.

"Of course," Martine said disdainfully. "Then Gloria say the dog doctor make Kumquat asleep so they cut it up."

"Veterinary surgery," Nico said.

"Nico go meet his father in Manhattan. Then Gloria get last phone call from Vanessa. Kumquat die in this . . . surgeny. Gloria try make Vanessa feel okay for long time. But when Gloria get off phone, she go crazy. Miguel, he drink beer at the table with other boys. Gloria yell and yell at Miguel. She call him animal and sick and stupid and other names. She say, what he have against little dog, who never hurt him, only bark. She say, Vanessa be never same. She say, Miguel and all the other boys, they have no feeling, they not people. She act disgust. Gloria is so angry, she is no afraid of Miguel. But this is mistake."

Martine lifted her bowed head and looked at Patterson. "I know this boys. Gloria yell in English, and Miguel speak no English. But there is sound in her voice he understand. In Honduras, boys like Miguel, they are little kings. Woman there, we keep mouth shut. We make fun of them, with each other, but never when boys are there. So Miguel, he is not used to woman shout to him. The sound in Gloria's voice is disrespect. This is language he speak. This is language they all speak. Is the most bad thing you can hear or say. Also, Gloria say this voice to him in front of other boys. They also speak no English, but they also speak this language that is same *en español*. Miguel embarrass with his friends. He let woman talk at him like dirt.

"I am behind kitchen counter, and I watch. I see look on Miguel's face. Better for Gloria he yell back, and call her names back, but he no yell back. He just get this look. The other boys at the table think Gloria yells are very funny. But not good funny, for Miguel.

"Gloria is still mad, and she go upstairs, bang, bang, bang with her foots on the steps. I think she want be alone in her room. But I see Miguel go upstairs also. I think for now I stay away, but I get more bad feeling.

"After no long time, I hear scream upstairs. I run upstairs. The door to Gloria's bedroom is open. I run down hall. Miguel tear Gloria's dress. He lie on top of her on the floor. He try keep his hand on her mouth. She still scream and try bite his hand. He open his jeans. He pull up Gloria's dress. Is easy to see what he want. He make her pay for disrespect. He show her who boss. The boys downstairs can hear the scream and fight, but I know they no care. They only think Gloria get what she ask for. They think what Miguel do to her is funny.

"Gloria is very good to me. Gloria give me home in America. Gloria do big help for me. Now I do help for Gloria. I turn off safety. I point the SIG at Miguel and say if he no stop I shoot. He shout, like, 'Fuck, Martine, which side you are on?' and 'Put the gun down, you stupid bitch'— but *stúpido coño* mean more like 'stupid cunt.'"

Martine sighed and her posture sagged. "I no know what different I do when I look back in my head, but this gun point, is no so smart. Now the boys know I have the gun, they can take my gun. Domingo will be mad I have the gun. They will think I stealed the gun. Miguel is still on top Gloria, and her clothes half off. But at least he stop open his jeans."

"Sweetie, you tried to keep our mother from getting raped," Palermo said. "I don't see how you can look back on that as a mistake."

"Is better you be rape and alive or no be rape and be dead?" Martine said. "I am no so sure I do Gloria favor."

"Miguel stopped assaulting Ms. Bonaventura, then," Bower said. "How did the situation get so out of hand?"

"Alonso is in the bedroom across the hall—" Martine said.

"Who is Alonso?" Bower asked.

"Alonso is *crew*," Martine said.

"You have a last name?"

"I no know last names. Even first names, they are maybe fake."

"Is yours?" Bower asked. "Is your husband's?"

"Let her finish the story," Patterson said.

"Alonso come see what is all this shouts," Martine continued defeatedly. "He see I point the gun at Miguel, and he try take my SIG 365 away. But is more hard than he think. Martine is very strong. We fight. Miguel still hold down Gloria on the floor. I am no sure just how it go, but Alonso get the gun from me after time. So I think Alonso was one who push the trigger. Maybe he no want push it. But the SIG shoot and hit Gloria in her face."

Vanessa's weeping accelerated.

"I am crazy," Martine went on. "I run to Gloria. I know I no can be crazy. I take my phone from other apron pocket and start call 911. Then I feel hard hit on my head"—she touched the matted hair—"here. The pain is bad. Before I understand, Alonso hit me again with hand end of the gun. I have black feeling, like time go away. I wake up, and there is no Miguel, no Alonso, no gun, no my phone. But Gloria is there. Blood is everywhere. I check, and I call her, and I listen to her mouth for the breath, but I think then that Gloria is dead."

"You think 'Alonso' shot Gloria on purpose?" Bower asked.

"I no can know," Martine said.

Well, Nico thought, she always was the queen of ambiguity.

"So where is Alonso now?" Bower said. "And Miguel—or whatever their names are?"

Martine's expression twitched. Under whatever degree of duress, no storyteller likes to get the turning points out of order. She resumed where she cared to. "I walk soft downstairs. I hear Domingo meet with his crew in the kitchen. I listen from dining room."

"And how many of these people are there?" Patterson asked.

"You should know," Nico said. "Last time you were here, you left all eight of them behind to keep terrorizing us. If you'd done your jobs then, my mother would still be alive." Were his mother still alive, she'd have upbraided him for the insolence. But she wasn't.

"Mouth," Bower said.

"I hear Alonso in the kitchen," Martine said. "He say: in Honduras, with dead person, you pay money to police, and then police do nothing. Also, you pay the money only if anyone care about some old lady, and in Honduras no one care about some old lady. Here in New York, he say, the police also do nothing about almost anything. They let all people rob, and take old lady's house, and they do nothing. But Alonso say killing is different, and the police maybe care about this old lady. Alonso say no one believe migrants if they say they shoot old lady in accident. Domingo and Alonso agree is time they leave Ditmas. They tell the boys pack up now.

"Domingo leave the kitchen and see me in dining room. I think he no care my head is hurt. He seem mad at me. He say all this my fault. If I let Miguel teach Gloria the lesson then nobody get hurt. Now is big mess, because I don't keep to my business. Then he say I need pack up my stuff, because we go.

"I say no. I say I no can leave Palermo, Vanessa, and Nico. I say they be sad. He say, *Whatever*, in English. He say, *Suit yourself*, in English. He say, I talk to police? They kill me."

"*Are* you talking to the police?" Patterson asked.

"What you think I do now?"

"Your husband threaten your life," Patterson said. "So you telling us the truth?"

Martine rolled her eyes. "How you know my husband threat my life? I tell you. You no believe what I say, you no believe that also. Okay, I finish? I almost finish. *Gracias*.

"I think Domingo no care if I come with him. I think maybe he go back to hit me, and I have enough of this. So I stay. In small time, a van come in driveway. Domingo have many friends, many *conexiones*. All the boys and their bags, they get in. They drive away. I call Nico on the landline. I think he need know first. But is too hard to say about Gloria on the phone. In minutes he come with his papa. They see Gloria. Nico cry. I call police."

Her ending was sporting on two counts. Nico hadn't cried, and the embellishment was a not especially creative but complimentary touch. And she'd made no mention of the pointless amateur SWAT team. His father not having said a word during the entire interview suddenly made sense. He didn't want to incriminate himself or his friends, but he also didn't want to get caught lying to the cops if Martine blabbed.

"Have any idea where these guys might have gone?" Bower asked.

"No," Martine said.

"You hear from them since?"

"No. They take my phone."

"Will you let us know if you do hear from any of them, even your husband?"

"*Sí*," she said. "But this no happen. For Domingo, I am bad, *traidora*. I point gun at Miguel. He no trust me no more. And you never find any of this boys. Here is big country, big city. They are good at this. They are better at this than you." She delivered the determination with satisfaction.

The police took a much shorter statement from Nico, who was obliged to admit that he'd rearranged his mother's clothing to protect her modesty. His father apologized, saying he was aware the scene shouldn't have been tampered with, but asking the policemen to imagine how they might feel coming on their own newly deceased mother in a state of undress. Nico could no better identify the men who'd absconded from the premises than Martine. Eager to wash their hands of a "squatting" dispute, these same officers hadn't even recorded the "tenants'" names, doubtless as fabricated as the "leases." Hardly inclined to preserve precious memories of the high old times the family had enjoyed with their uninvited visitors, Nico found no photos of the dickheads on his phone. His mother's surprise party had been such a catastrophe that no one had organized grinning group shots of the gate-crashers who ate all the shrimp.

His father's statement was shorter still, confirming Nico's version of events and embellishing as little as possible. Obviously, there was no reason to complicate the lives of the five decent men who'd arrived armed to the teeth to rescue their friend Carlin's ex-wife.

Everyone was banished from the house until law enforcement finished gathering forensic evidence. She might have dared a dash of "lipstick" trim, but the garish yellow police tape soon to beribbon her home's exterior doors would clash with Gloria Bonaventura's retro sensibility. Martine, Nico, and his father were advised not to leave the country.

Palermo and Byron offered to take Martine to NewYork-Presbyterian on Seventh Avenue to get patched up and checked for a concussion. Vanessa asked if she could drive to the hospital behind them; she didn't want to be alone. Palermo invited Martine to stay in Corona for now. His father said of course Nico would stay at his apartment in Manhattan.

Considering, the first few days with his father were all right. Taking time off from *Sanity.com*, Dad successfully discouraged his "new wife" from cutting her spa break short, the better to console his shattered son one-on-one. Dad paid for everything, including Nico's new set of clothes. They went to restaurants with almost normal food. Dad was scrupulous about saying only complimentary things about his ex until Nico implored him to lighten up on the sanctification already. Nico told his father about coming across that after-dinner footage of his mother finally laughing at herself over all that nonsensical trans crap. His father claimed that he used to be able to cajole her out of reflexive liberalisms all the time—she kept an eye outside herself, alert to hypocrisy or absurdity, especially her own—but when the times hardened and grew humorless, she hardened and grew more humorless with them. Still, she was a good woman, he said, and he didn't say that in the spirit of retroactive beatification. Her empathy wasn't all fraudulent. Haltingly, Nico explained that he and his mother had gone through a prolonged period during which she'd renounced him, but she came around near the end. Why, she *almost* admitted that the migrant sponsorship had been a mistake. She apologized. She actually said of her treatment of him, *I may have been a little unfair.* She . . . He allowed himself a tear or two, because his mother was dead and the only unacceptable reaction was not to have one. "She reached out and held my hand." It's biblical language, his father said, but liturgy has its place—because what you mean, he said, was the relationship was left in a *state of grace*.

All this *bonding* took a hit when Rita came home. She was a thin, pretty, stylish woman with a mysterious potbelly that probably drove her insane. She was one of those people who could be good fun, so long as she was getting her way. Having borne no children by choice, she doubtless disliked inheriting three through marriage. She'd never chafed at his sisters' decade-long boycott of their father's company. As for Nico, on the rare occasions they'd seen each other, her protestations that he really must stay for another drink only kicked in once he'd gotten his coat on. A bit of a prima donna, in social situations she delighted in holding court as a raconteur. She liked being the center of attention.

For Rita, then, this situation was not ideal. She wasn't even a secondary character in a story that made the *New York Times*—run reluctantly, no doubt, because the anti-immigration *New York Post*, in which his father had a column, made much political hay from the failure of the "deadly" Big Apple, Big Heart initiative (which was wrapping up anyway; with weak take-up and high overhead, the program hadn't proved an economy after all). Also, Rita loved splashy gestures of elective magnanimity, but she thrashed against nonstop niceness that tragic circumstances made compulsory. She didn't care for Gloria's death having desolated her husband after a divorce of such long standing. All told, with Rita back home a clock was ticking, and Nico planned to return to Ditmas at first opportunity.

Nico regularly got together with his sisters, though Palermo always bringing Martine along made these gatherings less therapeutic. Martine was prone to bouts of if-onlys. She had continually to be reassured that she'd merely been trying to rescue their mother from a horrific sexual assault, and that it wasn't her fault she didn't ultimately prevail against a hefty assailant like Alonso. Whether the crime was murder, manslaughter, or negligent homicide, Alonso was the culprit, Miguel an attempted rapist. Walloped upside of the head, Martine was simply another victim. For Nico, Martine's contrite hand-wringing grew wearingly one-note, and her immoderate mournfulness seemed misgauged for a "friend of the family." But when he alluded on the phone to the theatricality of Martine's bereavement, Palermo had no idea what he was talking about.

On the other hand, a subtle separation was developing between Martine and the two young women who'd so recently regarded themselves as her closest friends. For Palermo, nothing tested comradery like sharing a small apartment with no guest room for weeks, and being underfoot day and night cheapened the currency of anyone's company. Martine had no means of covering her expenses, and Corona Construction provided her hosts limited disposable income. Although Vanessa was the usual fount of generosity—she arrived at their first meeting at Manchego with a new iPhone for Martine that she couldn't afford—Nico detected a rare strain in his younger sister's kindness. Even her outpourings of undying affection for her *mejor amiga* felt, if not forced, then at least pro forma. Meanwhile, Vanessa's appetite for reminiscence was inexhaustible, while Nico and Palermo eventually grew desperate to talk about something, anything, besides their mother. Television! Rita's mysterious potbelly!

Alas, Martine would always chain the three siblings to a chapter of their lives that sooner or later they'd need to close. On WhatsApp, Nico had even mooted the proposition that it might be time for Martine to find her own place, and both sisters were surprisingly open to the idea. Without ever saying so expressly, the trio seemed to concur that their family's obligation to care for their adoptive ward had come to a contractual conclusion. The price the Bonaventuras had paid for fulfilling that contract had been extravagant. As Vanessa confessed on WhatsApp, "This has been so depleting . . . She's such a reminder . . . There's going to come a point where I just can't bear to think about it for a while." Looking ahead, Nico bet his sisters would keep up with Martine for a bit, if only to be able to tell themselves that their relationship with the Honduran had been genuine, but they'd both gradually lose touch, and be tacitly relieved to lose touch.

Finally, Nico got word that in two days the cops would graciously allow them back into their own family's property.

When the foursome reconvened at Manchego that evening, he was glad to deliver the good news but irked that Palermo had once again brought Martine. The whole point of getting together tonight was to ensure they were all cool with each other in advance of the meeting with their mother's lawyer the following afternoon. They could air any fears about the content of their mother's will and approach the depressing and fraught occasion in a state of sibling solidarity.

Their parents were even-Steven types, and aside from a few sentimental objects that might be bequeathed to particular heirs, like the pewter-and-crystal coasters to which Vanessa was partial but that had vanished into a Honduran backpack, they expected the estate to be divided evenly three ways. Yet one issue loomed logistically large. The biggest sentimental object was no easier to carve into thirds than Solomon's baby: the Ditmas house. In which a certain sibling had been living. Nico had entertained offering to pay his sisters rent, in the hopes that they'd refuse his money. But this wasn't a discussion they could conduct in Martine's presence. She was a penurious noncitizen from a shithole country, and she had no assets and no income other than that meager Refugee Cash Assistance. That was hardly an appropriate audience for talking turkey about the dispensation of a property worth $2.5 mil—if not, by now, worth even more.

Still, Martine's presence did allow him to raise the other issue that was . . . awkward.

"I admit it's going to feel creepy," Nico said, tracing a forefinger around the rim of his pint. "But at Dad's place, I've worn out my welcome and then some. So I guess, for now, I'll head back to Ditmas." He added to his sisters, "At least, if that's okay with you guys."

"Honey," Vanessa said, "sure you can handle that? Going back could be traumatic."

"I won't park my flag in Mom's bedroom or something. I was thinking of maybe"—he looked at Martine—"moving back into the basement."

"You want I move my things?" Martine said carefully.

"Yeah, I guess so . . ." Nico said.

In a dense microsecond, he fast-forwarded through an enticing scenario:

His sisters are in no hurry to cash out the property, an investment that will only rise in value. With their blessing, he and Martine both move back in as official caretakers of the building and grounds. They have the run of the house, except this time his mother is never returning from Phoenix. Once again they fall into a routine of having dinner together, and one night they lock eyes—only this time everything's on the level. Domingo's out of the picture, but no one's pretending he was never in the picture, and whatever side hustles Martine has going are on the table, too. As a lazy, unproductive member of society, Nico is anything but Mr. Perfect, but she's been running her own games, so maybe they deserve each other. The sex was good last time, and they allude to it casually, like no big deal. Before he reaches for her, Nico lays it out: the only rule is whatever she gets up to, she has to tell him about it, and she has to tell the truth.

This is where the frame froze. Because you don't make such deals with liars, who can always *claim* they're telling the truth, and then where are you? As for his estimation of this woman's character, the stakes had risen from a thirty grand ransom payment to, potentially, murder—which, to put it mildly, was a bridge too far.

"But I'm not suggesting you move, like, upstairs," Nico finished. "More like . . . out."

Given Martine's stunned silence, she hadn't expected to be jettisoned from her cushy setup in the basement. She might have plugged the same scenario into her own virtual reality headset, on the assumption that she could crook a finger and Nico Niñito, the lonely, artless incel upstairs, would come running.

"The Big Apple, Big Heart program is over," Nico went on. "Monthly payments from the city will no longer cover your rent and food. And it'll be freaky enough to be back there. I'd rather come to terms with what happened to my mom on my own."

"Only you, in house with five bedrooms?"

"Six, if you count the basement," he said. "I can wake up every morning deciding which john to take a shit in."

"And where I stay?" Martine asked.

"Up to you. Sponsorship was our mother's idea. Your accommodation is no longer our problem." If only this city could tell its two hundred thousand recently arrived tourists for life the same thing.

"Sweetie, I could help you look for a place," Vanessa offered. "For now, maybe just a room somewhere? Like, with an elderly widow who needs some extra cash."

Martine was clearly picturing this marvelous cupboard of a rented room with a mildewed mattress on the floor and a dementia patient who smells weird in the kitchen.

"I don't make no money," Martine said. "How I pay rent, buy groceries?"

"According to our mother," Nico said, "migrants are incredibly resourceful. She said you're 'problem solvers' and naturally 'resilient.' So I'm sure you'll think of something."

"You qualified for a work permit back in February," Palermo said. "Wait tables, wash dishes?"

"*Sí*," she said noncommittally.

"Also," Palermo added, "Byron and I have been super happy to put you up in Corona . . ."

"You want I find new place also," Martine filled in.

"We just don't have much room, and any couple needs, you know . . . time on their own."

Martine was surely disconcerted the sisters didn't campaign for allowing her to stay on in Ditmas. But pure altruism is a weak driver. Good works rely heavily on ulterior motives.

Nico gave Martine a week to find somewhere else to live.

"Thanks. That is very bighearted," she said, the deadpan striking an opaque note.

He promised not to move back in until she'd retrieved her things. Privately, he wasn't about to risk cohabitation and so tempt a rerun of playing house.

The cops still hadn't arrested anyone for the "wrongful death," and the case remained open. Maybe they put out APBs for "Alonso Somebody" and "Miguel Whoseits," but with no pics or surnames the gesture would have been pure paperwork. Though they asked her to the station to provide descriptions, the police never arrested the only person they could get their hands on who was present during the crime itself: Martine Salgado. So presumably their investigations hadn't turned up any forensics at odds with her story. Therefore, they bought the story.

Having rehearsed her version of events multiple times, Nico ran through it again on the subway back to his father's. The sequence roughly held together, and it gelled with what little he'd personally witnessed. But, a fan of Occam's razor, he didn't care for a narrative that was so complicated. Finding a gun left behind in a denim jacket that very afternoon was the kind of coincidence that marked detective fiction as second-rate. Her casting herself as Gloria Ador*abl*e's would-be savior jived too neatly with the role she'd embraced when fending off muggers with the hedge trimmer.

Martine's affect when the "liberation army" descended had been convincing. She was numb, dazed, and in shock. She delivered her statement to the cops with dulled, defeated sorrow, which she seemed successfully to battle, the better to impart the story not only to the police but also to the family. She didn't play up her despair with jags of uncontrollable weeping. If that was an act, it was the performance of her career. That said, he remembered her clear-eyed cool after Fucking Week—as if nothing had ever happened. She had talents.

It was possible to construct a story that fit the forensics with fewer moving parts. There was no need to concoct coming across a gun doing laundry if Martine and the gangbangers were in league; gangbangers have guns, *duh*. So, Gloria is in her room. Even if she locked the door, she'd open it for Martine. Either Martine herself, Domingo, or one of *los pandilleros* shoots Gloria. Martine asks to be pistol whipped to exonerate herself. The boyos cut out and lie low.

Yet this more straightforward tale failed the rationality test. Why would Martine stay behind? What would any of them get out of killing the homeowner—thereby involving heavy-duty law enforcement? Earlier that day, he'd warned his mother that her ex had organized some vague rescue for that very night. Nico had told her not to, but his trusting, blabbermouth mother might still have tipped off Martine. Yet Nico had furnished no particulars, including the incidental detail that the posse would be packing heat. Martine's pals had contempt for gringos, and the impending arrival of some tired-ass white guy would hardly have set them atremble.

Even if they'd anticipated dozens of fearsome vigilantes with AR-15s, why shoot a slight, harmlessly pissed-off older woman and flee? In what way was a murder conceivably in their interest? So maybe there really was an attempted rape, and maybe there really was a struggle over a gun, and maybe it really did go off by accident. The puzzle reliably curved full circle back to where it began.

14

Nico got to the slick midtown office of Hochman, Bell, and Nelson on West Fifty-Third a few minutes late. The receptionist ushered him into a meeting room with a long oval table and a prestigious array of windows. He was the last to arrive. His sisters had dressed up; Nico hadn't. To his astonishment, Martine was there, too—in a low-cut red frock he'd never seen her wear before that made her breasts look way bigger. His mouth twitched with annoyance. He wasn't hung up on protocol, but couldn't Palermo tell when to leave your pet illegal alien at home?

He shook hands with Tom Hochman, a lean guy in his fifties with a casual open collar who looked as if he played a lot of squash. "Have a seat, Nico. I've asked Martine to join us. I hope that's all right."

Nico shrugged.

"First, I want to tell you all how heartbroken I was to hear about your mother's death. I knew Gloria for years socially before she called on my help professionally, and I've always found her warm, passionate, and deeply concerned for other people."

Nico prayed that no one trotted out such a lame tribute when he kicked it.

"She was a lovely woman," Hochman continued, "and she died much too young in circumstances I still fail to understand. But I'm honored to carry out her wishes, even if I'm concerned that you heirs may be . . . unprepared."

The attorney handed Nico a white envelope. He recognized his mother's handwriting on the front, "For Nico Bonaventura," with a falling sensation. The touch of vertigo was precipitated not by anxiety about its contents but purely by the handwriting. Unlike most people's cave-drawing scrawl, her script was elegant, its slant even, each letter fully formed with a faint flourish. He'd always been captivated by his mother's cursive. She could dash off a paragraph quickly, yet the results bordered on calligraphy.

Living with Rita and his father had been psychically dislocating. Nico felt watched there, conscious of being stuck with the part of a young man whose mother has just been killed, and he wasn't sure whether at twenty-seven he was therefore called to buck up or fall apart. Awareness of playing a role made him feel outside himself. He had become a character, perhaps at long last a compelling one to other people, as if he cared. But her handwriting of all things brought his mother's death home. It recalled all the notes under a fridge magnet about when she'd be back and how he should help himself to the fruit salad, the birthday checks back in the days people still wrote such things, the hand-jotted letters sent loyally to Science Camp, the grocery lists dripping with exclamation marks (*tp!*), the insensibly long comments in the margins of *The Power Broker*, even the signatures on her divorce papers. Maybe the talent got misrouted into crocheted elephants, but it was in her automatic, unthinking actions—the way she iced a cake, tied a scarf, settled a belt at an angle on her hip, and, yes, wrote her son's name on an envelope—that best conveyed his mother was an artist.

"The rest of you will have to be patient," Hochman said. "Because I think we'd best let Nico read his mother's letter on his own first."

The letter was printed out. It was dated the third week in March:

Dear Nico,

I realize this is premature. Even coming up on sixty-three, I may be too young to be morbid. But having that Domingo fellow show up, about whom I have some reservations, and then having that Alonso fellow show up, about whom I have grave reservations, has been making me feel generally insecure, as if anything could happen. After all, anything often does happen, which is why Tom has encouraged me to always keep my will up-to-date, even when I'm in good health.

Making big decisions in anger is usually unwise. Yet I'm not acting today only out of fury that you used the extraordinary heroism of a woman I've come to deeply admire as a pretext for once again accusing her of far-fetched and premeditated deception. I can only conclude that you're jealous—jealous that Martine attracts your mother's admiration. But what have you ever done as an adult that a mother might admire?

Sweetheart, I was understanding when you returned from college feeling a bit lost, intimidated by having to take responsibility for your life, and uncertain where best to focus your energies. One's early twenties are daunting, and I was more than happy for you to come home to consider your options. I was taken aback when you seemed to lose faith in the environmentalism that attracted you to engineering, but I hoped addressing your doubts was part of the process of recommitting to a sense of mission with your whole heart. Then Covid came along and put all our lives on ice. I'm afraid too many people during that terrible time discovered how surprisingly easy it is to do absolutely nothing day after day, and you were one of them.

At no point during the last five years have I detected a sea change in you—a renewed enthusiasm for pursuing an engineering career or even an appetite for striking out in a wholly different direction. I don't sense you have any plans whatsoever. You seem willing to live the rest of your life wearing noise-canceling headphones and ambling downstairs for breakfast. Nico, this is a criminal waste—squandering such a sharp mind on buttered toast.

I've come to understand that I'm an enabler. Even now, I can't bring myself to kick you out (though I've thought about it). I worry you'd see that as a rejection, although it's only love that would impel me to throw you into the deep end. What I'm doing today at least guarantees that your seemingly infinite siesta faces an end point—even if I live to ninety, and you're not forced to face the music until you're fifty-four.

More candidly, I'm doing this for myself. You make me feel so helpless. Taking any action, even of an impetuous sort, makes me feel better. Before I make it official in midtown this afternoon, I can already tell that having covertly altered the unremittingly level landscape of your life will be a solace to me.

I think your sisters will be fine. I hope Vanessa finds someone soon, but even if she doesn't, she's so compulsively magnanimous that anything she might inherit she'd give away to someone who needs it more than she does in a matter of weeks. So I have no doubt that Vanessa will approve. As for Palermo, she'll be fine, too. I saw what she's made of during her agonizing recovery from the car accident, having to resign herself that she'd never be a professional gymnast after all. Palermo isn't a materialist, she's not inclined to self-pity, and Byron's business is supporting them comfortably enough. She shares my concerns for the less fortunate. We also share a discomfort with the whole notion of inheritance. It's always more gratifying to make it on your own steam. She and Byron are proud of their business, because no one handed it to them on a platter. Unearned wealth is a source of guilt if you have any scruples, and it's a vicious demotivator.

Nico, I'm leaving the house in Ditmas to Martine. I won't tell her what to do with it, but I have hopes that she'll turn it into a halfway house for new migrants to the United States who need a place to stay while they find their footing. If she takes my suggestion, I'll end up helping far more than the three newcomers I'm assisting now. We take our country—its functionality, its freedoms—far too much for granted, while migrants receive the bounty of America with the gratitude it deserves.

As for you, my dear, the best thing that could happen to you is anything that drags you out of your cozy rut. The last thing I'd want is for you to put your feet up, wait for me to succumb to breast cancer or something, and then live off your inheritance from me as you're currently eking along with your inheritance from your grandfather.

It's always possible that I'll get over my pique, make another appointment with Tom when I'm feeling less stirred up, and crumple this letter to the waste can. But for now, you deserve this. It may not feel like it right away, but I'm doing you a favor.

With more love than I can say,
Mom

Nico refolded the letter neatly into thirds and inserted it back in the envelope. It was addressed to him, so presumably he could keep it.

"My mother mentioned in May," he told Hochman, "that she'd done something 'rash.' She said as soon as she could get around to it, she was going to take it back."

"Did she say *what* she'd done that was rash?" Hoffman asked.

"No. But now it's obvious." Nico waved the envelope. "This."

"Were there any witnesses when she said she was going to 'take it back'?"

"No."

"Take what back?" Palermo asked. Sitting there for minutes as Nico took his time, she'd lost patience with the suspense.

"If she wasn't specific," Hoffman said, "and no one else heard her make that statement, I don't think you'd get anywhere in court."

"Didn't she write us letters?" Vanessa asked, sounding wounded. "Why only Nico?"

"I'd venture that she'd probably have left you and Palermo a note, too," Hoffman said, "if she thought she was in any immediate danger of . . ." It was weird that the very reason they were all gathered here could become unmentionable. "But she was physically well and in her early sixties. I assume there was no sense of urgency."

Nico badly wanted to leave. He'd not all-out bawled even on that grisly night in his mother's bedroom. Remaining in this office, he feared sponsoring yet another embarrassment before himself: after having been stolidly stoic throughout the aftermath of his mother's death, he sobs at last only because he's been disinherited. Now that, Palermo, is a proper materialist.

Still, sticking out the whole reading-of-the-will schmear might have been a legal obligation, and he didn't want to look like a big baby. Besides, the ritual might furnish valuable intelligence.

He gave no indication to the three women of what was in the letter, and neither did Hochman. The attorney read through a list of lesser bequests. Vanessa got the samples of their mother's knitted menagerie on display in the den's secretary; though Vanessa was the official animal lover, he was wistful that the crafty crocodile and the grumpy goat would no longer punctuate the backdrop of his Netflix binges. Palermo got the mismatched Victorian crockery, the product of many tenderly scavenged stoop sales and thrift shops, and nothing like a diss. Perhaps in partial compensation for the disappointing big reveal, Nico got the Toyota Prius—something of a thrown gauntlet, since he didn't drive. There'd be modest three-way distributions of what was left of her post-ransom IRA and whatever remained in her Citibank accounts, while they'd all get a small one-off death benefit from Social Security.

When Hochman reached the climactic paragraph, Nico didn't watch his sisters' reactions, though he'd have liked to have confirmed his theory that Palermo, at least, would not take as kindly to the will's benevolence toward "the less fortunate" as their mother expected. No, he focused solely on Martine.

She was stupefied. She was incredulous. She was overwhelmed, but she also threw in some apt chagrin in the presence of the three rightful heirs. There was the sharp intake of breath. The hands to the cheeks, a hand on the mouth. A quick, dazed glance around the room to confirm that to all appearances this was a real place and not a dreamscape. But she didn't overdo it. The timing, including an exquisitely subtle double-take at the outset, was on the beat; she didn't jump the gun, but neither did she lay it on heavy with not-possibly-having-heard-that-right. Physically, the dramatizing gestures were low-key. There was no whooping, no leaping to her feet. There were no tears of joy, no gasps of abashment. The whole number was tight, compact, and fluid, like one of Palermo's routines in gymnastics.

The Honduran was very, very good. He did not catch a single miscue. Pitch, scale, range of conflicting emotions: flawless. But then, she was also very good, from all reports, when receiving news that her children had been kidnapped. Receiving news that her children had been un-kidnapped. Battling hoodlums on Flatbush with a hedge trimmer. She had fucked the little boy upstairs with persuasive enthusiasm, and then she had unfucked him with persuasive amnesia. She'd been boffo as the devastated survivor of a violent altercation during which her friend and benefactor had been killed. Either (A) each of these junctures was simply what it appeared to be *or* (B) Martine Salgado deserved an Oscar—and how could such a multiple choice be solved with any certainty? Nico pitied anyone married to Hollywood's finest. Off-screen, it would have been foolhardy for anyone to believe a word from Meryl Streep.

"Mr. Hoffman," Martine said; whether she misremembered the attorney's name on purpose, how interesting that she reached for the lead actor's surname in a cinematic scam gone murderously wrong. "This is mistake."

"Maybe," Hochman said. "But if so, it's Gloria's mistake, not yours or mine."

"I don't know how to own whole big house," Martine said.

"You'll figure it out," Hochman tossed off. Given the trace of disgust in the lawyer's bearing, he'd probably tried to talk their mother out of, basically, leaving her house to the maid. Though Nico had read about worse bequests. Maybe better Martine than a poodle.

On second thought? He'd rather his mother had given the house to a poodle. Or to Kumquat, peace be upon him. At least then Vanessa would be next in line to the throne.

"The part about a halfway house for migrants," Hochman added. "That's merely a suggestion. It isn't binding."

"*Binding?*" Martine asked blankly.

"You don't have to turn the house into a migrant shelter if you don't want to," Hochman spelled out. "As if we need another one."

"We always need another one," Nico said. "Besides, our house has *been* a migrant shelter. For months."

"No more, I think. Ditmas is for family." After living there for a year, Martine still pronounced the neighborhood *Deetmas*.

"How quickly does this transfer of ownership take place?" Palermo asked evenly. She'd immediately put her feelings in lockdown. It was impressive. She wasn't going to let anything out. This was exactly her demeanor after the car accident. The back brace she wore for months was a metaphor. Inside, she held herself in place. She didn't move an emotional muscle.

"Your mother established a living trust," Hochman said, "so the estate doesn't go through probate. There's some paperwork I can take care of, but the title transfer is nearly immediate."

"I can't believe this!" Vanessa wasn't bursting with the joy of giving as anticipated. This sister wasn't given to battening down her internal hatches like Palermo, and if she was bursting with anything it was indignation. "Because Mom's putting Martine up for a year and paying a thirty thousand dollars ransom for her children wasn't enough, now she gets a five-bedroom Queen Anne?"

"Six," Nico said.

"And Mom said even the *furniture*," Vanessa said, "stays with the house?"

"All the accoutrements," Hochman said. "Though if there's anything it would mean a lot for you three to keep, Martine here might be open to negotiation."

"Vanessa Vivaz," Martine said. "The will of Gloria, this is not my idea—"

"I'd only have wanted a thing or two if I was able to move to a bigger apartment," Vanessa said, refusing to look at Martine. "I can't see how I'll ever do that now."

Chronically broke, Vanessa may have just learned how much she'd counted on a distant future in which the loss of parents was gently offset when a higher electric bill didn't mean the end of the world. Her fuming was a relief. Wow: his younger sister's largesse had its limits.

"We left the house in a hurry that night," Nico said. "The cops told us to leave everything the way it was. So I still have a bunch of my stuff in Ditmas."

"You no worry, Nico Niñito," Martine said. "I give you whole week to collect."

"Thanks. That's very bighearted." Nico's deadpan was anything but opaque. But the newly wealthy beneficiary was already impervious to sarcasm.

The loss of the house ended his sisters' friendship with Martine cold. Nothing stopped Martine from giving the place back, but it seemed Palermo's and Vanessa's affections were worth a great deal less than 2.5 million bucks. Both sisters were bitter—in Vanessa's case, startlingly so.

Their mother might have regretted the impulsive redirection of her estate, but the remorse couldn't mitigate a kick in the teeth that she'd never lived to call off. For all three siblings, it was difficult to disentangle feeling hurt from feeling robbed. They wanted their mother to have loved them. They also wanted the house. Either the material loss felt so savage because it was emotionally symbolic, or they were clinging to the emotional symbolism to ennoble shabby, material grievance.

Yet for once Nico hadn't time for such *observation*. Starting at 8 a.m. and doing six interviews in Brooklyn per day, within the week he found a room in Clinton Hill on Craigslist for $1,200/month—thus securing somewhere to schlep his stuff to. Thereafter, the three siblings descended mournfully on what was until so recently their family home. Vanessa retrieved her mother's knitted menagerie in the den, Palermo the Victorian crockery in the kitchen. If only out of resentment, and because they could, they gave each other tacit permission to pick up a few bits and pieces not bequeathed to them in the will—sentimentally loaded items like their mother's scarves and the relatively worthless costume jewelry the sisters remembered her wearing on dinners out with their father, but also practical things: a nearly full roll of duct tape, a wax-paper envelope of Forever stamps. Nico did a thorough search; *los pandilleros* might have cleared off in haste, but they'd still remembered to nab his laptop.

Boxing up his things, he took a perfunctory look under his bed, only to discover the "Tickita Ticketa" CD, the Yo-heart-NY baseball cap, and the discordantly pink cashmere packer. He could leave the gifts where they lay, so that Martine would eventually knock them with the vacuum, and she would therefore be assured that these totems meant nothing to the young man who left them behind. And why not? He also meant nothing to her. Or he could simply toss these weird items in the outdoor bin, thus sparing both parties recollection of what the knickknacks betokened for even a disconcerting moment or two. Instead, he slipped the three souvenirs into the open carton. He didn't know what they meant aside from the fact that they did mean something, if only that they were part of his life—which was rolling again, and any life with a future would also need a past. Funny, the shimmering ambivalence of the curios gave them an awesome power.

Home insurance had covered the cost of the crime-scene cleanup, and the team from Aftermath had decorously laid an oriental rug over ground zero in the master bedroom, but none of the siblings had any desire to lift the rug to check if all the reddish brown between the floorboards had been scoured away. Even aside from the harrowing misadventure that had occurred here—a history that, as Palermo noted with little sorrow, could give Martine trouble if she decided to sell—it was eerie to be back in a house now brutally ripped out from under them, which even take-the-shirt-off-my-back Vanessa regarded as a rank injustice. Before the trio's collective anger rose to combustible levels, they retreated to Manchego.

Once again, after ordering his usual pale ale and chorizo, Nico laid out his hypothesis. Their mother, he reminded his sisters, couldn't keep a secret for the life of her. Because she was so trusting, she enjoyed confiding in others. Besides, most people, even naturally generous people, like getting *credit* for being generous—and in this life. Might their mother have spilled the beans to Martine about having revised her will?

"Martine was obviously blown away in that lawyer's office," Vanessa objected. "She sure didn't see that bequest coming."

"So it would seem," Nico said neutrally. "But bear with me. Even if Mom did keep her mouth shut—since keeping her estate plans under her hat would make it easier to change her mind—Martine had access to Mom's email. Including her correspondence with Tom Hochman."

Once again, Palermo dismissed his cynical conjecture as preposterous. Having not transformed into a *completely* different person, Vanessa was so alarmed by the wicked implications of the puzzle pieces her brother had assembled that she put her hands over her ears.

His sisters were dead right on one point: Nico had no hard evidence. Not a speck—only a different story that fit the same facts. Nico rather liked his story, if only because it was so deliciously awful, and his sisters hated his story, if only because it was awful. The cops hadn't turned up any incriminating evidence, either, much less any of the other principles, who'd dissolved into the migrant chaos. So wasn't it fascinating that which story the family believed didn't make any difference? It was a taste thing, a temperament thing, an outlook thing. Whether their mother was murdered in cold blood for real estate was a matter of mood.

Meanwhile, his hovercraft had crash landed. Without thinking about it twice, Nico enrolled in an electrician apprenticeship program, which he'd need to stick out for four to five years before he could take the exam for a journeyman's license. He had the basics, certainly all the theory, but that was a far cry from knowing how to replace a circuit breaker panel. Whatever happened with the climate, people would always need wiring, and Nico was game for a sure thing. Maybe an electrician wasn't quite as well paid as an information security analyst, but the trade might still provide him a similar sensation of ordinary usefulness.

Obviously, Carlin Bonaventura would have been grateful for any display of initiative, even if his inert son had merely enrolled in a face-painting class. Better, Dad came to appreciate that, as Nico spelled out, "No one in my generation knows how to fix anything. Make anything. They can't hammer a nail or boil an egg. They want to run everything on electricity but can't replace a plug. Because everyone with degrees in, like, Queer Studies looks down on the trades, carpenters, plumbers, and electricians can name their price."

To Nico's relief, his father forwent "I'm *proud* of you, son," preferring to sit back in his banquette with a suspicious grunt. "Since when did you get so pragmatic, kid?"

"I've always been pragmatic," Nico said. "I didn't change a whit. The parameters did."

Beforehand, Nico had dreaded living with roommates, but he lucked out with three quirky, droll, and reflective young men, two of whom had also until recently lived with parents. Each of these guys came with his own set of bros, so Nico suddenly had access to a large, various social circle. He hadn't realized that he'd missed having friends, and he got in touch with Tyler to say, yes, he'd definitely come to the shoreline wedding in Chicago. He could easily afford the trip, because between alternate-side parking, larcenous insurance, and the theft of its catalytic converter twice in a row, he'd spurned sentimentality and sold the Prius. After all, the car had already served the purpose his mother intended: he'd learned to drive.

Instinctively, he avoided Ditmas, and not wholly due to its dark emotional residue of death and disinheritance. The period between Fordham and this more industrious era was firmly over. He felt oddly little nostalgia for his "contented" four-year hiatus, and he was relieved to put behind him year five's up-close-and-personal short course on the complexities of American immigration. Still, when invited to a dinner in East Midwood late that clement September, he decided to walk. Within a few blocks of their old house, from an uneasy curiosity, he swung by.

The light in the oaks was golden. The blooms of the hydrangeas had desiccated to a papery beige. The sun caught the lipstick-red trim on the window frames and along the roof of the deep wraparound porch, casting the structure in an Edward Hopper glow. Domingo was mowing the lawn; they'd upgraded to an electric riding mower that was murmurously quiet. They'd added a swing set and jungle gym in the backyard, where a little boy and two older girls were punching each other. Martine was unpegging the laundry from the clothesline. Doing more than her part to raise her new country's sluggish fertility rate, she was pregnant, he'd guess by around two trimesters. Nico counted on his fingers. It wasn't impossible.

Whatever the real story was, they had their better life. Nico had his.

ABOUT THE AUTHOR

LIONEL SHRIVER's novels include the National Book Award finalist *So Much for That,* the *Sunday Times* bestseller *The Mandibles,* and the international bestseller *We Need to Talk About Kevin,* winner of the Orange Prize. A regular on multiple podcasts, she's written fortnightly columns for the Spectator since 2017. Her journalism has also appeared in the *Wall Street Journal, Harper's, The Times, UnHerd,* the *Financial Times, The Free Press, Spiked Online* and many other media outlets. She lives in Portugal and Brooklyn, New York.